ALSO BY CRAIG ROBERTSON

The Forever Life
Book 1 of The Forever Series

The Forever Enemy
Book 2 of The Forever Series

The Forever Fight
Book 3 of the Forever Series

The Forever Quest
Book 4 of the Forever Series

The InnerGlow Effect

WRITE NOW!
The Prisoner of NaNoWriMo

Time Diving

Anon Time

THE CORPORATE VIRUS

It's a World Gone Mad

BY CRAIG ROBERTSON

Imagine-It Publishing
El Dorado Hills, CA

This book is dedicated to my beautiful, loving, and oh so understanding wife, Karen. You are love. Don't you dare change one little bit!

The Corporate Virus

Great nations are no longer led by their ablest men,
or by those who know most about their immediate affairs,
or even by those who have a coherent doctrine.
Democratic governments drift along the line of least resistance,
taking short views, paying their way with sops [bribes] and doles [welfares],
and smoothing their path with pleasant-sounding platitudes.

From Fifty Years Hence, *by Winston Churchill, 1931*

ONE

On a dreary early winter's morning I ascended the steps of one of the most prestigious medical school in America. I could not say why they chose to interview me, a mere mortal, a member of the common herd. Maybe it was some fortuitous clerical error. But I was not above the acceptance of charity. I was as nervous as a groom with two shotguns at his back. I walked with all the gusto of a condemned man down the interminable hallway toward the dean's office. The closer I got to the room, the greater the repulsive force the office exerted on my body became. I felt like I was climbing a vertical ice sheet barefoot and against a strong headwind.

But in the end, I passed through the open door.

As I entered the office, I spied an uncomfortable a group of overdressed young supplicants. They looked pitiful, morose, and painfully out of place. As I selected a chair and silently settled in, I was struck with the oddest thought. Had it occurred to any of these maximally stressed applicants that they were in an excellent position to murder several potential rivals? Pre-med students capable of any action that might increase their odds of success. The opportunity to knock off several high-level competitors was too great of a chance to pass up. My eyes scanned involuntarily for signs of weapons.

However, no mayhem ensued by the time a withered old secretary came in and asked us all to follow her into the conference room. Not one of us sat down until she had instructed us to do so. No one wanted to be the first to do something incorrectly. She offered us coffee or water. Everyone, naturally, declined the offer. We did not want to be perceived as thirsty, as that might suggest we did not prepare for the day with proper hydration. Plus, if you did not have a beverage, you could not spill it. Also, if you didn't drink, you wouldn't run the risk of needing to pee. No, we were all on our A-games, and A-gamers like us did not allow for any distractions.

Shortly, a rotund, elderly man waddled through the door and introduced himself as Vice Dean someone of something. I was too nervous to hear words. He extended a cordial, if funereal, welcome. Perfunctorily, and void of any conviction, he noted that we all certainly looked like "fine candidates." He told us that his secretary Marge would direct us all to our next appointments. A second-year medical student would take each of us on a tour of the campus. He dismissed us, and Marge turned us out of the Vice Dean's office with all the decorum employed to herd swine.

She pointed to the chairs in the hall that we had only recently left and asked us to sit and wait for our individual docents. Honest to goodness, the old bag called them docents. The second-year students trickled in over a few minutes and crowded into the waiting room. One of them greeted Marge and asked who got whom. Marge hefted a clipboard of considerable mass and scratched her nail down the paper. She read off an applicant's name followed by a student's name. The pairs found one another and introduced themselves as they left. I was assigned to Susan Watts. Sue was a young woman of slight build with a serious look more befitting a novice nun that a doctor-in-training. To my great relief, she tried to express some element of tepid warmth. That was an excellent sign. At least I was not paired with a sadistic jerk who could and would make me think I wasn't worthy of his lofty institution.

Sue escorted me to the library, the cafeteria, and the main lecture halls. All the usual suspects. I nodded attentively, continuously. Whenever conceivably possible, I asked insightful questions, to confirm I was a cut above my would-be classmates. A critical part of this game was to appear interested and curious, yet still seem like I wasn't all that committed. That was, of course, silly. I didn't want to tour the campus, and I didn't want to meet any deans. I wanted to be admitted to the school. I'd have been equally willing to attend if there were burning corpses nailed to every wall. What did I care about the odd local customs? But I had to act like I was interested in the school and still subtly convey that certain small factors might sway my decision one way or another. I was being courted, and the school was my suitor.

In turn, it was equally important that the school appear like it wanted to impress me. I, then, had to act like they were impressing me, and that they were, after all was taken into account, my best choice. They knew many applicants would sell their grandmothers to cannibals to be admitted. However, it was important to be courted and won over. It was gamesmanship, plain and simple.

The only interesting, albeit intimidating, part of the tour was when Sue led me to the Anatomy Lab. In college, I'd dissected a few live frogs and dead piglets. But I, like most of my co-applicants, had never seen a human cadaver, let alone a posse of them. I was quite uncertain how I'd react in the presence of a room full of dead, smelly corpses. I wouldn't win admission to prestigious programs if I passed out or ran screaming from the lab.

Sue opened the door for me and signaled that I should go into the lab. Maybe it was a test, or maybe she was just being cordial. In any case, in I went. I held my breath as long as I could, which was, of course, a silly gambit. I prayed with great passion that I did not faint from hypoxia or from the first deep breath I drew. The lab was not what I expected, but then again, I had no way to accurately know what it would be like.

The school had one hundred twenty members of each class. There were two pairs of first-year students assigned to each body. That meant there were thirty tightly swaddled irregular cylinders perched on waist-high stainless steel tables evenly spaced about the room. The air was cold and the smell was uninviting. There was no decay detectable, just the pungent, sickening-sweet smell of formaldehyde permeating everything. There lay thirty souls, resting not in peace, but in the basement of the medical school.

I assured myself internally that I could do it. Sue spoke in a respectfully hushed tone and pointed out the highlights of the facility. There were cross-sectioned bodies on display, voluminous sets of reference books available. As Sue started to add something to her narrative, the doors right behind us rammed open loudly. Even Sue jumped at the sound.

A young man ran in. He waved his arms maniacally above his head and began to shout, "There she is. Yes, there she is!" The young man then leaped up on one of the cadavers and ended up prone, as he straddled the body with his open thighs. He vigorously rubbed his groin on the plastic sheet and yelled at the top of his lungs, "Oh, Grandma, I've missed you so much! I've missed you so very much!"

Crimson-faced Sue balled her fists and shouted, "Kent *Pearson*! That is not funny! Get off the cadaver right now, or I'll go get the professor!"

That was the first time I met Kent.

TWO

Like the salmon that won the Darwinian contest to swim upstream and breed, I made it into medical school. Not only did I get in, I got in to one of the very best. Yes, against all odds, I was admitted into the very same school where Kent Pearson attempted carnal knowledge with a cadaver. There was, it turned out, a guardian angel for late-to-the-party pre-med students. Not only that, but said guardian angel really liked me.

After two years of hyper-intense classroom studies, tradition dictated that we brand new third-year medical students be thrown off a cliff, a very high and craggy cliff. In other words, we began the real work of transforming our civilian selves into medical demigods. We started our clinical "clerkships." I had no idea who came up with that archaic term. Those were the training rotations all medical students passed though in their training. Unlike our earlier classroom work, clerkships were six week apprenticeships in the various branches of medicine. There were required clerkships like Surgery, Medicine, and OB/GYN, and there were elective ones like Oncology, Gastroenterology, and Neurosurgery. We all needed some combination of required and elective clerkships to graduate.

Up to that point, medical school had been identical to our college years, only more focused and intense. During our first two years of medical school, we were asked to do something we were all proven to be good at, namely serial memorization paired with cagey test-taking skills. Those first two years were challenging, to be certain. Many of us were called upon to reach our personal limit for assimilating new material. The first two years of medical school were like memorizing the phone book on a tight schedule. Not hard, just immensely laborious.

Come year three, however, medical students were required to do what not one of us had done before—function as doctors. We, the neophytes, had no way of knowing that no one above us in the food chain would give us any credit or even think we could contribute to patient care at all. Unaware of that factor, we tried not to fail, unaware that failure was guaranteed. It awaited us with open arms, wore a big old grin, and threatened to break our spirits. Third-year students pretended to have prescient knowledge of all clinical skills and insights so that our true shortcomings were not discovered, but at a certain point, that façade had to break. Hey, we were third-year students, not board-certified specialist.

We put so much pressure on ourselves because we longed for the best residency, the next step up the ladder of success. If they found us less than stellar in a clerkship, we would not get a good grade. If we didn't get a good grade, we couldn't ask the attending physician for a letter of recommendation. If we didn't accumulate a critical mass of excellent letters of recommendation, we stood no chance of getting our choice of residencies. If we didn't get the right residency? Well, then our dreams would not be realized. We would have failed in our life's mission. Perhaps it was circular logic, but an ever-present reality to all proper third-year students.

We overdriven, obsessive clerks who had made it to that lofty level, where success was visible all around us, were unwilling to accept the cruelty demanded of us by whim and chance. We were determined to alter reality and dominate our fates by force of will alone. We would not be denied our sacred residencies. Though we were to fall flat on our faces, we refused to fall flat on our faces. We stubbornly created our own private nightmares, where post-traumatic stress disorder was a certainty. Like a drunken man determined to walk a straight line for a police officer, we defied reasonability and tried to present ourselves as fully knowledgeable physicians. The cruel twist was that positively everyone around us knew our impossible dilemma. They had survived their third year and knew the untenable position we were all in. Naturally, we became easy sport for their amusement.

An outside observer might not fully appreciate the importance of the *right* residency. A residency was the three- to six-year period that followed medical school. It was where we would learn our specialties. If we graduated medical school and passed all the state-required board exams, we got a piece of paper and a firm handshake. But aside from the ability to sign our names "Doctor," we were still just glorified members of the public. To be able to practice medicine, we had to do a one-year internship and pass more tests. Then we were qualified to do little more than nothing. Yes, we could see patients, prescribe medications, and perform simple procedures, but no respectable institution would hire us. To become an "RD," a real doc, we had to do a residency. Many would go on to do subspecialty training after residency. For example, an orthopedic surgeon could upgrade to a hand specialist or a pediatrician to a neonatologist.

There were, to be clear, two types of "right" residencies: the financial residencies and the prestigious residencies. The most coveted residencies were those known as the financial lottery-winning residencies.

Dermatology, ophthalmology, neurosurgery, and radiology led that list. Dermatology, the biggest plum, coupled massive earnings potential with no on call work, weekends, or holidays.

Opthalmology involved some on call, but the money made fixing cataracts in our aging society was overtly embarrassing.

Neurosurgery combined brutal hours with draconian surgeries, but the financial compensations promised to be astronomical. Winner, winner!

And then there was Radiology. There was a sweetheart career, to be certain. With a computer, call was done from home. Radiologists made money off every film read, and they could read them at the speed of light. Consequently, for those contented to sit alone in a dark room and print money, they had found their calling.

The second group of choice residencies were those at distinguished institutions. If one desired fame and prestige, one simply had to join one of the top-flight programs. The Mayo Clinic, Beth Israel Deaconess Medical Center, Michigan, and UC San Francisco were examples of the crème de la crème. If you wanted to play in one of those legendary sandboxes, you had better be at the top of your class. It also helped if you were related to royalty and fluent in all galactic languages. To pull down the best prestige residency, you had to be demonstrably better than the very best. Excreting feces that did not smell badly was a prerequisite, and the ability to walk on water was a definite plus.

To be anything but abject failures, we medical students had to secure the best residency possible. To do that, we had to be the top dog. To be top dog, we needed to shine brighter than all the other brilliant students alongside us, so we were all trying to crawl over each other's backs to get that sweetest of fruits. Dog-eat-dog was an inadequate analogy. In a dog fight, there was only one other dog biting you. In medical school, we struggled to best our extremely talented classmates in a world fraught with lethality. Our superiors, also wanted a pound of our flesh. We had to deflect, though we were perfectly incapable of doing so, the harsh critiques and murderous questions from our superiors. Third-year students were heckled by the fourth-year students, ridden by the interns like rented mules, confounded by the residents for their amusement, and actively ignored by the attendings as a matter of policy.

To be fully clear, the senior physicians ignored us except for when they were "pimping us," which was all too frequently. Lovely term, "pimping." Pimping, in medical-speak, was where a superior being higher up the medical hierarchy asked us a series of questions. Sounded benign enough, right? They asked us questions. What could have been more casual, more acceptable, than one colleague asking questions to another one?

But there were only two goals of pimping. Neither was for our benefit. The first function of pimping was to make the attendings feel better about themselves. The second was to utterly humiliate and disgrace us, their intended victims.

During pimping, they would hurl progressively harder questions at us. Importantly, the questions were asked in an overtly challenging, threatening manner. The outcome was always the same. Because we were merely third-year students and they had years of experience, they always arrived at a question that we could not know the right answer to. What third-year student knew more about surgery than a surgeon? None. So, sooner than later, our idiocy was exposed publicly. The only thing left for us to do after a good pimping was to wither and die. And a good time was had by all. Well, all but us victims, because we were deceased and discredited.

The takeaway point here was that we third-year students were thrown into the greatest torture test of our previously stress-burdened lives. We needed to excel at everything, although we could not possibly succeed. We also knew the attacks were coming around every corner and that we would survive almost none of them. So, by the end of our third year when the application process for residencies began, most of us found ourselves excluded from ever securing any of our top spots. I'm amazed any of us survived at all. We struggled, most of us failed, and all of us suffered mightily. Sound like fun? Well, maybe you should consider becoming a medical student.

Anyway, I began my first clerkship, my first step into a larger world, the fall of my third year. We've all seen doctors, right? What did Dr. Marcus Welby, Dr. Philip Chandler, and Dr. Meredith Grey all have in common? They—all great physicians—wore long flowing white coats. Historically and practically, those flowing white coats were worn to protect doctors from splattering blood and flying body parts experienced in the daily practice of medicine. In our modern age, a white coat no longer served a useful purpose. OSHA mandated extensive personal protective gear to protect physicians from coming in contact with noxious material. Nonetheless, a pristine white coat was emblematic of doctorhood. As a student doctor, we third-years were finally allowed to enter the fraternity. We could don a white coat. But, because every silver lining was accompanied by a huge, dark cloud, life was not to be too charitable to us. We had to sport a short white coat, the so called "Eisenhower cut" style. Everyone else, the RDs, wore the long, flowing doctor coats.

I assumed costuming us in silly little coats was intended to make us feel that much more out of place. Wearing the short coat was a "pimp me" sign that made it easier for everyone to identify the fresh meat that needed to be pounded raw. To say that I was nervous the first day of my third year would have been a massive understatement. A bride on her wedding day was nervous. A condemned man led slowly to the gallows was very nervous. A pilot who looked out the cockpit window at the ground in front of his plummeting plane was extremely nervous. I was beyond all three. My mouth was dry, my hands trembled, my armpits dripped sweat, and in spite of having stopped at every restroom I passed, I was in persistent danger of peeing my pants. I was on the verge of vomiting all morning. On three separate occasion before noon, I forgot my own name when asked. I think that if I had been one any more nervous, I would simply have died from a total system failure. I would have welcomed the reprieve.

For anyone, choosing their specialty rotation was critical. It had to be a field they would never pursue as a career. That way they could look their worst where it counted the least. Like misbehaving away from home, no one would hopefully know or remember their poor performance. In my case, as I was certain I wanted to go into Internal Medicine, I decided to do Obstetrics and Gynecology first. OB/GYN was one of the few specialties I knew early on I did not want to pursue. I quickly confirmed that it involved long, boring hours waiting for a few minutes of panic. Moreover, I was covered with amniotic fluid, blood, urine, and feces more often than I was not. It was not my cup of tea, thank you very much. However, on OB/GYN, I expected to get a lot of hands on clinical experience, like starting IVs and examining live patients.

For the first few weeks of the rotation, I did not crash and burn horrifically, so I was ecstatic, but the pimping was brutal. Nothing less would have been acceptable. The hours were arbitrary and unfair. Welcome to Dodge City, cowboy. And the assignments were intended not to teach me but to break my will. Who didn't see that coming? But, I had not screwed up royally once. I proved not to be invisible, and a couple of the interns treated me like a human being. But no clerkship was to be endured without suffering, so came the day in which my honeymoon was officially over.

One of my team's post-operative patients developed a nasty infection. I was given the last-minute assignment of "presenting" her to the infectious disease consult service. To "present" a patient was to inform another doctor or group about the patient's full medical history and their progress, or lack thereof, up to that point in their hospital stay. It was often done at the bedside, so the patient heard the presenter talk about them like they were an insect pinned on a board. It could be supremely dehumanizing to both presenter and patient. Anyway, the attending for infectious diseases was a really old relic named Wilfred Bottomsworth. I kid you not, that was the old goat's name. Wilfred was supposed to be some bigwig world authority. But that had to be a hundred years ago because now he was just a humorless, surly, and fully disagreeable mummy who walked around and made the world suffer for being in his presence.

I felt like a tiny sea lion pup bobbing helplessly above a hungry white shark whose mood reflected that he was having a particularly bad day in the first place. The senior resident on my service, Philip Cartwright, looked to Wilfred and announced unenthusiastically, "Noah here," he pointed at me without looking, "is going to present the case, Dr. Bottomsworth."

With that cue, I looked up from my notecards to see ten thousand sets of eyes boring down on me. Tunnel vision rapidly closed in, and all I could see was the attending's ancient, weathered nose. All those gray hairs protruded out at chaotic angles and rustled with each breath. They mocked me as they waved to me. Honestly, those accursed nose hairs occupied the totality of my universe at that moment. It was just me, that huge bulbous red nose, and those taunting hairs. The rest of reality was a frozen gunmetal gray void. Eons passed in icy silence. Stars were born, burned their entire allotments of fuel, and died in the time I stood there transfixed and reviled those misbehaved nose hairs.

Finally, after time began to move again, the lips just out of sight below that nose said, "Well, be on with it, young man. I haven't got all day!" He turned to the person next to him, and demanded, "Are they allowing dimwitted mutes into medical school these days?" As ill fortune would have it, the intern who stood next to Dr. Bottomsworth was none other than Kent Pearson. Remember Kent, the guy who really missed his grandmother back in the anatomy lab?

The fact that he was positioned directly next to the codger who was about to disembowel me broke my mind-lock. I was about to start speaking, when Bottomsworth turned haughtily toward my resident. My resident, you know, my immediate supervisor, the overworked man trying to succeed at all costs, the man who held my life in his hands? He lashed out, "What sort of slipshod trick are you attempting to pull off here, Doctor Cartwright? Did you *instruct* this idiot to publicly mock me as some sort of fraternity prank? Well, if you did, I can assure you that Dean Rutherford will hear of it directly. Heads will roll, I tell you. Heads will roll!"

At that juncture, my incompetence not only threatened my career but it also placed Philip's hope for future success in serious jeopardy. None of us had any idea whether the dean, or anyone else for that matter, took the dinosaur seriously. But finding out was not a proposition any of us relished. What should have just been just another unpleasant browbeating now threatened to escalate into a first-class disaster for several of us.

Into that confusion, uncertainty, and peril stepped Kent. Kent, who had the audacity to hump a cadaver, cocked his head slightly and winked at me. He placed a hand on Bottomsworth's shoulder. That bold act surprised the attending so completely that not only did he stop howling, but he also turned his head to stare with incredulity at Kent's offending appendage. Time, the actual stream of time which governs all our actions, halted for the briefest moment. Finally, he spoke.

"Gentlemen," he nodded to a nearby female resident and added with a smile, "and *lady*. Come now. Let us all allow cooler heads to prevail. There is a reasonable and comical justification for our present mutual misunderstanding."

He stepped over to me, wrapped his arm around me like we were reunited brothers, and pulled me closely to his bosom. He made a grand show as he released me and stared tenderly into my eyes. He shook his head side to side and said, "How silly this will seem to you, Professor Bottomsworth, once the truth of things comes to stand in the bright light of your informed understanding." He lingered his gaze on me several more loving moments and then physically rotated me to face Bottomsworth. He flung his right arm into the air and wrapped his left arm around my shoulder in an embrace. He reached all the way around my torso and deftly snapped the name tag off my lapel.

Kent boomed, "*Dr.* Bottomsworth, allow me to personally introduce you to this jewel-in-the-rough student physician. Our fine institution was fortunate enough to bring him here, as part of the Meredith Johnson-Smitherfield Endowed Visiting Clerkship Program. This stellar prospect is Igor Pensiscuff!" Kent placed his right hand on me and shook me like I was a piggy bank unwilling to release its last coin. "Igor Pensiscuff, comes to us all the way from Albania to study our way, to learn at our heels, and to carry our mission statement back to his quaint hometown of Vlorë, nestled picturesquely as it is on the bountiful Adriatic Sea." He whipped his head around, and asked, "Dr. Bottomsworth, do you know of fair Vlorë nestled on the Adriatic Sea?"

He either stammered in profound befuddlement or life-threatening rage. Bottomsworth said, "Why…why, yes. I know of Vlorë. I visited there as part of a medical exchange program back in the late 1950s. The Albanian government was having a devil of a time with a yellow fever outbreak and asked me to tour the country, beings as I was an authority on that particular infectious diseases." Bottomsworth realized he might have been drawn into a ruse of some sort and spoke more pointedly, "But I don't see—"

Kent thrust his arm skyward once again. "Yes, you were a world authority on infectious disease, yes indeed you were." He allowed his arm to drop back down, and proceeded more conversationally, "Yes, we all know that once you were quite the expert. But, as no doubt you will recall from your personal experience, the presenting of medical cases in Albania is done in a fundamentally different manner than it is here. It is quaint, I'll grant you, but it is also unfamiliar to us gathered here in the United States of America."

He let the briefest moment linger in the air for quiet self-reflection, then vaulted forward. "I'm certain you will recall that, out of pious respect for the senior faculty in Albanian hospitals, the underling physicians never begin speaking until their master has asked them an open-ended question. You know, for example, like, 'So, fine young country-boy physician, tell me how is it that this woman came to be here?' Or, 'I wish to know of this woman's plight. Can you inform me?'" He shrugged his shoulders and admitted with considerable regret that it probably sounded better in Albanian than it did in his rough translation. "So, kind, gentle sir, please be culturally sensitive of

Igor Pensiscuff. Judge him not rashly but in a manner consistent with our universities EEOC policies of non-discrimination." With that, he lowered his head like a seasoned Shakespearian actor at the end of a soliloquy and fell silent.

Dr. Bottomsworth was no one's fool. It was not possible to scale the mountain of academia to the lofty heights he had without a commanding a firm grasp of gamesmanship and the inclination toward a skeptical outlook. For several long tense seconds, he gesticulated his massive eyebrows as if he was trying to fly. His shoulders bobbed erratically. Finally, all spectators could breathe again as he said, "Why yes, now that you mention it, I do seem to recall something along those lines being the case." Less tentatively, he then pontificated with greater conviction. "Damn silly practice if you ask me. A waste of time and a hindrance to the economic progress of patient rounds." Addressing nobody in particular off to one side, he added, "No wonder Albania is still a third world piss hole." He scowled at me and added, "No offense intended, Igor. That was more an observation than a remark." Back to his former condescending self, he demanded of me, "Well, get on with it Igor. Can you please inform me of this accursed patient's sad state?"

Kent was still holding me by both shoulders. He dropped one hand down and pinched me quite painfully on my butt. He whispered so I alone could hear him. "Good luck with the accent, penis-cuff. Oh, and better pray to God the old fart doesn't remember any of his Albanian." He marched like royalty back to stand alongside Dr. Bottomsworth. All eyes were on me, yet again. In surely the worst parody of a Transylvanian accent ever performed, I presented the woman, the accursed woman, who stared in horror and disbelief at our senior professor with eyes the size of dinner plates.

That was the second time I crossed paths with Kent Pearson.

THREE

Two years later…

I must have been both smarter than I realized and luckier than I had any right to hope for. I applied for and was accepted into residency in Internal Medicine at my very own world-renowned institution. Candidates from across the globe schemed, plotted, and sacrificed domestic animals in their attempts to achieve what I did. But insecure and hesitant me pulled down one of the juiciest plums in all of medicine. Internship, which was just another name for the first year of any residency program, began each year in mid-June. After a touchy-feely picnic with our families and a welcome dinner, I reported to the hospital on the third Monday of June.

As I entered the building, poof, I became a real doctor. I was scared out of my mind, hopelessly in over my head, and about as far from my comfort zone as a redneck who'd strayed into a gay bar. But technically I was an RD. The interns received their first rotation assignments at the picnic, so we at least know who was on call and who would start off with an easy consultation service.

I was assigned to the wards. This was hospital speak for the service responsible for the care for any patient on the general medicine ward, which was different than patients in the ICU, on the surgery service, or admitted specifically to oncology. The wards were equivalent to the storied trenches of World War I. The service was every bit as unpleasant, grueling, and interminable as the cold, wet trenches too. The wards were where the gritty, laborious, and endless task of routine hospital care was administered. The wards were also where, as medical tradition decreed, civilians like me became proper doctors. We did so via superhuman endurance, herculean effort, and biblical suffering. Anything less was unacceptable. It would be like a visit to Paris without seeing the Eiffel Tower.

When on the ward service, I was on call every third night. That sounds so terribly reasonable and innocent when viewed on a sheet of paper. Every third night. No big deal. Every third night call was, in fact, a soul-crushing nightmare.

Here was the drill. I was on call day one. During the day, I was hit with scattered admissions, I still had to attend the usual educational conferences, and I had to look after those patients already on my service, i.e. those patients already assigned to me personally. In the dark of night, I had to additionally cross cover all the patients on any ward team, since those doctors had left the building. All the while continuing to be peppered with new admissions. Sleep? Yeah, that wasn't going to happen. Day one was invariably a long day.

Day two began as a continuum of day one. At 7:59 a.m. it was still day one and I was on call, then, bada-bing, at 8:00 a.m., day two began.

On day two, I was required to do my usual work and attend all conferences. The labor of day two consisted of "tucking in" my new charges, while at the same time making forward progress with my previous patients. If fortune smiled on my sorry ass, I might stagger out of the hospital by 6:00 or 7:00 p.m. Immediately upon arrival home, and hopefully not while I drove, I slipped into a coma.

My alarm woke me—unrefreshed—on day three, and I migrated blindly to work. Day three was my "gift" day, my day of leisure and relaxation. I was only required to do my typical ten-hour shift. I managed my patients, did formal rounds with my team's attending physician, and mixed in morning report and a noon conference. Again, with any luck, I was home by 7:00 or 8:00 p.m. I was free to do whatever I pleased. Usually, I favored passing out cold while eating dinner, but occasionally, I opted for falling asleep thirty seconds after turning on the TV.

The next morning, promptly at 8:00 a.m., I was on call again. Wash, rinse, repeat. Yeah, the wards really sucked. The only upside to being on the wards was that I got, whether I welcomed it or not, a massive amount of hands-on experience.

Though it was mostly unbearable, there were two other perverse upsides to call. The first was that during the wee hours, there were no attendings, fellows, consulting residents, or anyone else around to boss, belittle, pimp, and harass me. They were all at home sleeping in their warm, comfy beds. They dreamed of golf or Maui or anything other than being on call on the wards. The second upside of call was that, due to the absence of any other physicians, I was the go-to guy—by default, not merit. Nurses, respiratory therapists, lab technicians, or anyone else who needed a decision or disposition came to me, Dr. Noah Taylor.

Many a struggling patient gave up the ghost in the middle of the night. As only a physician could legally pronounce them dead, even if they were ice cold and stiff as a board, I was needed. I had power and authority. I had chops. That was a nice feeling for a beaten down, exhausted, overworked, and underpaid lackey.

Morning report. What was there to say about it? Every weekday on the wards, life began at 8:00 a.m. sharp with morning report. Morning report was the venue where the team coming off call presented a handful of "interesting" cases from the previous day. I stressed the word "interesting" for cause. I might have had ten admissions, but all ten could be demented patients with pneumonia or readmissions for heart failure after the patient spent the day gorging on pizza. Truth be told, hardly any patient seemed interesting and presentable after being on call. In any case, coffee and donuts were provided, bagels if we were lucky. All the personnel assigned to the wards were expected to attend. Specifically, every student, intern, and resident was required to be there. I once missed two consecutive morning reports and received, before noon the second day, a call from the Chairman of Medicine himself. This was our conversation.

Hello, I said.

You missed two morning reports. All of my residents attend morning report every day. Do you have any questions?

No, sir.

Click.

A smattering of ward attendings or consultants from Neurology or Cardiology were there on an irregular basis if they were so inclined. House staff was the term used to include all of us not who were not yet fully fledged doctors. In effect, "house staff" referred to interns and residents. It was coined because, in bygone days, all the doctors in training literally lived in the hospital, or "in house." As recently as the 1960s, interns—from the Latin word for *internal*—and residents—because they resided in the hospital—were lucky to get five or six days off per year.

A typical night on the wards at my hospital was similar to an upside-down metal garbage can placed over me, which was then hammered with a crowbar. The last thing I wanted to do when exhausted, smelly, and dispirited was to sit through an educational conference.

Of course, at 8:01 a.m. on that third Monday of June, I was, for the last time in the next nine months, rested, collected, and ready to go. I listened attentively to the cases presented but dared not say a word by way of question or comment.

As a student on the wards, I'd learned the risk of participating in morning report. If I asked if the patient was green, the presenter would say that, no, the patient was not green.

Before the conversation could advance, one of the popinjay attendings would challenge me with, "Since you bring up the subject of green, what is the differential diagnosis for green? Also, can you summarize for us the treatment for greenness? Moreover, I cannot understand why it is you are so dull as to ask if this clearly non-green patient is green?"

After I sailed anonymously through morning report (called Boring Report by the non-brown-nosing house staff) I had to join the other members of my team. Call was every third night, so there were three teams, Red, Blue, and White. I was on the Red Team. We were told at the end of morning report to get together under the appropriately colored piece of paper affixed to the wall in the hallway, just outside the conference room. In Ancient Rome, when the gladiators entered the Colosseum fifty percent of them would never leave.

They paraded before the Caesar, and shouted, "We who are about to die salute you!" As I passed out of the doors of morning report that third Monday in June, those words echoed in my head. Little did I know how prophetic they would be.

I found and approached the red sheet of paper taped to the wall. It wasn't until I was almost there that my gaze wandered down to notice the solitary figure present, already under that red sheet of paper. There, wearing scrubs, a long white coat, and sipping coffee from a red mug, leaned Kent Pearson. My heart sank. Sank, however, implied my heart dropped some distance and then came to rest. Mine fell to the center of the Earth before it was forced to stop. After my last run-in with Kent, we had not crossed paths much.

Nightmares were populated with dark breasts, scary images, and frightening nuances. Never, in my most crippling nightmare, however, could I have dreamed I would cut my teeth in medicine under the tutelage of Kent Pearson. The man was a scoundrel and a psychopath. Han Solo meets Hannibal Lecter. It never occurred to me to find out in advance who my resident would be since I had no control over the assignment. I figured, what the heck, I'd just find out Monday. If I had at least taken to time to discover that he was going to be my resident, I would have had the time to get properly drunk. It was a cruel joke, and I was the punchline. Kent, the crafty SOB, knew my feelings. He saw them in my eyes as I shuffled to a halt directly in front of him, stunned. Perhaps because he recognized the misgivings I emoted was why he had that devilish, cat-eating-shit grin on his face. He could have been just perennially mischievous and wore that look by rote.

Before my sorry fate could congeal in my mind, he chuckled. "I thought it was you, Pensiscuff, the moment I read who would be on my team." He took a long sip from his red mug, rolling his eyes skyward. "Well, let's say I hoped it was you, Igor. If it wasn't you, Penis, I might have had oh-so-much duller a month on the wards." The other members of Red Team looked either to the floor or to their coffee cups, unclear what was going on. They heard but could not understand the meaning of the words he spoke. They also saw the ashen color of my face and had to wonder what he meant.

Kent released my stare and addressed the group as a whole. "Morning, peoples. I'm your new god. You will hear other people referring to me as Kent Pearson, M.D. But to y'all for the next three weeks, I'm god. As I am speaking please note I say "god" with an uncapitalized "g." I am a humble, if not benevolent, lord and master." He shot a menacing a look at the Red Team, then continued. "Okay, now that introductions are out of the way, let's go over the ground rules."

The second intern assigned to Red Team, a person so forgettable and inconsequential that I cannot even recall her name, interrupted him. In a warm and civilized manner, she asked, "Aren't we going to … you know, introduce ourselves too?" She smiled wistfully and shook her mane of blonde hair. "I, for one, am new to the area and don't know a soul. I feel it would be really neat if we knew each other's names and maybe even a tiny bit about who we are. You know, our interests and that sort of thing."

He made it a point of holding his mug to his lips for a socially unacceptable period of time.

This forced what's-her-name to ask nervously, "Well, don't you think…" She trailed off uncertainly.

He lowered his mug and glared at her a moment. "You done speaking, princess?" Not surprisingly, she did not respond. She just lowered her head. "Well, I personally am glad to hear you're done. Damn glad, truth be told." He rolled his free fingers in the air alongside his head, squinted one eye almost shut, and continued, "Because I thought I decreed the introductions formally concluded." He thumped himself on the chest. "You all know me. I'm your god." He looked down thoughtfully, then addressed her again. "Perhaps in your limited and sheltered life experience, princess, you do not yet know that we gods, well, we are a powerfully focused on being in control and having our way."

He gestured widely to the Red Team. "You non-god people are completely insignificant. You're anonymous road kill rotting by the side of a lonely desert highway. You're, and I say this with true affection, nothing more than the piss overflowing a busy outhouse on a hot afternoon." He pointed at the other intern. "Do you take my meaning here, cupcake? I really hope you do because time's a wastin', and my feet are beginning to ache. So, if the princess here has no further objections …" His hand tauntingly beckoned her to respond if she needed to. She didn't respond. He concluded. "Well peachy keen, and somebody massage my swollen hemorrhoids! I think we can advance the program the patient care portion. I am now most encouraged and pleased. Y'all follow me."

He turned and sauntered away, and Red Team followed loosely in tow like ducklings. He walked just far enough to ensure that we were all in motion before spinning around on his heel. That forced Red Team to mutually collide to a stop. "Fresh meat." He then spun on a heel and headed forward again. Three steps later found him, once again, whipped around to address the Red Team. "That's what all your names are. fresh meat. If I want to talk at one of you, I will be addressing you by your new proper names, fresh meat."

He pretended to turn away but stopped halfway. "Anybody else, a patient or an attending, asks who you are, I want you to tell them, 'I'm fresh meat.'" He pointed a finger at us as a group. "I hope you are all perfectly clear on this most critical tenant of your sorry existences. You are nothing now but fresh meat to me and to any other member of this institution of higher learning." He let out a quiet laugh and pointed directly at me. "Well, except for Penis-cuff here. He will, henceforth and in perpetuity, be known only by that assignation and not as fresh meat." With that, he finally led us off to the wards.

That was the third time I crossed paths with Kent. On that occasion, and subsequently over the course of a very memorable residency, I was going to actually get to know him. We were to become, against all odds and laws that governed such matters, the best of friends.

FOUR

Eventually in life, we were all tested. We discovered if we were cut of hero cloth or something more akin to flannel. For me, it happened about halfway through my internship. I confronted the most challenging force of nature, the most rapid of quicksand, the most harrowing confine on planet Earth imaginable. I, like a matador squared off against a raging bull, was to cast myself into the Intensive Care Unit. The ICU. Also called "the unit" since there was no other unit in medicine so iconic or so formidable.

Working in the unit was the no-holds-barred cage fight of the medical field. It's a full-contact life where fouls and unorthodoxy are encouraged. A minor mistake or even a trifling oversight could end a human's life faster than one could say, "Well fuck me." The patients in the ICU were, as we loved to say, about as sick as they were ever going to get. To reflect that grim fact, there were any number of insensitive yet endearing descriptors employed by ICU personnel to help paint a picture of their temporary guests. "A hurtin' cowboy headin' for the last round up" or "one foot in the grave and the other on a banana peel" were time honored and applied liberally. The simplified version was to simply pronounce that the patient was "circling the drain." Most ICU staff members were, at best, pessimistic. They would work feverishly and passionately to save the lives of the people that they seemed, outwardly, cynically indifferent toward. There was always such an odd dichotomy present in the unit.

To labor in the unit was both an honor and a curse. At best, a medical goalie in possession of consummate skills could stop the Grim Reaper from kicking their patient's soul into the afterlife for only so long. There were limits to the knowledge, technology, and luck that could delay the inevitable. Some admissions to the ICU were not only going to die, but they also should have already been dead. So despite the miraculous tenacity of their care team, even truly superhuman efforts were rewarded with an empty feeling in the pit of one's stomach and a most dispiriting talk with the next of kin.

There were, for example, hospitals where it was understood that patients ill enough for the ICU had to be on death's doorstep. So, at such institution, the only patients admitted to the ICU were those completely bereft of hope. Conversely, anyone who might have actually benefited from ICU care was forced to rely on chance in the wards. It was always a lose-lose situation.

I had been pummeled and exhausted from my endless sentence on the wards. For the ICU rotation, I needed to add intimidation, indecision, and insecurity to my litany of personal demons. Sure, there were attendings, fellows, and residents galore in the ICU. However, each patient was assigned to one specific intern. They were the intern's patient, not the patient of the collective whole. In practice, what that meant was that any successes were attributed to the senior staff. The custodial intern, on the other hand, was liable for all outcomes falling shy of success. So, for the next month, I faced pressures I could not bear as I cared for patients I was completely ill-prepared to manage, all the while bridled with unrealistic, self-imposed expectations.

Remember that scene from the first Indiana Jones movie where Harrison Ford was running away from the rolling boulder in the cave? Yeah, that was me, with a subtle difference. I also ran toward a boulder rolling away from me. My confidence level could have been dubbed "low." My morale was lower. It was in the negative range on day one and marched in a southerly direction each subsequent day. As an intern in the unit, I knew before I even walked thought the sliding doors for the first time that my chances of a challenging yet rewarding month were around one-in-a-never-going-to-happen.

To make my perilous existence even more disenchanted, keep in mind that the medical pecking order was never more inviolately rigid than it was in the unit. Us lowly interns could discuss our patients only with our residents. The higher-ups, sure, they pimped us mercilessly, but that conversation was very much unidirectional. The residents, in turn, spoke only to the fellows, and the fellows were the only players allowed to actually discuss the patients with the attendings. The justification for the stilted arrangement was, I assumed, based on the covering of one's ass. If someone preempted the hierarchy of information exchange, there was the very real risk that the omitted player could be found to have committed an error. So, to inhibit me from letting something incriminating pass to one of my resident's bosses, I was denied the chance to do so. In the harsh reality of the unit, not only the patients' lives were at stake. Our careers were too. As a result, us flailing, foundering interns were never more dependent on another human being than we were on our residents when we rotated through the unit.

The nurses in the unit were a potent factor that all interns had to learn to manage if they were destined to survive. They were a potential boon or bane for an intern. Yes, a good nurse who kept an intern appraised of important changes was a blessing—a much welcomed succor. But, they were also capable of great mischief to us neophytes. Depending on how the newbie learned to interact with the nurses, our ICU rotations were either made or broken. It was just that simple.

Nurses in the unit were staffed either one-to-one or two-to-one with their patients. They spent so much focused time with the patient, they came to know them most intimately. As a result, they could also end up willfully possessive of their charges. An effective intern had to learn when to listen to and reward the nurse's input and when to tactfully acknowledge but discretely ignore their suggestions.

An example: I was looking in on a very ill patient on my service. He was decreasing his participation in the game of life at an alarming rate. His tactless nurse huffed up to me and demanded that the patient be started on triple antibiotics because he was crumping—going downhill rapidly—as we spoke. He, she speculated, might have been septic. The patient was crumping, to be certain, and at a truly breathtaking rate, but he was not expiring from an infection. He had end-stage heart, kidney, and liver diseases and was drowning in his own accumulated fluids. He was, as we termed it, made of "piss-poor-protoplasm."

As she was so angry and disrespectful (feeling disrespect was a deadly sin for an intern), I challenged her to give me an example of which three antibiotics she felt were needed. She replied indignantly that she didn't know which three, just that he obviously needed triple therapy. Over time, she'd heard the term "triple antibiotics" but never learned what that really meant or how medication choices were made. It was just an expression to her. If I'd have taken her advice, I would have been a fool. If I acted foolishly, there would have been about twenty people in supervisory roles above me who would have made it abundantly clear that I had screwed the pooch. I did not need any extra self-inflicted abuse.

Unbound by the physicians' hierarchical posturing, the nurses were free to discuss their patients with doctors of any rank. Many an attending in the unit started as interns in that same Unit with those same nurses. The nurse was supposed to ask the intern's permission to do most anything, but they could, in reality, also ask any senior physician for an order too. Consequently, if an intern's answer or attitude did not suit a nurse, she could appeal to one of his many bosses. Anything medical or personal an intern said could also be gossiped up the food chain to the rest of the unit team if the nurse was not pleased with an intern. Everyone, it seemed, liked the taste of fresh meat.

Until an intern earned the trust of a nurse, they were under constant scrutiny. So, the sorry life of an intern was made that much less bearable if the intern did not learn how to manage a nurse well.

I knew before I ever read the list of the monthly ICU assignments who my resident would be. For, as surely as a bridegroom wore nothing but a smile on his wedding night, I would be paired with Kent Pearson. Fate accepted nothing less from me..

In my month on the wards with Kent, I realized he was a competent, if not awe-inspiring, physician. To his credit, he was a good teacher of essential knowledge and skills, when he was so inclined to dispense them. After I endured his crushing wit for a while, he lightened up on me and actually talked to me like I mattered. Plus, truth be told, his humor worked best when he had an insider to share his jibes with. For example, remember the female intern on our ward team, the one whose name I'd forgotten? She received the lion's share of his abuse after he was done with me.

One day, she and I chatted as we were lying awake in a dark call room. Yes, there were coed call-room bunk beds. Neither of us could sleep from all the accumulated caffeine and adrenaline pulsing in our brains. She shared with me, for no reason other than punchiness, that since she started a new birth control pill the month before, her breasts had really gotten bigger. Mind you, in the bizarre setting of forced cohabitation with a member of the opposite sex you barely knew, such talk did not necessarily mean sexual innuendo. Well, she might have meant it as a come-on, but she may have equally have said it because it was what popped into her spent head at that moment.

At zero-dark-thirty after an interminable day, sleep deprived and isolated from whatever support we had outside the hospital walls, we could get weird. I hardly knew the woman. Her personal life and habits were an unknown country to me. But we both knew with great confidence that our pagers would scream out at us soon, so there was little time for sex. I chose to take her intent as nothing more than small talk. I told her that it was nice her breasts were bigger and that I'd try to pay more attention to them in the future. Sure enough, within a few minutes, there was a Code Blue and we were off and running.

Anyway, the next morning on rounds, Kent stared at her far longer than was socially acceptable. Finally, she was forced to ask, "Is there something the matter, Kent?"

He took a long look at her, thoughtfully drank from his red mug of coffee, then crossed his arms over his chest. Matter-of-factly he said, "Your breasts, are they bigger than they used to be?"

I swear I hadn't said a word to him up to that point about anything, least of all about Intern Girl's new and improved chest hardware. She knew it too, since we were together the entire night without interruption.

She roiled in offense. "How *dare* you!" She crossed her arms, partly to show anger and partly, I'm certain, to hide the topic of conversation.

Expressionless, Kent blinked a few times. "How dare I what?"

Flustered, she unfolded her arms and stomped one foot on the floor. "Oh no, you're not getting away with it this time, jocko. You have spent the entire month belittling me and making me the butt of your high-school-locker-room humor. But, that last remark is too much!"

As she paused to take in a shaky breath, he cut in. "I said your breasts were bigger, not your butt. There now, does that settle your frayed nerves? Is the little princess ready to tour her realm and get these rounds done with?" Several Red Team members failed miserably to suppress giggles.

She waved her finger back and forth at him, and stated, "Oh no, no, Mr. Politically Incorrect. You're not pulling that one off. You harassed me publicly, and I demand satisfaction." Immediately, she regretted having set him up so perfectly. "I mean, I demand a public apology. Then I will decide whether to take the matter up with the chairman!"

"Whoa there, Little Lady. Hold up."

A triumphant look crossed her face.

He went on. "I'm certain that if the chairman took note of your breasts previously, he would agree with me that they are bigger. But, decorum demands that I confess that I think it is highly unprofessional of you to drag the old boy into it, him having a weak heart and all. Why, having to stare at your breasts for a prolonged period in his decision-making process would give the old fart another heart attack. Think how bad you'd feel then, sweetheart." He paused to reflect. "However, I am willing to be reasonable. I am willing to be the bigger man here, if that's what it takes to jump-start rounds. If you are willing to swear here to everyone," he pointed around the circle, "that those breasts are not one tiny bit larger than they were only recently, I will apologize in a heartfelt manner that will leave not one dry eye in the house."

Her face assumed an even darker hue of crimson, but aside from that, she made no response.

He shrugged. "So, as much as it will pain me to say the words, I will concede openly here and now that I'm sorry as all get out that your beasts are every bit as itty-bitty as they have always been. My condolences to your unborn children, who seem at peril for malnutrition and its accompanying impairment of linear growth rates." He then flashed a look at his wrist, where a watch would have been if he owned one. "So, let's get a move on. Half the day's gone."

She held his gaze. Well, she would have if he would have looked in her direction for a few tense heartbeats. "That is the most insulting apology I have ever heard! Don't think this is over, Pearson." With that, rounds began, and that was the last I heard of the matter. I wasn't saying the way he embarrassed her was justifiable. But that was his humor, cruel and wickedly funny. I was just glad he had focused his laser beams somewhere else other than on me.

Anyway, back to the ICU rotation. Kent found me well before rounds started and went over my assigned patients. He'd been on-service a couple weeks already and knew them well. After we finished our discussion, he got a very serious, fatherly look on his face. I knew something was about to hit. He patted me on the shoulder and said, "Maybe now's as good a time as any to go over the ground rules. That okay with you, buddy?"

"Sure. What rules are those, Kent?"

He drew a wide arch around the room with his arm, and responded, "Why the rules of this fine intensive care facility!"

"The ICU has rules?"

Clearly taken aback, Kent said, "To be certain. It most assuredly has rules." He thumped me on the chest. "And if you learn them and abide by them closely, you just might survive this month."

"And if I do not heed these alleged rules, what then? Do I turn into a pumpkin or something?"

Aghast, Kent physically recoiled. "No! Nothing so benign as pumpkination would befall you, my poor fellow. No, that would be a blessing should you stray from the straight and narrow. You see, my boy, if you don't follow the rules and you end up killing a patient, you will get a bad review at the end by the attending."

"Okay, big guy, I'll bite. What are the 'rules'?" I hacked air quotation marks around "rules."

"Well, all right then! Rule one: *No big moves.* Rule two: *Every move's a big move.* Rule three: *Never take an ICU nurse's advice. Never!* Corollary one of rule three: *You must appear to listen to the bitches, but never...*please refer to rule three."

"Very kind of you to share. I don't know how to even begin to thank you. But seriously, the nurses know the patients the best. They spend all day with them. Doesn't that buy them some credibility?"

He scowled at me. "We are not having a discussion. We are reviewing the rules. Now hush up." He tapped his chin. "Where was I? Oh yes, rule four: *Do the right thing.* Rule five, my personal favorite: *Don't fuck up.* This leads us nicely to rule six: *Make sure to set up someone to blame when the patient turns into stool.* Respiratory therapy is the easiest and most common whipping boy. They are almost never present, and they control the ventilators. Trying to affix badness on a consultant can be tricky, but again, they are never around when to feces hits the fan, so they are unable to offer a defense." I raised my eyes, as if to speak. "Silence, meat! We're doing the rules. Rule seven: *You can't pace steak.* If a patient is deader than the proverbial doornail, stand down. Call the time of death and move the parade on down the road."

I had to interrupt. "Pace steak? What the hell's that supposed to mean?"

As if addressing a very small, very stupid child, he said, "You cannot reanimate a corpse, ya moronic toad. Once a participant expires, placing a pacemaker in the heart won't bring 'em back. So don't do it." He sighed wearily. "Rule eight is a longer rule, so listen attentively. *When, in the course of a code blue resuscitation, it becomes painfully obvious that the Grim Reaper has taken both the day and the patient, administer to the recently departed an ampule of everything on the crash cart. Then call the code off.*"

I had to protest. "An ampule of every drug on the code cart? Why? You mean to say I give them a drug simply because it's in a nearby box, not because they need it?"

He slapped me gently alongside the head. "You're the thick one today, aren't you, boy? The corpse doesn't need the meds. They're dearly departed and immune therein to the effects of medication. Recall rule seven, if you will. No, you give the patient one each of all the bright shiny bursto-jets and call their life's journey complete because you look thoroughly and commendably intelligent to those laboring by your side. All present will remark privately to themselves, 'Why, I would have forgotten to give both the calcium and the atropine. Isn't that intern a smart young physician?' Become a leader, meat! These simple folks need us to be their leaders."

Resigned, I was unwilling to resist any further. "That about all the rules, sensei?"

"Yes." He then corrected himself. "Yes, aside from rule nine, the most important of all rules." He allowed a moment to pass for dramatic effect. "Rule nine: *Never, never, ever, come bounding thought the doors of the ICU and yell out loud, 'I need a hot woman and a cold beer.'* Never, you hear me? You clear on that, bright eyes?"

I cocked an eyebrow. "I would never say such a stupid thing. But since you brought it up, why is it that I am forbidden to make that specific type of fool out of myself?"

As serious as a football coach during Super Bowl halftime, he wedged a finger under my chin. "Because that's *my* line, meat. Mine, and mine alone."

It promised to be an eventful month, remarkable in many ways.

FIVE

I mentioned morning report earlier, in a less than stellar light. It was actually an excellent vehicle for both learning and camaraderie. At least it had the potential to be. Attendance at morning report on my non-call day or when I was on a consultative service was fine, desirable actually. But, to be subjected to morning report after I had just survived all-day-all-night call? Well, that was just cruel and unusual. There I was, hair going every whichway, breath bad enough to stop a charging elephant, and my mind so addled it could easily be mistaken for tepid mush. I had to endure pimping and derision from people who were both more educated than me and who were in possession of a well-rested brain. However, any objections we hapless house officers might have raised against the system were batted-away like gnats on a warm summer's eve.

Morning report was run the way it was run. It always had been and it always would be. Arbitrary traditions were sacrosanct. There existed, even to that day, old medical codgers who lamented the fact that house officers were given regular days off and could live in their homes like normal people. They felt medicine could only be learned though bitter hardship and toil. Luckily for the universe, those blights died off eventually.

One pleasant upside to morning report was that I was able to maintain relationships I may have been otherwise been too busy to maintain. One anonymous morning, toward the end of my second year of training, I ran into Kent at morning report. We were both on electives, meaning both of us were free from the pressure of working on the wards or in the Unit. We were reasonably well-rested and mostly unbroken. I was seated in my usual spot, way to the back in the last row, farthest to the right-hand side of the room. This location allowed me as much invisibility as could be had. That made it less likely I'd be called on to answer questions.

Kent, not surprisingly, made it a habit of having no such predictability. He would sit anywhere when the moment inspired him. Occasionally, he would plant himself awkwardly right between two attendings who were clearly annoyed to have him there. That morning, whim directed him to sit by my side.

In his typical world-weary tone, Kent asked, "'Sup, Noah?"

No one else could hear me. "Abso-fucking-lutely nothing, my man. I sit here pining for knowledge, only to be disappointed, yet again, by these sorry excuses for slackers." I passed a hand in judgement broadly over the assembled crowd.

He elbowed me. "Don't be so hard on these peckerwoods. It's hard to reach their lofty positions before early dementia sets in. These poor SOBs are well-off enough to afford clean incontinence pads twice a day." He sipped at his coffee then looked straight ahead at nothing in particular. "Personally, I hate the smell of fermenting bodily waste. I could not be happier for the privilege of working with geezers with such fresh crotches."

I knew it was futile, but not to be outdone in the sarcasm department, I pointed at a senior citizen in the front row. "Not ol' Doc Hamilton there. The man smells like the Paris sewers."

He scoffed. "Hamilton's not incontinent. He just wears diapers to be cool. Why, he told me himself that he wear adult diapers because the astronauts in space do." He pointed again to Hamilton. "Dude just wants to be an astronaut. Never forget that a man's gotta have dream and aspirations, lest life become overly burdensome."

After I snickered appropriately, I raised a finger to either side of my head to simulate antennae and employed a mechanical voice. "Take me to your morning report, Earth doctor." Then I beeped a few times. At least I won a smirk from Kent for my efforts.

He scowled. "Could you cut it with the horseplay here, Noah. I'm trying to expand my horizons. All you seem to want to do is mock my close and personal friends."

Our chatter had gone on a bit too long to be ignored by our chief resident. One of her duties was to moderate morning report. Robin was a nice enough person, I guess, but she was quite the mother hen about her morning report. She took roll daily and allowed for no levity.

Abruptly, she said, "Noah, you and Kent there seem to be having quite the discussion about the differential diagnosis for this patient. Please share some of your collective insights, so that we might all be that much better informed."

Sideways from Kent's mouth came the whispered observation, "Bitch."

What was the case? Where were we in the presentation? I thought I'd heard a smattering of the discussion, so maybe I could wing it. A septic woman? No, but a woman, something—

Kent cut in, "Marion, if I might, as I am feeling a warm perkiness this fine morning, take a swing at that pitch." He called Robin "Marion." He told me that the name Robin brought forth images of Robin Hood for him. He opined that, as she was a woman, Robin must hence be known as Marion. Circular logic, to be certain, but that was Kent. She and he were the only two people, beside me, who knew why he called her Marion. Casual listeners probably imagined it was her middle name or a pet name they shared. She positively hated being called Marion. Whenever he addressed her as Marion, I could see little puffs of steam rise from her ears. He could too, naturally. That's why he called her Marion as often as possible.

She hissed through clenched teeth. "No, Dr. Pearson. Thank you, but no. I called on Noah, and I anticipate he will respond."

There existed in medicine several obscure, ill-defined, and decidedly rare disorders that were famous for having various and sundry presentation. "Great imitators," we called them, as those maladies could mimic many other more common diseases. Hence, the great imitators often went undiagnosed. I had learned, mostly from Kent, that if you wanted to either sound smart or were, as I was, backed into a corner, you would just about never be ridiculed for suggesting one of those rarities. In that defensive spirit, I listed of the possibilities. "Well, I—we—were thinking maybe porphyria, TB, or tertiary syphilis could be the cause here." I smiled disingenuously and folded my hands on the table to demonstrate finality.

If Robin's teeth were until now clenched tightly, she now threatened to break them all, such was the force of her bite. She knew that was a trick response as well as anyone did, only a year out of training herself. But she knew equally well that it was difficult to publicly reject the suggestions without appearing to be closed-minded and petty. "So, are we to understand that you feel this woman's fever, seizure, and preterm labor might have been a result of..." She took a deep breath to steady her disgust and anger, "tuberculosis or latent syphilis?"

In for a dollar, in for a dime. I raised an index digit. "Or acute intermittent porhyria."

She shook her head and nettled with strained credulity. "Or AIP."

"Yes," I agreed, as helpfully as I could.

"So, you don't think she has a kidney infection or the flu, which is going around, or even meningitis. You think she has... syphilis?" She was growing mightily hot under her matronly collar.

With a look on my face as serious as a judge passing a death sentence, I corrected her. "No. Well, those are good ideas too. Kudos to you for that. But I thought you were wanting to know the *entire* differential, not just the *obvious* diagnosis." I shook my head weightily in thoughtful reflection. "I don't feel morning report is a place to come to rapid judgments. I envision it more a forum of intellectual discussion and mind-stimulating brainstorming. But, if you prefer..." I trailed off dubiously.

Floridly irate, she thanked me. "Well, of course, we are here to think *outside* the box." Determined, as the vengeful woman she was, she asked, "But, how could TB or syphilis cause the patient to present as described? Please, Noah, I'm absolutely interested in hearing your line of reasoning." She crossed her arms and began to tap a foot.

I stretched my arms back over my head, then rested my hands atop my head. "Well, naturally, either syphilis and TB could cause a seizure by mass effect on the brain. That could result in a fever, and these two combined could initiate early labor." Hey, it was not impossible that was the sequence of events which lead her to our door.

She was of a mind to draw more blood. "And porphyria, how could that even possibly cause this clinical presentation?" She had an excellent point there. I had to yield her that.

Kent busted out, now as uncontainable as a nuclear chain reaction. He waved his hand maniacally in the air. "Call on me, pleeeeease! Call on me, Marion, pretty please. A cherry on top, if that what it takes, Marion. Meeee!"

With hateful revulsion, Robin looked at him and spoke. "Of course, Dr. Pearson. You are, as always, welcome to participate. Come, tell us all how AIP can, in your wildest estimations and delusions, cause this clinical presentation."

"Well, you see, Marion, it's like this. The patient was not actually in preterm labor. Her AIP caused abdominal pain *mimicking* labor. AIP is most common in women in this very age group." To be consummately annoying and to burrow even deeper under Robin's skin, he questioned her. "Did you not know that, Marion?"

Her fists were clenched, and her foot tapped loudly on the floor as her teeth began to shatter. "And how does that account for the fact that she had a fever and the fact that her cervix was fully dilated?" She added in purulent anger. "And yes, I am actually quite familiar with the demographics of AIP. Thank you for asking."

"Marion, please!" He bent over until his forehead touched the table. Head thus planted, he said, "It's *so* obvious! Wait," He looked suddenly serious and vulnerable. "Are you mocking me here in front of my peers and supervisors and friends, Marion?" He allowed a moment for that to sink in and continued, "But, Marion, I shall give you the benefit of the doubt and assume this is not the case. As you, in fact, asked so nicely, I will tell you. The muscular efforts she had from the pain and the rush of adrenaline caused her fever, and the fever caused the seizure, which, in turn, initiated early labor."

As frustrated as humanly possible, she shuddered. "And so…what? You think we should order a twenty-four-hour urine for porphobilinogen and ignore the head sticking out from between the woman's legs?"

He savored, yet again, his victory over maid Marion. He beamed a huge, warm smile. "No, Marion, I think she should be started on antibiotic for her urinary infection and the baby should be yanked out and whisked off to the NICU. Why do you think we need a twenty-four-hour porphobilinogen? Sounds to me like an expensive waste of limited recourses on a real shot in the dark there, honey."

"But *you*…Noah…suggested AIP, not me. You cannot deny you specifically mentioned AIP. We all heard it plain as day." She raised her arms to the stunned-silent audience by way of appeal.

"Marion, *Marion!*" He spoke paternally. "You seem vexed and distraught this morning. Anything you'd like to share with us?" He gestured around the room. "We're all family here. I, for one, am never too busy to help a comrade in distress."

Raggedly, she stiffened. "No. Thank you all the same. Nothing is bothering me. I just want to make certain report progresses intelligently and not like an episode of *The Three Stooges*." Stiffly smoothing her white coat, she added, "Sorry if I seemed to raise my voice, gang." Her smile was unconvincing. "I am just so darn passionate about getting the facts straight." She sipped her coffee and announced, "Okay, let's move on to the next case." She pointed to the lifeless resident who presented the first case. "Bob, if you will. Were there any other interesting cases last night?"

To complete his rendition of irritating and disrespectful, Kent raised his arm halfway, to signal he had a question. "Ah, Marion, one last question." He pointed to her cup. "That's decaf, right?"

She hesitated a long, pitiful moment, uncertain of whether to disembowel him then and there or to proceed with report. Hesitantly, she stared at him. "Please … proceed, Bob."

"Sure." Bob took a moment to yawn. "Oh, sorry. Long night. So we admitted a thirty-nine-year-old woman with fever of unknown origin."

She exuded excitement. "Really? How interesting. Please do tell us about her."

Bob rubbed his brow like he was kneading bread dough, probably to keep himself awake and focused. "So, she's an unmarried elementary school teacher

36

from the suburbs who has a two-month history of a thirty-pound weight loss, hectic fevers to one hundred four degrees, and night sweats. Pretty uneventful medical history and…"

Robin cut him off. "Please *inform* us of her history and let us judge if it is uneventful or not."

He stared at her, shrugged his shoulders, and filled us in. "No major medical conditions. Her only chronic medicine is her oral contraceptive, no surgeries except an appendectomy age eight." Least Bob expose himself to further reprimand, he added, "Social history, as I said, she's a teacher, lived around here all her life, and her stable sexual partners have been male. Nothing kinky going on when the bedroom doors are closed and the shades are drawn, at least none she owned up to."

Someone in the front quipped. "Too bad."

"No significant family history of cancer, heart disease, or anything else." He looked up to Robin. "Well, that's about her."

To those assembled at morning report, she asked, "Any questions as to her presentation?" There were none. "Okay, Robert. Why don't you give us the exam and labs."

He ran a hand through his shock of disjointed hair and complied. "BP one ten over seventy-six, pulse a little tachy at one hundred nine, respirations sixteen and unlabored. Well-developed, well-nourished female…"

Kent elbowed me and whispered, "I wonder if he took her word on that or if he checked himself as to her womanly development?"

I snorted nasally.

"Appearing her stated age. Head and neck exam unremarkable, lungs clear, heart regular rate and rhythm without murmurs, rubs, or gallops. Her abdomen showed large minimally tender hepatosplenomegaly but was otherwise normal. Bimanual GU exam was unremarkable; rectal was negative for blood. Neuro exam within normal limits. Everything else was too."

She turned to the room. "Any questions now?"

An attending asked if there was a history of IV drug use to hint at the possibility of AIDS. None was reported. With no other questions pending, Robin asked Bob for a summary of the labs. "Basically, everything was within normal limits. Blood count unremarkable, aside from eosinophils being a tad high. Chemistries picture perfect, chest X-ray clear as a bell. All rather anticlimactic, if I do say so myself."

"It would be better if you presented the labs and not your opinion of them, Robert. It will have to do for now, I guess. So, what did you do with her last night?"

Bob shrugged noncommittally. "Not a whole heck of a lot. We cultured her up and tucked her in. That's about it."

She attempted to disguise her next baited question with conviviality. "And did you start antibiotics?"

Bob was seasoned enough to avoid that trap. "No, we did not. We considered it for a time. It was very tempting to do so. But, in the end, we knew it would be a shot in the dark, since we had no idea what was wrong with her."

She was clearly disappointed at not being able to rip him a new hole because he started empiric treatment. "So, if you don't think she has an infection, what is your differential? What does she have?"

He was clearly ready for this question. "Well, numbers one through five on my top-ten list are cancer, cancer, cancer, cancer, and cancer. Next would be an occult infection like endocarditis or osteomyelitis, but these wouldn't account for the huge liver and spleen."

"How about hepatitis, cirrhosis even?" She folded her arms.

He scratched his head, cocked it sideways. "Not likely. Not with such normal liver tests. I'd expect she'd have some bump in LFTs or some other stigmata on exam."

She turned to address one of the Gastroenterology attendings who was quietly munching on a bagel. "Dr. Pinsky, what do you think? Could this be a presentation of cirrhosis?"

He wiped his mouth hurriedly. "Could be, if a whole bunch of factors lined-up just right, but I doubt it. In really advanced disease, it's hard to bump the LFTs because there's so little functioning liver, but I'd expect anemia and ascites would be present."

Back to the resident, she asked, "So, what type of cancer do you suspect, since you are fairly certain that's what the patient suffers from?"

"I'd wager a month's meager wages she has a leukemia hidden in her marrow. Lymphoma is possible, but my money is on leukemia."

"With such a normal complete blood count?"

"I'd like to see something odd on the CBC, sure, but it is not mandatory. A lymphoma could definitely present with a normal CBC."

She then addressed a middle-aged woman near the front of the room. "So, Dr. Li, as an oncologist, do you agree with this assessment?"

"I have to admit that Bob did buttonhole me earlier, so I know something about the case. A cancer of some blood component does seem most likely. A chronic leukemia would be top of my list. She's a bit too young for a myeloproliferative disease and too old for a lysosomal storage disease like Gaucher's. Sarcoid would likely show on the X-ray, and lupus this pronounced would have affected the other labs. Bottom line, she needs a bone marrow."

Robin asked broadly of morning report. "Anyone else have a different option? Any other ideas?"

A brave, totally foolhardy medical student asked, "How about sickle cell disease or a thalassemia?"

Robin responded as condescendingly as possible. "Not likely with such a normal CBC, don't you think?" The student did not respond verbally and only squirmed in her seat uncomfortably. "Okay then, some form of hematological cancer it is. Make sure to keep us up-to-date, Bob. Won't you?"

Robin started to make an announcement. "A couple of quick updates—"

"How about leishmaniasis?" I said this, to my considerable surprise and consternation.

Fresh from her earlier interaction with Kent and me, Robin was in no mood for a repeat performance. She snapped back at me, "How about leishmaniasis what, Noah?"

I sat up straight. "The woman we are discussing. She could have leishmaniasis."

She squared her body to face me and arms folded tightly. "Are you serious, or are you two simply attempting to have a bit more fun at my expense?"

Kent pointed both index fingers at me. "Him, Marion. Noah here is flying solo. I absolutely *love* your diagnostic conclusions, dear."

No less annoyed, she repeated her objection. "Then, Noah *alone*, why do you feel the need to add such an obtuse diagnosis to the differential? Hmm? Trying to impress us, yet again, with your unparalleled brilliance?"

"You are way too kind, Robin. Thanks for the compliment just the same. No, I mention Kala-Azar disease because she might have it. We can't make her better unless we treat what's wrong with her, right?"

She was clearly disenchanted with my continued existence on Earth. "Thanks. I didn't know that. I thought we could treat whatever we want to and leave the rest chance." She realized quickly she'd gone too far with that last snarky comment and replaced the mechanical smile on her face. "Seriously then, all my kidding aside, you don't for one second think this schoolmarm could have leishmaniasis do you? She has zero travel history to support that diagnosis. Where would she contract the bug? Can't get it from a toilet seat, now can she?" She turned to Bob and confirmed, "You said no travel history, right?"

"Nope, nothing big. Uh, the medical student went over her history in more detail." He scanned the room and pointed. "Debbie, no travel history, right?"

Caught off guard, the student stammered, "N... no, sir, Bob. No travel history."

I addressed the frightened Debbie as gently as I could. "No foreign travel ever?"

"No, none really. She went on a European cruise two years ago, but she spent almost the entire time on the ship. She toured Venice and Barcelona but was otherwise never off the boat. Aside from that, she hasn't even been to Disney World."

Robin dismissed me. "There, you see, Noah, no leishmaniasis. May we move on now?"

"Whatever. I'm just trying to be thorough, no stone unturned and all that. It's your party. You do want you want."

"Humph. Okay, back to announcements ..."

Four months later, my stomach churned with a thousand butterflies. I sat down after morning report to take over the ward service from a very relieved intern, Slim Steward. He was the only person I ever met who went by "Slim." And, yes, he was tall and extremely thin. So began my next sentence on the wards. Another month of pain. I felt exactly like the condemned man who walked up the wooden steps to be hanged. My lot was to be all that much worse, since it was mid-winter. The days were short and the temperatures freezing. Plus, in winter, the burden on hospitals increased. Cold and flu season would fill the hospital with life's hangers on and all the holiday revelry would throw many heart failure patients into the nearest ambulance. The service I inherited was unusually large to begin with, so coupled with the season, I knew I was about to be crushed, big time.

Four weeks of hell, I repeated like a mantra. *It's only four weeks in hell*. It wasn't six weeks in hell. No, only four weeks. I was doing a lousy job of encouraging myself.

My attention returned from my muddle of self-pity to Slim, when he said, "Then we have Cancer Lady. She's yours now, thanks be. Not much going on, Hem-Onc is still following along, but even they are losing interest in her. Infectious diseases finally said to stop calling unless something grows from a culture. They're tired of hearing about her. She gets bone marrow biopsies all the time, so you will at least get a lot of practice."

Before Slim went on, I had to stop him. "Cancer Lady? Who's that?"

Dumbfounded, Slim said, "You know…Cancer Lady. Everybody know her."

I shook my head. "I'm not everybody. Who the hell is Cancer Lady?"

"What planet have you been on, dude?"

"Planet vacation, planet nephrology rotation at the VA hospital before that, and planetoid ER rotation before that. Haven't you noted my absence from boring report lately?"

"Not particularly. No. Well, any way you look at it, you are about to inherit the hospital's dullest and most unfulfilling case. Cancer Lady."

"What," I asked, "is dull about cancer?"

"Nothing is dull about cancer, but she ain't got it."

I was in no mood. I stared down both barrels of a shotgun called a month on the wards. "Slim, just the facts, please. If she doesn't have cancer, how can she be Cancer Lady?"

With both hands, he soothed the air between us. "Easy, Tex. Keep your britches up 'n tight. Okay, Ms. Hope Chalmers has been in the hospital for several months. She must have cancer, but it won't show its fool head. She's had every test twice and most a dozen more just for good measure. CTs, PET scans, bone marrows, and enough blood tests to fill the Red Sea. Still nothing."

"You are kidding, right?"

Hands to heaven, Slim swore. "I only wish I were."

"So, that's it? She spikes temps, you culture her, and nothing shows up? Anything on physical exam?"

He shook his head piously. "Nope, nothing except the darn old hepatosplenomegaly."

Her! "Is she the school teacher Bob admitted for FUO months back?"

"Bob wrote the first H&P, so, yeah, that's probably her."

Well I'll be, I thought. The gauntlet was thrown down to me.

After I met with my team and felt halfway confident that all my fires had been put out, I sat down to study Hope's exceedingly voluminous electronic medical record. If it were still the days of paper charts, she'd be on volume ten, at least, and each chart would be thicker than an NYC phonebook. In the end, I had to agree with all the great minds that preceded mine.

Cancer was most likely, but every known type had been effectively excluded. She had five hundred thirty-seven negative blood cultures, two negative bronchoscopies, eight negative endoscopic studies of her gastrointestinal tract, and too numerous to count negative urine samples. Well, when all else failed, examine the patient. So, off I went to meet my new charge.

With professional aplomb or something not far from it, I strode into her semi-private room and introduced myself. "Hello, Ms. Chalmers, I'm Dr. Taylor. I'll be your new intern in charge of…"

"In charge of jack shit!" snapped Hope.

Now that caught me completely off guard. "Excuse me? I was just introducing myself as your new—"

"My new wet-behind-the-ears-know-nothing-ass-wipe intern." Impatiently, she added, "I know the drill, junior. You know next to nothing about medicine and are lorded over by higher-paid morons who haven't got one damn idea what's wrong with me after bleeding me and my insurance for all we're worth." After taking a breath, Hope continued further up my colon. "If you all had a shred of decency, you'd at least send me home to die of god knows what. But no! I'm stuck here giving doctor lessons to weak-cheese pukes the likes of you."

There were many ways to proceed. Even at my tender age and with my limited experience, I knew there were options. One was to assume the higher ground. "I understand your frustration, *generic patient*. Please, continue to vent so that I might help you." Too New Age for me.

Then there was the high-and-mighty. "Mrs. *Stupid ass patient*, I am a top man, and you're lucky to have me. Behave or I'll cast you down to a lesser practitioner." Nice, but there were always the complaint letters. Who needed them?

I could always play the wise ass card. "Really, is someone having a bad menstrual cycle this month?" Nah, even worse letters, trust me.

I decided, I'd just talk with her honestly. What the hell. "Wow! You do know the drill, Hope!" I clapped my hands. "Yes, I am your chump-of-the-month. I work for the bloated-morons-of-the-month. Yes, Hope, we are both sadly stuck with each other, you and me, for the next thirty days." I reached out my hand again. "My name is Noah. Glad to meet you."

She did not budge. "You're a lousy liar. You know that, kid?"

"Au contraire, you are a lousy judge of character. I am glad, honored even, to meet you."

She cautiously took my hand. "And just why would that be the case, boy?" She released my hand and continued, "You are stuck on the wards with me as a patient, and still, you are tickled pink to know me. How so?"

I sat on the end of her bed. "Because you are a remarkable woman. That's why I'm proud to know you."

"This hospital is a no-smoking zone, sonny boy. Don't be blowing it my ass."

"Hope, here you sit knowing you face certain death, desperate to go home but more afraid of not doing everything in you power to find out what is going on. You realize we are collectively clueless, but you also know that we are your best chance to live. If you walked out that door," I pointed to the door for effect, "where would you go? Any hospital in the United States would ship you right back here because we are, despite being deaf-dumb-blind morons, quite simply, number one."

She began to applaud me. I'm certain for the first time in months, she smiled, just a tiny impish smile, but a smile nonetheless. She pointed at me. "You, I like. The rest of them," she batted the back of her hand at the air, "can go straight to hell!"

"This I can work with."

"So, Noah-my-only-hope, what is the matter with me?"

I nodded my head a few times and puckered my lips. "No freaking idea. Not even a poor excuse for one, my friend."

She tried to game me with a stare down, but she couldn't hold back a laugh for very long. Soon we both rolled on her bed laughing like a couple of preteens. A nurse even came in to see what the commotion was about. She was met with a commanding, "What, Nancy? You never seen a patient and her doctor discussing her differential diagnosis before? Now scram before I lodge a confidentiality case against your skinny ass." After the nurse was out of earshot, Hope said, "My only true friends in the whole horrible mess have been the nurses. God bless them." She wiped at a tear. "Without them and their support…well, I'm just grateful to them all. Especially Nancy there. She is among the very best."

"That's good to hear. It's nice us wannabes have such excellent backup. You deserve the best."

"You better watch yourself, boy. I might just ask you to scoot up closer in bed and say that like a man."

I rose slowly to my feet. "No way, that's gonna happen. I don't want to catch whatever you got."

She laughed again. "I'd be so lucky if it was contagious. At least then you doctors would be motivated to find the diagnosis."

After we settled back down, I did my physical exam. Sure enough, everything was normal except for her large, hard liver and spleen. Well, honestly, I assumed they were hard. I had felt so few of either organ it was impossible to say from experience. They sure felt firm. "I know you've had every test and answered every question, but—"

She held up her hand. "Hold it right there. You're my doctor. You need to know everything, so if you have a question, you damn well better ask it. I'm not paying for just your pretty face. I want results."

"Okay, thanks. So, no drugs, no alcohol, no bad habits you forgot to mention."

"No." She pouted. "I wish there *was* something like that. At least I'd have enjoyed myself into this pickle."

"And no weird family history of any kind?" She shook her head decisively no. "And no travel?" Before she could answer, I said, "Well, just that Mediterranean cruise a couple years back, and you only got off the boat in Venice and Barcelona, right?"

She slapped her hands together. "Damn, you *are* good. You picked that out of my endless chart?"

"No. I remembered it from morning report the day after you were admitted. The med student was so serious and certain. I never forgot."

"All the more impressive, Dr. Taylor. I am most impressed. I have a tiny glimmering of faith way down in my belly that you may yet be my savior."

I held up a hand. "Let's not get ahead of ourselves. Having a good memory and being a clinical star are two very different things."

"A girl can hope, can't she?"

"It's funny. I remember I got ridiculed for making a suggestion about you too. Have you met our chief resident Robin yet?"

She rolled her eyes and whistled. "Bitch has a diamond-handled stick so far up her ass it would take King Arthur himself to pull it out."

"I see you've met her. She was pissed off when I suggested you might have Kala-Azar disease."

"Kala-*what*?"

"Sorry, visceral leishmaniasis. It's an infection in Egypt, the Indian

45

subcontinent, and other romantic destinations like that. Bad mojo, Hope. A real nasty disease."

She snuffled a quiet laugh.

"What?"

"You mention romantic destinations and bad mojo. Well, that's me. I'm a total stay-at-home Nancy, as you well know. Remember my dream cruise of the Med? Well, some dickweed twice my age I used to work with asked me to join him on that trip. He was going to go with his brother, but bro cancelled last minute because of prostate trouble. So, my ex-friend asked if I would like to go in his brother's place. He had only the one cabin, but he swore it would be a 'just friends' cruise." She made air-quotes around friends. "Right! The minute the ship's gangplank was pulled back, he pulled his out and yelled 'all aboard!' After a few nights of 'please excuse my hand, that was a cramp' and 'I thought that was my thigh,' I was done. I either slept in the lounge or, on the rare warm night, up on deck."

"Sounds like the cruise from hell," I chuckled.

"Boy howdy to that. Why are men such pigs?"

"Men!" I sniffed. "Don't get me started."

I was about to change the subject to get back on task when something she said registered as odd. "You said, 'rare warm night.' So, most nights were what, cold?"

"Yeah, most were bitterly cold. It was late autumn, and the weather had definitely turned."

"So why were there any warm nights? Seems odd to have a warm night out of the blue."

"Struck me funny too. And when it was warm, it was really warm. Warm and windy."

"Warm and windy then cold and not windy?"

"Yeah. Crazy European weather or something, I guess. And I'm here to tell you, it wasn't windy as in, mess your hair up windy. No. It was like howling gale force winds, pin your ears back, then, puff, nothing. Gone like a forgotten dream."

My back stiffened like electricity was shot down it. "Where in the Mediterranean were those strong, hot winds?"

"I'll tell you exactly where. Both times we sailed past Malta is where. I even asked a deckhand what was up with the winds, and he said something like 'Zoloft'. The only Zoloft I know of is a pill for depression. The man spoke nothing but whatever he spoke to his mother, so I don't know what he was trying to tell me. That mean anything to you?"

I mumbled. "Not Zoloft, Hope. *Xlokk*."

"Say what, honey? I can't understand what you said either, but you do sound kinda like that deckhand."

Animated as a circus monkey, I bounced. "The deckhand was trying to be as correct as possible. Maybe he was even a local." I was shouting at that point. "Hope, *xlokk* is what they call the *sirocco* in Malta."

She immediately lost any pretense of amusement. "You just stepped firmly on my last nerve. What in the name of all that's holy are you talking about?"

"Don't you see? No, of course you don't. How could you?"

She seized one of my wrists with sufficient firmness and buried her nails deep enough to get my full and immediate attention. "I say again, Dr. Taylor. To what are you referring? It's sounding to me like you blew some kind of gasket up top."

"No, no. I just figured out what's wrong with you." I stood and addressed her with formality. "Mrs. Chalmers, it is my duty as your physician to inform you that you suffer from visceral leishmaniasis, aka Kala-Azar disease, the black fever, alternately known as Dumdum fever."

"But you just said it's only from Africa and India. How can I have a disease I've never been exposed to?"

"Hope," my words raced like my pulse, "guess where the sirocco blows from."

"I have no idea what a sirocco is let alone where it hails from."

"The sirocco is the name of a legendary wind that blows from Africa in spring and fall. When the wind blows hard off of the desert of North Africa, it can carry with it not just hot air and dust, but a tiny little fly, the sand fly. That's the bug that transmits the disease." I pinched my fingers together to indicate something very small. "Its bite is so tiny it's hardly ever felt, and the parasite can grow so slowly that it takes months, even years to produce disease.

In general, the sand fly is nocturnal. Don't you see? You slept on the open deck while sand flies were being blown at you from Africa. You have Kala-Azar."

"So, Dr. Taylor, how do we prove I do, and more importantly, can I get rid of it?"

"Well, let me think. You can see the parasite in the blood if you look just right, but nowadays there are serological tests that are pretty good. Shouldn't be a problem proving it."

"And what about treatment? Come on, you got me to the brink of hope. Is it curable?"

I had to reply honestly. "I've never treated anyone with leishmaniasis before, so I don't know. There are a couple of orphan drugs reputed to work well. I'll call Infectious Disease, and we'll both find out. No worries."

"You've never seen a patient with leishmaniasis, but you know the name of the wind in Maltese and how to treat it. No one else had the slightest idea for four months in this whole place full of overpaid stooges, and you pull it off on day one of your rotation?"

I could only shrug noncommittally.

"Well, I'll be damned. If you were single, Noah, I'd invite you up to my place for a drink."

"I am single, Hope."

She swatted a hand my direction. "Get over it already, Noah. Our moment has passed." She winked at me. "But if anyone ever asks me who the best doctor in the whole wide world is, kiddo, I'm telling them it's Dr. Noah Taylor."

It took the better part of a year, a somewhat toxic treatment course, and countless phone calls to specialists all over the world, but by the following September, Hope Chalmers was finally cured of her visceral leishmaniasis for good. More importantly, she was back in the classroom where she longed to be.

I thought about rubbing Robin's nose in my glorious achievement, by the way. I could blind side her at morning report, casually interrupt her when I found her talking with a higher up, or send out a general FYI email. I chose to let it pass. My goal wasn't to get even, even though it would have been brilliant. My goal was to help my patients. Pissing off my chief resident didn't further that goal. I figured, in the end, I'd just have to be an adult.

SIX

Three years later …

I finished my residency in one piece, physically at least. Up until that point, the career choices I had made were so straightforward they basically made themselves. Go to college, get into medical school, and then fight for a good residency. I had been running a sprint while looking at my feet. I never glanced up at what lay ahead. I was fairly certain I wanted to practice general Internal Medicine. However, I lacked real world skills. I could pass any tube, place any line, and I knew which antibiotic killed which super-bugs. But I did not know how to treat pink eye or a sore back.

I decided the best way to remedy my shortcomings was to do a fellowship in Primary Care. As I had spent my entire medical training in the same, albeit distinguished, institution, I elected to venture to parts unknown. So, it was off to San Francisco I went for two cold years in the fog and wind. New England winters were bone-chilling, but they eventually ended in a pleasant spring. A fairly nice summer usually followed that. San Francisco was cold all year long. It was, to be certain, a beautiful city. Just too darn cold.

After I was done in San Francisco, I moved back home to New England. My next decision in terms a life plan was to see if I wanted to remain in academics. I accepted a position as a research associate with one of the high rollers back at my alma mater. Her area of focus involved cholesterol and its effects on populations. It wasn't exactly my first choice of subject matter, but it would look good to have worked with a big name like her.

So, on a brisk late September morning, I presented myself to Dr. Ruth Farbstein's office to begin my open-ended tour of duty. Ruth, who was aging gracefully, possessed an inviting smile and had a genuine warmth about her. As she had a reputation of being fair and thoughtful, and I very much looked forward to work under her tutelage.

Ruth received me in her office. Her group had some laboratory space assigned to it, but most of the work was done at a desk. She waved me in. "Noah, so good to see you! Wow, it's been months since your interview, hasn't it? How time does indeed fly. How've you been?"

"I couldn't be better. And you? Hey, did your son get into Yale? Last we met he was sweating out word about their MBA program."

She smiled. "There's that great memory of yours we all missed while you were gone. Yes, my Abe is down in New Haven as we speak. Thanks for asking."

"That's marvelous. I'm sure you're a proud mom."

"Proud-shmoud. He is paying for this degree, so I'm a *happy* mom." After our chuckles died down, Ruth asked, "So, are you ready to sink your teeth into clinical research, my boy? Ready to roll up those sleeves and plunge in?"

"Up to my shoulders."

"That's what I like to hear. But, we'll see if a few months under my vicious boot heel doesn't lessen your enthusiasm."

I fanned my fingers toward me, palms up. "Bring it on."

She laughed. "If only I were mean and cruel. Maybe I'd get a lot more done." She pointed toward the ceiling. "Do you know Hugh Silverman, right above us?"

"No, can't say I know him. Why?"

She leaned back in her chair. "Here's the line he uses with his graduate students. Play along. Hey, Noah, do you know what the best thing about Friday is?"

"No, Ruth. What is the best thing about Friday?"

She tried to look stern. "There's only two working days until Monday."

We both had a chuckle. "Sure glad I didn't sign on with him."

"That wouldn't have happened. Not in a million years."

"Why not? I'm a good postdoc choice, aren't I?"

"Yes, you are." She held up a hand and counted her reasons. "One, you're very bright. Two, you are proven to think outside the box. Three, you're a genuinely nice guy and easy to work with. Four, you are a tireless worker. Five, most importantly, you accepted my offer to work for slave wages."

"So, what? Silverman doesn't fancy a talented bargain?"

"He wouldn't take you on because you have options. If I piss you off or abuse you, you'd bolt. You could get a medicine job tomorrow and make real coin. Silverman will only take people who are stuck with him—literally trapped. He specializes in foreign nationals on visas provisional on their continued employment with him. They only get their degree when Silverman is good and ready to grant them. I befriended a really talented student of his a few years back. I watch Silverman dangle and withdraw the carrot so many times that the poor girl finally cracked. She bailed out after six years with nothing to show for her efforts other than the disgrace of failure."

"And the administration let's that sort of thing happen?"

Ruth smiled sadly. "Ah, the naiveté of youth." She stared thoughtfully out the window for a moment. "Silverman churns out three or four peer-reviewed journal articles a month. The grants he receives are so large that his bosses kiss his butt, embarrassingly loud and wet at times. He is 'The Real Deal' around these parts. No one in academia is ever going to question how he handles his grad students." Ruth throated a quiet, derisive laugh.

"What?"

"If Silverman mentioned to Dean Johnson that his teenage daughter was looking particularly nice, I bet Silverman would find her in his office the next morning wearing nothing but a bow."

"Ruth, I don't believe I've ever said this to any of my bosses before, but you're disgusting."

She snapped her fingers and pointed at me. "And don't you ever forget it. I'm capable of much worse, mind you, but the day is young, and I am, lamentably, still sober." She rose to her feet. "We're not catching up and sitting around here chewing the fat. Let's get you tucked in and productive."

I followed her out of the room and down the hall on an impromptu tour.

"My secretary's office is over here, as you know. The lunch room is down there, microwaves, fridges, and a sink. The usuals. These offices are for the grad students and miscellaneous flotsam a project the size of this gathers. Statisticians, dietitians, you name it."

"Does Dean Johnson's daughter have a cot in there too?"

Ruth wagged a finger at me. "You, I'm going to have to watch." Back to a casual tone, Ruth said, "These rooms are for my top assistants like you. A big old office all to yourself."

"I'm honored."

"Don't kid yourself. Here in the ivory tower, having your own space is a big deal. You, my friend, have made the jump to hyperspace."

"Duly noted, Captain Solo."

She opened a door and signaled me in. "This is your brand spankin' new office." I stuck my head in far enough to note an off odor. "Please overlook, for the time being, the coffin-like size, its lack of windows, and the fact that this used to be someone's mycology lab." Ah, yes, that was the off smell: ancient mold and fungus. How very entry level.

"However, before I turn you loose, I'd like to introduce you to a new addition to our little family. He's a junior faculty member with his own start-up grant. He'll be teaming up with me until he's ready to fledge on his own. Nice fellow. Wacky sense of humor like you." Ruth knocked on a door. There was something about the voice that said, "Come in." "Dr. Noah Taylor, I'd like you to meet—"

I shouted, "Not you!"

She shot a look of confusion between us, then finished her sentence. "Dr. Kent Pearson ... who I guess you already know."

He vaulted to his feet and extended a hand in greeting. "I taught him everything he knows, Ruth. I guess one could fairly summarize that I'm kind of a father figure to the boy."

She set her hands on her hips. "Well, then you should fit in perfectly to your new roles here. A father/son team. I rather like that."

She turned to me and said, "While I'm your ultimate supervisor, you'll be working more closely with Kent than me. He's starting an arm of our project that looks in fine detail at the constituent makeup of HDL cholesterol. We want to figure out which specific part or parts are responsible for the beneficial effects they have on cardiovascular risk. Traditionally, HDL, taken is said to confer protection. We suspect there are a whole lot of subcomponents, only some of which are active. That's what he's working on."

He cut in. "It's all very needle-in-the-haystack. No telling how many active parts there are if you look down to the nanomolar levels. You and I are going to get real up close and personal with genetically mutated mice. Now doesn't that sound like a hoot?"

Before I could answer, Ruth patted my shoulder. "With that, I'll leave you two old chums alone and get back to my office." She pointed to me as she parted. "You need anything, you let me know. Okay?"

Kent stepped in front of me and made a show of pushing her out and shutting the door behind her. "I'll show him where the bathrooms are and even how to wipe his butt, Mother Ruth. Never you worry." After we were alone, he balled up his fists. "Man, I thought she'd never leave!" Running to his chair, he landed in it, spun around twice, and pointed to another chair. "Grab some pine, meat. We got a lot of catching up to do."

I was stunned. "I can't believe it, finding you here. You of all people."

With his trademarked wise-ass smile, Kent asked, "Why does it strike you as so tremendously odd, my judgmental associate?"

"You…here…tenure track…a cholesterol researcher? Blah!"

"You remain as unfortunately sub-articulate as I recollect you to be."

"But you, all fancy and unconventional, a mainstream man? I figured you'd end up running a VD clinic in Tijuana or, I don't know, selling out to Big Pharma." I flung my arms around. "But this? The very center of respectability and conformity? No way."

"If I cared one gnat fart, I think I'd take offense at your implied slight. But as you present a potentially valid point, I might just be forced to own your observations."

"So, what gives? Why all this?" Again, I gestured globally.

He shrugged. "Well, truth be struck by the harsh light of day, I felt this was the best place for a soul the likes of mine."

"How so?"

With feigned gravity, he said, "This is how I see it, Noah. The manner in which I perceive it to be. While I am not averse, per se, to toiling to earn my daily bread, I am equally no fool, or so I hold. Consequently, after carefully reviewing all possible options the universe had so graciously set before me, I selected academic research." He held a hand up to forestall the questions that were competing to jump out of my mouth. "Please hold your peace and allow the story to build naturally. It carries, in such a manner, more gravitas. I think you'll come to agree."

What a piece of work was Kent.

"The manifest benefits of a career in academics include a slow-paced life. I am not called upon to see a patient in seven and a half minutes regardless of the severity of their condition. All research consists of, at its core, is spending grant money. The art of grant getting is, in my opinion, learning the application bullshit. It's not so much talent as it is sufficient quantities of said bullshit." Kent patted his chest. "I consider myself to be a consummate master of the art of bullshit. I know you can attest to that fact with significant conviction, based on our previous experiences together. Hence, let us face the facts as they actually are. I am a fundamentally lazy man. I am only marginally gifted intellectually, and I wish to engage in no activity that might produce sweat. Hence academia and I are as well matched as whores are to sailors."

I attempted to understand Kent's mind, which was impenetrable. "But seriously. Research can be difficult, very tricky. First off, you have to produce results. Publish or perish, right? So, that means you must have ideas, be curious, and find answers to unanswered questions. That requires much more than the application of bullshit. You have to have creativity and insight, which do not fall from the sky like manna."

He raised his hand to stop further protestation. "You have hit upon why I chose *cholesterol* research. You see, one does not need extensive training, a driven intellect, or brilliant imagination in this field. All one needs do to succeed in this arena is enroll enough cattle into larger pens, and one will always have publishable results. Even if I spend my entire career only validating the work of others, I will make tenure and command respect. Win-

win, Noah. I declare that to be win-win. I work little, think less, and climb the academic ladder with both grace, alacrity, and ease." He bowed his head. "Care you to join me, my esteemed junior colleague?"

Though it was always difficult to glean what he actually thought or felt, I took him at his word regarding his career choice. I was not, at that juncture, ready to decide where my future was to take me, however. Plus, he had nothing of substance to offer. He was as unseasoned and unproven as I was. If I joined him, it might have been to link my fortune to the mists of a dream, not to a rising star. "Hey, this is like my first day here. Lighten up already. I'm working under Ruth to decide if research is even my thing. Let's let the future worry about itself for now."

Squarely, Kent agreed. "A fine and a sound plan, compadre." Then he got that mischievous glint in his eyes. "You say you came to work under Ruth, is it?" His torso shook violently. "Sounds like an appalling and disillusioning prospect to me, but hey, to each his own. I must confess, it paints a most sobering image—one I don't like to picture." He placed his finger deep in his throat, to suggest he wanted to vomit.

"Very droll."

"So, if the future is not yours to say, kind fellow, can you at least appraise me as to what your immediate past has been?" He rocked his eyebrows up and down luridly and asked, "Any disgraceful jail time, tawdry affairs, or regrettable addictions to disclose?"

"No. Sorry. No skeletons in my closet, as you suspected. Why is it you always assume the worse of a person?"

"Because I hate to be disappointed. Others will act as poorly as they can. I refuse to be caught off guard."

"Poor baby."

"Thank you for appreciating my peril, true friend Noah. So, what did you do since you were last seen in these parts? I heard you went west, but I never put forth the necessary effort to learn the reason."

"I did a two-year fellowship at UCSF."

He held his hands up to indicate our immediate surroundings. "In cholesterol research?"

"No. In Primary Care."

Instantly, his face went deadpan. "In what, say you?"

"You heard me, you moron. In Primary Care."

Kent sniffed in a loud, snotty breath up his nose. "While I might understand and even condone criminality and debauchery, I'm not certain I can abide a person who has completed a fellowship in Primary Care as a component of a man's past."

I folded my arms. This promised to be good. "What, pray tell, is the problem with a Primary Care fellowship? Aside from the crummy weather, I learned a lot and met a lot of great people."

By way of sarcastic confirmation, Kent said, "In your Primary Care fellowship?"

"Yes, in my Primary Care fellowship."

He shook his head demonstrably. "Could there be anything more lame or pointless than wishing to do advanced study in primary care? Such an undertaking is, considered kindly, the advanced study of the perfectly obvious, of the perfectly dull and insipid. Wait, let me think." He rubbed his chin firmly for several moments. "Well, perhaps the advanced study of yarn production and the knitting thereof would be comparably feckless. No…no." He corrected himself. "I take that back. Compared to Primary Care, the yarn sciences are an enticing area of study, writhe with wonder and prospect. You seem to have chanced upon the most vacuous and least productive way to misspend two years of your life, which, like the seasons, inexorably advance to nothingness."

"And now I am here, working with you."

"How fundamentally disappointed your parents must be in the spawn of their loins."

SEVEN

The old saying goes that for every man there is a woman. It turned out to be verifiably true. Kent Pearson was getting married. About a year into my work with Ruth, he made it official, to the manifest disbelief of everyone who knew him well. By then, I considered him a good friend. Many others found him a playful and cheery spirit. But, I don't think any of us thought of him as marriage material. The man was too sarcastic, glib, and flighty. Further, he completely lacked the ability to act like an adult. Clinically, we would say he failed to complete the tasks of adulthood.

And wouldn't you know it, his betrothed turned out to be a wonderful person. Linda Ferguson was a fourth grade teacher at a local Catholic school. She was a sweet, attractive, and engaging woman. In fact, as far as I could tell, she was the complete opposite of Kent. True love did indeed conquer all, it would seem.

A few weeks before their wedding, he asked me to be a groomsman. His older brother Ned was to be the best man, though he told me I was his first choice for that duty. But, his family positively would not hear of such a betrayal. Ned, it seemed, had failed epically in life. Debt, substance abuse, and illegal misadventures were his stock-in-trade. His parents hoped beyond the limits of credulity that accomplishing of this one function might jump start Ned into becoming the man they were certain he could be. The fact that Kent despised Ned was immaterial to his parents.

Linda's parents spared no expense for their daughter's wedding. The wedding was held at Cathedral of the Holy Cross. That venerable Gothic structure was an inspiring venue, to be certain. Everything was top drawer, from the flowers to transportation. The reception was held at the most exclusive country club in town. I was quite impressed.

When the couple's first dance drew to a close, his father located Ned and me, as we chatted in a corner. He reminded Ned of his duty to toast his brother's good fortune and went over in some detail the key points he should cover. Ned was drunk—very drunk, in fact. He swayed gently and smiled giddily at his father's words. But he was clearly not capable of retaining any of his advice. I did not just have a *premonition* that things were going to proceed badly. I *knew* they were. But I wasn't in any position to alter the course insisted upon by his parents. I could only dread the consequences for my friend.

As the applause for the dance died off, his father shoved Ned in the direction of the newlyweds. I was dumbfounded to see his father smiling proudly as his pathetic son staggered toward certain disaster. He missed at his first attempt to spear the microphone from the director's hands. Once he held it, he twirled in his fingers and tapped the top to get everyone's attention. I inched closer to him, not that I had a plan, but I wanted to be able to act quickly if I felt the need. Kent and Linda were seated up on the dais, in their place of honor. She smiled happily, but Kent had the unmistakable look of concern on his face. He knew his brother all too well.

"If everyone will grab an adult beverage, it will be my pleasure to toast the lovely new couple, Mr. and Mrs. Dr. Kent Pearson!" He threw his arms in the air, twirled, and waited for the noticeably subdued applause to pass. It seems others knew him just as well. "Okay, okay," he waved his arms downward, "that's enough of that. I can't hear myself think." He gyrated around to face the couple and weaved in place as if aboard ship. I moved to within a few feet of him.

"Dearly beloved…no, wait, that's not my line, is it?" He stabbed the microphone into Kent's face. "You're already married, aren't you?" He snickered wetly. "So, as I was saying, I am here to toast this beautiful couple. First, a few remembrances, if you will." He toasted the now silent crowd and belted back most of his cocktail. "I am here to toast my cute little brother and his wew nife. I remember when Kent was this big." He stooped and flattened his hand a foot above the floor.

"One thing about Kent is that he's always been Kent. You know what I mean." He pumped his arms in circles to elicit a response from the spectators. None came. "Yes, Kent has always been a real smart one. He's a winner…always a winner. No, not like his big brother. Nope. Kent's a big shot, you know. Yeah! He's doctor and everything. That's a fact. You can look it up." He gave us an animated nod. Yup, Mr. Big Shot. But, I want to share with you that he's not big enough that he can spare a kind word for his big brother. Nope. Not a penny." He pinched his fingers together in front of his eye.

"But, hey, that's okay because I love him anyway. Yup, he's my baby bro, and I will always love him, now and forever!" He placed his palm over the microphone and said, as if privately, "And have you had a look at his woman? Hubba hubba, Bubba!" He rocketed his hips in a disgusting Elvis parody.

I turned to his sister, who had migrated to ground zero instinctively. "I'll grab the mic, you grab the idiot."

"In fact, when she was in my hotel room just last night, she told me she was a virgin—"

I ripped the microphone from his hands, and his sister spirited him away before his dulled senses knew what hit him. "Airline stewards." I smoothed back my hair. "Well, not really, Linda told us she always wanted to be a stewardess for Virgin Air. But, she heard the calling and became an elementary school teacher instead. And the world's a better place for it, I can promise you that."

"But enough about Linda. Ned asked me to help him with the toast to Kent, since Ned has such bad case of stage fright." Lame, true, but it was at least plausible. "So, I am pleased to do so. Kent, I've known you for years. Despite yourself." This drew light laughter. "No, seriously, Kent, it has been an honor and a privilege to know you and work with you. I can honestly say I would not be half the physician I am today if it hadn't been for you, buddy." That drew a round of applause. "For those who don't know Kent as well as I do, let me tell you he's an amazing man and a true friend. His sense of humor is infectious, his mood is always upbeat, and his dedication is ever present. Trust me, at three in the morning on call in the ICU, that's no mean feat. Me," I rested my hand on my chest, "I'm a pill. The nurses all say I'm like a bear woken suddenly from hibernation." I made a claw motion in the air.

"Now, I could tell you colorful stories all night about Kent. Yes, he can be a ton to handle, but I'm here to tell you that when the going gets tough and disaster seems all but a certainty, there's nobody on Earth I'd rather have at my side than Kent Pearson." I raised my glass, first to him, then to the crowd. "So, here's to the man I'm proud to call my friend and to the beautiful woman lucky enough to call him her husband." The room exploded in applause.

Much later in the evening, I was standing outside, alone, cooling off after a whole lot of dancing. It turned out that being a good-looking single doctor at a wedding was quite the hot item. I didn't hear Kent approach. He slipped his arm around my shoulder without saying a word. Then he pulled me sideways toward him and bumped our heads softly together.

"Noah," he began, "I really owe you. You saved the day, my friend."

"Kent, you owe me nothing. I was proud to help." I bumped his head gently with mine. "You'd do the same for me— probably'll have to someday."

After a brief silence, he spoke quietly. "Man, when my loser brother started spouting off, I looked into Linda's eyes and saw her pain and her fear. She was about to break into tears and bolt from the hall."

I looked over to see tears streaking his cheeks.

"If he'd ruined her princess wedding, there'd be no fixing it. I couldn't have fixed it, Noah. But you did."

He turned to face me squarely.

"You are my friend forever, Noah Taylor. Please know that. If there is ever anything, however small or however large, that I can do for you, please let me know. It will be done." He looked away into the night.

I shoved his head playfully to the side. "You bet your sorry ass I will, you big old sentimental guy."

EIGHT

Six years later …

During my time with Ruth, I learned how to do academic research. I also came to realize it was the path I wanted to follow. The sense of purpose, of being on the cutting edge of important knowledge and working alongside bright and energetic teammates became my dream. Cholesterol research, however, was not my cup of tea. There was nothing wrong with the field. It simply didn't stoke my fire.

I always suspected I'd end up studying immunology. The subject fascinated me. Innovative methods to diagnose and treat diseases that were unimaginable a decade earlier occurred daily. I knew, however, I was not in a position to work in immunology after my two years with Ruth. I needed state-of-the-art training to be the researcher I wanted to become.

So, I was off to the Bethesda, Maryland and the NIH. My CV was good enough, and more importantly, Ruth's connections were powerful enough to land me a postdoc fellowship in their Immunology department. The three years I spent there were the most challenging, stimulating, and rewarding years of my entire life. The NIH facilities were the best on Earth. The resources were endless, and the enthusiasm in the air was palpable. I worked two or three butts off in my time there and came out a competent researcher.

Following the NIH, I worked for a couple of years at the Scripps Institute in San Diego to get my sea legs. San Diego had the best weather on Earth. The sea was warm, and the culture was relaxed. When I completed my stent in San Diego, I had to make a big decision. In what area and at which school did I want to put down roots? The west coast was nice, but I was from the opposite coast. My family were all back east. Also, I finally met *the* girl.

Karan was working at Scripps with one of the oceanography groups. We met at a staff party and quickly realized we both had ties to New England. That kept the conversation going. As the evening progressed, we both sensed something special was cooking between us. For her part, she was witty, charming, and drop-dead gorgeous. For my part, I fell for her like an anvil dropped into the ocean. Luckily, she was impressed enough with me to agree to dinner that weekend. The rest, as they say, was history.

I interviewed at several universities in New England, but as fate graciously allowed, I ended up with a tenure-track faculty appointment at my old alma mater. I was provided a small seed grant, modest but serviceable lab space, and functioning, if not new, equipment. I was one happy camper.

Typically, the faculty of a university have dual tasks. Part of a professor's duties were teaching, service on committees, and, in the case of academic medicine, seeing patients. A negotiable portion of their time was allotted for research. Only the best were allowed to do research one hundred percent of the time. Mere mortals like myself, however, had to multitask. I never wanted to lose my connection with patients and students anyway, so I was in my own personal Wonderland.

Midway through my first year, I received my first committee assignment. I was to sit on The Curriculum Committee—TCC for short. The structure and inner workings of academia could neither be intuitive nor familiar to those outside of it. It was an ancient, inflexible, and closed-minded world, changing little from its origins in the Middle Ages. Witness how the funny caps and robes persisted against of all odds up until the modern day. The drape-like gown we all graduated high school in were designed to keep students and professors warm in the frigid classrooms of antiquity. Despite the invention of central heat, those robes have not been retired.

Similarly, rigid protocols and useless traditions dictated faculty roles and lives. But I didn't make the rules. I just had to live by them. Another point of orientation. On the surface, to serve on the TCC, assigned as it was to shepherd and guard the curriculum of my fine and venerable institution, might have seemed desirable. TCC should have had its finger on the pulse of new educational trends. And it would have, save for two very critical facts. First, no university committee had the potential to arrive at a consensus on anything, ever, even if it absolutely had to. Say the first item on a committee's agenda pertained to the refreshments served at the next meeting: coffee and donuts versus coffee and bagels. You could even add a third option: donuts *and* bagels. Still, no two overly stubborn and suspicious members would ever agree. Everyone would haggle like they were wagering at a cock fight. Long standing personal animosities and grudges were absolute impediments to progress. Hence, no refreshments would be available at the next scheduled meeting.

The second factor that doomed the committee to irrelevance was that, if a miracle did occur and some decision was reached, the administration would never agree to it. The committee's proposal would be dubbed too radical, too conservative, or too expensive. Sometimes all three. Anyway, professors looked at committee work like nothing productive could possibly happen. An uncomfortable time was to be had by all.

Maybe I was too negative, too cynical, and too given to hyperbole. After all, some changes had taken place in the recorded history of universities. But the Pope was more likely to convert to paganism soon than any new idea being adopted by an academic institution.

The first scheduled meeting of TCC was cancelled because it was too early in the academic year. Everyone was far too busy. The second meeting was postponed until the third meeting for reasons incomprehensible to me. I think the Earth's axis of rotation was too small or the air in the room was too big—some purely mystical reason. Then, the third TCC meeting was rescheduled until after the holidays because everyone would be away or was getting a new tattoo. Not that I minded the non-meetings, but it was annoying, nonetheless, to be made part of such capricious behavior.

Finally, after more misstarts than heavier-than-air flight, TCC met. There were twelve other permanent members who could vote on topics. Additionally, there were a bevy of non-voting advisors and representatives of various interest groups. Anyone could, if they were daft, foolish, or masochistic, attend TCC as an observer.

Given the significant delays, many participants braved a cold winter morning to attend. Our chairwoman, Barbara Celestial (I kid you not), gaveled us to order. "Good morning, ladies and gentleman. If we could get started, I'd appreciate it. We have a lot of points to go over, and I'd like to adjourn on schedule." She looked out the window. "The storm may arrive earlier than predicted, and I don't want us to be snowed in."

By ever-precious protocol, she took roll and double checked that the recording secretary had tabulated the tally accurately. Next, she laboriously read the printed agenda, which each and every person had in their hands. Then, she read a tedious summary of the minutes of the last meeting, which had taken place in prehistoric times. She called for a second to vote on the approval of minutes of said venerable documents. A second was offered, recorded, and a roll call vote taken. To no one's surprise, the minutes were accepted unanimously. Next it was on to new business. Okay, I thought, we TCC members would come off life support and actually do some work that added to the quality of our fine institution.

Silly me.

Barbara began. "The most important item pending today is a matter forwarded to TCC by Dean Yellin. He has asked us to review, consider, and suggest options for implementing the new state law mandating that all medical students have sufficient training in end of life care. I have—"

For reasons unclear to me, the neophyte in me said, "I second the motion." Silence fell as if a once bustling crowd saw a mushroom cloud rising nearby. Looks of confusion, horror, and incomprehension focused on me. The response I engendered would have been less dramatic if I had, instead, said, "I like to shove live kittens into the garbage disposal."

The worst part was, of course, that I had no idea what hideous malfeasance I had committed. Some dean wanted students to learn something in compliance with the law. We sort of had to comply, right? I could not have allowed the venerated TCC members to be locked away in prison for flaunting of the law. Most of the members I eyed around the table wouldn't last very long in the slammer.

After one or two eternities of anguished silence, I asked my chairwoman, "That was a motion…right?"

She tapped her pen on the documents she held in her white-knuckled fist and glared at me, presumably trying to kill me with a thought. Finally, she pinched her thin lips tightly. "Nooo, Dr. Taylor. What I just said was the farthest possible thing from a motion in the universe." More icy glaring interspersed itself between painful silence. Finally, she asked me in a stunningly condescending manner, "This is, I will assume in your defense, your first committee assignment, is it not, Dr. Taylor?"

I beamed like a guilty schoolboy, hoping to charm my way out of ignominy. "How'd you guess? I even bought a new tie." I lifted my tie to share with all present.

Humor seemed lost on my chairwoman, and forgiveness was clearly not domiciled in her frigid heart. "How very droll, Dr. Taylor. Thank you for the moment of levity you have brought to TCC today amidst all of its otherwise pressing workload."

She let those words hang in the air a moment. Finally, Madame Chairwoman said, "As I was about to announce to TCC, we are tasked to review, consider, and opine upon the new state law. After thoughtful debate, we are to forward recommendations to the dean as to how this goal can be met." She returned her scornful gaze once again to me and continued, "I shall begin the discussion by inquiring if everyone has read the full text of the law, which I forwarded to each member last week? A show of hands please. Who has read the full text?"

I slowly raised my hand to join Barbara's as the only ones aloft.

Her threatening body language provoked someone to speak. "Barb, I read the full summary you attached. Does that count?"

"I suppose it will have to, Mark. So, has everyone at least studied in detail my summary?" All hands present in the room rocketed up. "Well, Dr. Taylor, you seem to be the only member as familiar with the law as me. What are your initial thoughts?"

I reflected at some length prior to my response. I assumed she would most appreciate a vague and noncommittal statement. The law was both clear and directive, and the implementation was obvious, at least to me. So why not cut to the chase and be on to the next topic on the agenda? In my naively simple mind, I decided, what the hell. What could she do, fire me from that unpaid assignment no one on Earth would possibly want?

"Well thanks, Barb, for that vote of confidence. The law is both brief and clear." I quoted verbatim, "'Schools of Medicine, Osteopathy, Dentistry, and Podiatry are herein mandated to provide and document in their graduates familiarity with and competency in the major issues surrounding the humane, cost-effective, and multidisciplinary delivery of End-of-Life Care.' Since I was a medical student here, I know that Margret Peters and her staff in Medical Ethics are already charged with training in these matters. I think she does a spectacular job. Based on this new law, I would move we advise the Dean to forward Dr. Peters a copy of the text of the law and ask her to implement any needed changes and report back to the Dean and TCC with her progress."

I could not tell for certain where the sources of discontent and anxiety telepathically relayed to me originated from. Possibly from Barbara, who was again attempting to kill me with her thoughts. Possibly from the entire TCC, who seemed to be in collusion with her. But my brain felt the beams of negative energy focused on it like so many lasers.

To make the situation more toxic, some anonymous voice said, "I second the motion."

If our chairwoman was, prior to that second, fit to be tied, she was subsequently fit to be shrink wrapped then. I heard and felt the rumblings generated from the impending torrent of wrath which was soon to find me. She glowered at me while she shot dagger-glances around the table to see which depraved soul had seconded my motion. He was in for it too, the poor sod.

As it turned out, based on Robert's Rules of Order, debate had been cut off. I was hopeful that this would delay Barbara's disembowelment of me. After taking that vote, should it be in the affirmative by a two-thirds majority, the matter would be closed with finality. To close a topic without benefit of our chairwoman's magisterial input was as unprecedented as catching the wind in a net. Such an act was so impossible, yet the impossible had, because of me, just happened. The members of TCC knew we were in for a manifestation of chairwomanly eruption on the scale of Mount Vesuvius.

She shook like a terrier with a rat. "Oh, so...so I hear a s...sss...second t... to...to Dr. Taylor's...ssssss...motion? Will the secretary please call for a vote?"

The emaciated, lifeless man to her left stood with slow gravity. "All in favor say aye." There was a hushed chorus of many 'ayes,' which were barely audible in spite of the empty silence.

"All opposed say nay." After a tortured delay, the chairwoman hissed nay. Clearly more prescient than most of TCC of the cataclysm which was about to strike them, he said, "The record will additionally reflect that the secretary votes nay." He paused, cleared his throat. "The ayes, however, have it, Madame Chairwoman." With that, he sat back down.

I learned lesson one of survival in a large organization that day. To be correct was meaningless, to be bright was pointless, and to make an enemy was an eternal commitment. A corollary to lesson one was that if a supervisor asked someone their opinion, only return the boss's view. Disregard all original ideas. They were poison. All poisons must be discarded.

Also, and most critically, never-ever-never make one's boss look bad, foolish, or silly, even if she manifested all of those qualities. Never. Don't do it.

New ideas were new. Hence, they were not part of the Current Order. If not in full agreement with the Current Order, it meant there was dislike or disagreement with the Current Order. As the Current Order was envisioned and rolled out by the supervisor and, more importantly, by his supervisors, it was best not shake even a tiny portion of its foundation. One excellent way to torpedo a career was to present the boss a new idea publicly. A subtler and less direct method to end a career would have been to slap the boss across the face while laughing at her hysterically and wearing a chicken suit.

I learned that painfully and at consummate personal cost across subsequent years. But, back then I was cursed with the incautious optimism of youth. Most regrettably, I was chock full of innumerable good and innovative ideas. Also, I felt that I had the right to voice my own opinions.

Indeed, I felt an obligation to help my institution become better via my insights and wisdom.

In retrospect, the most lamentable fact was that I was impervious to the Corporate Virus. I always remained Noah Taylor. This proved regrettable. My life would have been less ladened with regret, loss, and isolation if only I wasn't immune to that bite. But, at least in the case of TCC versus Noah Taylor, the black die was cast. I could not very well take back what I'd done.

There were, however, positives in my early career. New faculty members were encouraged to participate in an orientation program. Throughout my first year, my wife and I were invited to dinners and picnics designed to make us feel welcome. Also, I went to a few meetings designed to orient me to how academic governance was structured and to learn about my benefits package. Professors from all departments of the university were mixed together in the orientation, so I met not only the medical new hires, but also those in Letters and Sciences and Engineering. That year there were twenty-five of us newbies. I quickly became fast friends with two new professors, James Blodget and Evan Miller. James was fresh from his PhD in economics at Yale, and Evan was a mid-career transfer in Medicine. Though Evan technically outranked us, we were all equally nervous and intimidated, so there were no barriers in our little group.

I recalled the cute conversation from our first lunches together. After a morning session of orientation, we chose to forego the complimentary boxed lunch and checked out a nearby cafe. Between nervous small talk, we outlined to each another our goals and dreams, having made it to the bottom rung of the ladder leading to academic heaven.

Evan went first. With a dreamy-eyed stare, he said, "I hope to make this place my last stop, professionally speaking. I've worked a couple other places, but I was really just staging myself to look good enough to be hired here. From my fellowship on, I've been lining up my ducks to land this appointment. I can't believe I actually made it here."

James spoke along a similar vein. "What about me? I end up here right out of training. Guys with PhDs in finance are a dime a dozen. Every time you thank the barista making your latte, you're probably talking to someone with a PhD in economics. You either boat one of these rare academic gems or you end up a whore on Wall Street making minimum wage. I cannot stop pinching myself."

"I bet your smarts had a lot to do with what you're calling luck, Jim," I said.

He shrugged. "Possibly. But I basically won the lotto of life." He hunkered down conspiratorially. "If I mind my Ps-and-Qs, publish enough drivel, and kiss sufficient butt, I could become one of those tweed-coated Ivy League cronies you see in those Norman Rockwell pictures." He rested back. "I can be fat, happy, rich, and modestly famous, all on the university's coattails." He nodded to me. "What's your story, Noah?"

I was hesitant to tell the whole truth. These guys had dreamed of being part of the university for their entire lives. I was born in its hallowed halls. "Me? I went to med school here then did my residency here. I came back here as faculty after my postdoc."

Both men had deer-in-the-headlights expressions. "You've basically been here your entire working life?"

"Yeah, basically...sort of."

"You're the luckiest son-of-a-bitch in the entire universe."

I tried to minimize my status. "Er ... well, you know, I suppose there was a good deal of luck in it too, you know."

James harrumphed. "No shit! But, still, dude. You are the luckiest cock in the hen house!"

I bristled a little. "Sure, but I had to compete for everything fair and square. Nothing was handed to me." Calming, I added, "I'm sure you two wouldn't be here either if you weren't top-notch and brimming with promise. And now we're all home free."

Evan did not agree. "Shows what you know, Mr. Assistant Professor. I've survived eight years in this jungle and am here to tell you it's a constant struggle. If you show anyone your back, they'll put a knife in it on general principle. Worse yet, if you pose even an imaginary threat to a somebody with an ounce of power, you're as good as dead. Piss someone off above you on the food chain and they'll make a show of canning your ass. You can bet on that."

Evan pointed a resolute finger at us as he finished.

James asked, "Aren't you being a bit over-dramatic here? I mean, sure, we know about politics and how petty it can be, but you make it sound like the mob."

"Not the mob. It's worse. It's an old boys' club—an old boys' club with extreme attitude."

"I've been here a long time, and I haven't seen anything like that."

Evan was impatient with my naïveté. "That's because, up until now, you didn't exist. You were a tool, a transient one at that, to be used and discarded. Now," Evan raised a finger skyward, "you're a potential threat. If no one has your back, it will become a popular target."

"I'm not too worried. It can't be all that bad."

I was to find out the hard way.

NINE

I survived my year on TCC and, specifically, I did so without being disemboweled by Barbara Celestial. More importantly, I was beginning to find my research stride. My small team was composed of crack scientists who were good people. As larger and more long-term grants came my way, I lead my group in innovative and ground-breaking directions. We were looking into immune system regulation as it pertained to new threats, like viruses or cancers. Specifically, we could identify a family of genetic mutations in mucosal-binding subunits, which also controlled broad classes of cell changes. Certain mutations made it all but impossible to arrest a growing cancer.

We were developing a system by which those mutations could be corrected. We used a harmless virus to insert the corrected genes into an animal's previously dysfunctional DNA. We were on the verge of completely rebooting the immune systems of deficient organisms. In effect, we were within striking distance of producing a vaccine to cure cancer, at least certain surface types.

In fact, Pepe Romero, who began his career as a postdoc in my lab, won the Nobel Prize in Medicine a quarter century later for completing the work I began. Ideas which were my own, but which I was … well, work which I was unable to see to completion. Had my life turned out differently, maybe it would have been me wearing a penguin suit shaking the King of Sweden's hand.

But more of such matters later. I wouldn't want to create too negative a tone, too early in my tale. I was, at that point, still young and full of energy and hope. The world was my buffet. I did not yet perceive the shadow that loomed over us all.

Within a few years, I was promoted to associate professor. That was no mean feat. For those unfamiliar with antiquated university structure two basic rules prevailed: first, there was bountiful chattel at the base of the pyramid to be consumed and discarded. Second, there was precious little room at the top the pyramid for more than a handful of survivors.

The true goal of any academic career was to obtain tenure. Tenure was, quite simply, gold. Non-tenured professors could be discharged on a whim at any point. Tenured faculty were free to act in any manner that struck their fancy. If they came to work with no pants on and lectured about soup, they could not be fired. Tenured faculty could not be terminated or forced to mend their ways without both an act of Congress *and* divine intervention.

An academic rose along a series of intermediate "steps" from assistant professor to full professor. They only "stepped up" if they followed the two cardinal rules of academic advancement: first, "publish or perish" and second, not make too many enemies.

Publish or perish was the catchphrase of academics. The theory held that if they were top notch, they would produce lots of great results. If they had lots of great results and published them, they would have documented their worth.

As to the not making too many enemies part, well that one was harder than the publishing part. In academia, there existed two ever present, negative factors: fear and jealousy. Professors were under-employed. They had summers, holidays, and weekends off. So, while successful researchers like me stooped nose-to-the-grindstone, less time-encumbered coworkers spent a lot of time studying my back to judge how best to stab me.

There were two basic strategies to avoid the jealous curse of success. You could become everyone's closest friend and most loyal ally. That was tough to accomplish, as you were dealing with a gaggle of prima donnas.

Alternately, you could try to kiss a lot of butt. One key factor limited that tactic. It could be hard to kiss enough derrière, as there was always such a long line near the buttocks of everyone in power.

My naive approach to dealing with the negative emotions my coworkers amassed against me was to work hard and hope for the best. That was, it turned out, a most unsuccessful strategy.

There came a day I needed to present myself for general inspection and institutional appraisal to the powers-that-be. I was already tenured, but there were still certain formal reviews that everyone was subject to. On a rainy, thoroughly dreary Wednesday morning, I was called to appear before the Committee on Committees (CoCs). Yes, universities have CoCs. They are charged with: *the nomination, selection, and, subject to Legislative Assembly approval, the appointment of the Chair, Vice Chair, and all non-ex officio members of each standing committee of a given Division.* I hadn't the foggiest notion what that sentence meant. I could not fathom what it was the CoCs actually did. But, that was none of my business. I simply had to show up, do or say something, and leave as quickly as possible.

I was slated to appear before the CoCs at 10:30 a.m. Right on schedule, the secretary of the CoCs rose and called my name aloud. Cute. I was the only non-committee member in the large room. Why not just wave me forward? Then again, only a busy person with better things to do cut pomp and protocol.

I was directed with marginal civility to be seated at the far end of a rectangular table. The CoCs members were on either side of the table. The chairman was opposite me in a high-backed, ornate wooden chair. It looked like a throne. It was hard for me to tell, as it was too far away to make out the precise details. The chairman was Simon Philipot. I'd never met him. He looked like a long, thin dill pickle wearing an over-voluminous wool sweater. He had short little arms and a puckered-up face, along with a disposition that looked just as sour.

He opened a manila folder, which contained information about to me. He spied down through his reading glasses at some written material a good long while. Then, he looked over his glasses at me. Finally, the pickle spoke. "Professor Taylor, so nice of you to join us this morning. We trust you are well."

No, Sim, I have meningitis and am finding it difficult to see.

Instead, I opted to say, "Yes, thanks. And you?"

He attempted a smile, which was clearly contrary to his nature and physiology. "Yes, thank you. We are well."

We? How many people are in poor Simon's head? Maybe he is telepathically linked to his CoCs members. Or, maybe there is an actual pickle-to-pickle link with wires coming out the back of their heads?

Stay focused, I chided myself. If I acted silly, I would just prolong my suffering.

"I assume you are familiar with the CoCs functions and responsibilities…"

Simon, I have no freaking clue what you do or why, even in a universe of infinite possibilities, your CoCs exist.

"So let's dispense with the formalities and get down to brass tacks."

Who says "brass tacks" this century? Oh, the chair of the CoCs does, that's who.

"We see…"

Again, with the "we." Does Simon speak as royalty? Is the chair of COCs that powerful a post? Wait, maybe he is possessed. Yes, the evil spirit of Constipated Dullness lives in his head…

Focus!

"You are, Dr. Taylor, sitting on the Academic Planning and Resource Allocation Committee, is that correct?"

I could be, if you mean the committee that gathers every fourth Tuesday afternoon to suck the joy out of all that lives. That convocation which brews not evil potions but mind-numbing resolutions. The group so pointless and ineffective that, were it sucked into a black hole, no one would ever miss, remember, or lament it?

Alternately, I went with, "Yes. That would be correct." Even too incautious for my own good, I added, "And if you ever need a, you know, a *plan* or an *allocation*, Simon," I tapped my chest, "you know who to ask." I winked at him.

He sat up from his profound slouch to a swaybacked hunch. "We do not take your meaning, Dr. Taylor." He looked to his right and left. "Could you rephrase your comment, please?"

Oh boy. Now what? I hadn't a hole, but a grave, it would seem. How was I to not fall in?

Before I could answer, the man to his right placed a palm on the back of Simon's arm. "I believe Dr. Taylor was making a joke, Dr. Philipot." Kent! It was Kent Pearson to my rescue, yet again. I thought I'd recognized him went I came in, but the missing hair and his lack of recognition toward me convinced me it was simply a man who looked like Kent.

Simon settled back into his former unhealthy looking posture. "A joke? Ah. Thank you, Dr. Taylor, we are certain. Now, where were we?" Kent whispered something in his ear. "Ah, yes. You sit on the APRAC. On that committee, you are a voting member but not an officer. Is that correct?"

No more nonsense. "Yes, sir. That is my role."

"Very good. As I am certain you know, it is the job of the CoCs to appoint the chair, secretary, and other officers of the committees on campus. We have called you here to address two matters. First, we are charged to inquire if you are happy with the leadership of the APRAC. Second, we wish to inquire if you would like to seek an appointment in the leadership of the APRAC." He set down his pen. "Not that you would then *necessarily* be appointed to such a position, mind you. We only wish to know if you are interested in a leadership role."

"Naturally, I'm sure."

"So, as to the first matter, that of committee governance. Are you satisfied, Dr. Taylor?"

Well, I suppose so. I'm not terribly fond of the mandatory group shower, during which the chairman keeps dropping his bar of soap and squealing, 'Oh, I'm a bad boy and someone needs to punish me.' Aside from that and the ritualistic cannibalism, the leadership is fundamentally sound.

"Yes, Dr. Philipot. I am."

"And might we query whether you are interested in advancing your position of the APRAC by aspiring to an administrative position?"

Not if my life and the lives of all my family depend upon it. Not if a nuclear-tipped ICBM were set in my mouth, to be ignited if I refuse. Not if I am forced to drink liquid nitrogen while boiling-oil is poured over my head.

"As much as I'd like to consider such a course, I'm afraid my research, teaching, and clinical commitments make such a move unwise at this particular juncture."

If, however, the current Miss APRAC finds she in unable to continue to fulfill her role, I will be honored to assume the title of Miss APRAC in her stead.

"So be it." He looked at his watch. "The CoCs will take a ten-minute break and meet here at precisely 11:09."

As I had not seen him in years, I sped over to catch Kent before he slipped out for a potty break. Turns out, I needn't have rushed. He spent most of the ten minutes conferring in hushed whispers with the Philipot. The chair finally excused himself, suffering no doubt from a prostate larger than Kent's. Kent rose and stretched his no longer so sleek frame. Only then did he notice me standing nearby. I stepped forward and seized his hand. "Kent, you son-of-a-thousand-fathers. How are you?"

His tepid reaction took my completely off guard. As quickly as socially tolerable, he released my hand. "Noah. Noah Taylor. So good to see you, old boy."

Old boy? Limp handshake? Oh, wait, this was the setup for a Kent-ism. The old bastard was clever. Yes, he was pretending to be distant, and then, bam, he'd give me a wedgie.

Well, two could play the cat-and-mouse game. I dropped to a matching flat tone. "So how have you been, old man?"

He pulled up his trousers and rocked on the balls of his feet. "Fine, fine, Noah. Couldn't be better. And you? I hear good things about you and your research up at the dean's office."

I blinked first. I couldn't stand it any longer. I placed my hands on my hips. "Are you trying to imply you are passing time with Dean Westmore and his phony, dim-witted cronies? You, Kent Pearson, ninja-master scoundrel?" Before he could respond, I held up a palm. "Wait, you're in the dean's office so he can call your parents and tell them what a bad boy you've been. Does he make you write on a blackboard five-hundred times *I will no longer be a screw up. I will no longer be a screw up?*" I punched him on the shoulder and giggled.

He rubbed absently at his arm. "No. Don't be ridiculous. Why would Carl do that?"

"Oh, it's *Carl* now, is it?" I danced my index fingers back and forth. "You and Westmore all, what, buddy-buddy BFFs?"

He checked his wristwatch. "Well, truth be told, Dean Westmore and I are good friends. He's a great leader and a reliable North Star. Say, I think I have just enough time to hit the restroom and still make it back on time."

"What, the CoCs can't begin again without you, Mr. Big?"

He limply shook my hand as he backed away. "Well, no. It can't reconvene without its recording secretary, now can it? I take the minutes. Really great to see you, Noah." He pointed at my face as he was turning to leave. "Hey. You and I have to do lunch sometime."

He was gone. Soon after the break, my review, or whatever it was, ended. There was no reason for me to linger. I shuffled out the door and back to my life. But, I had to wonder what had just happened. I could not have suspected back then, but the man I knew, the rapscallion Kent Pearson, was gone. He had fully succumbed, somewhere along the line, to the Corporate Virus.

TEN

Around the midpoint of my career, a very improbable and, as it turned out, miraculous event bethumped me. I met Cletus Abraham Lincoln Black IV, M.D. Bubba, to his friends, was a huge and colorful person. The man was a mountain with tree trunks for legs, a fire hydrant for a neck, and a chest as expansive as a kettledrum. Cletus also possessed as joyous a laugh as God had ever gifted a man. It could rattle windows blocks away. In physics, there were five traditional forces: gravity, electricity, magnetism, and two nuclear attractions. To that list, I would add the "Bubba Force." He was just that impactful.

When Bubba was in a room, he was never less than the sole focus of everyone's attention, even if he was silent. It was curiously undeniable, however, that when one spoke with Cletus, I instantly became oblivious to his heft and was taken in by the gentleness that was Bubba. Love, warmth, optimism, generosity, charity, piety, and a powerful sense of service to others began to herd together the elements of what it was to be Bubba. A kinder, gentler, more worthy soul has never walked this Earth.

I attended what turned out to be my last Faculty of Medicine Holiday Celebration, referred to by all as the Christmas Party, but officially labeled with a more generic title, for reasons of political correctness. Karan and I were having an acceptable, if not a riotous, time. We mingled, saw old friends, and put names to faces for several prominent members of the faculty. As Karan was the designated driver, I had a touch of happy-holiday cheer going. Just enough, mind you, to match the festive mood demanded. Not a drop more.

I was listening politely to one of nature's duller creations, Joan Clarke, Assistant Dean of Something or Another. She sang the praises of what she opined were the passing year's most momentous accomplishments with regard to the university. Abruptly, inconsistent with a firm grasp of proper etiquette, Karan grabbed my elbow and spun my torso toward the door. With awed reverence, Karan said, "Who on god's green earth is that?"

I turned back to Dean Clarke and apologized. "Sorry. Will you excuse me for a moment?" I turned back to my wife. "What is so important that you had to do that?"

Karan pinched my cheeks and forced my face toward the entrance. There stood, in all his considerable glory, Bubba.

"I have no idea, babe. I've never seen him before in my life."

Joan laughed cordially. "That, my friends, is Dr. Black, Assistant *Clinical* Professor of Medicine in the Primary Care Department." She emphasized the adjective "clinical" quite clearly. I was meant to understand that Dr. Black was one of *them*, the great unwashed, on the clinical track. "Dr. Black certainly does cut quite the figure, doesn't he?"

I wasn't sure if I gleaned racist undertones or whether she referred simply to Cletus's size and the significantly unconventional suit he wore. It was so garish and bright I could not look directly into it. In retrospect, I knew she meant to join any number of malignant innuendos into one negative condemnation. But, back then, I was inclined to give everyone the benefit of the doubt.

"Oh, my." After a moment, I added, "That doctor is huge."

Joan smirked knowingly. "As you find the man so engaging, come. Let me introduce you to him." She snaked thought the throng of revelers and walked up to Cletus.

"Dean Clarke!" boomed Bubba. "As I live and continue to breath. It is wonderful to see you!" Her shook her hand. "And may I ask how you and your wonderful family are on this blessed evening?"

"Fine, Dr. Black. Thank you for asking." She did not return the social inquiry back to him. Instead she turned and pointed to me. "I'd like you to meet Dr. Noah Taylor and his lovely wife Karan."

His attention shifted toward us like a runaway locomotive switching tracks. He enveloped my entire forearm like a giant clam snatching a guppy. "Wonderful to meet you, Noah!" I felt we were already old friends and that he would cut off his arm if I asked him to. "It is truly an honor and a privilege to make your acquaintance. And, as for you, my daring, Karan," Bubba gestured for Karan's hand and then gently kissed the back of it, "it is an even greater pleasure to meet you."

Joan simulated a laugh, and then coolly excused herself. "I see Provost Marshall over there. If you'll pardon me, I have something I need to discuss with him." With that, Dean Clarke was gone. But with Cletus, there was never the possibility of a quiet moment or an awkward silence. He took my hand and forearm again in more of an embrace than a handshake. "What is it that you do around here, Noah? Oh," he released my hand and thumped himself on the forehead, "where are my manners? I may call you Noah, mightn't I, Dr. Taylor?"

"Yes, by all means, ah…" I rolled my fingers toward him to indicate I wondered as to how he wished to be addressed.

He tented his fingers to rest on his chest. "Me? You must call me Bubba. Most folks do." He pointed in my face. "Just don't call me late for dinner!" He laughed deeply and grabbed his over-ample belly. "No one ever does, as you can most plainly see. Now, back to my *original* question. What is it that you do around here?"

"I'm an Associate Professor in Immunology."

"And what is it that you do there in Immunology?"

"I'm afraid I don't take your meaning."

"You know. What activities and endeavors occupy your days in the illustrious field of immunology?"

I was unclear as to what nuance Bubba was getting at. "I teach a few classes, do a lot of research, and see some patients."

"And where do you fit in around here?"

My lack of clarity was grading into overt confusion. "Like I said, I teach…"

He raised an enormous paw to halt me. "As I am confident you know, in this fine institution there exist a few distinct species." Beginning with his thumb, he counted off fingers on his hand. "One, there are the professor types. They spend all day with their heads in the clouds and hope no one will ask more of them. Two, there are the researchers. They hide in their labs all day and pray no one asks more of them. Three, there are the doctors, who spend their lives laboring to help others, hoping they will be asked to help even more folks. Four, there are the unspeakables, of whom it is best not to speak."

He piqued my curiosity. "Unspeakables, eh? We have unspeakables walking these halls? Could you whisper me a clue as to what they might look like, lest I entangle myself with one unwittingly?"

He set a stern face. "Why, Noah, I am not certain if you are mocking me. Here I'm trying to be all discrete and diplomatic. I'm not certain how to process such conflicting thoughts in the context of our budding new friendship."

I shrugged my shoulders. "All right. Let me state that I am a little bit of species one through three. I certainly shudder in terror to think I might have some species four in me too, since I do not know what it is."

Bubba giggled like a teenage girl and patted me on the shoulder. "One through three and maybe some four! Man, I can see I'm really going to like you, Noah. Gonna have to bring my A-game though, if I expect to keep up with you." He ran both hands back across his planet-sized bald head. "Well, group four consists of those useless, humorless, shiftless, and altogether worthless repackaging of spineless humans with morals so minuscule as to be fully undetectable. In other words, I refer to the administrative abominations." He looked with disgust at the path the assistant dean took as she departed. He was only missing the bible in one hand and the handkerchief in the other with his oration to fit the very prototype of a Baptist minister, which, as I later found out, he was.

I liked this man very much. He was honest, brutally so it would seem. But he coupled that with both passion and humor. I placed my left hand on my elbow, set my right thumb and index finger to my chin. "So, let me review. I might be one of two men trembling in a corner, petrified that someone might make me work. Alternately, I could be a dispassionate zombie, or I could be a working man with an actual soul. Does that about sum up my choices?"

"Amen I say to that! I do believe you have taken my meaning."

"So, Bubba. Why is it you would ask a perfect stranger if he was either lazy, a horrible abomination, or a good person? Especially," I gestured expansively around the crowded room, "during this season of peace and love?"

"Because I always want to know which type of person I am in the company of." He pointed in the direction of Joan. "Especially since you were introduced to me by the likes of her."

I could not suppress a playful smile. "You mean to suggest, Cletus, that Assistant Dean of Thumb-Up-Her-Butt is a zombie?" I slapped both my cheeks. "No way. I distinctly felt her pulse when I shook her hand not ten minutes ago. Zombies don't have pulses."

Karan noticed I was acting a bit too flamboyant with a perfect stranger. She looped an arm through my elbow and pulled me close. "And where is it that you fit in here, Dr. Black?"

Bubba slapped one knee and spun around three hundred sixty degrees on his heel. "Dr. Black! Don't you call me Dr. Black, pretty lady. You are my friend. It wounds me to the foundation of my heart when a friend calls me that. Bubba, yes. Cletus, maybe. The Good Lord's gift to womankind, to be certain. But never Dr. Black."

When Karan stopped laughing, she corrected her misspeak. "So where is it that you fit in here, *Bubba*?"

"I, my wondrous vision of captivating beauty, am most emphatically a doctor." Bubba abruptly grabbed my shoulder, pulled me closer, and pointed in my face. "Noah, I need to get this straight. Are you a doctor or a physician?"

Bubba was perfectly still and fully concentrated on my mouth to hear my clarification. Of course, I could not imagine what distinction he was making. "Aren't those two words for the same thing?"

Bubba's entire body trembled, making him look like the planet Earth after being struck by an asteroid. "Lord no, Noah! How could you think such a thing? Doctors and physicians the same manner of being? Is hot the same thing as tepid? Is delicious the same thing as ain't-too-bad? I say they are not! Around these parts, people like Clarke are physicians, at best. Me? I'm a doctor and I work for a living. I see patients and help families. I'm not some hollow pretense of a healer. Those lost causes wouldn't know a hemorrhage-age from a hemorrhoid!"

"Okay, I think I take your meaning. I guess I'd have to claim to be a doctor too. But, you'll still love me if I am a doctor *and* a researcher, as long as I don't put on too many airs?"

"I do believe I can."

"Cletus, we've just met and already you're growing on me like a bad case of leprosy."

Bubba laughed joyfully. Then he looked around the room with suspicion in his eyes. "Your challenge will be to keep on being a doctor in a den such as this, filled as it is with people like your Dean Clarke." I was certain that if it had been socially acceptable, he would have spat on the floor.

For reasons I cannot understand, I rallied to Joan's defense. "I barely know her. Met her maybe twice before. But, she seems harmless at best, talentless and over-ambitious at worst."

For the first time in our brief acquaintance, I read disapproval and maybe even anger in his eyes. "You should think long and hard before ever defending a person like Joan Clarke, Dean of Sodom."

"Wow, you sound kind of serious all of the sudden there, Bubba."

Karan tried to aid in my defense. She asked, "You don't like Joan, Bubba? Do you two have history?"

"Her? No. I hardly know the woman. In fact, tonight is one of the few times I have spoken to her."

"Ah, Bubba, I'm kind of confused here. If you don't really know Joan and haven't had any real dealings with her, how is it that you can have such strong negative feelings toward her? It doesn't sound, pardon me for being blunt, very Christian of you."

He stroked his chin in a moment of concentration. I was struck with his similarity to Rodin's statue *The Thinker*. With no trace of his former ebullience or frivolity, he weighed a paw down on of my shoulder. "First off,

Noah, never apologize for speaking the truth. It is one of the few powers which is for our use and not theirs. Second, I suppose, in a certain sense, you are sadly correct. My feelings towards the likes of Dean Clarke are not infused with Christian fellowship. Truth be told, I struggle with this mightily. I can only assure you, my friend, that I do not condemn her lightly or without powerful justification."

Cletus stared off for a long moment. "Are we asked to be Christian even to demons?" Before either Karan or I could respond to what was a rhetorical question, he smiled again. "Here I am going on so doom and gloom. There appears to be a Christmas party raging all about us. What say we all find us the food portion of the night's entertainment and do some real damage to the president's precious budget?"

"That sounds like a marvelous idea, Bubba," Karan said.

"Greater minds than mine have spoken. Who are we to argue or stand in protest?" I seconded.

After twenty minutes or so of intense consumption, mostly on Bubba's part, Karan went off to speak with an old girlfriend of hers from Scripps who happened to be there. That left Cletus and me alone for the first time. I sipped a glass of red wine as Bubba downed a river of punch. He nudged me with an elbow. "So, the part about you being a *doctor* and not one of those lesser forms of medical providers. Did you mean it or were you just putting on airs?"

"Why, if I did not know you as well as I do, I might take offense at that remark."

"I run a community clinic out of an RV, with this institution's name printed on its side, mostly working the inner city. I could stand the aid of another body, assuming said body was another doctor and not just another talking head."

I never saw that request coming. My instinctive reaction was to defer as quickly and as tactfully as possible. For some reason, instead, I took a second to consider his offer. Maybe it was the wine talking. "Sure, why not?'

He slapped his knee and then extended his hand to me. "Well all right then, Dr. Noah. Welcome on board! So, when do you think you can start? We serve the community mostly Saturdays, so any time would be fantastic.

And, least you ask, yes, the university covers your malpractice and fully condones any participation."

"Well, give me your card and a couple weeks to massage my schedule, and I'll let you know."

He squinted an eye shut. "You're not planning on blowing me off once I'm out of sight, are you?"

"No way, Bubba. My word is my bond. Plus," I gave him a wink, "it would take a hurricane to blow you off. I could never muster that type of force."

"Well, I think I have encumbered you enough for one evening. I will mingle a moment, then take my leave." He shook my hand. "It has been an inspired pleasure to meet you, Noah. I hope to hear from you soon. Give my best to your darling wife, if you would be so kind."

I held onto his hand, not letting him leave. "Cletus, one last thing. All night you've been casting vague accusations and evil innuendos at the administration, or at least the people associated with it. What gives?"

Bubba freed his hand. "Do you really want to know?"

Did I? Why should I care at all about this fellow's disenchantment with the higher-ups? In university life, malcontents abound even more than the outside world. Bubba could be nothing more than another of the grousing geese. My instincts suggested that I should let this go. But, since when did I ever heed reason? "Yes, Cletus the Fourth, I do."

"Good! Then you and I will have something to discuss when we're working together in my outreach RV." He held forth his massive hand. "Picture it, Noah. You and me exchanging clever repartee while doctoring to the good Lord's less fortunate."

And so began the most unexpected and rewarding chapter of my life.

ELEVEN

On a frigid, thoroughly miserable Saturday morning in early January, I pulled into the New Hope Baptist Church parking lot. It was not hard to find the idling bus that had been converted into Bubba's outreach clinic. Though it did indeed bear the name and logo of our university on both sides, they were the only, let me call them "conventional" trappings the vehicle displayed. The term Joseph's coat came to mind, based on the colorful patchwork of colors and designs.

There were biblical quotes at odd angles surrounded by every loud color imaginable. Reasonably good reproductions of Martin Luther King Jr., Mother Teresa, Rosa Parks, and John and Bobbie Kennedy arm-in-arm exploded from the exterior. In the dark of night, during a blackout, in a driving snow storm, and blindfolded, it was impossible to miss Bubba's clinic. That was, of course, the point.

I parked next to the bus and hazarded the ten icy steps to the forward entrance. As I staggered and slipped forward more than backward, I flashed back over my winters in San Diego. Why, I asked myself harshly yet again, did I choose New England? New England, where bones froze during a strong winter storm as did exhaled breaths. Where frostbite was a constant danger, as was hypothermic death. Just commuting to and from work was a struggle for survival that one rightly felt proud to survive.

I knocked as best I could, given the gloves I wore, the pain generating in my chilled hands and the wobbliness of the door panels. It took two attempts, but finally the doors swung open. Bubba loomed above me like the Himalayas.

"Noah, come in, my friend! Why are you standing out there in the cold? You could catch your death if you're not careful. Then what use would you be to me?" He pulled me up the three steps and directed me to the center of the bus. "Here, right here." He positioned me like a piece of furniture. "It is the warmest spot we've got. Stand there a minute or two. I'll get us some hot coffee. That should do the trick."

He had to walk sideways most of the way to the kitchenette area because of his expanse, but he returned directly with weak steaming hot coffee. As I pounded my feet on the floor to aid in their revival, he said, "It is so wonderful to have you on board, my friend. A blessing and a gift from God!"

"Hold up there. I haven't done anything yet. Thank me and praise God after I've done something other than stand around trying to warm up."

He smiled as wide as the horizon. "Ah, but you have already, Noah! You indeed have already done something truly marvelous!" He gestured around the cramped confines of the bus. "You have joined our small yet formidable crew!"

"So," I flipped my head widely from side to side, "how about a tour while I thaw?"

His eyes danced like a child's on Christmas morning. "Ah yes, the grand tour!" He pointed to the front of the bus, where four seats were welded to the wall bench-style, directly behind the driver. "That's our luxurious waiting room."

"Modest in capacity but warmer than the sidewalk, so that's a plus."

"It has to be so, Noah. It is most challenging to find room for the 'must haves', let alone the niceties. Mostly patients must wait outside. If the weather is less cooperative like it is today, we at least try to park near the entrance to a public building. Across from those seats are a few racks of educational handouts and community resource information. Shelters, soup kitchens, substance abuse centers, whatever might be helpful."

"I couldn't help noticing there are a few church fliers in there too."

He wagged a finger at me. "Aren't you observant. Why not, I ask you, avail yourself of the opportunity to save not only a man's life but also his soul? We're a one-stop people shop." He realized he might have overlooked an important factor. "Not a problem for you is it, Noah, my partaking in a bit of old-fashioned religion?"

"No, you big oaf. Relax. I tend to shy away from bold-faced evangelicalism as a WASP. But if that's your thing, I respect the heck out of it." I winked at Bubba. "I just want to let you know I'm paying attention."

"Of course. Nothing the matter with knowing exactly what you are committing your leisure time to doing." Bubba tapped the side of his head. "Most prudent of you, my friend, most prudent, if you ask me. Shall we continue our tour?"

He turned and gestured to the back end, where an open drape revealed a small exam table surrounded by a few instruments. "That is our sole exam room. It has always been adequate. With the two of us here now, we will just have to see what happens. Whoever needs more privacy can claim the exam room, and the other can do his exams over there." He indicated a chair next to the nurse's station. "Finally, in the center here are the work stations for us to chart or look something up on the Internet. As you can see, we attempted as best we could to erect walls and such to make the space as private as possible." He heaved a profound sigh. "That, Noah, is also where the hardest work you do will take place. That is where you break all the bad news to the patients. That is where you watch as loved ones weep, the patients bargain, and many a soul cry out in rage and frustration." The mighty Bubba fell quiet and still.

I thumped him as hard as I could on the back, which was probably imperceptible to him. "Yo, that's where we will also say, 'You're not dying.' Plus, I get to reassure people, 'No, you don't have to take Bubba home with you.' It will be our happy place too."

As he stared at me with ever-increasing bemusement, I went on with my impromptu pep talk. "Yes, Cletus the Fourth, anyone can draw blood, dispense meds, or scrape off a Pap smear. But you and I," I signaled back and forth between our chests, "will dispense many a glad tiding from that very spot."

He laughed as if to put Santa Claus to shame. "We most certainly will. We most certainly will!" When we were both through chuckling, he smiled hugely. "The good Lord knew what he was doing when He sent me you, young Noah. Our adventures shall be most amazing!"

I raised a digit. "Ah-ah, like said before. Wait for me to do something productive before you go singing my praises. So, are we done with the tour?" I tilted my head to the as yet silent woman leaning on the stainless-steel counter, dressed in scrubs, arms crossed, who stared at us like we were a pair of unruly teenage pests.

"Ah yes. Allow me to introduce to you our nurse, Tinisha. Tinisha, this is Dr. Noah Taylor."

As we were shaking hands, she grumbled, "I am your medical assistant, Tinisha, not your *nurse*." She scowled mightily at Bubba. "Someone here is too damn cheap to hire a real nurse. So, you're stuck with me, Dr. Taylor, until the good Lord sees fit to correct that man's glaring oversight."

"I'm sure you're all we need, Tinisha. Please, call me Noah."

She glared at me as though I'd made a lewd remark. "I will *not*, Dr. Taylor, be calling you by your given name like we just met at some bar, thank you very much. You, sir, have spent three-quarters of your life in school learning an honorable profession like doctoring. The way I figure it, that earns you the proper respect from me whether you like it or not."

Bubba cut in. He hugged her warmly from behind. "She's a feisty one, ain't she, Noah?" Then he kissed her on the top of the head. "But we do so love our Nurse Tinisha."

She looked toward the roof, to go eyeball to eyeball with him. "Dr. Black, I'm a married woman, and I will thank you kindly to avoid such amorous advances in the future. It is hard enough to maintain a professional atmosphere around here when even the little children call you Bubba and half the girls flirt with you so shamelessly that I am tempted to kick them off this bus."

His eyebrows bobbed up and down. "As I said, a feisty one." He released her. "But enough of this frivolity. We have serious work to do and on a tight schedule, to boot. Let us be off on our mission of endless mercy!"

"Tight schedule, my sweet aunt Sadie's ample behind! Within no time at all, this man'll have us an hour behind our so-called tight schedule." She rested a hand on her hip and pointed at him. "You think this blow hard talks too much to you and me? Wait until you see him with those who can't protest his advances because they come to him for free help." She visibly shuttered. "Lord give me strength! It's as painful a spectacle to witness as you'll likely endure, Dr Taylor."

He mouthed the word "feisty" to me as she ranted.

"So where's our driver?" I asked.

Tinisha brushed past me with focused intent. "You're looking at her, Dr. Taylor." As she buckled herself into the driver's seat, she continued to complain. "You know that certain cheapskate doctor I alluded to earlier, too cheap to hire a proper nurse? Well, in case you haven't guessed it yet, he's also too damn cheap to hire a driver so I can spend more time pretending to be the nurse we haven't got. Park your butts and buckle up, so I can get this two-ring circus of monkeys on the road before sunset."

As the bus churned out of the parking lot, Cletus again mouthed "feisty" to me and pointed toward her, his palm forming a barrier to shield it from her view.

"You know I can see you, Dr. Black?"

And so we were off.

TWELVE

Bubba dubbed us Heals-on-Wheels. Over time, our little trio gelled together nicely. Most Saturdays, the occasional Sunday afternoons, and the rare national holiday, we motored about, rounded up the suffering, and tended to the disenfranchised. Bubba proved himself to be a tireless worker and, as Tinisha warned so prophetically, he was also a tireless talker. Whether he addressed one lone teenager who was only there for free condoms or if he regaled an entire church congregation in pursuit of donations to further our cause, Cletus was never able to stop flapping his gums. Most amazing of all, no one, aside from Tinisha, ever seemed to mind, or even hint that they longed for him to wrap it up. His jovial nature, purity of conviction, and boundless energy were captivating.

Bubba proved himself a competent physician. Whatever he might have lacked in first-rate skills, he more than made up for with his efficiency and manifest concern. A word along those lines. You could have been the smartest, most correct physician in the world, but never achieve your goals. To be truly effective, the patient had to take the last step and actually buy what the doctor intended to sell. The patient had to want to do what the provider requested of them, or the doctor achieved nothing for the patient. Cholesterol pills and hypertension tablets lowered nothing if they remained in their bottles. High-risk sexual behaviors inevitably continued unless the patient wore the condoms dispensed. No tumor could voluntarily jump out of its host. So, unless the doctor convinced the patient to show up on the day of their surgery, the tumor won—not the patient.

In that capacity, I've always prided myself to be a high achiever, but Bubba was much better than me. He was a superstar. He charmed, frightened, browbeat, embarrassed, cajoled, or otherwise compelled most patients into to doing exactly what he asked of them. Maybe people were just so intimidated by his size that they figured it was in their best interest to not risk his ire. But hey, all was fair in love, war, and the effective delivery of healthcare. Bubba, by hook or crook, made a patient better, often despite themselves.

One day, I was sitting at our little work station polishing a draft of an article I was about to submit regarding a recent set of experiments my group had finished. Heals-On-Wheels was officially closed for the day. At the last minute, Bubba ran off to make a house call. It seemed a Mr. Freeman had come by and asked him to look in on his wife, who was too ill and incapacitated to make the journey herself.

We were committed to hang around for what promised to be a very long time, as we awaited Bubba's return. Tinisha asked me if I wouldn't mind seeing a straggler. That was our pet phrase for a latecomer. No problem. I was there to see patients, not to write journal articles. I finished correcting a few more lines of text as Tinisha put the patient behind the curtains at the back of the bus.

Within a few minutes, Tinisha informed me that Mrs. Prudencia Arroyo y Lopez Vega was ready to be "placed through the wringer." I was uncertain what she meant by that remark. I grabbed my white coat and headed back while I scanned the chart. Then I understood. The patient's chief complaint was for the all-too-familiar "STD check." I recited in my head, for the millionth time, my when-will-they-learn admonition. I parted the drapes and was instantly jarred by the vision that confronted me from atop the exam table.

There sat a matriarch, overly dressed in formal black, chisel-faced—an altogether withered woman. She seemed as much as possible to accelerate the natural aging process we were all subject to by sheer force of will, there, as I watched. The element that completed the emotive picture I studied was the fact that Mrs. Arroyo y Lopez Vega still wore her voluminous, tattered wool overcoat. I was also struck by the way señora Arroyo y Lopez Vega clutched her black patent-leather purse. It was cinched tightly in both hands against her chest, like a protective talisman designed to ward me off.

One option was to summon a master portrait artist to capture that timeless image of transfixed intimidation and icy repulsion in oil on canvas. If done right, it could make the artist famous for all time. As an alternative, I introduced myself. "Good afternoon, Mrs. Arroyo. I am Dr. Taylor. How are you today?"

Eons came and went as the obdurate señora glared lethally at me. Stars were born, burned their Methuselahean lives, and went nova as I stood waiting for a response. The locked jaw of the señora churned back and forth, placing her teeth at great peril of being ground to dust. Finally, Mrs. Arroyo drew in a sharp, parched breath. I believed it to be the first she had since I entered her space.

More dispassionately than I would have thought possible, she said, "Please, Dr. Taylor, may we dispense with the trappings of pretense and cordiality? It is with profound shame and the complete absence of pleasure that I present myself here before you today, groveling for your pitiless assistance. I should not like to draw out longer than possible our interaction. Further, I will ask of you to note that my name is Mrs. Arroyo *y Lopez Vega*. If you would please be so gentile as to recall this in the future, I shall be grateful."

Ouch!

"Very well, Mrs. Arroyo y Lopez Vega. What brings you in to see me today?"

Another eternity of tense silence threatened to suffocate all existence. "Am I attended today by an illiterate physician? If so, I will take my leave of you without further imposition upon our respective times."

I could tell by her foot steps that Tinisha was about to burst through the partition in defense of her floundering provider. If she did, the huffy señora would definitely meet her match. "I'm s... orry, Mrs. Arroyo y Lopez Vega, if I've said something to offend you, I—"

The señora spoke frozen words. "I stated my complaint to your assistant. I can see it plainly written on the top of the paper you hold despite it being upside down from my perspective." She aimed a brittle digit at the chart I held as she ripped further into me. "So, I must assume you are unable to read. The only other, significantly less charitable explanation I can conceive of, is that you're asking because you wish to hear an old woman speak vulgar words for your entertainment. Which is the type of man you are, Dr. Taylor? Illiterate or cruel?"

I attempted to exert some manner of control. "*Neither*, señora Arroyo y Lopez Vega. I am a man who is running though the script of a physician speaking to a new patient. It is, I have found over the years, always best to hear a patient's story first-hand. Any and all clues to establishing the diagnosis are helpful." I let that hang a moment before plowing forward. "It is a pity I had neither the foresight nor prior inclination to match your desire for a socially abbreviated, testy interaction. I am the type of person who does not appreciate being berated and abused by someone until I have done something worthy of rude treatment." I allowed a five count to pass. "So, Mrs. Arroyo y Lopez Vega, what say we begin again?" I held out my hand in greeting. "I am Dr. Taylor. I might add, volunteering on my day off to provide you free medical care. What brings you in to see me today?"

The stony señora contemplated my words for a few, tense seconds. Rather than storming off as I had assumed she would, and wished she'd do, she said flatly, "Of course you are correct, *médico*. Please accept my apologies. I have spoken without due respect and with inappropriate harshness." The señora breathed heavily. "Perhaps it is the humiliating nature of my visit that has prompted such unacceptable conduct from me. Again, I pray you will forgive me." She snapped her shoulder back. "I am here to be examined for the presence of any and all possible sexually transmissible diseases. Specifically, I fear that I might have contracted SIDA, pardon me, the AIDS."

"Thank you, señora, for the confidence you have placed in me with your report. May I ask first if you have any symptoms which might be due to an STD?"

No, she replied. There were no specific symptoms.

"So, why is it that you think you might have been infected with an STD? I will assume for brevity's sake that you do not participate in any high-risk sexual behavior, such as unprotected intercourse with multiple partners."

Fiery bile surged in the back of the señora's throat, but she held it in. She confirmed flatly that, no, she did not partake in high-risk sexual behaviors, herself. Ah! There it was.

"Do you think your husband might have contracted an STD and passed it along to you unwittingly?"

If she was closed and unforthcoming before, she became positively sphinxlike at that point. After some considerable thought, she acquiesced. "Yes. It is my fear he might have. Infidelity is at the core of my presentation before you today."

Don't judge, I reminded myself. *Don't take the low road and snark in your head about how profoundly gross the image is of her partaking in intimate relationships of any kind. Everyone must make it through the day as best they can. Even Prudencia and her spouse.*

"Are you certain you husband has strayed from the marital bed, or is it simply that you suspect he might have?"

She circled her wagons with finality and reformed an impregnable facade. "The whys and hows of the matter are unimportant, Dr. Taylor. They are not the subjects of further discussion. I have voiced as many of the intimate details of my life to a stranger as I care to. I would now ask to be subjected only to your medical evaluation." She nodded to the stirrups at the end of the table she sat on.

I suppressed a guffaw of laughter. Regrettably, I must have let slip some of the visceral response I had experienced, as a curse from her eyes struck me. She tensed and began to rise.

"No, wait, Mrs. Arroyo y Lopez Vega, please. It's just that, well…things have changed since your last…err, screening." I gingerly encouraged her to sit back. "Nowadays, we require only a blood and a urine sample. No physical exam in required if you are having no symptoms."

As if the weight of the Great Pyramids of Giza was lifted from her shoulders, she nearly imploded with relaxation. The old bat thought I was going to have her up in stirrups with her dignity flapping in the breeze. Bless her heart. She had been transfixed with mortification about what she presumed a strange male was about to do to her.

Her relief was so profound that she seemed close to fainting. I summoned Tinisha in as back-up. "Oh, T, could you come help us?" Since she was still lingering just outside the curtains, she appeared instantly. "Ah, Mrs. Arroyo y Lopez Vega will need a blood and urine for STD screens. After that, if you feel she's ready, she is free to leave." Tinisha understood that I meant if the patient could walk without passing out, she could depart.

Placing Prudencia's arm around her own neck, she guided our wobbly patient toward the nurse's station. She rolled her eyes so only I could see. "You got it, Dr. Taylor. I'm all over this one." She looked down on the listing head of her new charge. "You come with me, sweetheart. I'll fix you up in a snap and get you going quick as a wink."

To my considerable surprise, when Heals-on-Wheels arrived at the same location the next month, Mrs. Arroyo presented herself again. She knocked on the bus door shortly after we'd closed for business. Bubba popped up, eager to help any stray soul, but I pushed him back into his seat with a hand on top of his head. "I got this one, Bubba. With this one, I have history."

Tinisha's arms were crossed, and her foot tapped as she looked back to me for guidance. "Show the señora in, if you would be so kind, T." Mrs. Arroyo gave me the slightest hint of a nod as she and Tinisha squeezed past me, heading to the exam area. Within a couple minutes, her vitals were recorded and I held, yet again, a chart topped with the chief complaint of "STD Check."

I stepped through the curtains and greeted her. "Buenos dias, señora Arroyo y Lopez Vega." We briefly shook hands, her side of the interaction being particularly limp and prefatory. "If I may be so bold. Is it fair of me to assume your late arrivals are not by error but are planned so none of your neighbors will observe you seeking our services?"

She spoke sternly, like the formidable mother superior she so resembled. "Very perceptive of you, Dr. Taylor, and correct. It is very much against my nature to be tardy to any occasion. My late arrival here with you is very out of character." She scowled over one shoulder. "There are idle minds that seize upon any novel activity to generate all manner of malicious gossip. I would, if possible, spare myself such unwelcome and painful scrutiny." She focused on me a most forbidding expression. "It is also my hope that we can forego the extraneous pleasantries and unnecessary badgering which punctuated my last visit?"

Okay, even charitable old me had to say it. What a bitch.

"As you wish. But as your attending physician, it is my duty to make certain I am caring for you the best I can. So, if you would indulge me a couple of quick questions. You did receive Tinisha's call last month, confirming that all the tests were negative?"

She removed a handkerchief from her purse and dabbed her lips. "Yes, I did. Thank you for that service."

"Then, why is it you feel a need to be retested? While we are here to help and the test themselves are not all that expensive, I would hate to waste our meager resources unnecessarily."

To that challenge, she exploded with only marginal restraint. "Dr. Taylor! I will not be subjected to your cruel and belittling degradations a second time. Let me make my circumstances clear to you for the last time. I find myself at a station in life where I must seek charitable medical services. Fate and ill fortune have dictated that I have no alternatives. I can assure you that if I had the means to go elsewhere—anywhere else—I would not relegate myself to seek care metered out from a medical *bus.*" That last word stuck painfully in her throat. "That I am treated so poorly, I freely accept as part of my payment and my penance." A less willful woman would have allowed herself to cry at that point. She was not such a person. "If I could pay you for the testing to quiet your judgmental tongue, I would do so gladly. But, and curse you for making me say the words again, I cannot presently afford such a luxury." With that she fell as silent as a corpse frozen solid, deep in its grave. She neither visibly breathed nor moved. What was very much alive about her, however, were the hateful, penetrating stares she burned into the back of my head.

"Prudencia, please hear what I am about to say to you." Her gaze softened ever so slightly from white hot to simply scorching. "I know you are in a world of pain, both because of your need to come here and with whatever the crisis it is in your life which causes you to ask for medical help. But, please, I would ask that you grant me the privilege of helping you. I have never wished to make you uncomfortable. If I have, then I apologize sincerely. I don't know exactly what I said or did to make you despise me so completely. But, I'm sorry I gave you those incorrect impression. I ask you to please give me a second chance. Can you do that?" I let her consider my words a few tense moments. "Now, if all you want is for Tinisha to do the tests again, say the word and that's what we'll do. If, however, you will allow me to reach into your heart and ease some of your pain, I would be honored to do so." Another pregnant pause passed, then I finished. "Which would you prefer?"

By some practical miracle, her rigid body language melted to one of passive indifference. "I will consider your gracious offer, Dr. Taylor. However, for now, I would prefer only to have your nurse collect the samples, and then I will take my leave of you and allow you to get on with your day." She held her hand out to me. When I gave her mine, she cupped the back of my hand with her left. "Thank you, Dr. Taylor, for your kindness and your *humanidad*. I can see that I misjudged you. You are clearly an honorable man."

When Heals-On-Wheels arrived the following month, I could not help but kept one eye out for Prudencia. To my disappointment, she did not show. My day was, hence, proportionally easier, and shorter, but more empty.

The next month was chaotic for me with the crush of work, family, and countless deadlines. I was so sufficiently distracted that I was caught off guard when Tinisha stepped to my side that Saturday. "Dr. Taylor, your *girlfriend* is back."

I startled up from my laptop. "I wasn't aware I had one, T." Collecting myself, I elbowed Tinisha's ample hip. "Is she cute?"

She folded her arms across her chest and angled her head in judgement. "I don't know about cute, Dr. Taylor. She's kinda long in the tooth. I estimate she's well past being anybody's idea of cute."

I frowned. "Sounds like I'm selling myself short in the infidelity department, doesn't it, T?"

"I'm afraid you might have. I'd say a man with your looks and income could acquit himself better in choosing a mistress. Not that it's any of my business, mind you." T returned to her proper business demeanor. "So, do you want me to put the Lady Arroyo and something-or-other in the exam room, Dr. Taylor?"

The lost señora! "Of course, T. I am dying to be pummeled about the head and neck again. I have only just healed from our last encounter."

A few minutes later, I parted the curtains with too big a smile on my face. "Prudencia, it's good to see you again. How have you been?"

She measured me up and down with an impassive gaze. "Are you really, my good doctor, glad not to be rid of me?" She spoke as seriously as an executioner sharpening his axe. "I will take that in its best sense, at least for now, Dr. Taylor. And, before you can ask, yes, I could forego a visit last month, bolstered, no doubt, by your kind words."

"But…"

She afforded me the thinnest of emotionless smiles, and cut me off. "However, my mind has not been able to remain concern free, so I again make this journey for your aid."

"Do you have or have you had any symptoms suggestive of a sexually transmitted disease? Any fever, rash, discharge, or skin lesions?"

"No."

"Has, and forgive me if I ask too boldly concerning such a private matter, your husband confessed to any… transgression that might cause you to worry?"

"No."

"Again, forgive my bluntness, but have you and your husband had intercourse since we last met?"

"No."

"Then why are you burdened with this obsession concerning an STD?" I omitted, in the best interest of productivity, the various quips that ricocheted about in my head. *You do know you cannot get them from a toilet seat*, right? *You, Prudencia, possibly contracting an STD. You should be so lucky.* No, those observations were unlikely to advance the conversation along positive lines.

Sternly, she glared at me. "So, it is an obsession now that I suffer from a potential disease of the flesh?"

I back peddled quickly. "No, sorry, Prudencia. That was unfair of me. What I meant to say was…"

She threw her palm up now to halt me. "What you meant to say, Dr. Taylor, was how is it that an old woman, one as sexually unappealing as I, fancies she might possibly be the recipient of a disease requiring intercourse to contract?"

You know, I really had to admire the old battle-axe. She was sharp as a tack and as straightforward as a beggar. "Yes, I believe that is at least some of what I was thinking, if not what I might actually have meant to say."

Her first smile of any worth preceded her response. "Despite my better judgement, and strong inclinations to the contrary, I believe I am growing to like you, if only just a little."

I bowed deeply at the waist. "That, señora Arroyo y Lopez Vega, will be the grandest gift I shall receive this day."

"Which still leaves the question you ask hanging in the air." She sighed. "You are a man, Dr. Taylor."

That caught me off guard. "Last I checked, yes."

One eyelid squeezed partly shut at my flippancy, but she mellowed quickly. "Perhaps I should have said *as* a man, Dr. Taylor, I assume you will understand my line of reasoning. Men are given to animal instincts throughout their lives. It is lamentable that such bestiality stays a part of even an aged, broken, man. But, as it happens, he will still be possessed by it. Such passions do burn in a man's heart well past the time when such attentions might be anticipated or reciprocally appreciated." She paused for a long time before making an attempt to be cheerier. "Don't you agree, both as a physician *and* as a man, Dr. Taylor?"

I nodded equivocally and contemplated a response.

Luckily, she continued directly. "Well, Dr. Taylor, my husband of fifty-seven years is neither immune to nor above such base and degrading motivations. Like many a younger woman, I too was not completely averse to such advances. Plus," she raised a finger, "I always knew the toleration of such actions was required of me." She drooped her head noticeably. "I know such attitudes are no longer held to or popularly spoken of. I am from a passing generation whose values have outlived their utility. I share my thoughts with you now, as they are central to my presentation to you these past months. You comprehend me, yes, *médico*?"

Her concrete facade finally failed and the dam burst. She collapsed upon herself like a wet paper doll. She began to sob, then to moan, and then to wail inconsolably. Tinisha cleared her throat loudly just outside the curtail, inquiring if I needed any intervention on her part.

"We're just fine, T," I said.

I let Prudencia pour forth whatever contentious demons she had amassed behind her powers of containment for untold decades. As with all powerful barrier once breached, there was much which needed to escape before any semblance of peace could return to her. Ten minutes later, she found herself looking up at me from my moist shoulder as I stood next to her. She still sat on the exam table. As if from a far distant dream within a dream, she drew her bearings, began to focus her gaze, and straightened slowly back until stiffly erect. She groped for her handkerchief, but I was ready with a box of tissue, which I presented to her.

"How are you doing?"

She blew her nose and swabbed the sheet of tears from her cheeks. "I am fine now, thank you. I cannot imagine what came over me. Please forgive such a schoolgirl-like outburst, *mi médico*. It is improper of me, and it wastes your valuable time watching such a spectacle. Again, my sincerest apologies."

I grinned. "Apologies for what? For being human?"

She shook her head in playful scorn. "I fear you miss precious little, Dr. Taylor, precious little indeed."

I looked neutrally at the chart I had picked back up. "Now, you were beginning to say something concerning why you have worried about STDs these last few months. Please continue from just before we were interrupted."

"My husband of over half a century, Jorge, has so far lost none of his passion. Though the effects of time upon him might suggest he should not have, the man remains a bull in that arena." She fell just short of adding "to my profound disappointment." I could see the words dance briefly across her eyes. "It is because of this I come to seek your aid."

"How so?"

"Please know these are difficult words for me to speak." Okay, now my interest was a little piqued. Despite years of practice under my belt, I had no clue where this was heading. "It has now been over six months since Jorge has…presented himself to me for the fulfillment of my marital obligations."

"So… you mean you figure since Jorge has not required you to have sex with him, he must be having that service delivered elsewhere? And, if Jorge is testing the waters of another well, you fear the possibility of being gifted some tainted waters as a result."

An undiluted irritation returned to her tone. "I do not believe you could have put it more crudely, Dr. Taylor, but yes, these are my fears."

"Sorry. I take your point. You are worried that Jorge's lack of demand upon your marital obligations means he's satisfying his urges elsewhere. So, why not simply ask him?"

She was flabbergasted. "Such things are *never* spoken of."

"What, you aren't supposed to talk about sex, a major defining point of marriage, with your husband of fifty-seven years?"

"Not if we were married a *thousand* and fifty-seven years."

"So, it is preferable to ask me to screen you for STDs rather than to simply ask Jorge what's up with his libido?"

In defense of the indefensible, forces other than reason were often summoned. Culture, religion, and established tradition were helpful in that effort. To that end, she glowered at me fiercely and proudly threw back her shoulders. "Dr. Taylor, mock the cultural system that has sustained my people through centuries of trial and torment if you will. Such casual disregard does not alter the strengthening monolith that they are to me."

"Okay, well if you cannot discuss sex with Jorge, bring him here. I can."

"What? Am I to ask Jorge to accompany me to a medical bus because I wish him to discuss with my doctor why his flame has suddenly extinguished? Dr. Taylor, certainly you understand such a thing is absurdly impossible."

"Then don't tell him why, exactly. Tell him you need him to come here to get a physical. Or, maybe say it is to discuss *your* medical condition with him present."

"Not likely to work. Jorge complains of nothing but age, so he will see no motivation to go to the doctor. Jorge would not see it as his place to participate in my care, so enticing him in that manner would not work either."

"But, you won't know for certain unless you ask him, will you?"

"No, but still…"

"Look, Prudencia, please try. Maybe he'll surprise you." I switched to my most doctorly tone of voice. "Maybe there is some important medical issue Jorge needs to discuss, but his pride holds him back."

"Point taken, *médico*. Now, may your sour assistant Tinisha take my sample now? Then you and I may both be free of each other's irritation today"

"As you wish."

The next month passed without a Prudencia sighting. But five weeks later, I was thrilled to spy her mounting the steps of Heals-On-Wheels leading a stooped man. She was right on time. We had just closed. After Tinisha recorded both sets of vital signs and placed them in the exam area, I stepped in and greeted Prudencia first. "Wonderful to see you again. And this must be—"

"This is my husband, Jorge." We shook hands. She vaulted over any perfunctory niceties. "Jorge has accompanied me here today because I have told him that the stability of our marriage is threatened. I have told him that you, Dr. Taylor, have volunteered to set matters straight, if such a thing is possible."

Speech did not come naturally to Jorge, but he could grumble. "Though why such matters could not be instead discussed with our pastor is beyond my understanding."

She slapped his arm. "Because, you old fool, we *have* discussed such matters with the padre more than once. Nothing has come of it. I talk, he listens, and you sit there like an embalmed toad, saying nothing. So, we are here to see if my doctor can save our marriage."

I just wanted to pat Jorge on the shoulder and tell him I felt his pain— maybe offer to buy him a beer. I was confident, however, that such favoritism would not go unpunished for either of us. I cut right to the chase. "Jorge, do you know precisely why your wife brought you in today?"

He shrugged unreadably.

"Let me start again. Jorge, how are you today? Do you have any serious medical complaints or other issues I might help you with?"

He grunted, "Never better."

"Jorge, you're a man of eighty-one years. It is not possible that you are 'never better.'" I pointed my finger off to the far left. "You were always better than you are now." That did elicit a begrudging giggle. "Would it be better if I asked Prudencia to wait outside, so we may speak privately?"

Jorge harrumphed resolutely. "The woman can stay. It would take a better man than either you or me to drag her away."

"Behave! It is not enough that you must humiliate me in front of our friends, now you must scorn me as a burdensome shrew before my physician?"

"Ah, let's all stay focused and positive here. There's nothing to be gained in bickering," I said.

Another, louder, harrumph came from Jorge. "Welcome to my world!"

"*¡Cállate, bruto!* You waste not just my time now, but that of my doctor." She gestured toward me.

"Okay, executive decision here. Prudencia, you go have a seat out front. Jorge and I will stay here and talk. Now shoo! Doctor's orders."

She looked stunned, offended, and uncertain all wrapped up in one ball of consternation. To her credit, however, she did finally shuffle away from us, though quite slowly.

Alone with Jorge, I could sense his body language snap more tightly closed. His grumpy-old-man playfulness evaporated. He sat there like a rock—hard, silent, and unyielding—and he gave every indication that he'd say nothing for all of eternity.

"Jorge, give me a break here. You know as well as I do that if you don't talk to me, your sainted wife will just drag you all over creation and back until you tell *someone*. Plus, the woman will peel my skin off and feed it to the crows for not finding out the problem."

He flashed a crooked smile. "You know my Prudencita well, *médico.*"

"So, why not save yourself the time and me the flaying? Let's be done with it here and now. Your call, my friend. Either way. But, if it was me, I'd spare us both unneeded suffering."

He straightened from his profound slouch and began to say something, then shook his head violently a few times. "No! There is nothing wrong with me that time alone cannot explain." He looked over his shoulder toward the front of the bus. "May I go now?"

So be it. "You're an adult. I can't stop you. Crawl back under your rock and hold on tight. You just know your wife will be tugging at your feet trying to pull you out, kicking and screaming. Go with my heartfelt condolences, one married man to another."

He stood up, pawed his wrinkled shirt, and took one step toward the curtain. Then, as if meeting an invisible palm against his chest, he stopped and slumped in defeat. He sat back down. He sat there a long while, gathering his thoughts. "I imagine she has brought me here today because she is confused and upset by the absence of my advances on her womanhood." He snapped a look to me. "Is that not so, Dr. Taylor?"

"Yes, Jorge. That is precisely why she brought you. She assumes that since you are not interested in her favors, you are finding them elsewhere. She worries you might give her an STD."

"Hah. That relentless witch!" He shook his head in disbelief. "I should be so lucky!"

That struck me as quite the odd attitude to espouse, given the accusations I had just leveled. "So, what is going on? Why the sudden loss of interest in sex? I know you're not cheating on her. For that matter, so does she. She came to me out of desperation. Come on. What gives?"

"Can't you just tell my wife that I am as faithful as Don Quixote? Assure her I have no medical problems that you can detect." He looked absently to the floor. "Then we can all proceed with our lives, such as they are."

"It's a bit late for that. For one thing, I doubt very much that's the case. Unless I'm sure you're fine, I won't lie. Look, is it erectile dysfunction? I mean, if you cannot—"

Jorge cut me off angrily. "I know what ED is! I cannot avoid those pornographic television ads. You do not need to paint me a photograph."

I pointed at him. "That's it. You do have ED."

He physically batted away my finger. "No. I do not have that problem, at least not in that sense." He mumbled something else I couldn't quite hear.

"What? I didn't catch the last part."

"Nothing! I said *no-thing*."

"Jorge, come on, say it. Once you do, it will be all downhill. I promise."

"You live in a strange land of dreams, Doctor."

"Then *what*? You're not having sex, but you aren't cheating, and you don't have ED. What else is there? Why—"

"Because I can't perform any sexual act with any woman ever again. God give me strength!" He pounded his chest as he crossed himself.

"Why, Jorge? Because you've lost interest? There's treatment for that t—"

He wailed with enough volume to be heard outside the bus and probably two blocks farther. "I have lost a good deal more than my interest!" He issued forth a series of short, ragged breaths laced with spittle. "In fact, I have literally lost everything."

He shot to his feet as if his chair was electrified. He jerked and wrestled frantically with his belt buckle. After he had that open, he tugged at his zipper so hard his fingers flew off the slider several times. Once open, he harshly pulled his trousers and underwear down in one tearing motion. He grabbed his penis, or, rather, what was left of it, and held it toward me. "There! Are you happy now? Are you proud of yourself, Doctor? Will God grant that it shuts you and my infernal wife up, finally?" As he yelled, he shook the irregular flesh attached to his crotch which had once been the base of his penis. "There, I have proven it to you! I cannot cheat on my wife. I cannot make love to my wife or to any woman." With that, he collapsed into the chair, a ball of tears, his pants tangled around his calves.

Jorge clearly had squamous cell carcinoma of the penis. I would wager he was never circumcised, though that didn't matter now. The cancer almost certainly began near the tip of his penis, under his foreskin, and had slowly eroded back toward the base. An angry, heaped up cuff of white tumor cells formed the end of the hideously deformed remnants of his masculinity. Even later, when Jorge calmed down enough for me to examine him closely, I could not find where the urine, which bubbled up from his stump, exited from.

I allowed him a good long while to weep and moan before I helped him pull up his pants. I patted him on the leg. "I'll do the talking, okay?"

No doubt, the cancer had already spread throughout his body. That type, at that stage, always had. He would, all too soon, die from the cancer's insatiable hunger. I knew with certainty there existed no cure for him. I could offer him some palliation, but it would be minimal, at best. Some urologist would insist that what remained of the festering penis be removed and a permanent urine tube be placed. They always did. Jorge would, as most men before him, refuse to even consider those options. They always did.

When I went with Jorge and Prudencia to Urology the next day, we would all act out that sorrowful, pointless play. The oncologist would hem and haw unsatisfactorily. She would dispassionately list chemotherapies and potential radiation treatments, and would agree with the surgeon that the disfigured stump must be removed. She would, however, lack the strength of conviction to make those interventions sound even remotely like something she recommended. Without doubt, long before his time came, Jorge would pray for death to speed up the inevitable and more mercifully end his private hell.

But, before any of those unbearable scenarios could take place, it was my job to bring Prudencia back to hear the unbearable. I was to be the unwilling witness, once again, to the impotent railings of a loving family faced with the unfaceable. I could not make things right, but I could make them better. I could be their doctor. Their *médico*.

Those moments always struck me as odd. I was to tell Jorge what he already knew and what would traumatically eviscerate Prudencia. I then had to say to them some complement of words, words I never knew in advance and words I always prayed would come to me at the last minute. Then I had to pretend to myself that those words could even be bolstering enough or clear enough or reverent enough to justify my sending them back to their once warm and comfortable lives. I would sound positive, within reason. Jorge and Prudencia would somehow find their way home. The front door would close behind them, and they would be numb. The family would be totally alone and fully unprepared to deal with the nightmare I had just escorted them into

They would cry. They always did.

One day in early spring, with ice still gleaming in the shade, Jorge was laid to his final rest. I stood behind Prudencia, with my hand on her shoulder, as she desperately clutched her children close to her, and we all wept.

THIRTEEN

A few Saturdays later, I found myself sitting in the RV's kitchenette, as I shared after-hours coffee with Bubba. By then, we had become great friends. Before he succumbed, Prudencia brought Jorge in dutifully each week for a check-up. Afterwards, she stopped coming altogether. I suppose that was natural enough since she had no real reason, other than friendship and obligation, to visit. Careful not to look directly at me, Bubba asked, "So, are you okay with your Jorge's passing and all?"

I sniffed thoughtfully. "Me? Yeah, sure. No problems." I took another sip. "Those two sure were a cute couple, though, you have to admit. But, Jorge had a bad disease. He let it go too long, and it cost him his life. I know better than to take it personally."

"No regrets or second-guessing on your part?"

I sat back and pondered his question. "None but the obvious ones we all get, I suppose."

He honed in. "And what might those be?"

I stretched my arms. "I know I did as much as possible for them, but you always wonder if there could have been more. But, this is not my first bull ride on the back of the Grim Reaper. Jorge's number was up. At the final tally, we're just physicians, not miracle workers."

He stared out the window. "Yeah, but it still sucks. They were good people. You're right on about that."

I reached my mug across the void between us, and we clinked stoneware. "I'll drink to that."

I had passed his brief screening test for burnout, so he switched to a less gloomy topic. "I hear you are one busy bee in the research department. Lead author on a paper in *The New England Journal of Medicine,* no less." He waggled his melon of a head back and forth merrily. "How my little boy has grown up. And so fast too!"

"Gee, thanks, Dad. Oh, the hospital called. They said there was a small clerical error when I was in the nursery. They said the man who thinks he's my father should give them a call."

"With our strong family resemblance? Nah, there's no need to even check, son." More conversationally, Bubba went on. "That's good stuff though. Real big mojo. *The New England Journal!* You should be proud."

"You have to know I am. It is sort of a watershed event in my life, like losing your virginity or your first visit to Paris."

"If you say so. Personally, I'd rather lose my virginity a few more times than publish any darn article you can imagine."

"Why, Cletus, I never knew you were such a hedonistic pig. I may have to reassess the wisdom of remaining your friend."

He set a placemat-sized palm gently on his chest. "Me? A hedonistic pig? Why I have never! Here I am a simple man with simple goals that are objectively superior to yours, and for that, I am assigned a pejorative label?" The bus nudged side to side as his negative response of twists and head shakes rocked the vehicle. "There's no justice in it, Noah, no justice at all."

"I can only pray your delicate constitution is not permanently injured by the gaping wounds I so unjustly inflicted."

He smiled wider than the horizon at sea. "You'd know why I felt the way I do if you saw the girl I lost my virginity to. Lord in heaven, she was three beauty queens, two exotic dancers, and one spewing volcano all rolled up into one stimulating package. That young lady had a body built for sex and a mind to make me happy!" The walls vibrated as Bubba joyously slapped his hands together and laughed.

"Careful. You're drooling on the table there. If you form a puddle, T's going to make you clean it up."

After the raging lust passed from his eyes, Bubba became very serious. "You know I love you, right?"

Uncertain where he was headed, I replied noncommittally. "Yeah, sure."

He spied up at me surreptitiously. "I didn't at first, you know."

"At first, when?"

"When we first met. When you first started working here. I wasn't sure of your motives."

I cocked my head. "Not sure about my motives? What's that supposed to mean? I began working with you because this sounded like a worthy cause. What other motivation might I have had?"

"Well, you were with that *dean* woman. She made a specific point to introduce us, if you will recall," he admitted sheepishly.

"I'd think I was being insulted here if I had any idea what you were talking about."

He had absolute honesty in his eyes. "How was I to know whether you and she were the best of friends?"

"Me and Joan friends? No way! My impression of her is that she's a heartless political bitch using the knives she's just placed in people's backs to climb over them as she struggles to reach the top of Crap Hill."

"I know that now. But I didn't back then."

"And exactly why are we having this conversation?"

"Nothing. Probably nothing," he grumbled vaguely.

"And since I am not a mind reader, what exactly amounts to 'probably nothing?'"

He stared at me. There was something in his look I would have thought impossible. He was afraid. "I don't know exactly. I just can't stop imagining I'm hearing coyotes sniffing around my chicken coop in the dark of night."

I became concerned. "Bubba, help me out here. You're making no sense at all. What are you even talking about?"

He scratched at his chest. "I can't say exactly. But I get the uneasy feeling that the university is looking into my business." He placed the butts of his palms together on the table and opened his fingers toward me. "It's like I just popped up on somebody's radar screen, and now they are watching my every move. I can't give you any specific examples or anything, but I got that feeling you get when you think someone's watching you."

I knew better than to tease, with him being so serious and frightened. "First, why would the university be dogging your ass? Second, why do you even suspect they would? Third, and most important of all, what does me possibly conspiring with Dean Clarke have to do with the reality we live in?"

He replied with a burst of anger and incredulity. "Why would they be harassing me? Are you serious?"

"Of course, I'm serious. What would you have done to elicit any attention from the university? You are a free spirit, sure. You're definitely an iconoclast, but it's not like you're a threat to them. Unless you've done something bad you're not telling me, how could you have anything to worry about?"

"There, you just said it. I'm an iconoclast, a non-believer." He addressed the ceiling. "Just like the Inquisition, our bosses burn non-believers."

"I'm getting more confused and a little bit freaked out, Bubba. The Inquisition was centuries ago. Nobody's burning anybody at the stake these days. Could you please back up and tell me what's going on?"

He and I stared at each other several seconds. He shifted uncomfortably on the bench a little. "Okay, this is it. I'm guessing you're unfamiliar with the true nature of the forces that have focused their unwelcome attention on me." He struggled to make clear what he was about to say. "Look, man, what I was getting at with Dean Clarke is that I wasn't sure I could trust you at first. Now, I know you'll take a bullet for me. You're a true and a valued friend."

"Thank you. That means a lot to me."

"What I'm saying is that lately, I have the distinct impression that the university is snooping around my past and subjecting me to undue scrutiny. These are bad people at their cores. When bad people come a-sniffing, the next thing that happens will never be good. They focus on you today, and tomorrow you go bye-bye."

"I don't know, Bubba. I think you're being a little dramatic. I wouldn't want to move next door to any administrators, but they have better things to do than harass you or me."

"Not by my way of seeing things. I don't say they're bad people or evil people lightly. I am a man of God, as you well know. For me to condemn them, you have to believe I've reflected upon this at some length." He was dead serious.

"Bubba, I respect your conviction, and for sure they're not our friends, but—"

He raised his hands to stop me. "These people, the deans and other administrative types, they are not your friends."

"I know they're—"

"No, man, I don't mean they are not your friends but that maybe someday they might be. No, I mean they can *never* be friends, not with the likes of you and me."

"That's a bold condemnation of my personality, don't you think? I am really quite likable—lovable at times."

Irritated frustration boiled over. "No, it's not you. It's them!" Easing back a bit, he continued. "Look, it's like this. Let's take Dean Joan as a case in point. When you two were chatting at the party, what were you discussing?"

"I don't know, Bubba. That was over a year ago."

He pointed at the tabletop. "Think! What were you two discussing?"

I relaxed and tried to recapture my brief interlude with Joan. "Let me see…just before you squeezed through the door…she was asking me how my work on the Curriculum Committee was going. Yes. That's it. See, nothing earth-shattering. Just small talk."

"And what did you tell Dean Clarke?"

"Nothing really." I could see him physically rising upon hearing my neutral response. "I think I replied something to the effect that, thus far, I had managed to stay awake."

He slapped a hand over his eyes to shield his vision. "And what did your *boss* Joan say in response to your ever so witty remark?"

"What?" I defended. "I was just being my usual cute self. Charmingly and disarmingly clever, that's me."

Hand still over his brow while beckoning me with his free hand. "And what did she say back at you?"

I was annoyed at the course the conversation had taken. "Joan said something like that's not what she'd heard. She heard that I kidnapped the committee and went over Chairwoman Celestial's head right in front of the entire committee."

"Oh Lord, this is worse than I could have imagined!" He peeked through a couple digits. "And what did you say in response to that, young and naive Noah?"

"I said that I never went over anyone's head, not intentionally at least. Yes, maybe I had spoken a few misunderstood words, but that I never had any intention of breaking protocol or trying to disrespect the chair."

"To which she responded?" Bubba said very sarcastically.

"Words, Dr. Taylor—"

"are a powerful thing. You shouldn't use them lightly or use them at all if you are not certain what you mean and what actions those words might ignite."

I was stunned. "You couldn't have possibly overheard her. For the record, Joan actually said, 'set in motion', not 'ignite.'"

"Man, you are significantly dumber than *me*. I did not think such a thing was possible. When Joan asked how the committee work was going, she wasn't asking because she wanted to know. She was just listening to see if she received back the correct code words."

"Code? What code words? You're starting to sound a bit paranoid."

He shook his global head. "You only talk like that because you do not know them. The code is to confirm quickly to an insider whether you're one of them. As far as one of them sees it, being an outsider is like having leprosy and syphilis rolled up into one big old infectious ball, with a dash of mental illness tossed in for good measure." Before I could interrupt, Bubba leaped ahead. "Listen, Noah, your correctly coded answer to Dean Joan would have sounded more like, 'Just fine, Joan, thanks for asking. The work is daunting, but our team is really committed to working together.' You ever hear a person talk like that?"

"Like what? Like the speaker was a lobotomized cretin and a committed team player?"

He vaulted up. "Yes! That's it. See, you do know how they speak."

"Know what, Bubba, that administrative clones all talk the same, saying nothing and accomplishing even less?"

He pointed at me with significant emotion. "Yes, they all do. Don't you forget it!"

"Bubba…"

"Don't you get it, Noah? They're not just talking like robots. They're sniffing at each other's butts like a pack of dogs." He gestured to one side. "If you smell like one of their pack, then you're over here." He pancaked his palms together and placed them to his right side. "But if you answer like some wiseass immunologist and say that the work is boring, then you're over here, and most assuredly not a member of their pack." His hands lurched over to his left side. He shook his hands over the second area. "Here is not a good place to reside. As far as they see the world, the folks standing over here are the great unwashed. Do you take my meaning?"

I relented, as whatever he was on about was important to him. "So, you're saying the admins look and talk alike so they can tell us from them. Big deal. They can have their little tea party, wear pretty dresses, and not invite me. I'll be better off and a heck of a lot happier."

A thoughtful Bubba corrected me. "No. It's not that benign. This is not like high school where the cool kids harass the nerds. No, these people need to identify outsiders so their hive can deal with all the bad bees." He looked at me with great consternation. "Don't you see? They either gotta fix us bad bees or get rid of us, because that's what is best for the hive. Sure, they may humor us a spell, waiting to see if we come around and become good little bees." He rested his face in his palms. "But if we don't come around, or worse yet, if we cause even a tiny bit of trouble for the hive, we must be dealt with. I'm serious, Noah. I only know two ways of getting rid of a bad bee. You can either boot them outta the hive, or you can sting them to death. There's no other way around the problem. It's not publish or perish. It's *conform* or perish." With that, he fell silent, fully drained.

"Bubba, you're kinda freaking me out here."

"For that I am sorry, my friend. But these people…" He paused, trying to hold his emotions in check. "These are not nice people."

I reached over to my friend and rubbed his forearm. "Easy there, buddy. I hear what you're saying, and I thank you for worrying enough about me to point it out. But, I'm certain both of us are perfectly safe. The powers that be may not like either of us much, but they're stuck with us, so stay strong." I tried to sound convincing. "Plus, I got your back. That's gotta count for something, right? More importantly, Tinisha got both our backs. No one's getting past that woman. She'd bitch-slap the devil himself to keep us safe."

That drew a faint, if unconvincing, smile. Then he became serious again. "I wish I was just being paranoid, but deep in my heart, I do not believe that is the case. I hate to play the race card, but, you gotta remember, my people were slaves. I think that makes me more sensitive to what's going on than someone like yourself. My nose is telling me someone's trying to be my master, like back in those hateful times." His voice rose and bristled with emotion. "But they are not just trying to be *my* master. They want to be *your* master too. They desire nothing short of being the master of everyone who is not one of them."

"Cletus, I can tell you're upset and that you feel these things…"

Gently, just barely above a whisper, he held up the time-out sign used in football, to stop me. "Your finest doctor-talking isn't going to work on me. Not with me and not when I speak the truth. I know you want to help, and I love you like a brother. But seriously, don't waste your time trying to ease my pain." He struggled uncharacteristically to find the right words. "Just be careful. Be cautious who you choose to trust, and be even more careful who you choose to be honest with."

"Me, Bubba? I'm on the road to certain success. No one is going to mess with me. Remember, I'm now a lead author in *The New England Journal.* I have grant dollars pouring forth from my behind, and my teaching reviews read like I wrote them myself."

With grim finality, Bubba looked deeply into my eyes. "You may see yourself as the golden child in a catbird seat, as safe as a king in his mighty castle. But never forget. Just as the Pharisees betrayed Jesus, your leaders can have you crucified at their whim. If you walk with your eyes shut and your ears closed but insist on leaving your mouth wide open, you are no more secure than Christ himself."

FOURTEEN

A couple of weeks after my unusual and unsettling discussion with Bubba, I received a note in my inbox from, of all people, Kent Pearson. I had neither seen nor heard from Kent since that odd encounter at the COCs a while back. Frankly, I had put him out of my mind completely. Our friendship when we worked together in Ruth Farbstein's cholesterol group years ago, turned out to be not so close. After I left, we completely lost touch. That was not too surprising in retrospect, I suppose. We had totally different personalities. Sure, we were bosom-buddies in the trenches of warfare that was medical training. But those times were long gone. He was, in the end, too crazy, too rebellious, and too unpredictable for my taste. The most off-putting aspect about him was that he was just too cynical and narcissistic. He did not give a rat's behind about any person, place, or thing that wasn't Kent Pearson. So, we drifted apart.

Anyway, the note said to meet Kent in his office the following week to discuss *personnel matters*. That did not strike me as terribly odd. My secretary, though as marvelous person, was less than stellar when it came to the clarity of her messages. I assumed she had meant to write *personal matters*.

Maybe he wanted to rekindle our friendship or relate some news concerning a mutual acquaintance. Who could know when it came to Kent? In any case, I presented myself to his office that next week. I tried to simply walk into his office, us being old chums, but his receptionist simply would not have it. He halted me with a high-pitched squeal so shrill that I thought

I must have stepped on his tail. The humorless functionary then pointed to a chair. He waited haughtily for me to be seated before he would even announce my arrival to his high lord and master. The spindly gnome informed me that Dr. Pearson was "finishing something up" and would be with me "shortly." Shortly turned out to be twelve minutes. I noted the delay precisely because I was so annoyed at being made to wait that I referred to the wall clock almost continuously.

Finally, the preposterous receptionist escorted me the ten feet from where I sat to Kent's door. He knocked softly, then, only after hearing a verbal confirmation, opened the door like he was about to enter the Oval Office. Silently, he signaled me to enter.

"Will there be anything else, Dean Pearson? Can I bring you some water? Coffee?"

Kent did not look up from the paper he was writing on to answer. "No, Harold, we're fine. Shut the door on your way out." With that, the pipsqueak retreated.

Kent did not lift his attention from his writing. "Just a second, Noah. I want to finish this paperwork. There, done." With that, he set down his pen, stood halfway up out of his chair, and extended a hand across the table. "Good to see you, Noah. Thanks for coming on such short notice, old boy," he said with striking hollowness.

I waited dumbly for a moment, anticipating some punchline. None was forthcoming. "A week's not really short notice, Kent." His blank stare was unreadable. I stumbled ahead. "And what's this *Dean* Pearson crap? I didn't hear that you had ascended to such lofty heights."

With a passionless smile, he batted one palm down toward his desk top. "Actually, it *Interim Assistant* Dean Pearson. Since that's such a mouthful, Harold just addresses me as *Dean*."

"Interim assistant dean. Interim assistant dean. Interim assistant dean. Gosh, Kent. My mouth seems to be able to say it pretty easily."

His smile reduced itself to an even more desiccated husk of its former paucity. "Well, once Dean Chamberlain is back from his medical leave, I'll be just plain old *Professor* Pearson again, if that makes you feel any better."

I leaned forward. "No, that wouldn't make me feel better or any worse. I'm playing with you, but you ain't playing back. Lighten up already. It's me, Noah, Peniscuff...fresh meat." I spun my hands in the air to ask for acknowledgement. "Any of this sounding familiar?"

He lost all expression on his facade and spoke with stunning blandness. "Ah, yes, residency. Those were good times, weren't they?"

"No, Kent, they were horrible times. Almost everything about residency sucked with tremendous force and frequency. But you and I, we were okay. You having a bad day or something, my man? Migraine headache...erectile dysfunction...the insecurity of fecal incontinence making everyday life a challenge?"

He attempted what had clearly become a chore for him: to seem convivial and cordial. "No, old chum. I'm having a bang-up day, really. I imagine it is just we had gotten older and I have, naturally, been too busy of late to 'let my hair down.'"

"Kent, bubby, have you looked in a mirror lately? Fraid there's not much left atop your noggin to be letting down."

Whatever previously posed for forced civility evaporated like water cast upon a hot skillet. He chuckled humorlessly. "As I implied, growing up *can* be hard." I had to wonder if he had been required by the CoCs or the Council of Deans to take powerful psychotropic medications before he assumed his present position. What a stiff he'd become in his middle years.

He shuffled his papers like a news anchor and went on. "Well then, as to why I called you here today. We need your input on a certain personnel matter. It turns out you are in a unique position to afford us key insights that could be most helpful to the team. This pertains to a faculty member you have worked with closely, one whom we have become quite worried about as of late."

I raised my hand to signal that I had a question. I actually had several of them all of the sudden. I did not wait for him to call on me before I began. "First off, I thought this was a *personal* matter. I don't wish to sound pissy, Kent, but who are you to be conducting a personnel investigation? And who is this 'we' you keep referring to? Royalty and editors call themselves 'we,' not interim assistant deans. They all still refer to themselves as 'I,' just like the rest of us workaday folk. And, what do you mean *you called me here?* I came because you asked me to and we used to be friends. I was not aware I was being summoned by fiat based on your power and might."

A stern, displeased look briefly passed across his face but disappeared as quickly as it had appeared. Some abomination of a smile preceded his attempt to address my challenge. "Noah, please, remain calm. Those are excellent questions, and I'm happy to address them all, one at a time. I guess in my newness to this job, I made assumptions that I shouldn't have in terms of your familiarity with the situations involved."

Huh, what did Kent just say?

"First off, let me assure you the personnel matter I *requested* you to come here to discuss with me does not in any way concern you directly. We know you are a loyal and valuable asset to this university, naturally. We have not had an occasion to raise a collective eyebrow at anything you've said or done that we know of, to date."

"I never figured it was about me. But, gee, thanks for the ringing endorsement. It's just peachy to hear the university still loves me, especially based on the fact I heard it from a man of your station. But, I'm hearing that 'we' again, Kent. I'm still sitting here wondering who 'we' is?" I sat back defiantly. "This is the weirdest conversation I've ever had."

Kent folded his hands together pursed his lips. "Noah, let me backtrack so we can get back on track. I'm certain I can clear the air a bit. I sit on the P&T Committee. You know, Personnel and Tenure."

I know, puke, what P&T stand for. I had to present myself to them before I received my tenure. Hell!

"Part of Dean Chamberlain's duties place him on that committee too. When DC, oh, excuse me, I am referring to Dean Chamberlain, took medical leave, the Provost felt I was a logical choice to keep Chamberlain's chair warm, pending his return."

"Wait. I thought you were on the CoCs, not P&T."

He smiled with self-congratulation. "I sit on *both*, as well as a few others we have no need to discuss now. So—"

Incredulous, I cut him off. "You sit on more than one committee? Dude, we're only required to suffer through one. What kind of stupid are you?"

He seemed to require some inner mantra to settle his irritation. Quickly though, he spoke blandly. "For the good of the university, I elected to do more than the bare minimum. Others might, but not me. Look," irritation involuntarily crept into his tone, "I have another meeting in ten minutes, so I'd like to forgo any more banter and get straight to the purpose of our meeting. Do you think we could make that happen?"

I swept an ushering hand. "Go right ahead. Your circus, your monkeys, Kent. The next ten minutes of my life belong now to you, this university, and 'we.'"

He was patently unamused. "Fine, thank you." Automatically, he returned to his bloodless civil intonation. "We would like to pick your brain about Dr. Cletus Black. We understand you've worked closely with Dr. Black for more than a year as part of his outreach efforts. Is that true?"

That caught my attention, sort of like a hydrogen bomb going off in my face. "Yes, as you knew before you asked, I have worked with him for a while."

"I am sorry if you misinterpret my remark as overly formal. I am simply establishing a coherent line of thought and a factual trail. So, you have partnered with Dr. Black, yes?"

"He and I work together at least once a week doing Heals-on-Wheels. If you call that partnering, then that's what it is." I shook my head in disgust. "I can't imagine why a man with a college degree would call working together 'partnering,' but there you have it."

He beamed as if he just discovered a thousand-dollar bill on the street. "Excellent!" He slipped seamlessly back into melba-toast mode. "I am confident that as an established asset of value, you can aid us with needed insights." He morphed his face into that of a worried father. "Noah, we, by that I mean to say the P&T Committee, are concerned about Dr. Black."

The hairs rose along the back of my neck. I leaned forward. "How so, Kent?" Their concern for Cletus could not be good. "What do you mean by 'concerned'?"

"Well, by concerned, we mean to say that we are concerned for him." He must have felt a need for further clarity. "We direct that concern, naturally, in the best sense of the word."

I was lost, a babe in the woods. I had no clue what he meant to say. "Ah, Earth-to-Dean KP, you're sort of babbling. You know that, right? You can't use a word in its own definition."

He flipped effortlessly back to a default reply. "I am sorry if you see it that way, Noah. Perhaps in my newness to this job I have made—"

I halted him with a raised hand. "That's okay, Kent, I know. You're new at the dean business and not up to snuff, in fighting trim, shipshape, as right as rain, or found your sea legs quite yet."

Displeasure erupted in him like an ice volcano. "I would prefer it if you did not give me the distinct impression that you were mocking me, Dr. Taylor." He rapped his fingers on his desk in the style of an irritated Mother Superior addressing a naughty child. "As I was saying. The committee is concerned that Dr. Black's performance has dropped off somewhat of late. We wonder if this lack of performance might reflect some fundamental unhappiness on Dr. Black's part."

"Unhappy?" I blurted out. "Bubba, unhappy? He's as happy as any ten men you're ever going to find, all duct-taped together into one great big bundle of happy."

He met my exuberance with steely indifference and waited impatiently for me to finish. "What we are asking of you would be, oh, say, a few first-hand details concerning Dr. Black's hindered performance."

I scoffed. "Hindered performance? What in the blue blazes are you smoking these days? Cletus is a fabulous doctor. He is a tireless worker, caring to a fault, and as good an advertisement for this university as you will find anywhere. What more could anyone ask for? Oh, and did I mention the man is physiologically incapable of being anything other than extremely happy?"

Kent responded mechanically. "It's not a matter of what we want…check that, it is, naturally. What we want is for all our faculty to be happy." With the warmth of a funeral director, he summarized. "We, naturally, want to make sure Dr. Black is *happy* here. That is our mission. If he were not happy, then, as a valued member of our team, we'd want to set in motion actions to ensure his being happy once again." He opened his hands in a gesture of welcome. "You see, Noah. Nothing sinister or covert is going on here. We simply want Dr. Black to be *happy.*"

I concealed my trepidation as best I could. "And if 'we' come to the collective conclusion that he is not as happy as a butcher's dog?"

"Then it is tasked to the P&T Committee to decide what actions best fit the facts in terms of a mutually beneficial set of solution-parameters and options-bases."

I could not help it. "What, maybe y'all will send him to an indoctrination camp? Or force a happiness transfusion into his head? Even better, how about a brain transplant?"

Kent balanced his internal fuming with an outward look of concern. "Noah, this is not the time nor occasion for humor. I must take offense at your general tone. I am conducting an employee-intervention investigation, and naturally, I wish to be as impartial and thorough as possible. It is with regret that I see that you hold my efforts in a certain amount of contempt." His jaw muscles strained mightily and crushed his teeth together audibly, by way of manifesting his unhappiness with my performance. "We would have thought that you, as Dr. Black's purported friend would have wanted to cooperate more fully and more substantively to our efforts to ensure his personal and professional happiness." He stared intently at me for a moment. "Such a shame."

I narrowed my eyes. "Well ex-squeeze me, Professor Interim Assistant Dean Pearson. You speak in dark veiled nuance about a good friend's performance. You invite me, like Judas before me, to betray a good man. And 'we' are off put by my reluctance to help 'we' destroy him?"

With petulant irritation, Kent exhaled. "I sense this meeting has passed its productive end."

"Not productive, you say? *Eu contraire!* You asked about Bubba's performance, and I was able to assure you that the man is both highly functioning and ridiculously happy. 'We' got all that 'we' wanted, right? The fact as they truly are, right? I'm as sure as a gambler on a hot streak that 'we' would not want me to state the facts in any other manner, would 'we'?"

I sat forward threateningly. "Unless of course 'we' didn't want the truth. Maybe 'we' were hoping for salacious gossip? Or maybe, wet dream of wet dreams, 'we' were lusting for false accusations and backstabbing? Maybe your damn P&T Committee has already decided what they will do and just wants to backfill the justification?"

Kent stiffened impassively. "I trust, Dr. Taylor, you will have no problem finding your way out. On behalf of the Personnel and Tenure Committee, I would like to thank you for your valuable time and your considered opinions." With no further notation of my existence, he picked up the phone and tapped a button. "Harold, is my three thirty here yet?"

FIFTEEN

Over coffee the next Saturday, Bubba informed me that he had been terminated.

Sonsabitches!

For the first time since I'd met him, Bubba was quiet and reserved. Staring at the table, he broke the ice. "Well, now's as good a time as any to let you know that the administration has let my rather considerable ass go." He looked up to me, tears flooding down his cheeks. "I was too different, so I had to go." He tried to finish his next sentence. "This is my last…day on…to be with…" He broke down completely.

"Bubba, God! I'm so sorry to hear that. I thought you were a little moody this morning, but I had no idea. Are you okay?"

Half accusingly, he sobbed like a harpooned walrus. "No idea, eh? They didn't forewarn you of their dirty little deed? You weren't *in* the loop?"

"I know you're upset, but what are you suggesting? You can't think I had anything to do with this, do you?"

He quickly reversed himself. "You're right, you're right. Sorry, man. You didn't deserve that. Please forgive this sorry excuse for a friend."

I reached across and patted the back of his hand. "No excuse needed. No offense taken and none possible between two friends."

He sniffed a torrent of snot back up his nose. "I know that. You wouldn't actually have known they were out to get me if I hadn't told you myself, right?"

Oh boy. That mortar round landed pretty close to my exposed testicles. Should I have said something about my interaction with Kent? Of course. I had to come clean with the man who had quickly become my best friend. I knew Bubba would appreciate my candor. At least I prayed he would, as opposed to him flattening me.

"Yeah, you did mention that someone was snooping into your business, looking for dirt." I waited a few heartbeats for divine inspiration. None arrived. "After that, I did meet briefly with an assistant dean. The jerk tried to pump me for information about you. But I told them nothing but superlatives. That pissed him off royally, I can tell you for nothing."

As if a boulder had fall from on high and dam a mighty river, his tears ceased abruptly. "And you didn't think to tell me?" He slammed a fist down hard enough to split most surfaces. "And here I thought you were my *trusted* friend. Shoulda known better than to take an elite academic into my confidence. As God is my witness, I shoulda known better!"

I was torn. Should I bolt out of the door in self-righteous anger at his hurtful outburst? Should I apologize, sit quietly, and let him vent? What should I do?

From nowhere, a commanding, window-rattling voice boomed forth. "You should be as ashamed of yourself as Pontius Pilot himself, Dr. Cletus Black! If you weren't so damn big and I wasn't so damn old, I'd lay you across my knee and tan the hide of your behind so red that it'd shine like a second sun in the sky." It was Tinisha. She was mad. Though the bus was too small for secrets, T always gave us our space without butting in. As she saw it, we were only wasting time flapping our gums while she had real work to do. But not today, boy-howdy.

She placed a wagging digit an inch in front of his nose. "Now you apologize to Dr. Taylor right this minute or I will forget that I am a lady and dress you down with language more befitting a drunken sailor than a professional woman."

His eyes bounced in confused concentration at the finger bobbing before him. He shook his head back and forth rapidly. "Woah, Tinisha! I am sorry. You're right."

"Of course I'm right, you overgrown rhinoceros. But I haven't heard any apologizing going on yet. Cat got your tongue, Dr. Black?"

He looked up at her as shame flooded across his full moon of a face. He dropped his head. "Oh, Noah, can you ever forgive this wretched and childish soul? I am a fool and struck out at a good man who is not at fault."

T folded her arms and leaned back in triumph against the counter.

"Bubba there can be no insults here. You are upset because you were treated badly, and you struck out. That's perfectly understandable." I seized his tree-trunk-sized forearm firmly. "We'll get through this together, the three of us."

With that, all of Bubba began to blubber-quake. The bus swayed with his motions like a seismograph documenting a massive tremor. By the time he was done, Tinisha had slid in next to him and was crying like a baby herself. Her head was lost somewhere between his arm and neck. Not one to cry, I sat quietly apart from the two of them and watched.

Eventually, his crying jag ended. T extracted a solemn promise from him that he was okay, and she left us alone.

He spoke slowly, as if waking from a paralyzing dream. "So what will become of us? Of Heals-on-Wheels?"

"That I can't say. It's too early to know. But we'll muddle on somehow, I'm sure. I, for one, will soldier on until my cold-dead fingers are pried off the door. Who knows, maybe they'll let me bring you back on as a volunteer. It's hard for even assholes to say no to free help."

"Ah, Noah, my friend. Naive young Noah. You may stay, but I am as gone as yesterday's trash. They wouldn't let me clean the toilet out in the dark of night if I paid them for the privilege. That's not how it works."

"Cletus, that's not how what works? What is the it that I'm not getting?"

He appealed to me from puffy red globes. "Don't look to me for answers to that. I'm just a tired, broken old man. If I knew anything wise enough to tell another man, I don't think I'd have ended up the way I have."

"Look, Bubba, I'm as sorry as hell about all this. It stinks to high heaven, but there's nothing either of us can do about it. I just wish I understood what you keep *not* telling me."

He rubbed at his face so forcefully I half-imagined it would peel off. He shook his head back and forth like a bloodhound trying to cast off a tick. "I can't tell you anything definitive. All I can verify is that there is something going on." He stopped to formulate his next sentence while he rapped his fingernails nervously on the Formica table. "Like I said before, being a black man in a white man's world has made me over observant, or at least oversensitive." He angled his head. "What I'm trying to describe is real subtle, and it's grown slowly, but…" He trailed off again and tried to articulate what it was that he wanted to say. He continued uncertainly. "It's like now, as opposed to a few years back. All the bosses are beginning to look the same and act the same and even think the same as each other. Do you follow me? Am I makin' any sense at all?"

"Not too much."

He pointed a finger at me in affirmation. "Honesty is good. It is essential in times such as these." With a pensive look, Bubba began again. "I guess all I can say is there is no current premium on individuality. No," he softly slapped the sides of his head, "that's not it either. There is a penalty for being different. Yes, that's more like it."

"I don't want to disagree, being you just got fired and all, but I think maybe you're overgeneralizing and being a tad dramatic. My impression of a boss is that they usually don't welcome dissent, sure. But there is no big conspiracy afoot that—"

Emphatically, he cut me off. "But that's just my point! There *is* a conspiracy, or at least a common mindset that binds them all together like rats glued into one big ball."

He was clearly being paranoid. Poor guy. But, as a good friend, I felt I needed to validate what he was saying, so I played along. "You mean here at the university? All the managers and administrators are…I don't know…are all acting strangely?"

A strained anguish crossed his face. "Yes and no. It's not just here though. It's not that they're acting strangely. It's like all the politicians and all the CEOs, even all the shift managers at the local fast food restaurants, they're all sounding the same. Haven't you noticed?"

"Can you be more specific?"

He snapped his head back and forth. "No, I don't think I can be." He slouched back and pondered his last remark. He sat up and corrected himself. "No, I can be, at least a little. They all talk about 'the company' like it is an actual living being, like some graven idol they want to please. They all use the same buzzwords and make positives out of everything. Where you and I would use 'but' in a sentence, they all substitute 'and,' because it doesn't sound as negative." He tore at his bald scalp feverishly. "Hell, at the meeting where they fired me, someone said they wanted to 'establish an action plan' to make me a better employee. Then the cold-hearted snakes fired me! I know I sound crazy. I most likely I *am* crazy, but what kind of sense does that make? Setting up a plan to make me a better employee which includes my termination?" Wearily, he shook his head. "I see this dark and consuming force befalling the world. All the foolishness and scheming and inhumanity, it can't be a result of random chance."

"Tell me about it! They told me they were worried because you might not happy, when what they really wanted to do was fire you without any good reason."

That caught him off guard. "What?"

"You mean the bosses now, they make proper sounding statements like they want you to be happy, when they actually don't like you and want to get rid of you."

He squinted one eye shut and tentatively agreed. "Yeah, I guess that's a specific example of..." A light suddenly when on. "Wait, that's not—"

"what Interim Assistant Dean Pearson said when we met concerning you."

"And what did you tell Interim Assistant Dean Pearson about my status of contentment?"

"What do you think I told him? I told him to go screw himself!"

He folded his hands in front of himself on the table. "Okay, Noah, deep breaths. Let's take a few moments to focus our thoughts." After a brief pause, he began with unmistakable concern in his tone. "Now, I am certain that you have regaled me an accurate summary of the *spirit* of the message you delivered to this dean fellow. However, what, in a less graphic and a more verbatim summary, did you *actually* say to him?"

I shrugged. "I don't know, Bubba. I told him the truth. I said you were one hell of a doctor and a great human. I told him you were so happy, I probably needed to start giving you injections of sad to make you be like the rest of us."

"Okay, fine, and thank you for your unadulterated support, but I want to know exactly what you said."

"Why?"

Like a very serious mountain, Cletus rested his knuckles on the table and leaned forward. "Because I want to know if I have unwittingly dragged you into this sea of human excrement you see me disappearing into."

"Don't you go worrying about me! I can fend for myself. This is a free country, and I am tenured. If I say something Pearson does not like, he can shove it up to the midpoint of his colon. I'll even gladly assist him."

"Brave words, my friend, but unwise ones in these times. Before you can correct me and say how wonderful things are, just listen instead for one minute. While I appreciate deeply you acting in my defense, please know two supremely important facts. One, it could not possibly have helped because these folks do not change their minds. Two, such actions are foolhardy, even for one such as yourself. Your support of me only draws their menacing eyes toward you. This you do not want. It's like with Frodo in *The Lord of the Rings*, you know? When Frodo places the ring on his finger, *zap*, Sauron can see him."

"Bubba, you really didn't just reference Tolkien, did you? And me, Frodo?"

"Do not try and be funny. I am extremely serious. Your support of me was as strong a beacon to the powers that be as was Frodo activating that ring was to ehe Eye of Sauron or those Nazgûl."

I childishly had to grumble. "I just can't picture you as a Middle Earth groupie."

He set his face with a biblically stern look. I took that as a powerful signal and confined my further remarks to the helpful and omitted any attempts at levity. "I know the dean, or knew him, from way back. So, I felt I could be pretty straightforward with him. I basically told him that you were a

130

wonderful asset and sent him the clearest message possible that he was wasting his time 'investigating' you. I don't recall if I said it in so many words, but I definitely tried to leave him with the impression that he was acting in a foolish and ill-advised manner."

He placed his face into his joined palms. "That is *exactly* what you should not have done. Look, this Kent fellow was out for my scalp. You told him he was wrong in doing so. You basically informed this up-and-coming administrator that you were right and that he and all his senior buddies had their heads up their asses, right?"

Sheepishly, I had to agree. "Yeah, I guess that pretty much sums it up."

"And for that bit of enlightenment, he thanked you, right? He was ever so grateful for the 4-1-1, for your pointing out his error in the discharge of his duties as an aspiring underling?"

"Not really."

"Why am I not surprised?"

He was beginning to convince me he was right, which was disquieting. "I'm certain you are overreacting." He started to respond, but I stopped him with a raised hand. "I realize they just fired you, so you have every right to be upset. But I do not think for one minute that I'm—"

"What? You think you're better than me, so you don't have to worry? Is that where your mind is headed? Well, I will save you the trip. Y'ain't! Get over any thought of that right here and now. When it comes to those weasels, the only difference they see between you and me is that I *have* been terminated and you are *yet* to be terminated. Period. And before you say it, I will save you the time a saying that too. Yes, you've got tenure, and yes, you bring in a boatload of grant money. But, none of that matters one infinitesimal bit. With these devils, you're either friend or foe. You're either with them or against them. And you, my foolish friend, just officially cast your vote as to which side of the line you're standing on. To them, you just became a problem. As we have just witnessed," he pointed both fingers to his chest, "problems need to be dealt with for the good of the company." He crossed him massive arms. "And that's the all there is to the story."

I had nothing left to say. Somewhere, way in the back of my brain, I heard a pesky little voice whisper that he was right and that I should be worried. But it was just a silly little foghorn that warned me about the rocks in my path. I ignored it. Sooner than I should have, I shut out the alert with the sure certainty that I was untouchable. I could not lend any credence to what he claimed about dire consequences headed in my direction. Me, at risk? Bubba was at a low point in his life. Of course, he saw danger in every move, hazard in every word, and evil in every shadow. There was no point in continued argument, in his being dragged through that unpleasantness any longer. I reassured him several times, as convincingly as I could, that I would heed his warning. I would be studiously cautious. I promised him I would never presume that I was safe.

How different my life would have turned out if I had only kept that promise.

SIXTEEN

The weeks following Bubba's dismissal, Tinisha and I muddled along together as best we could. It was impossible to replace his spirit, productivity, and sheer force of will, but we provided care for some people who needed it. We did good. Perhaps a month into our downsized mission with Heals-on-Wheels, I was asked to meet with the Associate Dean of Development & College Relations, one Steve Martin. I assumed, as it turned out presciently, that he was not the famous comedian. Both Ebenezer Scrooge and Captain Ahab had more vibrant, humorous, and likable personalities than Dean Steve Martin. He had all the *joie de vivre* of the embalmed Lenin on display in his mausoleum.

Scrooge was dour, cold, and petty. Ahab was monomaniacal, obsessed, and cruel. The man who greeted me combined all those untoward characteristics combined. He was the very poster child for disagreeability, disdain, and disapproval. His demeanor was bleak and void of any humor or humanity. He was the very image of a plague cart driver hauling away the dead. To meet him was as unpleasant as being reminded of our own mortality. Instead of a hello, I expected Steve to say, "Bah! Humbug! or No more porridge for you, Olive Twist! or Off with their heads!"

Were there, in some perverse mockery of human affairs, a *Mrs.* Associate Dean Martin, my mind tried to envision her perverse nature. She had to be unimaginably unattractive in physical appearance and reprehensibly repugnant in all personality traits. But, surely her single greatest shortcoming was her fatally flawed taste in men. But, to speculate was to digress.

The dean puffed up his jowls in...

No, demanded my brain. It would not be halted in its mission to paint the fullest picture of his surely hypothetical spouse, if she was possible. In a universe of choices, some good, some not so good, *Mrs.* Dean Martin must have made, in her selection of him for a husband, the worst choice allowable. The forlorn woman had to have been bereft of any other choice, other than that of spending her days alone. Alone would have been any sane person's choice, but inconceivably it was not hers. Even if *Mrs.* Dean Martin lacked eyes with which to see him, and arms with which to feel him, and ears with which to hear him, it was not possible that *Mrs.* Associate Dean Martin could be so oblivious as to his unsuitability as to possibly chose *Mr.* Associate Dean Martin to be her mate. No! In a universe of choices, I had proven logically that a *Mrs.* Dean Martin did not and could not exist.

There, better.

The dean puffed up his jowls in a tragic parody of a smile and greeted me. He half-stood with a half-extended arm, which resulted in a precarious teeter forward. I feared a calamitous fall was imminent. Notwithstanding his teeter, he spoke. "Thank you for coming, Dr. Taylor."

He had not so much a voice as he did a sandy-abrasive-throaty-rasp generator. He was the high-level executive in the academic hierarchy tasked to squeeze donations from the alumni and generally outreach to a community? He was a most improbable choice for that job.

I sat down. "Please sit, won't you, Dr. Taylor?" He looked at me, impressed by the speed with which I sat down. Then he began in earnest. "We have been following your progress closely here at the university, Dr. Taylor. I must say we were quite pleased with your progress, for the most part at least."

Oh crap, the imperial "we" again, just like Kent.

"As it is in the flow chart of my direct supervisory duties, I have followed with notation your work in terms of medical outreach on...oh, what do they called it? Ah yes, Meals-on-Wheels! A most catchy title, I must say."

Oh my. Out of respect to my instructions from the recently departed Bubba, I refrained from either correcting or laughing at the dean, at least at that early juncture.

With more serial belches than spoken words, Steve continued. "Yes, fine work." There passed several silent, hollow seconds, void of any obvious meaning yet undeniably awkward. I had no idea where the relic was heading, but from the general sound of things, I surmised that it would not be a pleasant direction from my point of view. "So, now that Dr. Black had elected to leave our institution, we were curious as to your plans, Dr. Trailnor"

"Elected" to leave? He was fired, you idiot. As to my plans, well, I plan to have dinner with my family tonight. I plan to get very drunk afterwards, thanks to you. I plan on outliving you, good sir.

"Ah, Dean Martin, could you be a bit more specific?"

There came from him a parched rumble, approximating speech. "Certainly, I could."

Another void of hopeless, empty time passed before it registered with me. This man-like apparition was such a dick. "Ah, Dean Martin, *would* you be a bit more specific?" He must have taught in the English Department when he was still alive.

He formed a smile-like perturbation of his face, similar to a prosecuting attorney's grin when he heard the judge decree capital punishment. "Certainly, Dr. Trailer. We were wondering what your plans for the outreach clinic you seem to have inherited will be?"

My plan is to paint it psychedelic colors and drive to San Francisco. Or, maybe I'll sell it in Mexico and blow the proceeds on cheap booze and even cheaper women.

"I'm not sure I take your meaning, Steve. Why wouldn't my plans remain the same? My assistant and I plan to continue to deliver quality medical care to the underserved."

I hoped that using his first name would have a slap-across-the-face effect. It did. The old fart recoiled as if goosed. Perhaps, he'd simply forgotten his first name was Steve and he was confused who I addressed

"We speculated as much, Dr. Taintor. As noble as that work was, we have reviewed your mission and feel that it will benefit from a little revamping, some updating, if you will."

You mean like your toupée, Steve? Here, let me slap that mangy rat off your pointy little head before it bites you and it dies.

"Dean Martin?"

Lord, doesn't that wax figure get it? Dean Martin, like the drunken 1960s comedian? Your name combines the essence of two great jesters, Steve and Dean Martin. Yet you are humor's antiparticle! Why is it that irony was always so lost on those who generate it?

"Yes."

"You referred to my mission in the past tense. I have to confess, that concerns me a bit."

"It does, does it? Very perceptive of you, Dr. Traver." He switched to a haughtier tone, one from a library of abrasive tones he possessed. "I'm confident you know that this is the Office of the Associate Dean in charge of our university's community outreach efforts. Hence, it falls to us to, from time to time, to reassess and redefine the various forms of outreach we wish to extend."

I hate the word 'we'! I'm never saying the word again.

"To that end, we wanted to solicit your opinion as to how the mobile clinic concept…"

So now it's not a bus helping people, but a concept?

"…could best be extended to serve a greater good."

The old goat folded the spindly remains of his hands in front of himself on his desk and stared at me, wheezing quietly. I forced myself to keep in mind that Bubba would be fundamentally disappointed with me if laid into the buffoon. "I think we're doing a pretty good job already. Why is there a need to change anything?"

The automaton, like one those in the Hall of Presidents at Disneyland, spoke. Only the dean's lips moved, and even then, they moved unconvincingly. "Change is inevitable, Dr. Trenure."

Trenure? Now my name is Trenure? That's not even a word in human.

"Without change, we'd all be running around the jungle, living in caves, and parading around wearing animal skin loin cloths." He shook his head in the negative and his dangly skin whipped around like a Bassett hound's. "No, Dr. Trenure, change is essential, and those who oppose change oppose the promise which burns so brightly in all of our hearts."

Hey, Steve, that's a mixed metaphor! And you used to teach English. Shame on you.

"That eternal desire for change longs to burst forth from the hearts of all good men and women, hoping to sweep across the face of the Earth, ushering in a new era of betterment." The clown pointed a finger toward the ceiling and suffered me to hear further meaningless rhetoric. "To stand against change is to remand yourself to the past, Dr. Trensor, not to place yourself in the future, let alone the present."

Where did this zombie come up with such mindless drivel?

"So, it falls to you to ask yourself, Dr. Trensor, will it be the future or the past which you will long and strive for? Surely, logic and Dr. Darwin argue that you must join us in the future."

Nothing, I got nothing.

It took me a few moments to decide that he was done saying words. No time for wit or snark. The man sounded powerfully serious, in a word salad sort of way. "Ah, Dean Martin, I believe you said you wanted to solicit my opinion on the mission. It sounds, however, that the mission has already changed and that you're asking if I'm on board or not. Which is it?"

He was determined to confound me further. "Which *what* is the *it* to which you refer?"

The freak was doing an Abbott and Costello routine with himself. "No, Dean Martin, I'm asking did you ask my opinion as to whether the mission should be changed or are you telling me it has changed and wondering if I want to be part of the new one."

Steve replied mystically, "Yes."

Enough. I promised Bubba I'd play nice and be a good egg, but I was officially pissed off and about to whoop some archaeological butt. "Listen carefully, you desiccated old hack. I'm though with your games. If you do not stop being a Class 1-AAA asshole, I'm outta here. You go that? Tell me what it is you're not saying like you are a native English speaker and then let's be mutually free of one another's unpleasant company for good."

Like the viper which he was, Steve coiled. "So, we are not to be friends, are we, you and I, Dr. Taylor?"

Wow, I am suddenly back to Taylor. Perchance you're more lucid then you were letting on?

"Not in a million years, even if you were the prettiest girl in town with a see-though dress and a purse full of condoms."

Icy contentment laced his words. "What very vulgar and base words to come from a man of your presumed standing in our academic community."

"Save the dark innuendos and veiled threats, bucko. I've still got the keys to the bus, the loyalty of the staff, and excellent support from several charitable groups. The mission statement is this: I'm driving the damn bus, and it's going to aid the sick and ill otherwise excluded from healthcare. Any questions, numbnuts?"

He sat lifelessly for the better part of an eternity before he began to clack together the bony appendages that were his hands. "Well spoken, young Dr. Taylor. So passionate. Such bravado!"

"I asked you once, nicely, to cut the crap. The next request will be more tactile then verbal, if you catch my drift."

"Of course, I take your meaning. And, in case it hasn't fully struck me, thank goodness I had the foresight to tape our little get together. What, with me being so old and feeble of mind, I'm certain you'll understand."

Shit! Double shit. No, triple shit. I walked right into that baited trap, and it just snapped shut on my crotch. "Now wait a second, Martin. I have to object strongly to you secretly taping this meeting. I—"

He lashed out. "You what? You wanted to be able to physically threaten with impunity an old man who is simply trying to solicit your opinion? Is that what you object to, hum?"

Son of a *BITCH*! "What is it that you want?"

I was certain he had just ejaculated in his pants, such was his joyful expression. "That is what we like to hear, Dr. Taylor. Did you know that? We love to hear the wicked and the weak grovel! It is such a sweet sound, such an eternal sound. Mmmm. How sweet it is." He leaned forward and squinted his eyes. "What we want, we always get. Always! What we want from you, for now, is the set the keys to your precious bus on our desk, and then we want you to tuck your tail between your legs and slink out of here a broken man.

Then, Dr. Taylor, we want you to live in fear of what we have planned for you next."

I tried to explain what had happened to my wife that night after the kids were in bed. Neither she nor I knew what to make of the meeting. Karan was not clear as to exactly how she felt about what had happened. At least that was what she said. I wasn't so sure I believed her. Her face was set with the beginnings of concern, while the first wisps of worry danced in her eyes. Never good signs from your wife after you delivered less than stellar news.

She knew, on an intellectual level, that I was a secure tenured professor with an internationally recognized and rapidly growing body of work. She knew I brought millions of coveted grant dollars into the university. Still, she was a mother of three small children and, at least on an instinctive level, greeted any challenge to her children's safety poorly. She knew jackbooted university police were not going to storm in and drag me away in the middle of the night. Still, genetic forces were powerful and not necessarily subject to reason. I was going to have to put out the fire of her concerns quickly.

If worse came to worse, I could always pick up the phone and land any number of jobs at other top institutions. Any university would fall all over itself to add me to their talent and income stream.

Wait. What was I thinking? What had I just thought? I had a minor run-in with some has-been dean, and I was ready to bail on the only real home I'd ever known? What was going on? I was overreacting by a factor of a hundred. So, what if Dean Martin accused me of workplace violence? Any fool who listened to his silly recording could tell instantly I spoke with hyperbole based on his irascible badgering of me. At best, there might occur a tempest in a tea pot. If anything came of it, most likely his superiors would berate *him* for being so irresponsible as to provoke the incident in the first place. Where had my impulse to flee town come from? Maybe I was still shell-shocked about the lousy way they had treated Bubba.

But why the sudden fear?

A few days passed, and I received an email from Kent asking me to come to his office as soon as my schedule allowed. The nature of the meeting was that nebulous "personnel" matter again. At least that time I had a pretty good idea what we were going to discuss at our meeting. I was shown in a little late by the same jerk as last time, Harold. As I entered, Kent sat impassively with his hands folded in front of him on the desk. I sat down without being asked. It was then I noted the name plate on the edge of the table read "Assistant Dean Pearson." I pointed at the desk ornament. "You left off the 'Interim' part."

He grinned humorlessly. "No, actually I did not. I am now officially the Assistant Dean."

I furrowed my brow. "But what about ole Chamberlain, the guy on medical leave? Won't he sort of notice?"

Kent shrugged inscrutably. "Unlikely. He's dead."

"Wow."

"His medical leave went more poorly than anticipated."

I guffawed. "No shit! Death is a pretty bad outcome. They really don't come any worse." I grunted a short laugh. "I bet Chamberlain would second that notion."

He was still void of any visible human emotion. "That's neither a proper arena for humor nor the reason we need to speak."

I lowered my head and tried my best to look offended by his tone. "Duly noted, Assistant Dean Pearson."

A smile meant to convey cordiality materialized on his mouth. "Come, let's not get off to a bad start again, shall we, old friend. Can Harold get you some coffee, water?"

I responded that I wanted nothing to drink.

"Very well." He leaned his chair back, and got to it. "We've been asked to discuss with you the unfortunate interaction you had with Dean Martin the other day." The Kent of old could never have passed up such a perfect set up for a joke. Who was the man in that chair? "Would you like to tell us, in your own words, the events as you perceive them?"

"Yeah, an arrogant old shit-bird burrowed his irritating beak under my skin a little too far, and I let him know it. End of story."

"Would that this ended the story. Would that it were." He leaned his chair farther back, rotated a small turn to one side, and addressed the fingers tented before his face. "As we understand it, you threatened physical violence to the man, to the feeble, old, senior faculty member of a man."

I raised my hackles like a threatened cat. "I'm tired of everyone pretending there was more meaning to what I said than there was. I did not *threaten* the man. I simply used hyperbole and a figure of speech to express my frustration. Everybody does it, all the time. There is nothing on which to build a federal case. Let's all just move on, shall we?"

"That's our goal. That is precisely our goal." He motioned his hands back and forth between us. "There. You see? We're all on the same page here. We all want to move forward." He took a practiced moment to reflect. "Now, and this is just between you and me, I'm tending to take your side in this matter. I know you're not a violent man. Moreover, I could grant that you employed a colorful, if perchance injudicious, but basically harmless expression." He leaned forward to signal a shared confidence. "I think Dean Martin can be a tad overbearing and imperious at times myself." He shook his head in lament. "However, it is always best if cooler heads prevail. Dean Martin is a solid fellow, loyal as a hound, and he's contributed mightily to the integrity and cachet of this university. You and I can both learn a lot from him if we remain open-minded and team spirited." By the end of his mini-lecture, Kent was bobbing his angled forehead in my direction paternally.

"What the hell are you talking about? Can you please point the ship of fools you are so comically piloting in the general direction of the port known as We're-Done-Here?"

He was clearly deflated in an irritated manner by my irreverent stance. "We are talking about the future here. *Your* future specifically, Noah. We want to make certain that a treasured asset such as yourself is on board...er...that you are fully committed to a shared future, one charged with promise and collegiality."

I leaned a third the way across Kent's desk. "Let me repeat my last question. Kent, what the hell are you talking about? Please note I employed the second-person singular 'you' and not its plural form 'we,' which you continue to employ most annoyingly."

He glowered in a fashion designed to reflective mounting concern. "Now let's not have a repeat of your decidedly suboptimal interaction with Dean Martin. We...I don't—"

"You don't what, Dean Kent? You, who once held me in a headlock and tried to force my face into a female cadaver's groin in the anatomy lab, are concerned with personal space issues and workplace safety imperatives? Get over yourself! Talk regular to me. I know you can." The last sentence was delivered with my best Mister Rogers impersonation.

He tried not to bristle. "It is only because of our long and warm personal friendship that I will brook such insolence and disrespect form you, at least for the time being."

"Okay, now *that* was close to human speak. I knew you had it in you. Just please cut the high-and-mighty crap, because it fits you like a live-skunk scarf."

He drummed his fingers rapidly on the desk in unintended manifest irritation and stared at me a good long while. Finally, his hands folded together, his shoulders eased down a few centimeters, and he could talk in a composed manner. "Very well. I know you're a busy man and need to get back to whatever it is you do. I too am a busy man, as I'm certain you can imagine. I will be concise. We are willing to completely overlook and dismiss any and all potential err … concerns we might have otherwise been forced to take more seriously if we can secure a few—oh, let's call them concessions."

He let that tortured sentence resonate in my head a few heartbeats before advancing. "Please keep in mind, we only want what is best for you and what is best for the university." I wondered if those were even the same things any longer. "So, in exchange for a formal apology from you to Dean Steve Martin as well as your personal reassurances to remain a team player overall, we will consider the matter closed."

"Just like that? Simple as liking chocolate ice cream?"

Clearly unsure of what to make of my odd analogy, he replied cautiously. "Yeah, just like that, I suppose. So, what do you say, old boy?"

I snatched a pen and paper from in front of him with cobra like suddenness. He recoiled. I angrily scribbled the words *Sorry Dean Martin if I spoke rashly and scared you.* I ripped the sheet from the pad and slammed it down in front of him. "There, apology accepted!"

Taken back at my ferocity, he read the words. "Oh…okay, Noah. I guess that will fulfill one requirement. Now, as to—"

I cut him off. "And as to the other mumbo jumbo that slid past your forked tongue and dripped from your fangs, I wish to honestly share my feelings, old boy. I am a tenured full professor of medicine at this fine institution and will damn well do whatever I please. I may support you, I may wear a sandwich board daily denouncing you, or I may ignore the waste-of-space empty-headed lot of 'we' like I ignore dog crap on the sidewalk." I stood. "Any questions or concerns, DP, before we adjourn our little witch hunt?"

"No, no questions. We think you've made your point and declared your position with abundantly clarity." I turned to leave. "You may go now, Dr. Taylor."

Screw you and Dean Martin, and the horses' asses you both rode in on.

SEVENTEEN

Stripped as I was of the keys to Heals-on-Wheels, I had to call Tinisha and let her know we were, at best, on hold. Ever the irascible soul, T remarked something to the effect that she was actually glad to hear it, as she could use some rest in her weary life. Moreover, she knew that whoever thought a couple of juvenile monkeys could run a clinic was just plain crazy in the first place. Eventually, it had to end in disaster. We made it a lot further than she'd thought we had any right to hope for. I asked if she would be okay financially. She thanked me for my concern but appraised me of the fact that working with us was not a source of income, but must have been penance for some calamitous past misdeeds. She would be fine and was half-glad to be rid of the both of us. I missed T even as I hung up the phone.

A few weeks later I received a broadcast email from the Development Department. They trumpeted the news that their charity bus had been completely revamped. The announcement read:

After fulfilling its mission to temporarily aid those medically less fortunate than others, the university's Meal-on-Wheel clinic is being re-purposed! The mobile healthcare-mobile has transformed itself into the Friends of the University Community Outreach Fraternal Services! *FUCOFS will be outreaching to many exciting new locations. The FUCOFS bus will visit suburban malls to raise awareness of the university's world-class resources to members of the public unaware of what they're missing! Free blood pressure and blood sugar screenings will let everyone know how committed the university is to keeping them healthy!*

FUCOFS will additionally be stopping by local farmers' markets and craft fairs to spread good cheer! It is our hope that such services will be rewarded with many new patient-clients changing their PPO, HMO, and individual or group insurance plans to us! My-oh-my how the university's future looks bright! It will need sunglasses!

How was it I knew Steve Martin penned those words personally? So, desperately needed medical care would be terminated to the marginalized and destitute, and the clinic would be turned into a PR hook to add coins to the university's coffers. It was insult added to injury in the worst sense. Plus, how was it possible no one notice what the project's acronym was? It was plain to my eye.

The ignorant must be blessed with a built-in safeguard against their own stupidity. One might have ignored the proposition that the university would need sunglasses. But the acronym? In the weeks and months which followed. I heard various admin types speak glowingly of the FOCUS Van Clinic. No, people, it included an F. The clinic's nickname was FUCOFS, not FOCUS. Seriously, a university proved that, collectively, it could neither read nor write. Maybe in administrativese, second Fs were silent?

I just gave up wondering.

In retrospect, it was from the best that the clinic was repurposed and named so ineptly. That sealed the fact that I had zero part in its future. I sent the announcement to Tinisha, but otherwise tried very hard to forget about the FUCOFS project. It took me longer than I would have liked to stop seething. Fortunately, my research was at an all-time fever pitch in productivity, so staying busy was not a problem.

But, it still fried my bacon. What group of "doctors" would set adrift thousands of medical indigents to try to encourage well people switch health plans? It was not simply immoral, it was amoral. The administration was free to do whatever it liked. Fortunately, I played no part in leadership. The blame for their reprehensible behavior was not tied me. But I continued to ruminate unhealthfully on their betrayal. Those managers had become physicians, providers with no interest in helping the infirm. They must have either drank the Kool-Aid or signed a contract with the stench of sulfur on it. They worked for what they thought was the greater purpose. They labored for the Company. That the Company was a university did not matter. The focus of their lives' work was to help and advance the Company, not to offer healthcare to the poor.

Another example of the new order committed to business even at the expense of the public's health was their stupid flu shot program. Everyone has seen the barrage of ads for flu shots around the holidays. Flu shots were safe and effective preventative measures against influenza. It was a medical fact that the vaccinations worked over a rather short period, no more than three or four months. I received a broadcast email announcing that year's launch date. Vaccinations for patients and employees were to begin in July. The insanity of the early shot administration was more than I could let pass. Back then, I thought I had a right to air my opinions. So, I called Infectious Disease, the department in charge of the vaccination program. The following was my conversation with the man in charge.

Me: "We are giving the flu shots too early. You know we are, and you know I know you know we are."

Idiot: "We are simply reflecting the mood of the community."

Me: "What the hell did you just say?"

Idiot: "We are launching our campaign at a time where we will be medical trendsetters, not medical followers. We are, after all, the university. We must set the tone and send a clear message."

Me: "But if you fool everybody into getting their vaccines too early, they won't work. Thousands of people will suffer needlessly and some will die because of your deceptive marketing plan."

Idiot: "We don't know that for a fact."

Me: "Yes, we do! Read the package insert that comes with each vial."

Idiot: "Well, we'll just have to agree to disagree."

Me: "No, wait, we can't agree to disagree on facts. That's why they are called *facts*!"

Idiot (sarcastically): "According to you."

Me (my head pounding): "Why don't we start offering the flu vaccine in November like we are supposed to?"

Idiot: "Look, pal, I cannot allow the major pharmacy chains and our direct competitors to get the drop on us. Think how silly we'll look refusing to offer our members a flu shot when the provider right down the road is passing them out like Halloween candy."

Me (with tears in my eyes): "But they're wrong in doing so! Starting the flu campaign too early guarantees it will not work. It is the same as not offering flu shots at all."

Idiot: "But we do offer the flu shot! They are proven to be safe and effective. What kind of doctor are you, suggesting we not vaccinate the public against influenza?"

Me (add crying inconsolably): "But that's exactly what we are doing. Giving the shot incorrectly is the same as not giving it. Just skipping the administration step would be a whole lot cheaper and easier, all the way around."

Idiot: "In your mind, but not mine. We will simply have to agree to disagree." He paused, all smug and contented. "If you feel so strongly, just have your patients get a second booster shot in December."

Me (misbegotten hope fluttered in my heart): "So, you'll agree to tell people you've tricked into getting a useless early shot that they need to get a booster that will actually help them a few months later? God, I misjudged you. Here I thought you were a soulless demon, when in fact, you do want to help potential flu victims."

Idiot (aghast): "I will do no such thing! Such a disclaimer might cause us to be perceived as foolish, or worse yet, as independent thinkers."

Me (on the floor, writhing): "You just said that you know a booster is needed if the initial vaccine is given too early. But, if you dispense a written disclaimer, you will be medically and morally in the clear."

Idiot (indignation flared): "What a ridiculous notion! If we did that, people would assume that our flu shots were not as strong as our competition's or that we didn't know how to give them properly. Then how would we look? Pretty darn silly, that's how."

Me (in a fetal ball, motionless on the floor): "Do you happen to have a handgun I could use to shoot myself in the head?"

Idiot (supremely smug): "Indeed not! Guns kill people, people don't kill people! This is a zero-tolerance area for workplace violence and are a drug-free zone."

Me (as my life passed from me): "How can we be drug free? We're a hospital. We exist to hand out drugs…we're doctors…doctors dispense…med…."

Idiot (I heard faintly, distantly, as I freely yielded to death): "Well, we'll simply have to agree to disagree on that point."

Given what had happened to Bubba, to the mobile clinic, and to me with Dean Martin, I needed to move on. I held no influence over the ill-advised and supercilious actions of my administration. More importantly, it sure as hell was a bad place to picnic with the family, and I needed to not waste my time in any attempts to bring reason and compassion back to their minds. Head down, nose to the grindstone, and pull hard at the yoke. That was my plan. I needed to leave the fools to their delusional world and to create a safe little bubble for myself.

As it happened, the very next month I was the keynote speaker at the biggest annual immunology meeting, so I was more than busy enough to stay clear of my handlers. Earlier, I mentioned that my research focused on the repair of defective human genes. My group had a proven system in which a rare inherited disorder was fully "cured" by inserting a properly functioning gene in every cell of the victim's body. We were also on the cusp of publishing a "fix" for a common genetic error that caused most cases of colon cancer. I spoke with pride about these accomplishments to the main session of the meeting. I had to admit, it was surreal. I stood before everyone important, all the movers and shakers in my field. My groundbreaking news duly stunned them. It was, I must confess, a sensation that I would like to have repeated many more times.

That evening, at a formal reception in my honor, I wandered into a group of old friends and colleagues. They milled about and gossiped like a gaggle of women doing laundry along a river bank. There was Billie Ludo from San Diego, Grace Johansson from Yale, Alain Devereaux from Centre de Recherche en Cancérologie de Toulouse in France, along with a few less familiar faces. As I ambled up, Grace gave me a one-armed hug and kissed me on the cheek. "Are we to be privileged with an audience from royalty?"

I looked deeply into my plastic wine glass. "Well, maybe just a brief hi and goodbye." I scanned side to side. "I wouldn't want any important people to see me socializing with the likes of you all."

Billie leaned over and shook my hand heartily. "Not if your reputation and future fame are to be protected. One documentary photo of you in our midst would be like a torpedo to your career!" We all shared a warm laugh. "Seriously, Noah, I couldn't be happier for you or more proud to call you my friend. Absolutely brilliant work." He pointed around the group with his glass hand. "Here we all are, high rollers every lovin' one of us. While we're feeling about the problem like the famous blind men trying to describe an elephant, you see only the whole animal and send a snapshot to the world. If you weren't such a good friend, I'd hate you. But I just can't bring myself to poison your drink or slip a dagger in your back." He raised his glass. "Here's to the best damn scientist in the room and my best friend in the field, Dr. Noah Taylor!" Everyone clinked plastic and sounded a robust hear, hear. I had to admit, it felt good.

Alain discretely grabbed my elbow and turned me away from the group's center. In his delicious French accent, he added his praise. "Fantastic work, Noah. Really great stuff." He quickly raised a solitary glass to salute me, belted back the rest of its contents, and went on. "You know we are not an academic institution as much as we are a production facility. We could use a man of your vision and capability. The rewards you could garner would far exceed anything you could achieve in your current, humble position. Plus, I can personally guarantee you a magnificent budget and a completely free hand in your research."

I bowed slightly in acknowledgement. "Thanks for the compliment. I am truly moved. But you and I have been over this before. As much as I know and respect you and your company, I am not interested."

He protested cordially. "But, *sacré dieu, mon ami,* think before you answer so definitively! Imagine what we can offer. A gorgeous mansion near Toulouse, a driver, a cook, and private schooling for your children. Your salary would be beyond generous and supplemented with a percentage of your earnings." He elbowed me and winked. "And, I can assure you that I will personally select your private secretary. In my country, that job description is much more flexible than here in puritanical America, *mon frère!*"

Through my not-so-subtle blush, I patted him on the shoulder. "Okay, my friend. I will discuss your incredibly generous offer, once again, with Karan. I doubt she will be any more receptive this time, but we will talk."

He shot his eyebrows up and down. "Probably best not to mention having your own personal secretary handpicked by me, eh?"

I shook my head vigorously. "No, that wouldn't help." We laughed and clinked cups and giggled like a pair of schoolboys.

Grace walked over and interrupted. "How is it that I know what you two degenerates are laughing about?" She tapped her chin. "Let me see, is it less than twenty-five years old, blonde, wears a size two, has breasts the size of mutant cantaloupes, and the only words she says say are *oui* and *ooh la la*?"

I protested. "Grace, how can you even think that of us? Here, two of the greatest minds of interventional immunology are discussing the deepest secrets of life. How could you even think we are discussing anything else? I am so hurt."

Alain sniffed loudly. "I, too, am insulted. The size of cantaloupes indeed!" He pushed my shoulder. "Minds like ours would never think so conservatively." He placed his hands on his chest and pumped them up and down. "We speak of watermelons!"

She rolled her eyes. "They remain high school boys their entire lives when it comes to women. You two were bottle fed, there's no doubt in my mind." She pointed generally at us. "Here, two of the top names in innovative research stand giggling about oversized breasts. Why-oh-why is the world not run by women? With all the extra time spent not fantasizing about that which we will never have, we could get a lot more accomplished."

Alain twirled his fingers toward the floor in her direction. "Grace, I am not listening to your words, but could you please stand a little more sideways as you address us with such passion?"

"Okay, that's it! Noah, super congratulations again. I'll call you next week.

Alain, take a long cold shower," she scolded him sternly. Before Alain could say it, she added sharply, "Alone!"

No sooner had she left, Billie wrapped an arm over my shoulder. "Don't call her. Grace will use her womanly charms to try and lure you a few miles south to Yale. Next week you call *me*. I have no charm whatsoever, but I can try and lure you to sunny San Diego."

"I don't think I'll be calling either of you next week. Thanks, as always, for the compliment, but I'm perfectly happy in Boston."

He kept me nearby with an arm around my neck and pointed at me with his glass. "Noah, have you been through a New England winter?" Before I could answer yes, maybe thirty so far, he corrected himself. "Perhaps I should rephrase that. Noah, have you ever been through a *San Diego* winter?"

"No, well, except for the years I worked with you in San Diego, if you want to count those."

"Then I rest my case. Why would any rational man wish to freeze his nuts off annually when he could be soaking in the rays and the babes at a nice warm beach? Say, do you surf?"

Surfing was not a practical pastime in New England.

"Well, you could learn. Heck, I could teach you—your kids too. Man, they'd love you ten times more if you allowed them a shot at a life like that."

I turned and asked Alain. "Do they surf in Toulouse?"

His eyes twinkled. "No, not currently. However, if you join us, I will personally dig the one-hundred-fifty-mile trench to Narbonne so you can swim there and surf all year round."

It took Billie a second to get it, but he rallied quickly. "Surfing in Toulouse? Heavens no! They're landlocked an hour and a half from the coast right smack in the middle of Bordeaux. The closest you will come to a wave there will be a heatwave."

I pooched my lips. "You make that sound not so bad, Billie. Winery surfing in the middle of Bordeaux. Not too shabby, if you ask me."

"What, and work for that money-grubbing Alain? Why would you want to go and do that? The very thought of you getting a real job. How disgusting. You can relax in academics until you make Professor Emeritus, never having had to work an honest day in your life." He shuddered demonstrably. "With all that rich French food going to your arteries on top of the fact that you're required to punch a time clock? You wouldn't last until retirement. No, my boy," he thumped my chest, "you come to San Diego, and you'll live like a king and live forever!"

"Wow, forever? Could I get that in writing?"

"For you, anything is possible. You just say the word, and I'll see to it that immortality is written into our contract offer."

"Immortality. That's quite an offer, Billie."

"If that's what it takes to bring you home to San Diego, consider it my privilege to make it so."

"A guy would be crazy to pass up an offer of immortality from a major US university, wouldn't he?"

Billie, like a used-car salesman behind on his quota, howled in assent. "Crazier than a loon! Crazier than ten loons, whatever a loon is."

"It's a kind of duck. Makes a wacky call."

He squinted an eye shut. "You don't say?" Then, resolutely, he slapped me on the back soundly. "You definitely don't want to act like a duck with a lame voice. Absolutely not! You better come to San Diego before it's too late and you start sprouting pin feathers."

"I will certainly keep that in mind. First sign of plumage and I'm on the next flight out. Wait, maybe I can fly on my own then, saving the fare."

Billie wagged a finger at me. "Laugh now, Noah. But by then, it may be too late. No, better transfer *before* the process starts, be on the safe side. I like you too much to lose you to an annual migration."

"You're too kind, my friend, much too kind."

"Damn skippy! I'm too nice. That's just what I am, too nice."

As I began to walk away, I noticed Alain had a strained look on his face. "You all right?" I asked.

"No... yes, of course. I was just considering how I could top immortality in my offer to bring you to France."

I pushed at the air between me and him. "Goodnight, Alain. Don't sweat that part. If we move to France, I'll make sure I never die all on my own."

True to her word, Grace called me that next week. After general pleasantries were exchanged, she spoke forthrightly. "So, did either of those two jokers win you over yet? Have you begun packing?"

"I presume 'those two jokers' would be Billie and Alain."

"Two biggest jokers I know."

"Did someone start the rumor that I was looking to relocate or something? I'm slightly north of perfectly happy where I am now, you know."

"No, nothing is in the rumor mill, and trust me, of this I speak with authority." She always knew who was doing what and to whom. She was not a vicious gossip or anything, but she kept an ear to the ground when it came to gossip. "Why? Would you like me to start some buzz?"

"Hardly!"

"Your call, big guy."

"So, all kidding aside, how'd you know those two jokers were pitching me for a move?"

"Because that's what we were talking about just before you walked up."

"And just why were you *three* jokers having such a meaningless conversation?"

"Oh, come on. Don't be overly modest here. You're a superstar that's still rising. Did you know there's an informal betting pool as to how soon you'll win the Nobel Prize?" She did not wait for my reply. "Well there is. I bet on five years from now, so hustle up, or I'm out twenty bucks."

"But, why were you all discussing placing a hook in my mouth?"

"Because we would all do unspeakable things to land a catch like you. Plus, five years from now, your price will be out of our league. You big shots, with all your conditions and demands and entourages. You all are a bunch of spoiled prima donnas. You know that?"

"Uh, let's not get too ahead of ourselves, dear. Sweden hasn't called, as of today."

"So, cut to the case. Did any of them trick you into relocating?"

"As flattered as I was, no. I'm staying right where I'm really happy."

"Thank goodness! I was hoping right reason would prevail and you'd join me at Yale. It's your only real choice, after all."

"Do tell?"

"Of course! You're a New England boy, Karan's a New England girl, and your pups are New England kids. It would be a crime against nature to drag them to some lilting, sun-bathed paradise. They'd most likely melt. No, you are right in knowing you need to stay local. Hence, Yale's your only real option."

"Oh, so now it's *my* idea to stay near home and hearth?"

"Like I said, Noah, you're Nobel smart. I knew you'd figure it out, see the light and all."

"So, now that I've figured out where to relocate, I only have to figure out why I want to relocate. Let me run the numbers." Although Grace couldn't see, I actually held up digits sequentially. "One, I'm a tenured full professor. Two, I have endless, modern lab space. Three, I have a crack team of associates with whom I love working with already assembled. Four, my wife loves her job and the kids love their schools. That's actually four and five, but I'm working on the back of an envelope here. So, six is that I have a perfect house, in-laws down the street, a ton of great friends, and about a million other reasons to stay put. So, help me figure out how those numbers add up to move to Yale?"

"You're so stuck in your little rut you can't even see over the dirty edge to a world of new possibilities. Sure, you're *comfortable*, but you need to experience other places, other minds. A talent like yours needs to be constantly enriched, challenged, and redirected. Top people never stay in the same place for their entire career. Look, Einstein came to America, Feynman went from Wisconsin to Princeton, to the Manhattan Project, and then Caltech. Nobody who's anybody stays in one place forever. Come on, Noah, wake up and smell the moving van!"

"I would give that sales pitch a perfect ten, but the Russian judge's sign says only nine point eight. Tough luck, Grace. Maybe he dinged you because Einstein came to America to escape Nazism and World War Two. Feynman moved because he had a personal goal of sleeping with every woman in the world at least once."

"Details, details. The facts still speak for themselves."

"That's such a lame comeback, I won't even comment upon it."

"Look, all kidding aside, just keep Yale in mind if you ever do consider a change. That's all I want to say in neon lights with loud fireworks arching over in the background."

"Thank you, Grace. You're a kind person and a wonderful friend. Of course, I'll keep Yale near the top of my list, when relocation makes sense. You don't know what your support and loyalty means to me."

Grace said she needed to hang up before she got all teary-eyed and gushy because all the warm and fuzzies. I promised to keep in touch, which was prophetic, as it turns out, and said our goodbyes. As much as I was happy right where I was, it was humbling to know I had suitors beating down my door.

EIGHTEEN

One warm fall evening, Evan Miller and Jim Blodget, still good friends of mine long after our orientation program finished, came to dinner. They each brought their partners. Jim brought his lovely wife, Jill. Evan was accompanied by Isaiah, his most recent life partner. Evan, it turned out, defined "life partner" differently than those words might suggest to others. He swore to me he loved each man he paired with completely and absolutely and planned on spending the rest of his life with him. He just never did. In any case, Isaiah, who'd been with him for five or six years, was a fascinating character and a hoot to be around. Over glasses of wine, sitting near the spread of appetizers, Evan, James, and I engaged in one of our favorite contact sports—exchanging university gossip.

Like most academicians, we loved to hear gossip, spread gossip, and, when incredibly lucky, start salacious gossip. Jim had just revealed to us that the office assistant of one of the senior deans of Medicine had recently vanished without a trace. It seemed Jack Herbst's secretary was there one day and gone the next. A girlfriend of the secretary, who worked down the hall from Jim, let it be known that Jack was to be the accidental and not-so-proud father of a love child. The College Provost, heretofore a fast friend and ally of Dean Herbst, was heard threatening Jack behind closed doors. "Your head would roll!" echoed down the hallowed halls one morning. Oh, did he mention that Jack's wife was the Provost's cousin? They were as close as sister and brother since they'd grown up neighbors in the Hamptons. Juicy!

Evan shared that the chair of the Economics Department was blindsided at a recent meeting of the Chairmen in Letters and Science by some dean. The ambitious vice-chair of Econ had gone over her chairman's head in an attempt to place a dagger deep in the chairman's back. She had apprised the dean that some grant money was found in the account ledger of a sham-consulting firm. Facts were still being sorted through, but there were some very suspicious links from said shell company that led back directly to the chairman himself. Rather than allow the investigation to come to its natural conclusion, the dean leapfrogged due process by accusing the man of embezzlement right there in public.

Rumors maintained that the chairman had retained a top law firm and was "not being tossed under the bus because of someone else's incompetent bookkeeping or illegality." The hapless chairman was either, depending on which rumor one lent superior credence to, either on a long-planned holiday in the Caribbean, on administrative leave, or in a "quiet place" for "medical treatment" for an open-ended period of time. Now, that was sweet gossip, but not as good as the one with an inconvenient baby.

I was out of my league that particular evening. I had a couple of tidbits but nothing good. There had been a shouting match between a surgeon and an anesthesiologist. Stop the presses, right? It was said to have escalated to blows, but that wasn't known for sure. I also paraded out a lame story concerning an assistant professor's saber rattling that she had been passed over for tenure because of gender bias. She announced she was not going to bend over and let the department have their will with her. Her story was in the dime-a-dozen category, at best, however. Every hapless soul who was cast off the mother ship whined and cried foul when passed up for tenure. I received such incredulous looks from my dinner guests for insulting them with such a blasé, banal rumor. It popped into my head just then to mention the unfortunate case of Cletus. It wasn't really gossip, but it was, at least to me, a poignant and cautionary tale.

Jim and Evan sat in mute judgement as I rehashed the events leading up to Bubba's dismissal. I don't think Jim noticed, but I could tell Evan was aware that I was very close to tears as I neared the end of the story.

Evan said, "Wow, that's amazing and disturbing. I can tell he was a good friend and a good man. I'm sorry to hear he was treated so badly. Have you heard how he's doing? Did he land on his feet?"

I lowered my head. "I don't know. Shortly after he was let go, he moved back to the little town of Ocilla, Georgia, where he grew up. He never responded to any of my emails or calls. Tinisha, our medical assistant, told me she'd heard he was all right and was thinking of opening a practice in Ocilla. Then she told me that Ocilla was nothing more than a wide spot on a hot road. The only jobs in Ocilla were at the local penitentiary. Otherwise, most folks who lived there were dirt poor. She speculated that Ocilla's economy couldn't support a hamburger stand, let alone a fat lazy doctor."

Evan continued to be supportive. "That must be hard for you to take. I'm truly sorry it went down that way. You let me know if there's anything I can do to help." What a prince.

Up until then a forgotten part of the conversation, Jim spoke analytically. "Well, it's always unfortunate when someone's fortunes fall short of their plans, but this is the real world." More to himself than Evan or me, Jim said, "Not everyone is capable of achieving their dreams."

Quickly aware that Jim's insensitivity was not helpful, Evan snapped at him. "James, what does that even mean? And, for crying out loud, we're talking about a man's life here. At least *pretend* you have some empathy for him."

"What?"

Evan was annoyed. "Are you even listening to the conversation or the words coming out of your mouth?"

Jim shimmied up in the sofa. "Of course, I'm present and accounted for. Your remarks just caught me off guard, I guess." Jim squinted his brow and thought for a second. "Look, the man was let go. That's sad, but I'm certain there was good reason and just cause. We don't have all the inside dope the administration is privy to, you know." He turned to me in appeal. "I know this Black fellow was you friend, but it wasn't your fault he didn't measure up. Don't take it personally. After all, they didn't fire you."

Evan said, "Well I think it stinks to high heaven. Furthermore, I think we should drop the subject here and now."

Mercifully for our mutual friendship, Karan entered the room at that point. "The fact that heaven has now entered your conversation no doubt reflects a new and productive first for you three gossips. Hence, I regret I must drag you away. Dinner is ready."

I don't know why I dwelled so much on that night's conversation for the next few weeks. Maybe I just missed Bubba and still struggled for some resolution and some peace of mind. But, why had Jim just assumed the higher ups acted properly? I was close to the scene and knew that Cletus had received a hose job on the scale of Niagara Falls. I knew the facts, and I was unable to come away with any positive take on the administration's action. But Jim, levelheaded, fair-minded Jim, automatically assumed they were right, that Bubba was suspect, and that justice had prevailed, however unpalatable it had been on a personal level. Jim was, not ten years earlier, a leader in student protest movements of all sorts. He was very nearly expelled from one undergraduate program for insubordination. Why was he so ready to trust and embrace the higher ups? Maybe he was just growing up faster than me.

Despite whatever reservations and condemnations I had regarding my administration, I tried hard and successfully to not let them hamstring me. I had to pinch myself on a thrice-daily basis for the overabundant good fortune fate had dispensed to me. A perfect marriage, perfect kids, and perfect health. What else of value was there in life? I was a go-to guy in the hospital, a rising star in my field of research, and most important of all, I was the bright light shimmering back from my children's eyes whenever they looked at me. I was doing good, and I made a very real difference in many people's lives. I believed these things not in self-aggrandizement or to set myself above anyone else but because they were true. Little did I know at the time, I was poised, like a cliff diver in Acapulco at low tide, for a very long and a very traumatic fall.

NINETEEN

I guess it was based on some law of human behavior. If the boss was left alone in a cozy office with adequate support staff and no real work to do, he would invariably come up with some useless plan or program. I was not sure why we humans had that law, but there it was. I suppose that was only natural, if the matter was broken down to its essence. To illustrate my point, I could put myself in the boss's place, as distasteful as that sounded.

Okay, I sit in my office, hands folded on the desk. I have cleared my emails and answered my calls. It is only 10:15 a.m. Lunch is two hours away and quitting time is six long ones down the road. What to do? I could nap, but I'm not tired yet. I could go to a meeting, surely there is one nearby. But then I can't be all cozy in my office. I can do nothing, certainly nothing related to work. I can, for example, surf the Internet, call old friends, or zone out like when I was in college.

But, what if someone above me learns that I spent several hours doing nothing? Maybe my boss has as little to do as I do. If so, he may decide to justify his time by checking on the productivity of his subordinates. It hits me. I will do something! But what? It can't be anything challenging to my superiors, like a brilliant new plan. No, perish the thought. Imagine if I take an excellent idea to my boss that he didn't think of first. I will, in effect, call him out for being less bright than me. Wow, I can't believe I even thought those words. I hoped that words can't leak out of my head accidentally or become visible.

So, I must do something, but something that is inoffensive and insipid. It is best if whatever I do can be interpreted as inspired, if just the right lighting is applied. I have it, we should paint all the garbage cans green! Who doesn't love green? No one that I know. Hum, maybe before I launch my green can plan, no, my Green Can Plan, I should check whether all people like green. No, that is silly! I love green. Who doesn't love green?

I'll summon my secretary and start to dictate the necessary documents concerning the painting all our garbage cans green. But wait! Who will do the painting? The maintenance staff is stretched well beyond thin, and I cannot risk it if the word "overtime" appears in print with my name signed at the bottom of the page. Gosh, I can't believe I even thought those words. I hope that words cannot leak out of my head accidentally or become visible.

And, painting gives off fumes, so my actions cannot subject us to increased worker's compensation claims. Well, we can buy green trash cans, so they don't need to be painted green locally. No, that means capital outlay. I am not about to sign a death warrant on myself. Wait, wait! What if I simply issue a directive that all trash cans be green painted, not painted green. And if anyone goes to their boss and asks for the money to buy a green painted trash can, well that is on their budget. What is that to me?

Wait, wait, wait! Man, am I good or what? No wonder I have my job. Green is the color of recycling! So, my plan to deposit all non-recyclable trash in green painted trash cans supports recycling, in color if not in fact. Oh, I need a raise! I need to get started on my new Green Can Plan for the Environment Plan as soon as possible. GCPEP. What is a GCPEP? Doesn't ring a bell. Oh well, I'll work out the kinks later.

So, worked the mind of the motivationally impaired, aka, the boss. In the past, I had never let them bother me too much. Sure, I complained about the useless mental eunuchs, but only to my coworkers at social events. I used to complain about them to my wife, but Karan officially informed me that she wanted to be fully involved in my life *except* where it concerned my opinion as to the shortcomings of my bosses. That tiny segment of my life had to be either kept to myself or shared with people who were not her.

Anyway, when it came to the boss's inane actions, I'd always figured that they could do whatever floated their boat, if they left me the hell alone. I mean, if the boss decided my trash can needed to be green, who really cared?

It had to be some color, so, to press my parable, green was fine, as long as I was not asked to paint it myself.

I really could not say, looking back on it, when the paradigm shifted, when Elvis left the building. The exact moment when the bosses decided that I needed to be involved. When had disinterest become an institutional threat and indifference an actionable problem? Even ten years earlier, I couldn't remember my bosses concerning themselves with what I did on a daily basis. I was, as far as I recalled, off their radar screen. A warm hand clasp at the annual faculty party and that was about it. That was the only point where our worlds met. Something had certainly changed. Of course, it began fairly innocently and was definitely slow as it transformed itself. It all seemed so, I don't know, annoying, but it was harmless at first. Yes, I could remember the first time it struck me that the rules had changed. It was that damned satisfaction survey.

About half way through one academic year, everyone from chancellor to temporary janitor's assistant was required to attend a special meeting. We were to be gifted with an "innovative vision of the future." I was suspicious. I doubted the university was actually going to show us the future, in say, a large crystal ball. I suspected, instead, the future vision was what some underemployed administrator had dreamed up as their plan for our future. So as not to interfere with normal work flow, the meeting, inspirationally termed an "imperative," was held on a Saturday. The very thought of wasting a weekend day in "an imperative concerning an innovative vision of the future," made my stomach turn in dread..

The imperative was held in one of the main campus's larger auditoriums on an otherwise pleasant morning. After selecting my bagel breakfast sandwich and a beverage, I shuffled to a spot more toward the front than I'd have liked. The early birds all snatched up the more anonymous seats closer to the exits. They required me to be present, but that did not mean I had to listen. I, like several others, brought my laptop and a set of headphones. I planned on listening to jazz while I cleared my emails.

As it turned out, they anticipated that obvious ploy. There were ten or twelve women—secretaries in the administration—who walked around with long poles. The poles had bright red flags attached. When one of the women saw someone looking at a computer, she raised her red flag and pointed directly at the offending audience member. The nearest flag bearer came over to that individual and reminded them how much the chancellor wanted us to provide him with our utmost attention. I knew that was what they said because I was reminded three times before I decided it was not worth the hassle and closed my computer.

The imperative began with some lifeless associate vice-chancellor. He monotoned an introduction to a video tape of an assistant provost. That woman was way too perky and bubbly for such an early hour. It was, she declared, her honor to unveil to the world the bold new vision for the future. I was never totally clear whose vision she referred to. Possibly the university itself was having visions and had told someone. How the institution accomplished the communication was never specified. Maybe the speaker herself had the visions. She seemed, on first impression, crazy enough to have all kinds of visions. The only interesting aspect of her talk was that, during the entire ten-minute sentence she spoke to us, she never once stopped to take a breath. She was like a puffer fish in reverse.

After she was done, I could release the white-knuckled grip on my armrests caused by her death defyingly long sentence. The main speaker strode boldly on stage, and carried, of all things, a Superscope Bob Barker style microphone. Those were the long, thin microphones game show hosts sported last century. That type of microphone was popular back then because they seemed modern, they could be whipped about like a sword, and they obscured the speaker's face as little as possible. That was, of course, important to the celebrities.

The man who walked to center stage was Kent Pearson. No one in their right mind would believe for a second he could be the person selected for such an important role. The university had hundreds of administrators who could have made the presentation. It was unbelievable that my personal nightmare, Kent, was the one selected. How could it have been possible that he was so central to all those pivotal moments in my life? Remember the character of Javert in *Les Miserables*? Whenever Jean Valjean ran, hid, or tried to disguise himself, he was confronted by the police officer Javert. Javert came to symbolize the universal, generic manifestation of the state. So, it was to be, it would seem, with Kent and me.

I sat, slack-jawed, as he enunciated in a powerful but restrained baritone I'd never heard exit his throat before. "Great morning, my fellow visionaries! Are you ready to reach out and touch the future?" Based on his energy and conviction, I expected the crowd to rise as one and begin cheering and applauding wildly. Alternately, I could have also anticipated absolute silence, a cue-the-crickets moment, from the both sleepy and now stunned assemblage. He received a hybrid response. Twenty people, all seated together front and center at his feet, sounded riotous assent. From the rest of those in attendance, he received the aforementioned mix of silence, disbelief, and disinterest.

After a five count, the boisterous applause cut off synchronously, so much so that, if one was cynically inclined, they might have had the impression that it was rehearsed. If I were giving a presentation and five percent of those present responded so positively while ninety-five percent reacted so anemically, I would be given to pause. I might have even stopped what I was about to say and query the majority for some issue I was unaware of. Was I, for example, not wearing pants? Was I speaking in tongues? I would want to clarify the situation. Once again, Kent proved himself not me. He waved to the crowd as if every member were his best friend and charged ahead. "Thank you, university of the future!" He paused for a two count, possibly to allow for the applause that he anticipated, but which was conspicuously absent. If what he had bellowed so far was not surreal enough to set one thinking, his next revelation was downright creepy. "I love you!"

Oblivious to being so out of touch with the majority of his audience, he eased back on his volume knob. "I am proud to stand before you and have the privilege of pointing the Ship of State toward the future, which lies just in front of its bow." Incongruously, he snapped to attention and saluted like a complete moron. "And the future begins now!" The twenty or so who cheered in front clapped dutifully. Imbued out of proportion to that altogether tepid response, he surged forward. "Together, we *are* the future. As a wise mentor of mine once told me, 'we' is never 'us' without 'you'! Well, in kind, the I in our TEAM is always 'you!'"

I felt the first pops of a headache spasm to life. I placed my hand over my eyes in disbelief of, and in nascent pity for, Kent. I had received an advance memo covering some of what he was shouting about. I knew, therefore, that he was not referring to TEAM but TEIM, as in *Together Everyone Is Mighty*. That was the dubious catchphrase the university had come up with as its new rally call. Unfortunately, almost everyone else with ears had to have thought that he couldn't spell team correctly. Oh well, not my *faux pas*, not mine to fix, right? I mean, if a mime's pants fall down during a performance, was it an accident or part of the act? Not mine to say. He was a big boy and held the silly microphone, so it was all on him.

He raised his palm to the audience. "And just how, you ask, are we going to TEIM together toward the future?"

Saints preserve me, the acronym is now a transitive verb! My headache developed a pulsing throb.

"We shall TEIM forward by pulling on the rope together, comrades in arms, brothers and sisters, yo-heave-ho-ing as a team (or TEIM, I couldn't tell what the man meant to say. Oh, bother, yo-heave-ho was a new intransitive verb. My right eyelid began to twitch.) He plunged forward. "The key to our success, to the Ship of States not *not* sailing into the future it sees will be bold new initiatives coupled with our visions."

No. No way I just heard a college dean say "not not" sail to a future the boat "sees." I was employed by a boat with eyes. That wasn't in my contract. Plus, they were not just having visions, they were proud enough of them to mention them in public. Wait, maybe the Kent of old was doing this on purpose. He was erecting some dark Trojan horse, designed to show how foolish the administration had become. But, no. He would have been cleverer in his sarcasm and more devious in his setup. It promised to be a very long morning. I decided it would be best if I stopped to buy a liter of single malt scotch on the way home. Possibly two.

He paced to one side, looked thoughtfully at that segment of the audience, then spoke with candor. "The world is changing. Those who cannot change will suffer the same fate as the dinosaurs. Extinction. Our TEIM will not become extinct. No, our TEIM will change with the times. Wait, check that. Our TEIM will change *ahead* of the times. We will be leaders and define the paths others will follow if they wish to not extinct themselves. Yes, we will march ahead of the pack. We won't be doing today's work today. We'll be doing today's work yesterday. That way, we will be able to do tomorrow's work today. Vision, people." He pointed upward. "It's all about vision. Either one has vision or one doesn't, and we are here to tell you we *do* have vision."

Oh my, it is getting ugly. Sticks and stones may break bones, but these words are going to kill me.

He turned and paced in the opposite direction. He stopped, rubbed his chin, and spoke. "We will use our superior team (he had to mean team, but don't quote me), our network of excellence, and bold new metrics to forge the future into a new one."

Ouch! That sentence is painful.

"To help guide our hands, we will institute a transparent system of reviews and self-reviews. Whether you're the chancellor or the sanitation technician, we are going to measure your performance and give you thE feedback to power your change into a new and better you, a new and better part of the TEIM team."

Where is my revolver when I need it? First Kent, then me. I'll be revered as a hero and a martyr.

"Once those numbers are available to you, you will be able to alter your behavior so as to meet—no, allow me to challenge you to *exceed*—the universal goals for performance expectations."

Wait, that sounds ominous.

He turned to face us all squarely and lifted both arms skyward. "It is our goal that everyone be in the top third of performers in their respective metric categories."

What did he just say? I must have heard him wrong.

"After we are all at goal, the TEIM will be unstoppable. Our customer base will flock to our doors because they want to join the TEIM, the winning TEIM!" There was a pause, then Kent spoke conversationally. "What, Dr. Taylor?"

Startled, I snapped a looked up at Kent and only then noticed my arm was raised. I, it appeared, had a question. "Um, Dean Pearson, I was wondering—"

He cut me off with a treacle tone. "Ah, Dr. Taylor, this is a presentation, not a Q and A opportunity. If I could ask you to hold your questions for the breakout sessions that will take place right after the morning—"

I cut him off right back. I raised my voice to eclipse his. "No! I have a question for *now*." I did not wait for his permission to move forward. "You just mentioned the goal for performance will be that everybody will be in the top third, right?"

With a nervous smile, he bent toward me. "Okay, I guess one question is not unwelcome. Yes, Dr. Taylor, that is our goal." He started to straighten again. "As I was—"

"No, wait, Kent. That was not my question. My question is, are you aware of the fact that everybody cannot be in the top third?"

He turned back to me and had trouble concealing his irritation. "It *is* our goal, Dr. Taylor. To be certain, at least initially, some parties will be more compliance-challenged than others. But without goals to strive for, how can we achieve them?"

"I just—"

"That was a *rhetorical* question, Dr. Taylor. Now I really must insist you not co-opt this interventional presentation and—"

I stood. "This will just take a second. I am positive we'd all like to hear your take on my observation. In statistics, in any sample group, the whole adds up to one hundred percent. If you break the group down into thirds, there are three thirds. There is the *top* third, the *middle* third, and the *bottom* third. That's how it works. By definition, one hundred percent of participants cannot be in the top third. Two-thirds of participants *must* be in one of the lower two thirds. Everyone cannot be in the top third. Hence, your stated goal is impossible to achieve. I will sit to hear your response."

Sternly, he stared at me. Then a distinctly unfriendly smile appeared on his face. He squeezed the microphone with both hands like he wanted to choke someone. "Perhaps not, but it will be our *goal*, Dr. Taylor. Now, will you please allow us to continue. Please make it *your* goal to clarify your misunderstanding in small group later this morning."

No point turning this into a shouting match. I had only tried to be helpful. But really, how could he not see his goal was insane? It was like the scene in Orwell's *1984* where O'Brien said he would, before he killed him, make Winston Smith believe that two plus two equaled five.

Wait…crap, it was *just* like that! I—we—were in for trouble. Big trouble.

TWENTY

Earlier, I touched upon the committee work required in academics. Another administrative commitment was to attend the department's monthly meeting. An outsider might have supposed that those particular meetings were worthwhile. After all, I met with my concerned supervisor and my convivial colleagues. Surely that provided fertile ground for progress, understanding, and camaraderie.

If only it were so. Department meetings in academia were just as dispiriting as those in any industry or large group. My boss, like all his brethren, did not have the slightest interest in any problems or conflicts that were afoot. If he heard of a problem, he either had to fix it or ignore it. If he attempted to fix a problem, he risked unwanted attention and its criticism from above. Plus, if he tried to fix something and didn't, he looked bad.

On the other hand, if a problem was brought to his attention and he ignored it, he knew he could be reminded of it endlessly. Worse yet, someone might bring his dereliction to the attention of one of any number of bosses. Both the words *problem* and *poison* began with P." Other words that began with P were the typical rewards for bringing a problem to a boss: punishment, pain, and penury.

At department meetings, my boss had to appraise us of new policies. He might have disliked a new directive as much as we did, but one dark aspect of his job was that he needed to cram it down our throats like it may well have been crammed down his. In reality, no one wanted to be at these meetings, and everyone employed any plausible excuse to miss those meetings. Plus, as I mentioned before, academics were petty, jealous, and fearful. So, members were brought together in number at great risk, like fissionable material packed into a nuclear bomb. If too many of either faculty members or uranium atoms were brought together too tightly, there would be an explosion.

But I never minded department meetings. Don't get me wrong. They weren't like Christmas morning with cinnamon rolls in the oven and children crowded around an packed tree. No, but they were tolerable if not fun-filled. I had a chance to see people I didn't cross paths with very often, and it was always good to have some heads up as to what the future held institutionally. Well, I never minded department meetings up until the first department meeting after the dog-and-pony show that was the Saturday morning gala where gameshow host Kent and I clashed shields. From that point on, they ranged exclusively from decidedly unpleasant to disturbingly suicidal. One positive was that I was not to suffer though too many more before I was no longer allowed to attend them.

Our department met on Thursday afternoons in a large conference room down the hall from my chairman's office. Complimentary coffee and rock-like cookies were provided based on motivations unclear to me. If they were present to show how much we meant to the department, it showed that we meant very little. If they were a joke, it was in poor taste. I found the only value of the coffee was that sipping it scalded me awake. The cookies. What could be said? Their taste and texture were jarring, a mixture guaranteed to offend one's senses, and they were ladened with a huge dose of empty calories. I imagine everyone has had the misfortune of confronting these industrial cookies.

My chairman, Robert Williams, tapped a stack of papers softly on the table like a news anchor and called the department meeting to order. He was an affable enough man, at least at some past segment of his life. Ten years prior, Karan and I had even socialized with him and his quirky wife Hatch. But, we never really clicked, so nothing developed from the interactions. By the time of that meeting, Bob had grown closed, defensive, and supremely sure. He was, to my reckoning, unable to make a decision and was afraid to commit himself to anything spoken, written, or implied. But, he also made it a point to leave me alone, so I had no real problem with him.

"So, let's get started, okay? We have a lot to cover today, and I'd like us to be able to end at the usual hour, if possible. First off, everyone made it to one of the Saturday sessions, right?" Bob scanned those present and confirmed that everyone signaled that they had. "Good, then I can skip over some of the introductory material I've been given." He set the top five or six sheets in his stack off to one side. "No questions, anyone, on what was said at the sessions?" Reflexively, he raised a "hold on" hand directly at me. "Except for you, Noah. I don't want to lock horns with you like Dean Pearson had to. I'm not up for that, so please just let it go."

I was crushed. I had never heard Bob say anything so insensitive or unfair. As my stomach flipped a three-sixty. "Let what go?"

With a fierce intensity, I felt Bob turn on me. "I said *drop* it, and I mean it. You have no idea how much your smartass stunt has cost this department." He leaned his chair back and slid his thumbs under his waistband. "I hope it was worth it to you. In our meeting last week, Pearson said you had some vendetta against him. You sure as hell threw the rest of us under the bus to get at him, you jackass." He shook his head in slow, judgmental disbelief.

I had to challenge that. "Bob, seriously, what are you talking about? And how dare you accuse me of something publicly that isn't even true." I pointed at him. "You're better than this, Bob. You're better than this, and you know it."

He sat back up and stared at me for several seconds as he decided how to respond to my remarks. Finally, his face softened slightly. "Look, I'm sorry. You're right. I blindsided you with that, didn't I? You didn't have to endure the chief's meeting like I did last week. They're really hot over what you did. I'm talking solar hot. I was a convenient whipping boy."

"What I did was point out that their idiotic goal was mathematically impossible. That is a fact. They should be thanking me for pointing it out so early so they can reword their all-important message."

There were traces of wonder in his eyes. "You really don't get it, do you?" He appealed to the rest of those in the room. "He really doesn't get it, does he?"

Naturally, no one made the slightest reply. He addressed me softly. "When you pinned Pearson's ears back in public like that, calling him a fool in front of his entire universe, you sort of declared war on him. You know that, right?"

I could feel the color leave my face. My heart raced. "I didn't call him a fool. I simply challenged him to realize their goal was, err...I don't know...poorly thought out."

"Right. You called Pearson a fool with a fool's plan." He shook his head again. "They really don't appreciate being called fools, and especially not in front of God and country." After a moment, he said, "But, now we need to move forward and see if we can survive as a department. I hope it all blows over and is history. We'll see."

"Fine. Let's meet tomorrow to discuss this more, okay?"

"Sure. I'll let you know if I have an opening." He returned to his former blank expression. "So, I have here the new metrics they are rolling out." He handed a stack of paper to the woman on his left and she, in turn, passed the stack around after taking one. "Pretty straightforward. We have numeric goals to hit regarding patient care outcomes. Nothing too difficult to achieve or too controversial." He sneaked a one-eyed peek at me. "Ninety percent of eligible women need mammograms and Paps, ninety-five percent of clients need to be at or below blood pressure targets, and diabetic controls need to be where they are listed. All in all—"

"Uh, Bob," I said, "can I clarify something here?"

"I thought I told you to drop your holy crusade against the administration."

I bristled with anger. How dare he? "*Dr.* Williams," I began. I always reserved calling a colleague *doctor* for one of two reasons. One, if they were senior to me and truly renowned, I respectfully addressed them by their title. I met Sir Francis Crick when he was very old. I addressed him as *Dr.* Crick. More commonly, I used the title when I was pissed at them. "Please stop slandering and insulting me. I have half a mind to report your conduct to the Committee on Charges. First off, I do not have a crusade against anyone or anything. Second, I have a valid point to make on a matter being discussed at my department meeting. Third, if you can't handle the questions, get out of the chairman's seat." That felt good.

He glared at me a good while longer than before. I could see hate growing in his eyes, and I knew I'd just made another permanent enemy. But there was nothing for it. The man was out of bounds by a good measure. Through gritted teeth, he said, "What, specifically, would you like clarified?"

"These are fine goals, but we are a specialty clinic. We see immunology patients—you know, bad asthma, immunodeficiencies, and severe immune reactions. These listed metrics are for primary care to accomplish, not us."

He could sense a recognition pass through those present. Since I'd brought it up, they all wondered the same thing. "The administration feels we need to take collective responsibility of our customers. They think we have missed opportunities to improve customer perception and outcome in the past by over-compartmentalizing our service area."

I couldn't stop myself. "What did you just say?"

He swelled. "I told you before. I don't have the time or inclination to get into it with you today." He heaved a mighty sigh. "I am going to—"

"Hang on a second, Robert. If I might, I'd like to clarify what you said myself." It was Naomi Sanchez, a junior member of the department who was never a troublemaker. "What *customers* are you referring to, and what on earth is an over-compartmentalized service area?"

"While you at it," asked Jeff Shaub, "could you kind of clarify the *collective-responsibility* thing too?"

He looked at me as if he wished to kill me with his hands and teeth. I had never experienced such primal hatred or anger. I was so taken back by his ferocity that I dropped my gaze to the floor. It took him the better part of a minute before he was composed enough to respond in a civilized manner. "As to your question, Naomi, the customers are our patients. Over-compartmentalization means to say we've focused our attention too narrowly in the past but will not be doing so from now on." He breathed in and out a few seconds and glared at me alone. "Jeff, collective charge means we are all equal stakeholders in customer outcomes."

I don't think Jeff had any idea just how inflamed Bob was. If he had been, he would not have dared to ask his next question. "I'm afraid I don't understand that either. Why don't you just say it in plain English? Collective charge, equal stakeholders. It's all a bunch of corporate mumbo jumbo and gum flapping, if you ask me." He snorted in amusement after he finished.

Jeff didn't remain amused long. Bob slammed his fists on the table and stood to his feet. "Well, no one is asking you, Jeff. The words *mean* what they *mean*, and we will all do as instructed." He looked only at me. "And we will all be happy, or we will begin job searches first thing in the morning." He passed his eyes from person to person to make certain everyone perfectly understood his meaning. We all did. Naomi began to tear up. I wasn't far behind her.

Bob thumped back into his chair heavily and with resignation in his face. "So, bottom line here, folks, is that our fate is tied to everyone else's. If the customer doesn't meet the goals, we all suffer. If they do, we all benefit. This year, ten percent of your salary will be linked to these targets. Over the next five years, up to twenty-five percent of your salary will be dependent on meeting these goals." He eyed us all again, stopping on me. "Pretty cut and dry, really."

Jeff found his voice again. "So, are you suggesting that if a patient I see in the Immunology Clinic ends the year with a b/p greater than some arbitrary goal, *my* pay will go down twenty-five percent along with the Primary Care Provider's whose job it is to control the b/p in the first place?"

"No, Jeff. I don't mean to suggest anything. I mean to *state* that your pay will be restructured to reflect fallen expectations of compliance with outlined goals and metrics."

"I don't think that's even legal. Has this matter gone through the proper committees and been vetted by our union?"

"Jeff, do I look like someone who knows about that crap? That's many levels above my pay grade. I'm not here to sell you the idea or take your feedback to my dean. I'm one tired son of a bitch who's here to inform you of the plan, like Moses and the Ten Commandments. I have. We're done. No more questions, please, especially from you, Noah." He called over his shoulder as he exited. "Last one out, turn off the lights."

I came away with the firm conviction that I was in for quite an unpleasant ride in the immediate future.

TWENTY-ONE

"Are you going to get off the computer and come downstairs for a glass of wine? There's a lovely sunset tonight. Maybe we could even bundle up and sit on the deck a few minutes." I turned to see Karan resting an arm on the entry to my study. She gave me her best warm and loving smile. I was very tempted to join her.

I shrugged. "I don't think I'll make very good company tonight. You have the wine and enjoy the view. I'll be down for dinner in a while." I returned my attention to the computer screen, though I wasn't doing anything so important it couldn't wait. Okay, I was playing Candy Crush. But, I was on like level nine hundred fifty, so the game had gotten challenging.

She walked up behind me and started to massage my neck. "Not good company, eh? You have a bad day? Or you working on a new image of detachment and rugged individualism?" She paused, then speculated, "You're a bit young to be a curmudgeon and a bit too old to now manifest misanthropy. Ennui is possibly sprouting roots, but you just don't seem the type. You're an optimist by nature."

"Then it must be a bad day."

"Ooh, not even a clever comeback. Must've been some bad day."

"It was."

"You know, I read a scientific paper written by a *medical* doctor. He discovered that the best treatment for someone who'd had a really bad day was a glass of wine on the deck with his spouse. It must be true, you know, because he's a doctor."

"Couldn't be printed if it weren't true. Doctors aren't allowed to be wrong."

"All right, there's a little humor. You're not so far gone, after all. I bet that wine-o-therapy will just about do the trick."

I let it out. "They've all gone crazy all at once. Like lemmings jumping into the frozen ocean, they all went nuts." I stared ahead at the computer screen as I spoke.

She gently but firmly rotated my chair so I faced her. "Somehow, I get the feeling you're not talking about the wine-on-the-deck doctor, are you?"

I lowered my head. "No, hon, I'm not. Everyone at work has simultaneously gone insane."

She furrowed her brow. "Everyone?"

I tossed my head to one side. "Well, anyone in charge of anything is bananas."

She ran the back of her hand softly against my cheek. "Come on down and we'll talk. Well, you'll talk. I will listen attentively. We can skip the cuddling part if need be."

A few minutes later, we were seated in the family room in front of the fire and sharing a bottle cabernet. She began. "So, tell me all about the mean crazy people you work for." She smiled the smile that always melted me. How I loved that most perfect woman.

"Well, you remember that Saturday session I went to last month?"

She nodded as she sipped. "Sure, the one where your friend Kent screwed up the statistics?"

"He not my friend anymore."

"Really? I thought you two went way back and all? You were a groomsman at his wedding."

I raised my eyebrows. "That was definitely then and this is now." I poured back some wine. "It turns out the innocent seed I planted, intended only to help, has blossomed into poison ivy."

She squinched her nose. "What's that supposed to mean?"

"Today at the department meeting, Bob ripped me a new one. Seems dear old Kent and company took the greatest umbrage at my input. He accused me of trying to show them up publicly as fools."

She groaned ominously. "That can't be good."

"Not hardly. Turns out you're married to Public Enemy Number One in the halls of academia." I shook my head. "Bob said he was raked over the coals at the chief's meeting. He, in turn, wanted to make my meeting experience just as unpleasant."

She set her mostly full glass down. "And did he succeed?"

"He did indeed succeed most spectacularly. Seriously, honey, I've never seen a man so angry or hateful as he was toward me today."

"Bob? Mild-mannered, couldn't-hurt-a-fly-if-he-wanted-to, Bob?"

"Not so very mild-mannered, it turns out. I mean, he was so angry at me I was a bit frightened. Everyone felt it too, except for head-in-the-clouds Jeff Shaub. But, by the end Jeff was scared stiff. Poor Naomi Sanchez was brought to tears."

"This all sounds very unhealthy, honey."

"Tell me about it."

"Do you think Bob's actually a threat? I mean, do you think you're in any physical danger?"

"Up until today, I'd have said that question was ridiculous. But, after looking into those eyes and hearing how angry he was…"

"What? Finish your sentence."

"Look, I'm sure I'm overreacting. It was intense, but Bob could not be driven to physical violence over a pissing contest between Kent and me. That's ridiculous. *I'm* ridiculous for even thinking he's that mad."

"So, what happened at the meeting today? Was it all about you and your assailing of Kent?"

"No, Bob was babbling about some insane metrics they're going to dump on us. Lambasting me was just the warm up."

Concern laced her words. "You're using that word insane an awful lot lately."

Surprised, I said, "I guess I am."

As gingerly as she could, which wasn't all that gingerly, she wondered out loud. "Maybe you should cool it with the 'insane' this-and-thats. It is probably not so wise to go out of your way to goad these people."

She was, of course, correct. That did not change the fact that I was stubborn. I felt wronged, and I still felt that I had the right to voice my valid concerns in an open forum at the university.

"I don't know, sweetheart..."

"Hey, you're a big boy, and you can do whatever you want. I'm just saying it might be wise to avoid the high horse and walk the long way around the hornet's nest."

"But, honey, you have to hear their so-called metrics."

Determination sculpted her face. "Well, then you had better tell me about them." I know she had no real interest in the metrics themselves but was just curious to hear what I was willing to put myself at such risk for. Smart girl.

I sliced the air with my flattened palm. "Basically, they have set some arbitrary goals, eh, metrics, for patient care. They're looking at blood pressure and diabetic control, getting regular mammograms, that type of thing."

She angled her head. "So far, that sounds fairly reasonable. I mean, metrics can help standardize best practices."

"That's not the point. The point is how they are instituting them."

"Please excuse me."

I was being an ass. "Look, sweetheart, it's me who's sorry. I didn't mean to snap at you like that. You're trying to help. It's just that I'm really upset at the way Bob treated me *and* with the heavy-handed metrics."

She reached over and filled my glass close to the top. "Thank you for seeing the error of your reckless ways. Here, this will help." She set the bottle back down. "So, go on, keeping in mind I'm on your side, whatever side that might be."

I leaned over and gave her a quick kiss. When seated again, I continued. "As much as it grieves me to admit it, I have to concede that, yes, metrics can be useful. But medically, the metrics they've chosen are flawed. I wouldn't mind if they set valid goals. But, aside from that, the issue has more to do with the scope and harshness those lunatics purpose."

She cleared her throat.

"Oh, sorry. How about morons? No, strike that. I'll just call them the bosses. That better?"

She pinched one side of her lips together. "It will have to do for now."

"In the worst renditions of corporate speak I've ever heard, the bosses are going to hold anyone involved in a patient's care responsible for achieving *all* the metrics. On top of that, they plan to tie twenty-five percent of our base salaries to achieve their questionable goals."

She whistled quietly. "Wow, that is kind of draconian."

"Thank you! Now you see what I'm so worked up over."

"Can they even do that, cut your pay if you miss a metric?"

I crossed my arms. "Up until today I'd have said never. But now…I don't know. They seem awfully confident, cocky almost. It's like they're actually ready for a fight." I turned to address her squarely. "Who would want to start a big fight when there were no real issues to fight about to begin with? That's…well, it's insane. And, even if they can't pull it all off, it fries my bacon that they'd treat us so badly. No discussion, no input, no buy-in, nothing. Just bend over and take it with a smile."

As I finished, she was lost in thought. She swirled her wine slowly, holding the rim just in front of her lips. After a full minute, she spoke more to herself than to me. "Interesting." A moment later, she asked, "So, what's incorrect about the metrics?"

"Hang on a second. What was that 'interesting' remark about?"

"What?" she protested. "I can't think this is all very interesting?"

I squinted one eye. "That's not what it sounded like to me."

She shot up one eyebrow. "And just exactly what did it sound like to you?"

Oh boy. Danger, Will Robinson! "I'm not sure. That's why I asked. If you say it's nothing, of course it's nothing." Phew!

"Anyway, the problem with their metrics are sort of technical, but they are fundamentally flawed. First, they employing what are called surrogate measures. It's like this. Take blood sugar. They propose to measure it by levels that fall in a defined range. This assumes that if they are maintained in the proper range, the patients will have fewer heart attacks and strokes, that sort of thing. But we don't actually measure how many strokes occur, which is the measurement which counts. They are only following a surrogate that they *hope* reflects the real endpoint."

"So, do these surrogates accurately reflect real endpoints?"

"Sometimes, yes. Sometimes, no. It depends on the effect you wish to measure and the surrogates available. Take anemia, for example. If you look in a reference book, it will say the blood count should be in a certain range. If it is below the range, the patient is anemic. If I draw a sample from a patient and the results are that they only have ten percent of their normal blood concentration, I can assume they are anemic. So, I accept the surrogate—the blood count in this example—is a good indication that the patient is in trouble."

"So, what," she wondered, "is the real endpoint? Isn't it anemia?"

"No." I corrected. "The real outcome is, oh, I don't know, *death*, shortness of breath, altered mental status. But when I examine the patient, I don't measure if they are so anemic that they are short of breath. I measure the surrogate, worry that they might suffer shortness of breath, and then give them a transfusion."

"I'm beginning to regret I asked."

"Sorry. Like I said, it's technical. But, here, take their goal for blood pressure. They want the patients to be below 140/90. That's the standard recommendation from the experts."

"So, what's wrong with setting that surrogate as a goal?"

"The goal is fine, but not if they use garbage data."

"What garbage data?"

I shook my hands in front of me. "The garbage data we accept is a patient's blood pressure when they present in clinic."

"What, you people can't operate a blood pressure machine correctly?"

"Sure, we can place it on an arm and record the pretty numbers on the display. But, the fact of the matter is that we take the pressure in the incorrect setting."

"What? You take it with them sitting there right before you weigh them and stuff them in a room. That's how it's done."

"Yes," I said, "but that gives a spuriously high value. It's the wrong way to do it. Research has proven that the true blood pressure, the one the patient experiences ninety-nine point nine percent of the time, is lower than the one taken at the doctor's office. Here, look. I'll make you the patient. You're running late, so you run up the stairs to the office. You're rushed back by the medical assistant who places the cuff over your clothes while asking you if you're a victim of domestic abuse with me standing right next to you. To top it off, you know the next act will be to publicly weigh you. I bet you already know how women feel about their weight. The next act will be for the assistant taking your weight to call out its value. Am I right? Do you think it might just bring up that blood pressure a tad?"

"It sure does mine."

"So, ladies and gentleman of the jury, there you have it. We collect and accept garbage-data for blood pressure, which are, in turn, just surrogate measures in the first place. Now my livelihood will be based on this fecal-contaminated data?"

She smirked. "I see your point, champ. But don't you think you should bring it down a notch or two? I think *your* blood pressure is way high just now."

I shook my head. "Sorry, honey, but this stuff really gets my goat." I paused to gathered my thoughts. "These things matter to me. Health, patient care, fairness, and science. Most of all, it bothers me significantly that a bunch of doctor-bosses who are supposed to follow best practices and adhere to the scientific method choose to ignore the facts out of a sense of convenience."

"Maybe you should have gone into private practice, sweetheart." I looked up from my tirade to see her sassy smile. "Or, maybe you could have been a cowboy…or a prospector. You know, rugged men who work in near complete isolation from other human beings?"

"Very droll."

She placed her hand over mine. "My dearest, I know you are passionate about this. It's one of your best qualities, one I would never ask you to lose."

"But. I hear a 'but' in there, don't I?"

She pinched her finger and thumb almost together. "Just a little one."

"*But*, you think I need to keep that passion in check, realizing others may not share or appreciate it. Further, you opine that if I don't keep my gun in my holster, I may just get the gunfight I seem to be begging for."

She tapped a finger on one cheek. "Can you read minds? No, wait, perchance we've had this conversation *before*. No, wait, wait, is it that you are, just now, stepping full-fledged into adulthood?"

"You do know that when I said, 'For better or worse,' this is what I was talking about, right?"

She smiled wickedly. "Really. I'll have to watch our wedding video again to make sure. I'll get back to you on that, okay?"

"For better or worse, evil one."

TWENTY-TWO

I was determined to respect my wife's opinion as to what was good for me. Well, at least as best I could. But, I was upset, threatened, and, was cursed with the tendency to be a bit childish at times. So, I spent the next couple of days stewing quietly about my disenchantment. I tried to decide what to actually do about it. A clear, but devilishly unsatisfying option was to do nothing at all, simply lay low and keep my mouth shut. Not likely.

I wasn't hearing any watercooler chatter on the subject, so I decided I'd check with my old friends, Jim and Evan. I had always counted on their honest and insightful input. Plus, it had been a while since I'd spoken with either of them. Jim was in Economics, so he might not have experienced the same oppressive mandates as Evan or I had in Medicine. Nonetheless, he always kept an ear to the ground for trends and gossip. I emailed the pair

Dudes! How's it going? We need to get together for lunch or something real soon. It's been too long. : (Plus, I want to get your take on these new rules and metrics. Karan says I'm not supposed to call them idiotic or refer to our bosses as imbeciles, so please don't tell her I did!! Jim, I heard they dumped a load of crap on you people in the Social Science too, not just us Medicine slaves. What kind of ill-conceived and asinine rubbish did they come up with specifically? Anyway, let's get together soon. Your co-conspirator…Noah

By the next morning, I had received replies from both men. And so continued my education as to what happened to ordinary people during extraordinary times.

Noah, hi back atcha! Yeah, weird changes in the winds to be certain. My take is sort of a wait and see approach, I guess. Render unto Caesar and all that, right? Lunch sounds great. Let me know when and we can talk face-to-face. No permanent documents then, you secret conspirator...Jim

Friendly, noncommittal, and vague. Not typical of Jim. And what was with his concern about "permanent documents?" He was kidding, right? But if Jim's reply puzzled me, Evan's punched me in the gut.

Noah, nice to hear from you. Yes, we three have not been in any form of contact for a very long while, have we? I have not independently spoken with or contacted Jim in any form. But we get busy. I would definitely have to agree with you, Noah, that several innovative and far-reaching proposals are on the table. I am of the belief that time alone will prove the best judge of their nature. This, of course, is not to say we should act in any manner other than to give them our fullest support at this juncture. Change is in the wind, and I smell a fresh breeze. The possibility of lunch with James and you sounds nice. Do let me know when it might take place, so I can verify if I am able to break our long, mutual, three-way silence. James, I am not at all familiar with the metrics and proposals that are being instituted in your specific department. I would, naturally, allow you fill me in, if you so choose. Regards to both your wives...Evan

Wow! I mean, beat-me-with-a-stick-in-the-noonday-sun wow. That was the most distancing and litigious work of denial and duplicity I had ever read. He worded the letter like he knew it would be read back to him before the McCarthy hearings back in the 1950s. What was up with Evan? The last time we spoke—a year ago—he didn't seem mad at me. He seemed good-old Evan to me. Who was that man? I printed copies of both responses to show Karan. Her level-headed input was always a blessing. Maybe she could bring some insight where I was surely lacking, especially concerning Evan. I also sent them both the following reply:

How about lunch at the at Nine Tastes a week from Friday? We need to talk. Let me know ASAP. Thanks…Noah

That evening, I fidgeted in my chair as Karan read the two email responses. She first read one, then the other, then read them both again. She rested the papers on her lap and stared off into space. Occasionally, she mumbled something quietly to herself like she was trying to solve some unbreakable code. She scratched her forehead, sipped her wine, and picked up the sheets to read them a third time.

"Enough already," I said. "Tell me what you think. You're sort of freaking me out."

"Oh," she replied, as if I woke her from a daydream, "sorry. I didn't mean to do that." She shook the emails toward me. "It's just that these are so damn curious. Especially Evan's. If you hadn't told me who they were from, I'd have never guessed it was either of them. I mean," she shook the sheets again, "these are just not the Jim and Evan I have known for years."

"Tell me about it."

"What's your take on them?"

"I asked you first. What's yours?"

"Well, Evan's is bloody obvious, but Jim's, I'm…"

"Evan's is bloody obvious?" I blurted out incredulously. "I am more stuck on Evan's than Jim's."

"Really, Noah, you can't be that dense."

I had to protest. "What?"

She pursed her lips. "It's plain to see Evan is frightened out of his skin. He is cutting all ties with you and Jim too for good measure. Jim is your friend. Evan, as we used to say in school, is ditching you both.

"But why? Evan is one of my oldest and best friends."

"Not any more he's not." She held the evidence up as proof. "I imagine he was scared in the first place, and when he has heard that you're a problem child, he decided to skedaddle ASAP. He doesn't want to be associated with of your baggage. So, he documents clearly, concisely, and unequivocally that he was not and will never be part of your insurrection."

"My insurrection?"

She scowled at me. "Did you not sign your name as co-conspirator?"

"I was joking between good friends. You know that."

"Call it what you will, but you're a marked man, at least as far as Evan sees it."

Stupefied, I melted back into my chair. "And what about Jim?"

She tapped the papers lightly against her chin. "Jim, I'm not so sure of. You know he's this big kid at heart and is as easy to read as a Dr. Seuss book. He's willing to continue to be in contact with you, so that's something."

I scowled. "Thank god for minor miracles."

She patted my knee. "Be that as it may, sweetheart, Jim's not ready to throw you under the bus, but, I can't tell if he's just simplistically going with the flow or whether he's trying to tell you something."

"Well, I'll just ask him at lunch next week."

"Jim will show, but not Evan. You, love of my life, have seen the last of him."

"No way! Evan may be circling his wagons, but I'm sure he hasn't gone over to the dark side yet."

"I can't say Evan's gone over either, but he's at least aware of its threat and is reacting to it."

"Honey, you sound a bit too conspiracy-theory paranoid here. Overreacting a tad."

"Let me put it this way. If Evan shows up for lunch, you can pick this summer's vacation spot with no input from me."

"Even Vegas?"

She shuddered. "Even Sin City. If Evan isn't dropping you like a bad habit, you may drag your young and impressionable children and your disapproving wife to Las Vegas."

"And if he doesn't show? You choose, and I have to keep my mouth shut?"

She placed her palms up. "It would only be fair."

"Your mother's," I said like the words themselves were sour.

"My mother's what."

"If that jackass Evan stands me up for lunch, we're spending a month at your mother's house."

"It would be one of many possible options I would explore. Father would be there too, you know."

"It's only your mother who counts."

She trying to sound insulted. "Well that's a fine thing to say!"

"Tell me, have you ever met your mother? Spent any time with her? Longer than, oh, say, ten minutes in a row?"

"Are you suggesting that my mother can be overly formal, intolerant, and a ceaseless nag at times?"

"Ah, you *have* met her."

TWENTY-THREE

The following morning, I found two emails awaiting me. Jim's was a simple.

Sure, I'll be there at noon.

Evan's was far more tortured and convoluted.

Fellows, next Friday doesn't work for me. In fact, I had hoped to keep my private life out of this and to myself, but I'm not ready to socialize now or in the foreseeable future. Isaiah and I have just experienced a painful and chaotic breakup. I am emotionally distraught and physically devastated. I shall contact you, Noah, when I feel I have healed enough to, once again, be socially available. My best to your families...Evan

Crap. Four interminable weeks at her mother's! Oh well. At least I still had Thai food with my pal Jim to look forward to.

Lunch with Jim went much better than I expected. He was his usual affable, straightforward self. He hadn't even placed any special significance on Evan's apparent rebuff. Jim asked if I thought it would be a good idea for him to broach the matter with Evan. I asked him not to. If Evan had, in fact, dumped me, to call it out would only prove painful for all concerned. No, let the action play itself out naturally. We'd just have to wait and see. Jim was fine with that approach.

In terms of Jim's take on the changes proposed, he hadn't given them much thought. Typical Jim, nose to the grindstone and damn the torpedoes. He said he'd start to worrying if something happened that rocked his microcosmic world, but not a moment before. Jim mostly dismissed the administrators. He figured it was all a trial balloon, and it didn't mean they were actually going to do anything. God bless him, he just didn't let other people bother him as much as I let them bother me. He was less suspicious than I was of the human tendency to crush, kill, and destroy.

Before I could even say hello, Karan asked me what Evan ordered for lunch. I said he and I both ate crow. I asked if Karan wouldn't mind us all spending a month at her parents' place that summer. I missed my mother-in-law dearly, and a month there would do the trick.

She pumped her fists in the air. "I knew it!" Then she whipped out her cell phone and texted her mother that the tentative plans they'd discussed earlier in the day were a definite go. I know she did that in front of me to rub my nose that much more in the sand. She was such a poor winner.

For the next few weeks, I worked as hard as I could to ignore the evil omens and apocalyptic signs I saw all about me. I had shouting matches continually in my head with either Kent or Bob, sometimes with both at once. They would announce something stupid (Karan couldn't stop me from using that pejorative inside my own head). Typically, I would calmly point out how and why they were wrong. Then we'd yell at each other until I vanquished them. They always thanked me for caring enough to set them straight. They also groveled a lot. Naturally, I, the better man, insisted they not grovel, but to just not be stupid again in the future. I spent way too much time having those sessions in my head. It was bad for my well-being, but I was stuck in that rut.

I, for the most part, groused less in general after you-know-who ask me to cool it with the kvetching. That lasted up until I read an email for some dean I'd never heard of. He trumpeted a "bold new innovation to customer care and satisfaction." We were all to receive a list of patients who were delinquent for some test or procedure. These were not our own patients, but random patients presumably still getting their care in our system. We'd each get twenty-five names and phone numbers. We were to call these people ourselves. No delegation or letters were acceptable. We were to convince them to do what was in their best interest, tauted as "good, managed concern." Dollars would be "attached to" our completion of the list. The dean did not state whether the money at risk was extra or would be deducted from our base pay. That oversight irritated me all that much more.

The helpful, company-oriented individual that I was shot back a protest to the dean who sent the document. I asked why it was that highest paid person in the room had to do a task so menial. I constructively pointed out that a myna bird with training could perform the task equally well, and they worked for sunflower seeds. I also wondered out loud if the entire operation didn't violate the patient's privacy. We were, after all, letting someone not involved in their care know a sensitive detail concerning their medical history. I also asked him to reconsider the project because there were already multiple and redundant backup systems in place to do that type of work. The primary care providers, their assistants, letters sent, and calls made by underlings all followed up when important tests were not completed. I also asked him to confirm back to me, as I knew he had to be a dutiful fellow, that all the administrators were to receive a list of similar length.

That evening, I mentioned to Karan how much helping I had done. There followed a disconcerting period during where I worried that she might traumatically castrate me. She didn't anger easily or often, and I had really never given her cause to be truly mad at me. Let it be known that I shall always, in the future, think thrice before potentially upsetting my wife. The words mushroom head, shit-disturber, and egotistical narcissist left her mouth, as were the concepts of imposed celibacy, separate sleeping arrangements, and my ass being whooped. Fortunately, she cooled off much quicker than I expected. By the following evening, she was speaking to me again, albeit in only short, terse sentences.

To my adolescent email, the dean responded promptly. He also cc'd every administrator and chief on the planet. He thanked me for my concern. He relayed that the proposal had been discussed, decided upon, and vetted by everyone who was anyone, so it would be rolled out as planned. He said they felt customers would react disproportionately better to a call from a physician rather than from anyone else. Who wouldn't be impressed that a doctor was so worried about them that he took the time to call them personally? The fact that it might be a urologist calling to remind a woman about her mammogram didn't seem to register odd to them. As to my remarks about myna birds and administrators' participation, he mentioned nothing at all.

Late that week, Bob showed up unannounced at my office door. With the warmth and cheer of a truant officer, he informed me that I should come to his office at nine sharp the following morning. I started to point out that I had clinic. He told me unemotionally that I did not any longer. He then departed as abruptly and as uncivilly as he had appeared. There was, I quickly concluded, nothing good about to befall me.

That marked the first, but tragically not the last, time I would conceal from Karan what happened at work. It was not that I didn't want her to yell at me or be mad. No, I felt it was my job, my duty, and my honor to protect her from the sorrow, the pain, and the angst that I had brought down upon myself.

To this day, many a sleepless night and horror-filled days later, I am proud that I did that for her.

I knew she wouldn't have asked a martyr's role of me. It was likely that she wanted to support me through my trials. I might not have been able to put a stop to the humiliations, lies, and cruelties I was to face. I could, however, shelter the woman I loved from them. That way, the beast—the beast the virus had spawned—could not make her life the living hell mine was about to become.

TWENTY-FOUR

At 8:59 a.m. I presented myself to Bob's door. It was open. He was seated behind his desk, but joining him to his right was, of course, Kent. Bob waved me in and pointed to a chair across from the two of them. I believe Bob grumbled *morning*. He might, however, have just cleared some phlegm. He pointed his pen at Kent. "You two know each other."

On cue, Kent popped up and beamed a smile that could burn through a cloudy sky. He shook my hand like I'd just won the lottery. "It is *so* good to see you again, old boy." After he sat back down, he asked, "How are the wife and kids? Well, I hope." I reported that they were fine. Then he got down to it. "I bet you would like us to get to the crux of our meeting this morning, wouldn't you?"

I stared impassively, first at Kent then at Bob. The look on Bob's face reflected life-threatening constipation coupled with hemorrhoids burning out of control. Oh well, at least Bob didn't look like he wanted to murder me—yet.

"Well, Noah, Bob here," he gestured towards Bob, presumably so I'd know which Bob in the room he referred to, "asked me to drop in on this meeting with you." He pushed his palms at me like he refused to accept any more dessert. "Now, don't get me wrong. This *is* Bob's meeting, not mine. I'm just here as a sort of ombudsman, so to speak. Bob," again, a specific Bob was pointed out, "is aware you and I go way back together. He felt it might be helpful to have me here, you know, to grease the wheels, so to speak.

Naturally, how could I say no?" He shook his head in amused disbelief. "After all, you and I go way back together."

I instantly regretted eating breakfast. It was about to come back up.

"The fact that I am one of the deans over the division you work in and that I sit on the Committee of Academic Personnel do not necessarily reflect any motivation for my presence here today. If either of those factors were the case, which they are not, then I'd be required to inform you of that codicil or those codicils and I'd, naturally, offer and allow you the option of requesting the counsel and presence of your union representative." He looked at me to gauge my comprehension status, which happened to be sinking like the *Titanic*. "You understand that, right, Noah?" He folded his hands on the desk, and awaited my response.

I wiggled a finger in the air. "Could you repeat the sentence beginning with 'If either of those factors' please?"

He ruffled, looked at Bob, and studied the ceiling. "If either of those…"

I held up a hold-it-there hand. "Okay, Kent, stop. I just wanted to see if you could. I understood you all too well. If it is not too much trouble, and actually even if it is too much trouble, would one of you two clowns tell me what this is all about?"

Bob looked to him. Kent smiled warmly. "As I was saying, Bob here asked me to…"

"I know, grease my wheels. Seriously, what gives?" I looked at me watch. "I'll give you sixty seconds to come up with something understandable, or I'm afraid I'll have to move that we adjourn the meeting on account of its lameness."

Any pretense of civility evaporated from his face. "Noah, I don't think that is a healthy attitude to take at this time and at this juncture in your career." He eased back on the attitude slightly. "Perhaps you are not aware of the fact that Robert has summoned you to a meeting to present you with an Action Plan that will ensure your improved performance and professional satisfaction. Please know that is the purpose of Robert's meeting with you. I am here as a second set of hands to help steer your Ship of State in the best direction we can in order to help you."

Noticing that Bob became physically smaller with each passing moment. I pointed at him. "For someone running a meeting, he's kind of quiet, don't you think?"

"Be cautious as to the level of your flippancy and open disrespect. We should not want this intervention to take a drastic turn for the worse. You, we can promise with certainty, want that to happen less than we do." Never blinking, he asked, "Do we make ourselves perfectly clear, Dr. Taylor?"

I was in a quandary. I knew I had done nothing illegal or improper. Hence, any disciplinary action they might threaten was, in the end, just posturing. On the other hand, if I let them have their kangaroo court, maybe I could be done with them. That would have clearly been the safest, least painful path to choose.

"Very well, Kent. I will be a good boy, but only if we get one thing straight. You do not scare me. Okay, two things straight. You do not intimidate me. Crap—this is what I get for thinking out loud—three things straight. I have done nothing for which any intervention, or whatever you chose to label it, is called for. You," I placed an index finger as close to Kent's nose as humanly possible, "know that." My finger rotated to stop centimeters in from of Bob's forehead. "Bob knows that." Finally, my finger pointed toward my face. "And I know that. Now, Bob, please continue with your meeting."

Bob was not, in my estimation, a healthy man. He was flabby, pasty, and completely deconditioned. If I pushed him too hard emotionally, I might put his life at risk. He was sweating like man on the gallows with a noose around his neck. His hands trembled so badly, I worried they'd start thumping on the table. His heart had to be racing a mile a minute. Something happened at my moment of realization that both stunned and frightened me. As I sat there in his office about to be railroaded, hating both men with a passion, I found myself trying to decide whether I cared if Bob lived or died.

I heard the diminutive devil on my left shoulder. "Bob brought this on himself, the flaming jerk. He has no one to blame but his own sorry ass. He chose his bedfellows. Now, let him deal with the cost of his poor, anti-Noah choices." I weighed the relative plusses and minuses of his death. Bob, the man I'd supported for department chief. Bob, the man who did missionary work in Africa every summer. Bob, the man who came over and mowed my lawn after I broke my ankle.

What on God's green Earth possessed me to feel so inhuman toward him that I had practically willed his hand to rise and grasp his chest? I had actually pictured frothy fluid gurgling up from his lungs as he died like a dog there on top of his desk with me standing in judgment, arms folded.

Before he could say another word, I spoke to him in an even, neutral voice. "Bob, look, I'm sorry to have said that. It was completely uncalled for. You've always been a friend and as fair as possible with me. I'm sorry to have placed you in such an awkward and doubtlessly painful position. Please forgive me. Look, why don't you say whatever it is you have to say, we'll shake hands, and I'll be out of your hair. What do you say?"

He sat up and looked over to Kent, who shrugged his shoulders as if that was okay. "Thanks. No problem. I appreciate you saying that." He chuckled grimly once. "It was getting kind of intense there, wasn't it?"

Kent began, "So, you see…"

He placed a hand on Kent's shoulder. "I'll take it from here, Dean Pearson. You're welcome to stay, but I think I've got this."

Kent was stunned, and I would swear to it, he had a child's look of pouty disappointment on his face. He rested back in his chair, mute. Bob began. "So, here's the deal here, Noah. Lately, it has been brought to my attention that you are acting in a somewhat hostile and provocative manner."

I fought back mightily the urge to respond to that allegation. I counted to ten instead.

"Frankly, I have never had any problem with you personally or professionally." He tossed his head back and forth robustly. "Sure, I guess I got in your face at the department meeting, but," he couldn't hide a quick glance over to Kent, "well, I guess I was having a bad day too. So, what we…I mean what I want to do is outline an informal Action Plan to help you see if you are interacting with your colleagues in a less than optimal manner. No accusations, no blame, just a good-faith effort to make sure you're happy."

I suppressed my primal urge to strike out. "That sounds fine. What exactly do you need from me?".

He almost smiled. "Only that you take the university's two-day course in communication skills. You've heard about our Peers Helping Anyone Really Succeed program, haven't you?"

Yes, I had. It was one of those things like an IRS audit or waking up with Paula Dean in your arms. I never wanted to be involved with it. PHARS was one of those classes where overenthusiastic cheerleaders told participants how to handle problematic interactions. Then, to test newfound skills, a talentless actor pretended to be a difficult person so they could be handled. PHARS sounded about as fun as a barrel full of monkeys climbing my colon. "Yes, Bob, I have heard of it."

"Great. You know, it's a spectacular program. It did wonders for me, I can tell you that without a doubt." That high praise from the man who wished to choke me a few weeks before. "So, all I need to have you do is sign this Action Plan," he pointed to a blank line under my printed name, "here, and were good to go." As if he just recalled the eight-hundred-pound gorilla in the corner, he looked for approval from Kent.

While Bob signed the document below my name, Kent spoke. "Excellent, gentlemen. This is most encouraging. You know, Noah, that all we want— all any of us want—is for you to be happy."

Right, that's why you're dragging me naked over hot coals, Kent, so I can be happy. You lousy excuse for an insincere hypocrite.

"And, as I'm certain Bob will be offering too, if there is anything he or I, or anyone for that matter can do for you, you just let us know lickety-split."

Well, as you so generously offered, Kent, could you and all your cronies jump into an actively flowing river of lava, pretty please with a cherry on top?

"For now, I don't think that will be necessary, but it's sure swell of you to offer, Kent."

I left Bob's office and walked quickly down the hall toward the elevators. I needed to make it there or to the restroom halfway down the corridor fast. While I was sitting in the meeting, I did not have a problem. But, upright and moving, I saw lights explode in front of my eyes, and my legs were turning into jelly. I was not going to collapse or vomit anywhere my two persecutors could see. They would assume I was tipsy from the stress of the meeting. I was not going to give them the satisfaction of thinking they'd gotten to me, especially since that was not the case.

I crashed through the bathroom doors and stumbled into a stall and plopped onto the toilet. I didn't even bother to latch the door. I dropped my head between my knees and breathed deeply. I was uncertain why I was having such a dramatic reaction. I knew it had something to do with the awful things I'd thought about Bob. When I hoped he would drop dead and I could not have cared less.

Later, I came to know why I'd had that powerful, visceral response. The corporate virus had touched me. As it always did, it began with the lightest touch. All too soon, it took full control. I was a very lucky man that dark day. I successfully resisted it.

TWENTY-FIVE

I survived my near-swoon, and I survived the PHARS program too. The session was supremely annoying on so many levels. I did not physically die, but I suffered several flesh wounds to my soul. During the morning "sharing" section, the speakers repeatedly kept welcoming us to PHARS. How was it, I slammed my palm on my forehead, that they did not hear what they had just said? They pronounced PHARS the same way you pronounce *farce*. Again, lost irony. Where was self-reflection when it was so comically necessary?

It was all I could do not to walk out, but I knew I would just have to come back and PHARS all over again, so I sat transfixed between boredom and disbelief. We had some shriveled old woman as our "actor" to help hone our skills. She interpreted her role as needing to be as loud and as mean as she could be in the skits we suffered though. Fortunately, I'd done my share of high school and college plays, so I could both handle her and make it seem like I learned something. Fortunately, just as all good things come to an end, so, also, did all the bad things.

One part of PHARS was weird though. There was one German guy in my small group who actually broke down toward the end of the roleplaying. As he tried to interact with our actress, he was forced to face his personal demons. He sobbed about how he and his wife couldn't get along, their isolation, and the shouting matches they had daily. It was TMI, but he told us they hadn't had sex in three and a half years. As a result of that celibate hiatus, he suffered us all to know he felt swollen "down there." I really hoped I didn't run into that swollen fellow at work. Worse yet, I hope I never looked up from a gurney in the ER and saw him looking down at me. I might be critically injured, but he would be distracted with his critical swelling.

I wasn't sure how I felt doing PHARS without telling Karan. I mean, if I informed her I was doing the class, she'd want to know why I'd do such an uncharacteristic thing. I would have to tell her about my Action Plan and why one was leveled against me. It was simply part of the price I paid to insulate her, but it was uncomfortable. Fortunately, I did PHARS on a weekday, so I didn't have to invent a weekend cover story.

I was certain that, in spite of having completed PHARS, the administration was not likely done with me. They were not likely to forgive my transgressions so easily. According to Bubba's rule, I demonstrated that I was not with them, so I was against them. That was an act punishable with ostracization, for the good of the Company. I expected some form of continued harassment. My best hope was that if I kept quiet long enough, they would eventually lose interest in me. The problem was that I didn't know if I could still be on the sidelines when unpalatable changes were forced down my throat. It might sound maudlin of me to draw such a parallel, but I felt like a German citizen during the rise of the Nazis. If I didn't speak out against an evil government, I would share blame for their actions.

I vowed to try my best to refrain from confrontation. That would not be easy. New imperatives arrived more regularly than the US Mail. Yet, with each new imperative, I could hold my tongue. So, when the university became a "fragrance-free zone," I said nothing. I assume the administration meant don't wear perfume? Why they hadn't said what they meant just confirmed that they were clueless. Did they also mean our basketball team was not allowed to sweat? The players would certainly be "fragrant" if they did. What about my shampoo? Even the slightest residue caused my head to be *fragrant*. So, no more clean hair? Fabric softener sheets used in the dryer left a distinct fragrance on the laundry. No more cling-free clothes? I knew no one thought any of that through. They just nodded their big, fat, swollen heads and congratulated one another on their collective brilliance. But, hard as it was, I still said nothing. So, to sum it up, I worked in a fragrance, latex, violence, smoking, gun, drug, bullying, harassment, hate, gender/race/ethnic discrimination, GMO, nuclear weapon, and fear-free zones.

I got nothing.

Along the same vein, when all the department heads went on a one week, all-expenses-paid retreat to "rework" the "mission-vision statement," I did not protest. I forced myself to recall the parable of the workers in the bible—*Matthew 20:1-16*. I was able, with some effort, to ignore the fact that they'd had a free vacation at a posh resort with their spouses, while I did not.

When we were told that "warm greetings" in clinic were mandatory, I sealed my lips. Everyone from receptionists to chronic condition managers and even the janitor, if present, had to go out to the waiting room and "warmly greet" the customer—to really make them feel welcome. Never mind the fact that the patient might have been sick and did not want chitchat. No, go chew the fat with them, enough so that you made it clear just how much you, the supply clerk, were personally glad the patient was there for a visit. The rule pertained to everyone except the doctors. So, I just let it fall like water off a duck's back.

Ever-helpful me even came up with some imperatives of my own. Yes, as streamlined, customer-center concern (no longer "care," now it was "concern") was so important, I thought up a few. All female employees under the age of fifty would be required to work topless. Hey, we'd hook the male purchasers, right? Men would be more satisfied with their concern experience if they liked the view, right? Lest anyone complain that my topless imperative was both sexist and dehumanizing, remember, it was what was best for the Company.

Also, all visits would be free. Yeah, who didn't like free?

I wasn't sure if my next idea, that of a reality show office visit would work, but it was worth a try. I envisioned one patient and three doctors present for the history and exam. The doctors would then compete to see which of their diagnoses the patient liked the most. There were potential issues. What would happen if the patient chose the wrong diagnosis, or based their choice on the diagnosis on which had most painless treatment? I definitely needed to work out a few bugs from that imperative.

I had a great, metric-changing imperative too. Instead of mailing satisfaction surveys to the customers, I proposed we mail them to the providers. True, some accuracy might be lost, but at least we'd have great numbers. Say, if I took that to its logical conclusion, if everyone was at one hundred percent, they'd all be in the top third. Kent would be *so* happy.

And snacks! Yes, we were to have free snacks and lots of them. Sugary-sweet, deep-fried snacks were best since people liked them the most. Never mind the terrible message that sent, with a healthcare provider inviting the customer to destroy their bodies at their appointment. It would be best for the Company, so it would be good.

It was a shame I never shared my imperatives with the administration. They probably weren't quite ready for me.

There arose a series of situations, where I simply had to take a stand. The first came in the form of an email memo from the actual Dean of the School of Medicine himself. Rough and tumble Dr. Ryker Crumpler was one surly son of a bitch. He was sort a of John Wayne meets Al Capone type. Square-shouldered and square-jawed with eyes that warned that he was a sociopath and was capable of doing anything he needed to do to get the job done. He announced he was going to improve patient satisfaction by "innovating" access. His imperative had several provisions that were intolerable and one that was downright insane.

The first innovation he decreed was that all patients in the clinic would be seen. That part might seem obvious. But what he meant was that any person who came to clinic would be seen whether they had an appointment or not, whether they were two hours late or not, whether their complaint was even in the scope of practice for that clinic. If a man showed up in OB/GYN and wanted to be seen, he would be seen. Seriously, that's one of the examples he cited. Furthermore, registration-to-discharge times were to be thirty minutes or less. Period.

Consequently, we could not run behind schedule. Period. But, we all ran behind schedule routinely. It was impossible not to run late at least some of the time. That imperative also meant we had to dismiss a patient rapidly, even if their condition was serious and mandated a more thorough evaluation.

He said, specifically, ambulance transports out of the clinic were not an excuse to violate his imperative. I saw nothing good for providers on the frontlines. Even an ambulance summoned with sirens and lights took five to ten minutes to arrive. So, if a patient even said the words *chest* and *pain* in the same sentence, we would be forced to call 9-1-1. It was institutionalized insanity.

His imperative got worse the further I read. Email messages from customers should be answered in less than four hours. Period. As to weekends, vacations, and personal illnesses, he said the imperative was so imperative that it must be followed, "…in spite of there arising some potential variances from past practices and time utilization."

Crap. That meant I'd have to check my work inbox often, even on my days off. If I was on vacation, the person who covered me had to add my ridiculously large burden to his already full plate. In effect, I was better off and less stressed-out when I was at work than at home. No rest for the weary, it was to be.

The final straw for me was his imperative to increase "schedulable" appointment times. It seemed, he had noted with his penetrating insight, that when providers were not present at work, their "contribution to the continuum of appointment availability" was diminished. Huh? Of course, it was diminished—they weren't there. But, never fear, the man had a plan. "In periods where appointment desirability is reasonably assumed to be, or might potentially be, high, non-presence by schedulable personnel in the clinic setting will no longer be allowed." What? "Vacations, sick days, and other forms of non-presence in clinic are, naturally, anticipated and are not 'unapproved of.' If, however, the consequences of such non-presence is potentially impactful, rearrangements and reprioritization will be mandatory at the discretion of the administration."

What was he even trying to say in such tortured English? What I read was that I could take vacation as long as it did not affect appointment availability, which, of course, meant I could not take vacation. I think he was saying we were no longer allowed to be on holiday or ill. What if we died quietly in our sleep? Would Dean Crumpler allow that? What would he do to our corpse if we did not show up to work?

I printed the document and stormed into Bob's office. Turned out, I was not the first one there. Three of my peers were waving sheets of paper at Bob and everyone was shouting. Though no one probably even heard me, I chimed in loudly. "What's going on here?" They ignored me.

Bob rose to his feet, picked up a voluminous textbook, and pounded it on the table. Gradually, the shouting faded. He yelled, "Knock it off, all of you! If you cannot act in a civil manner, I will call security and have you all thrown out of the building, and I mean it." Silence prevailed. "I suppose it wouldn't help me to say I was not in favor of running out the new imperative the way it was."

Someone said, "What's that supposed to mean?"

He raised a hand. "Nothing. Nothing at all. Forget I even said it. Now, there aren't enough chairs in here, so I suggest we adjourn this free-for-all to the conference room." No one moved. "Come on, people, let's at least try to act like adults." Slowly, the other three shuffled toward the door. I followed. Bob came last.

Once we were all seated, he began. "Look, I know this is a lot to throw at you, and I have to say I question the wisdom of some of the proposals."

Someone said, "Some?"

"All right, Carl, that's not helpful. Crap, I will clear the air as much as I can, but I'm just the messenger here, folks. And keep in mind there are ten people who aren't here that I have to do the whole thing with over again. Try and cut me some slack, okay?"

Glenda Parker said, "Not likely, Bob. You asked for the damn job, so you might just have to man up."

"Thanks, Glenda. You're a real pal."

I cut in. "Bob, I know you had nothing to do with this bullshit." I held up my copies. "But can you at least tell me that this is just a first draft proposal?"

He shook his head sorrowfully. "No, it is not a draft. It is the real deal."

I gritted my teeth. "How can they do this? Not only is it insane, but it's arbitrary, unilateral, and probably illegal. I won't stand for it." I swung my papers in the direction of the other three in the room. "They won't stand for it."

He attempted to placate us. "Now, hang on there. Stop before anyone says anything they'll regret down the line. Look, I just found out about this last night. There were several conference calls where the higher ups told the chiefs about the new imperative. I can tell you firsthand the calls were neither pleasant nor brief. I personally raised holy hell, and it didn't do one god— let's just say my efforts failed to move any mountains."

"So, how long has this been in the works? And who, specifically, is responsible?"

He shrugged meekly. "They hatched this plan during that retreat we had a few weeks back. The top dogs had a series of closed-door meetings, and this imperative was the result. As to who the shot-caller is, well that would be none other than the man whose name is at the bottom of the page. This is supposedly the brainchild of Crumpler himself. Of course, now they all love the plan so much, you'd think they all gave birth to it simultaneously." He continued to tremble.

"I'm sorry you're in the middle of all this," I said, "but be that as it may, you're still our leader. Somehow, we all need to present a united front and make the dean back down. Some of these goals are not only unreasonable, but they'll be extremely hard to meet. Others are ridiculous, like a man demanding to be seen in OB/GYN on a drop-in basis. The position about vacations is both subliterate and untenable. What's our next move, *boss*?"

He squeezed his scalp with his palm so forcibly I feared he might pop his head. "I have no idea. None, nothing. And as for being your chief, my resignation of that position was offered and accepted last night during the hour-and-a-half shouting match. As of this moment, I have no idea who the next chief will be. No one else in our department has ever expressed much interest in the job, and that was before the position became *very* undesirable. Certainly, none of you are interested in the job?" Bob laughed mirthlessly. "I can't imagine anyone, *anywhere*, who would be so ill-advised and so stupid as to want to take my former job."

As if on magical cue, a cheery baritone voice came from the doorway. "Well then, Robert, turn to meet the man who is all that and more."

All five of us turned in surprise. I didn't know whether the man had only just arrived or if we were so preoccupied that no one had known he was there. But, there stood Kent Pearson with a smile so wide it extended past his face. He stepped over to the group, set his briefcase on the table, and extended a hand to Bob. Bob stared dumbfounded at his hand long enough that Kent withdrew it, unshaken.

"Hey, I'm as sorry as I can be about you having to step down so abruptly, Bob. Tough call on *both* ends of the phone, I can assure you." He looked off into an undefined distance. "We admire a man with the personal fortitude to take a stand nowadays. But, we'll have to agree to disagree, won't we?"

That was all I could take. "Kent, what the hell are you doing here?"

He grinned like I'd stepped directly into the trap he'd laid. "Why, as the new Chief of Immunology, Noah, I rather thought this was the proper place for me *to* be. *N'est pas, mon frère?*"

I was too rattled to spar with him. "This is not the time nor place for your shit-bird humor, Kent. We're in a real crisis, and you prance in like it's all a big fat joke."

Kent addressed me with unyielding sternness. "We are not taking anything to be funny. Nothing." Pleased to have halted my tongue, he proceeded. "With the roll out of an imperative of this magnitude, we had anticipated some initial pushback. Part of our contingency plans have always been to have boots on the ground ready to march into action at a moment's notice when the need presented itself." He clicked open his briefcase latches. "The need has presented itself, and I am proud and honored to be one pair of boots responding—clip-clop." The imbecile mimed his feet plodding forward with his hands.

I was so upset I shook. "Y…you mean to suggest that y… you're now chief of this department?"

Inner joy beamed in him brightly. He manifested a look of knowing concern. "I mean to suggest nothing." He handed me a sheet of paper. I looked at it and read the trembling page, written on official letterhead.

It is with great pride and pleasure that I have appointed Dean Kent Pearson to be the interim Chief of the Departments of Dermatology,

Cardiology, Allergy and Immunology, as well as director of the Neonatology Services Section of Pediatrics and the Employee Health and Safety subgroup of Department of Occupational Medicine, effective immediately.

It was signed by Dean Crumpler. There were more words in the text, but I stopped reading. It was not possible. A draconian new program was announced, there occurred a bloodbath in response to dissent, and Kent was placed in charge of half the school. No way that could have happened—zero percent chance.

I threw the letter at Kent's chest and stepped right up to his nose. "You cannot be chief of any of those departments. You are not an Immunologist, so you cannot lead the Department of Immunology. You are also not a Cardiologist, Dermatologist, or any other species on that sheet of paper."

He neither blinked nor retreated. "I can be, and I am. Please do not blur, in your mind's eye, the generic administrative skills needed to run a department as compared to the technical knowledge needed to teach in that department."

"What? That's bullshit!"

He allowed the reverberation of my voice to pass. "A common misperception, I can assure you. As chief, as with being a dean, one need not be an expert in all the skills of those you're in charge of to govern them wisely. Think how perverse the world would be if any administrator at any level had to be a subspecialist in every discipline he administered." Kent sat down. "Impossible, I tell you. You needn't answer."

"So, what, five chiefs bailed because of this stupid new imperative, and they put you in charge of all five departments?"

He knitted his fingers together and replied to me mechanically. "No. They placed me in *interim* charge of five of the departments that found themselves leaderless as of this morning. Others are now chiefs of the other vacancies that needed to be filled." Then he gathered up around him a charged atmosphere of malice and loathing. He looked only at me. "Now, if there are no further questions, I will ask you all to return to the work you do, which I am certain needs to be completed." He reached into his briefcase and added, "Bob, leave your office keys on the table. You'll bunk with Noah here until suitable alternative arrangements can be made." The despot looked up to Bob and twisted the knife. "All in the fullness of time."

With varying degrees of shock, they zombie-shuffled out of the room. I remained. When it was undeniable that I was not leaving, Kent asked without looking up from his laptop, "Having some problem with simple directions spoken in plain English, Noah? You would appear to not be accompanying the other sheep on their way back to the flock." He snapped his head up to address me and toyed with me further. "Hum, champ? Well, let me say it in y'alls language. Baa, baa, bleat-baa, baa, bleat. Now baa-baa, wooly little Noah."

I was calm, powerful, and resolute. I knuckled the desk and leaned as close to him as anatomy allowed. "You think you are all that and a whole lot more, don't you, Pearson? Well, you don't intimidate me. So, why don't you cut the horseshit and drop the facade. Then let us have ourselves a friendly little conversation."

He started off in his administrative monotone, but gradually graded into a rich sarcasm. "Well, I am not certain we can have ourselves a friendly conversation of any size. For, you see, you have left me confused and befuddled. First it is *bull*shit I am so wrongly accused of slinging, yet now you speak of *horse*shit. What precise form of *shit* are we to discuss, Dr. Taylor?"

I had to smile. "Why, if I did not know better, I'd swear I just heard the voice of the long-dead Kent Pearson"

"I have no idea what you are referring to, Dr. Taylor. So, if you will turn and depart with alacrity, I will not be forced to document your insubordination in your personnel file."

"No, Pearson, that's not how this ends. You and the half-wits you shower with have gone too far, and you all need to own up to it. I want answers, and I want them now."

He picked up his cell phone and tapped a series of numbers. "This is Dean Pearson. I am in the fourth-floor conference room in the Bishop Building. One of my employees is acting in a threatening manner toward me and will not follow my instructions. Please come at once. This is one of the Code Reds we discussed yesterday." He tapped the phone to end the call. He grinned at me. "There, now you've made me go and call the campus police. It is at times such as these that men's souls are tried. Some, as in your case, are also found to be lacking." He clicked his tongue. "Pity." He casually went back to reading something on his laptop. I could have been on the moon for all his notice.

I left quickly, but so as not to display haste.

TWENTY-SIX

I had never been so frightened and alone. Check that. I had never been frightened and alone. I was nurtured with kindness and support from my parents as I grew up. Karan lovingly supplied that bulwark now. Of course, I mentioned to Karan in general there were significant changes at the university. She needed to know, for example, that Bob had resigned his chair in protest of the totalitarian new order. But, I could not mention the harrowing situation I was in, lest I dragged her into what I'd pledged myself not to. I provided Karan with a watered-down version, void of any specifics. I had to try with all my acting ability to give the impression that detached disinterest was my only take on the direction set by a capricious, sociopathic administration.

Evan was obviously out as someone to confide in during this crisis. Also, I did not want to compromise Jim's position any farther than I already had. No one in my now embattled department could be trusted. None of them were, in any case, close friends. With the tyrannical Kent at the helm, any coworkers were as likely to sell me out as they were to console me.

My family would listen, but they wouldn't know the inner working of a university. They could only give generic emotional support as opposed to bringing any helpful insights to the table. Plus, I really didn't want to reveal to any of them that my so-far stellar career was in grave jeopardy. I know that might have been a vanity I could ill afford, but it would be humiliating to have them see me so vulnerable.

I could always hunt down Cletus. He was a great friend and would love to help. But, he had just recently suffered a similar fate. It might have been too painful to ask him to relive that dark passage in his life. Plus, he had so vehemently warned me not to do what I went right ahead and did that it would be hard for him not to scold me. Neither of us needed that.

I considered being my own, sole counsel, but experience dictated that an outside perspective was a great thing to have. Plus, the longer I kept all the pain inside, the worse my sense of isolation and desperation grew. John Donne warned that "no man is an island," but at great personal peril, I was rapidly becoming precariously insular.

As I mentally scanned the long list of every colleague, friend, or acquaintance I could recall over the past few years, Tinisha's name suddenly popped into my head. I initially dismissing her as a confidant. She was a medical assistant who had worked for me, not a peer. We had never socialized, so there was no friendship to revive. On the other hand, I really liked her, and in her own cantankerous manner, I knew she was devoutly loyal to me. After I had mulled it over a while, I decided consulting with T might not be such a bad idea after all.

I phoned her immediately so as not to lose resolve. She seemed mildly surprised to hear my voice. After a bit of small talk and reminiscing—and after we bashed poor Bubba mercilessly—I asked Tinisha if we could get together for coffee. I stammered my way through explaining why I'd called.

She, in classic Tinisha-style, asked with a little edge to her voice if there was a possibility that I was having marital problems "at home," which had "compelled" me to direct some of my "attention" toward her. She hoped and prayed that I wasn't so inclined. She reminded me that she was not only my senior by a "goodly" number of years, but that, more importantly, she was a married woman of "strong spiritual conviction." If I had not recalled that aspect of her personality since we last met, she asked me then to place them up front in my mind.

I'm not exactly sure how T took my laughter as a response. I smoothed over any ruffled feathers or misperceptions she might have had. I reassured her that my love life was perfectly intact and that I was most certainly calling as a friend. If she was at all uncomfortable, I would not resent it if she declined to meet with me. Tinisha, bless her heart, reassured me that she was not uncomfortable getting together with me. She just wanted to be clear. T did not want to disappoint my expectations, which she was most assuredly capable of doing "without batting an eye."

We met the following day at a coffee house near her apartment. After some chitchat, I got down to it. "T, I really have to thank you for meeting with me today. I know I sounded like a baboon on the phone, didn't I?"

She inched an eye half-shut. "Don't know if I ever heard a baboon over the telephone, Dr. Taylor, but most likely I have not. Hard to judge fairly." She smiled mischievously.

"I miss you, T."

"I have missed you too, Dr. Taylor, and that's a fact. We had fun, didn't we?"

"Yes, we certainly did."

"And despite that huge obstacle we had to work around!"

We tapped glasses, "To Bubba!"

"So, if this isn't a job offer or a romantic proposal, Dr. Taylor, what is it I can help you with?"

I rubbed the edge of my mug with my thumb and stared off into the distance through the window. "I don't know, T. It's like you and I went to war together." I raised a preemptive hand. "Now, I know it wasn't that awful, but we did work together, closely through some tough times and under a lot of pressure."

"So, what you're trying to say is that we have an *esprit de corps*. That we learned to watch each other's backs. Is it something along those lines?"

I perked up. "Yes, exactly." I shook my head. "When you have that bond, I don't know, you understand the other person in a way someone without that shared stress can't. So, anyway, I've really hit a situation, and I need to talk it out with someone who understands."

"Dr. Taylor, why didn't you just say you want to bounce a problem off a friend?" She placed a hand over her chest. "I *am* your friend. You know that. You still have a way of using twenty-five words to say one little thing, don't you?"

I smiled broadly. "Did I mention missing you, T?"

"You did, Dr. Taylor."

I twisted my face up conspiratorially. "I don't suppose there's any way of getting you to call me Noah now, is there Tinisha?"

"Short of me becoming a doctor myself, which is most unlikely for this withered up old bag of bones, no. Dr. Taylor it will remain."

I threw up my hands in defeat. "Anyway, I think I've gotten myself into quite a shi—"

She raised a finger. "Please remember, Dr. Taylor, that you're not talking to that thoroughly vulgar Dr. Black, if you would be so kind."

"Ah, sorry, T. Well, I'm in one proper pickle." As she listened studiously, I gave her a detailed, blow-by-blow account of the events that led to the most resent crisis. I included the part about how goofy old Kent Pearson turned into a Mafia kingpin and ended with him calling the campus police.

She sipped intermittently at her coffee but never interrupted once or even asked for a clarification.

"So," I concluded, "that's where I stand. The world has gone mad, all my accolades mean nothing, and I'm afraid for my job even though it is basically impossible for them to get rid of me."

As seriously as a hangman slipping on a rope around a client's neck, she asked, "Excuse me for being so bold, Dr. Taylor, but exactly how is what the university is doing to you not like the same thing old white men *always* do when they hold power?"

That was honest. "It's just, well, this time they're acting more suddenly and dramatically, I guess."

"Or maybe it's that it's happening to *you*. Remember, these are the same old white men who kidnapped my ancestors and shipped them over here as slaves. These are the same old white men who burned six million Jews in World War Two. I'm struggling to see the difference. These university bozos are a whole lot nicer than those other two bunch of deviants, if you ask me."

"Well, I guess if you place it in that context, this is small potatoes."

"Still, if it's happening to you, it has to feel pretty devastating."

"I got an amen for that, T."

She sat quiet for a while. I had the impression she knew what she wanted to say but was unsure how or if to express it. Finally, she cleared her throat and tilted her head. "You read your *bible* much, Dr. Taylor?"

That caught me by surprise. "No," I stammered, "not so much. I don't read it recreationally."

"Oh," she sat back, "so you sorta figure I'm reading Matthew or Mark as opposed to watching Montel?"

I flushed. "*No*, Tinisha. That's not what I meant at all. I'm so—"

With a relaxed look, she stopped me. "That's okay, Dr. Taylor. I didn't think you were the type a man to imply that, but I had to be certain." She rotated both palms toward me. "It's like this, Dr. Taylor. You read in the good book how mankind was vexed with demons. The Lord Jesus himself cast out many a foul demon."

"I'm familiar with the concept, T. Not sure how it pertains to my dilemma though."

She waved at me with an impatient hand. "Hold on. I'm getting there. I'd like to ask you one of those rhetorical-type questions, Dr. Taylor. Do you think Jesus said He cast out demons when they didn't really exist?"

I sat mute.

"'Course He knew they was real! My point is, nowadays, people figure the bible was speaking of the mentally ill or in metaphors. People just can't get their heads around there being a solid explanation for certain people behaving in certain manners."

"Are you suggesting the administration is possessed by demons, T? That's why they are acting this way?"

"Now where would you get a fool idea like that? I'm not suggesting anything of the kind. Heaven's sake, Dr. Noah, aren't you even *listening* to me?"

Wow. Was I confused. "Sorry, T. I mean, you were talking about..."

"I know what I was saying, and I now what I was talking about. Now, do you want me to finish my thought, or would you rather play twenty questions?"

"Sorry. Go on, please."

"All I'm saying is that sometimes there's a reason a group of people act the way they do. How else can a bunch of otherwise peaceful, mind-your-own-business folks get together and do the horrible things they are capable of doing?"

"Ah, I don't know. How can they?"

"How should I know? Do I look like Solomon to you?"

"But you just said…No, let me start again. T, I don't know how people can act badly together. Do you have any insights along those lines?"

She squinted and pointed at me with annoyance implied. "Are you making fun of me, Dr. Taylor? Because, if so, I surely don't appreciate it."

"No way, T. I guess I'm not taking your meaning."

"Okay, let me put it to you this way. You have just detailed to me how a bunch of previously boring supervisors have started to act in a crazy manner over a relatively short period of time. How is it you think that could happen?"

I finished her thought. "Given that people can be unwittingly influenced by unseen forces."

Tinisha nodded with utmost contentment.

"Well, let me…"

"No," she stated strongly. "Take a minute to think it over first. Then I want you to tell me."

"Okay. Weird, but okay."

I would give it a go. So, a large group of college administrators change in a short span of time. In five years, they went from being mousey, reclusive overseers into a hoard of focused, forceful, and likeminded maniacs. They started sounding the same, used the same buzzwords, and even began to dress alike. And their buzzwords made little to no sense, pure mumbo jumbo on a good day. And the horde said all it wanted was what was best for the university. Clearly, in their collective view, I was not best for the university, when realistically, someone like me was the poster child of who was good for any university. Okay, there was a horde that acted as one, but illogically so. At least they did not mean what they said. Maybe they just didn't *care* what they said. They wanted to lead, make decisions, and they wanted to punish people.

They acted in only their own best interests. They did not act in support of their subordinates, as seen by Bubba and me. They did not act in the best interest of the institution they claimed to serve either. So, they acted in support of themselves. That was not so unusual, right? Any for-profit company acts to line the pockets of the investors, not for the employees. They would even line their own pockets at the cost of devaluing the company. Krispy Creme, Enron, and countless other bosses ran their companies into the ground as they became personally wealthy.

Was what the university doing the same thing? No. There were no monetary gains to be had in academics. Presidents made embarrassingly high salaries, but there was not much wealth to be gained. It was not about money.

Why did people change into...zombies...no, animals...no, that was not it either. Normal people turning into...machines? Well, not machines, that was silly. They turned into, hive members? Hey, that was similar. A bunch of disparate grasshoppers became a colony of ants. Lame analogy. I was onto something though. Okay, normal, independent-minded individuals became a like-minded horde...of ants. Or zombies. They served neither the members nor the institution they claimed to cherish.

I flashed on the fundamental question. What did these drones serve? What motivated them? If they did not help the faculty, the university, or themselves financially, what was their allegiance to? Altruisms was easily eliminated from my list of choices. What did they labor to help, what cause did they forward? All they seemed to want was control, power for its own sake, and self-aggrandizement.

Whoa! Why couldn't those be their goals? Why did a child burn the wings off a bug? To see the wings burned and the insect suffer. The child had no global long-range vision and no greater motivation. He wanted to see suffering, and he wanted to be the one inflicting it. Control. It was all about the control of others, of systems, of the world.

What made people turn into a monomorphic clan with goals of control? I had no idea. Mass hysteria? No, that happened to the weak minded and did not lead to such conscious, sequential actions.

They could all have been brainwashed, like by a cult. No, that would be too slow and there was no way all those people could be affected.

Demonic possession? Hey, T brought it up. No, that was preposterous in the case of a university. If ever there were a group likely to be less cohesive than a bunch of college professors, it would be a horde of demons. Possessed academics would never accomplish one single thing.

How about, duress or blackmail? That would work, but who could hold a gun to their collective heads? Very hard to imagine anyone could hold such sway.

What made parts act against the whole, against the system that sustained them? Viruses. Viruses turned our own cells against us. The virus bred new viruses at the expense of the host with the sole purpose of reproduction. But that was silly. Maybe there was a virus for the common cold or cancer, but there couldn't be one for...for like-minded meanness.

Why couldn't there be? Well, there could be, it just—I don't know—sounded too weird. But so did demonic possession. Okay, it could be a viral infection. *Could* be. But, more likely, it was just a quirk of human nature. Put a group together, and all their compass needles just started to turn north. It was likely instinctive pack behavior and nothing more...unconventional. Kurt Vonnegut spoke of such types as psychotic personalities, or PPs, the persuasive guessers who ignored fact when expeditious. Their objectives were to make decisions, not caring in the slightest which choices were correct or incorrect, good or bad. PPs strived only to appear decisive, never in fear of the consequences. How could they? They were sociopaths.

I noticed that Tinisha stared at me most impatiently. "Yes," she said, "I did say take some time and get back to me. I kinda figured it would be before I died of natural causes, however."

"Sorry, T. Well, I came up with two reasons why unique individuals would turn into a bunch of bees, working together and stinging everyone who's not a member of their hive."

"Let me have the first one."

"I'll go with the least insane first. It could be an adaptive, instinctive behavior. Put a bunch of cavemen together, and they self-assemble themselves into a horde with one mind."

"So, now we a bunch of cavemen and cavewomen?"

"No, I just mean…"

"I think I know what you mean. I'm not crazy about that explanation. Kind of wishy-washy. What's number two?"

I took a deep breath. "Well, number two is a bit wacky."

Sternly, she said, "Let *me* be the judge of that, if you please."

I just said it. "It could be a viral infection."

"A what?"

I retreated. "You heard me. They could have contracted a virus."

"And instead of sneezing, they all want to fire you?"

In what ended up sounding more like a question than a statement, I said, "Yes?"

I heard her foot tap under the table. "I sat here long enough to learn a new language, and all you come up with is a virus or that's just the way it is?"

"Sort of." Then something she said came to mind. "At least it's no sillier than possession by evil spirits." I was hoping very much not to spit some teeth out after she loosened them with her fist.

Instead, she sat back, contemplative. Finally, she remarked, "You know, Dr. Taylor, you're right. There's no difference in substance between the two."

I wasn't so sure I was happy she agreed with me. My idea was extremely flaky. Of course, flaky didn't mean it wasn't true.

"So, there's a virus out there making every victim start thinking and acting in the same unusual manner, with goals that are contrary to what a normal human would have?" She began to nod. "I like it, Dr. Taylor! I mean, it's nuts, but so are you, and I like you."

"Thanks, I think."

"So, there you have it. You call on Tinisha, and she delivers. You're welcome, Dr. Taylor."

"But, even if it was a virus, that doesn't tell me how to stop it or what I need to do to prevent a personal disaster."

For one of the few times ever, I saw her become deadly serious. She looked at me with compassion and empathy and reached over to hold the backs of my hands. "Noah," she began gently, "what you are going to do is be yourself.

You are going to act like the proud, loving, and intelligent man that you are. You are going to pray for guidance, and you are going to be just fine. No matter what the outcome, you will be fine. You cannot let the virus take you, and you cannot let it change your soul. So, what you will do is hold your head high and proceed with honor, dignity, and integrity. If you arrive at some juncture where you do not know what to do or how to act, here's a little suggestion for you. Ask yourself what would Jesus do in this same situation. You will never go wrong if you act like He would have."

"Tinisha," I said, almost stunned beyond words, "I am not Jesus."

She raised her hands off mine and slapped them firmly. "A'course you're not! I didn't say *be* Him, just act like Him as best you can."

"But, my job, my career. What about those?"

She rubbed the backs of my hands again. "What about them, Dr. Taylor? In the end, they are not what you are. You've had jobs before and, if you leave this one, you'll have jobs again. Nothing is ever lost if you don't regret one minute of it. You'll move on knowing you are a better man for having experienced it." She smirked, something quite uncharacteristic for her. "What is it they say? Shoot them all and let the good Lord sort it all out? Let Him sort this out for you too, Dr. Taylor."

"But you don't really want me to shoot them, right?"

She withdrew her hand. "Not unless you really have to, Dr. Taylor. Not unless there's *no* way 'round it. If you think about it, most likely, Jesus Christ wouldn't blow a bunch of people away with automatic weapons." Then she winked at me.

TWENTY-SEVEN

Whether it was a result of corrupt human nature or nasty viral infection, it didn't take long for the Corporate Virus to demand my demise. The Monday following what became widely known as the Midnight Massacre and my latest confrontation with Kent, Jim Blodget called me. When I asked him what all the background noise was that was making him so hard to understand, he said he was at a bus depot. I had to ask him, as that struck me so odd, what was he doing at a bus depot. Jim said it was the closest place he could think of that still had pay phones. This explanation seemed ominous, so I followed up with the inquiry as to why he needed to call from a payphone. He said we could talk when we met. He told me to meet him at three p.m. at the first Starbucks Evan, he, and I had ever gone to. He didn't name the place or location. He coded me the message, as it was a place only the three of us would recall. As bizarre as the conversation had become, I had to then ask if Evan was coming too. He hung up the phone without a response. How very odd.

When I arrived at the Starbucks a little before three, Jim was sitting in the corner farthest from the entrance or windows. I waved to him, bought a drink, and joined him. Cautiously, I began. "This is all very cloak and dagger. When did you and I become spies?"

He toyed nervously with his cup a moment. "This is nothing to joke about. I took a big chance contacting you and coming here. Could you please respect that and be serious for a change?"

By that point in the collapse of my life as I knew it, I was used to my stomach dropping in my abdomen when I heard upsetting news. I fancied my stomach resided permanently somewhere down around my knees. Still, his remark sent it further south. "I'm sorry, Jim. No problem. So, what's this all about?"

He glanced reflexively over his shoulder, cleared his throat, then scanned the room. "You know when you emailed Evan and me, and you and I had lunch?"

"Yes. I remember the emails and lunch."

He hunched down and whispered, "Well, crazy as it sounds, I feel like I've been followed on and off since then. My office phone has been making funny clicks and snaps too."

"Why would someone follow you and eavesdrop on your phone calls?"

His only response was a silent, fixed stare and the visible grinding of his jaw.

"Jim, this is all getting so unbelievable and surreal. Look, I'm sorry if I dragged you into something ugly. But, I've done nothing wrong. You have to trust me on this. I am not involved in any criminal activity, period. The only thing I'm guilty of is speaking out against our insane administration when they need to hear the voice of reason."

"I'm sure that's what our founding fathers said about the British, but I guarantee that's no how the British saw it. Look, the reason I had to meet with you like this is because I was questioned."

There went my stomach, down closer to my ankles. "You were questioned by whom about what?"

"Who do you think I'd be grilled about, *Noah*?"

"Me?" I peeped.

"Yes *you*. Because of our friendship, I took the risk of letting you know about the investigation. They told me specifically not to contact you, so I'm being maybe extra cautious. Plus, they have no right to place a gag order on me, so to hell with them."

"Thank you for being such a good friend. Now, who is conducting what investigation concerning me?"

He scanned the room again nervously. "Two days ago, an investigator from Human Resources dropped by my office and asked about you. Yesterday someone named Kent called and asked a few more questions."

Stomach, next stop, the subfloor. "What sort of questions?"

He rocked his head and shuffled his shoulders. "About your loyalty, as to whether you had shared any subversive plans with me, and whether—I know this sounds stupid—but whether you were happy." He drew his left arm in while he shot his right upward. "Christ, they ask if you're an agent of destruction, then they want to know if you're happy. Craziest thing I ever heard of. Why would they care if you're happy, sad, or midway between the two when they are trying to prove you're an enemy of the state?"

"I have no idea." Actually, I did, but I didn't want to sidetrack our conversation. I needed to hear his story. "What did you tell them?"

He scoffed, "As little as possible without seeming like I was trying to say as little as possible. I did say you were happy, for whatever that's worth."

"Thanks. I agree with you that they are not concerned with my piece of mind, but thanks just the same."

He pouted. "I just thought you should know about this investigation."

"Seriously, thank you so much for telling me about it. They've said nothing to me about it."

"I thought as much. That's why they didn't want me to alert you."

"That way I'd have no time to prepare a defense, not that it would do me any good in the first place."

He squirmed in his seat. "Well, I told you what I came to tell you, so I'll be going."

Wow, that was fast. "You have no idea how much it means to me, you doing this, Jim."

"Hey, what are friends for?" I reached across the table to shake Jim's hand good-bye, but he hesitated. "Ah...one last thing..."

I finished his thought. "I will not contact you in any way, shape, or form until this is all behind us. You can count on it."

He looked to the floor. "I hate like hell to ask it of you, but...this is all getting so scary."

"Don't give it another thought, my friend. It's the wisest course, and it's

the one I will follow. So, until who knows when, you take care of yourself."
We shook hands, and he left quietly after admonishing me to take extreme
care of myself.

I had little time to ruminate over the meaning of the investigation. The
following day a letter was hand delivered to me by one of Dean Crumpler's
secretaries. The letter instructed me to be outside the dean's conference room,
located down the hall from his office, at nine o'clock the following morning.
I was told that I was to meet with Dean Crumpler and a "review board" about
certain personnel issues, though the specific issues were not mentioned. I was
to appear before them alone. No one, including legal counsel, would be
allowed to accompany me. My union representative, he assured me, would be
in attendance. That did not make me feel better. The scenario looked to have
all the positive trappings for me of the Salem Witch Trials, which were held
only twenty miles from where I read the letter. Convenient.

I was outside the conference room at 8:59. Uncharacteristically for me, I
wore a navy-blue blazer. To make the blazer look proper, I put on a collared
shirt and tie. Normally I am Mr. Casual, but I wanted the blazer for two
critical reasons. First, no matter what happened inside that Star Chamber,
they were not going to see me sweat. Second, its bulk nicely concealed the
two recording devices I had hidden in the coat. Why two? In case they asked
straight up whether I had a recorder. I could set one on the table and look
like an honest man. No way they'd ask if I harbored another. Plus,
redundancy was always a positive in a crisis.

Heads up, if you will, to anyone out there about to undergo a vivisection
similar to mine. A stop in the restroom was mandatory beforehand. An empty
bladder is a must, plus you can turn on your recorder in private.

Promptly at nine, the conference room door creaked open. One of Dean
Crumpler's secretaries, who was present to take notes, looked at me as if I was
a child-abusing priest about to meet Saint Peter. Then, wordlessly, she
signaled me in. I saw three figures seated at the end of the long conference
room table. Dean Crumpler was at the head of the table. I checked quickly to
see if he had a carving set in hand to use on me. Thankfully, he did not. To
his right was my old not-friend Dean Steve Martin. I presumed Martin was

not dead yet, but given his moribund appearance, I chose to wait and see before I decided for sure. To his left, as sure as there was a foul smell given off by sewers, perched Kent. His neck even crooked forward like the vulture he was.

Crumpler noted the time on his wristwatch. "Sit where you please, Taylor. I am certain you have some general impressions as to what this meeting is about. Let me fill you in on the specifics. Deans Martin," he pointed to Steve, "and Pearson," he pointed a pen at Kent, "and I have taken valuable time from our busy schedules to see if there is any way your career, which you have so recklessly and frivolously placed at risk, is to be salvaged. Not only have you wasted our time by being here today, but you have squandered the school's valuable and critically limited resources in terms of investigative and managerial time in gathering the facts." He set his pen down and buried one fist inside the other. "Am I expressing my perspective on this meeting in any unambiguous manner, Taylor? I hear you're one for clever repartee. Let see what you've got."

He was no man to toy with. Neither was I. I glowered at him. "Proceed."

Dean Martin was, it turned out, still alive. "Ouch! That was a good one."

He ignored the quip, and set his hand on a cardboard box that rested in front of Kent. "This is most of the evidence we've been able to gather concerning your sorry performance. I have to tell you right now that it tells a truly pathetic tale. As pay back for all the nurturing you have been showered with by this proud institution, I read only selfishness, spite, and skullduggery." He addressed Martin sideways. "Why, if this were feudal Japan, I think you would beg us to let you commit *seppuku*." That drew a parched, wheezy giggle from Steve.

"But, fortunately for you, Taylor, we do not have that as an options. I will not review the litany of malfeasances and departures from protocol and decorum you've suffered upon us. If that's all right with you."

I said nothing in reply. I did not even move.

"Tough guy, eh? Well, so am I. First, we will list off a few of the more egregious infractions you've committed, and then we'll hear your brief rebuttal, if you see so fit to further vaporize our valuable time."

You know, Ryker, I'm getting the distinct impression you don't like me.

"In no particular order, here we go. We see you threatened the life of my good friend Dean Martin. Bet that took some guts. I mean, you're forty years his junior, and he's a man committed to peace. You must have felt good about yourself. I also see you were guilty of insubordination, not once but twice. Strong work, son. Bet your mother is very proud of you. First you deliberately undermined the authority of your chairwoman, Dean Celestial at your very first meeting. Then I see you disobeyed a direct order from Dean Pearson to leave his acting office just last week. You threatened him with physical violence too." He patted Kent on the shoulder. "Fortunately, Kent here can take care of himself." Kent flashed a sheepish smile back at him.

He returned his attention to his notes. "I see also you suborned not only your department members but your close friend to organize rebellion." He scowled prodigiously at me. "You know, Taylor, I think you're the lowest form of coward I've ever had the misfortune to deal with."

Oh, there went my day. I've disappointed a pompous, blustering old fart.

"First you send emails to two old, trusted friends, begging them to be co-conspirators with you to subvert the proper authorities in charge of this university." He tisk-tisked me. "You're a dangerous man. Did you know that?" He smiled wickedly at his own cleverness.

"Next, at an informal meeting held by Dean Pearson last week after our new imperative was announced, you tried to induce those present to join you to, and I quote, "Bring down the walls of this false idol.""

That was more than I could sit through. I shot to my feet. I slammed my palm down to draw focused attention from these three stooges. "That, Ryker, is a damn lie." To Kent, I said, "How could you *dare* to present that lie as evidence? You idiot. There were witnesses who know I didn't say that."

Crumpler growled. "Sit down and shut up, Taylor, or I'll have you thrown out of your own disciplinary hearing. I said you could briefly rebut at the end of my summary. And, before perjuring yourself further, I think you should know Dean Pearson testified to the veracity of your words under oath at a deposition conducted yesterday."

I held my hands toward Kent. "There were witnesses—three of them. You can go to *jail* for lying under oath."

Crumpler started to speak, but Kent interrupted him with a light touch on his sleeve. "Dean Crumpler, I know you want to maintain the pace of these proceedings. However, if you would permit me, I'd like to take a second to clarify this point." Crumpler nodded consent. "Dr. Taylor, you made those remarks after any potential witnesses had departed."

What! "You're insane as well as stupid. If everyone had *left*, how could I stir them to rebellion with those words you invented?"

Crumpler retook the reins. "Taylor, we are not here to discuss or debate the evidence. We are here to present you with the facts and establish what we will do about them. Is that perfectly clear?"

I had enough manhandling and intimidation. "You listen to me, Ryker. You cannot confront me with 'factual' evidence that is easily to prove false. Furthermore, this is not a legal proceeding. I cannot perjure myself here, so get over yourself. Please try and allow the fact to enter your brain that I did not 'disobey' a direct order from Kent. I hate to be the one to break it to you, but we are not a military organization. Neither can I be 'insubordinate' nor can I 'suborn' a rebellion. Rebellions, as you clearly seem not to know, are against sovereign nations exclusively, not shit-for-brains administrations in at rapidly devolving university."

I could tell he was about to say something. "And before you say another word, I would like to remind you that I am a tenured full professor at this sorry excuse for an academic institution, and there still exists due processes that you are making a mockery of. I will not condone such disregard for the law and my rights. And you know, I am entitled to have union representation present. Your letter even stated they would be present, but you lied. I don't see my union representative present. I see only lies, empty threats, and three pathetic morons trying for the first times in their lives to achieve an orgasm by beating up on what they wrongly believed to be a defenseless man." I sat back down.

"You are so over," said Crumpler. "Even I feel sorry for you, you worthless crumb of bread"

Oh no, I'm a crumb of bread! My life is over.

He pointed at me. "You are going to regret each and every one of those

225

harsh words. Fact, not threat. To call me a liar to my face with witnesses? You're more a fool that I was led to believe. You want union representation? I'll give you your precious representation." He bounced up and down pointing at Kent. "Pearson is your new union rep. You called me a liar, yet there he sits. You are so over." He began to laugh hysterically. The man had lost his foothold on reality.

I protested righteously. "Kent can't be a union representative, you buffoon. He's management."

He slowly decrescendoed his guffawing and turned to face me. "Why, of course you are correct, Taylor. Kent is not your union representative. He's your *interim* union representative, until such time as a sanctioned election can be arranged. President Miller appointed Kent personally, since the former representative no longer works for this institution." He smiled like the lunatic he was. "These are desperate times. We must take desperate measures."

Kent stood and rested his finger tips on the table. "These proceedings have degenerated to a dangerous extent, Noah. As your union representative, I am going to respectfully ask Dean Crumpler if we can suspend this meeting until such time as you and I have a chance to better prepare your responses to these serious charges. Of course, if you waive the right to my counsel or choose to await the election of my replacement, I will certainly understand."

Crumpler slammed his fist down. "This meeting is over. But don't think for one second this process is over. Not for one second!"

I heard the trio cackle laughter as they faded away. Three things were crystal clear. First, I was in trouble. Second, I needed a lawyer, probably a whole room full of them. The insanity was only just beginning. It was impossible to predict its extent and its duration. So third, I needed to start job hunting.

TWENTY-EIGHT

Try and imagine what I said to Karan that night over dinner when she asked how my day had gone. *Oh, fine. My boss tried to crucify me but stopped just short of it. I think he wants a chance to torture me some more another day. How about your day?* Or maybe I could go with, *Ah, fine, fine. Well, I was threatened with termination based on trumped-up charges and false testimony. But the commute traffic was very light both ways, so there was an upside.* I had to say, dinner that haunting Thursday night was the lowest point of my life. Not only did I suffer mightily from the day's abuse, but I had to sit there and say nothing of it to my soul mate and best friend. As opposed to being consoled by my loving wife, instead, I outlined my plans for the backyard landscaping with particular emphasis on the sprinkler system. I also had to pretend to listen with interest as I learned that Karan's kid brother had been placed on academic probation at his high school for cutting too many classes. I was living a lie.

My pledge to keep Karan out of the fray seemed like juvenile posturing on my part, at best. The most crushing part was that someday, sooner or later, I was going to have to own up to the entire charade. The more substance of my life I excluded her from, the more, on my day of reckoning, I risked her refusal to even forgive me.

As I could not ask for her opinion on moving, I had to put out feelers for a new position very covertly. That, unfortunately, only heightened my sense of betrayal. Nonetheless, I was certain I needed to act. I suspected that the administration would fail in its attempts to terminate me. Still, it would have been foolish to wait and see if I survived before I began a job hunt. I was not dealing with rational people of good intent. Luckily for me, I was a hot commodity professionally and had many suitors banging at my door. I was sure to have no trouble lining up several wonderful job offers.

My first query was to Billie Ludo in San Diego. He had expressed interest in my transferring there. I knew San Diego well, loved it, and the school was world-class. A perfect fit. So, late that Friday morning I rang Billie. I used his cell phone number, so I got hold of him promptly.

"Billie! Hey, this is Noah Taylor. How are you doing out there in paradise?"

After the briefest of delays, Billie said, "Noah! Gosh, it's wonderful to hear from you. Unexpected too. I hope everything is all right with you and the family."

"Couldn't be better. How about you and yours?" Billie was pleased to report all was well at home. We chatted briefly about his publication in *Nature Immunology* the month before. Then I simply asked. "So, I was reflecting on how needy you were, trying to lure me to San Diego and all, back at the AAI conference."

I stopped to let Billie launch into his energetic sales pitch. All I heard was a low grunt. Odd.

I went on. "So, not that I'm on the auction block or anything, but do you have a moment to discuss the type of offer we're talking about here?"

More odd silence, aside from a scratching sound. Was he writing?

"It won't take the sun and the stars above, you know. Either one alone would be just fine."

Finally, Billie replied. "Well, darn it all, I knew you'd come to your senses eventually."

"Now, I'm not prepared to go that far, Billie. San Diego, yes. My senses, well, that's another thing altogether."

I paused for Billie to chuckle. Billie did not chuckle.

"Is there something wrong? Have I caught you at a bad time?"

"Heavens no!" he reassured me. "For you, I'm all ears. Well, I am sort of in the middle of an important meeting, now that you mention it. Ah, excuse me, Noah. Yes, Monique, what is it?"

A voice in the background spoke clearly and in a paced manner. "Dr. Ludo, your next appointment is asking how much longer it will be. He seems a bit impatient…I think."

"Monique, I'm on the phone with an important scientist. Tell the dean he'll just have to cool his jets a little longer." Heels clicked loudly, then Billie was back on the line. "Ah, where were we, Noah? Sorry about that."

"You were sort of in the middle of an important meeting in your office, after I reminded you that you were." I let a three-count pass. "Hectic pace out there in San Diego, nowadays."

"You bet it is, old pal!"

I cut to the chase. "So, any chance your school has a place for me?"

I had to hold the phone away from my ear, Billie responded so loudly. "Are you *kidding* me? Why, you're the biggest catch in the entire ocean."

"Why do I think I hear a 'but' somewhere in that flattery?"

He stammered awkwardly and tried to sound shocked. "A bu…but! Hey, Noah, what are you smoking out there these days? No one would be more pleased than me to be able to extend an offer to a man of your caliber. I…I just wished you'd called two weeks ago. I mean, what I mean to say, is that we sort of committed to a top candidate recently. What with the budget being what it is and all, I'm sure you understand? That's not to say I'm not going to cancel the rest of my morning and attempt to beat a fair offer for you from my administration. You know that much to be true, right, N…Noah?"

"Sure. I know exactly what you're saying Billie. Hey, thanks for your time. If you do hear anything, try and let me know, okay? Hey, lucky for you the dean is waiting to see you. You'll have a chance to ask him to somehow create a spot for me immediately." I hung up quickly, not waiting to hear Billie's inept response. That was one down. Two to go.

It was still early enough in the morning, Boston time, to ring Alain up in Toulouse. I knew I'd be taking a chance, as it was late on a Friday afternoon there, and he did live in France. But, most likely such a high-powered company with fortunes on the line didn't encourage employees to slip out a bit early any day of the week. Alain answered immediately. "*Bon jour*, Noah. It is great to hear from you!"

"Good evening to you, Alain. Did I catch you at an okay time? You weren't about to head home or anything, were you?"

Still joyous, Alain said, "Nonsense, Noah. It is barely past lunch, my friend. So, how are you and your precious little family?"

"We're all fine. The girls are growing so fast though. It makes me feel old every time I see how big they are."

"As we say here, *c'est la vie*."

"Truer words were never spoken. And as to your family? All is well?"

"Yes, wonderful! Thank you for asking. My oldest just won entry into the Sorbonne!"

"Congratulations! That is a great achievement. What is Pierre to study?"

"Alas, the poor boy is stricken with the ancient Romance languages, of all things. No effort on my part was able to direct him toward a more practical career path."

"Like, say, pharmaceutical research?"

"But of course! It has put food on his mouth and paid for his preposterously expensive education."

"Well, Alain, as I like to say, *c'est la vie*!" We both had a good laugh over that one.

"So, is this a social conversation, my friend, or is there another reason you called me for the first time in a while?"

"Ouch! Hey, I thought all the French were as cordial as they are chatty. You're beginning to sound like an American."

He feigned anger and roared his response. "If it is to insult me you have called, I must remind you of a Frenchman's reputation of having an explosively foul temper."

"Ah, now there's my Alain." After we stopped giggling, I got to it. "I'll be American and straightforward. I am calling to see if the job offer we discussed at the meetings is still on the table."

"*C' est incroyable*! The words I had all but allowed hope to die of ever hearing from you. But, of course! May I send my jet now to pick you up before you change your thinking?"

"Easy, slow down. I'm just asking. The house isn't packed yet. Heck, I haven't even discussed the idea with Karan yet."

Astutely, he wondered out loud. "If it were just the packing, I could bring several burly men with me on the plane. But, how is it, I wonder, that a man explores a major life change before discussing it with his wife? Ah, you are relocating with your girlfriend? This is fine with me, of course. I'm French. We do this all the time. But, *mon amie*, why not bring them both?"

"Not hardly. No girlfriend involved, I'm sorry to disappoint you."

"I am. But, I will recover soon enough. Having known you for such a long time, it is odd for you to conceal this call from Karan, no?"

"I'm not concealing the call…er, well, I guess I am. No. It's just that the call is very preliminary. No need to broach a tricky conversation with her if it's for naught, right?"

"I can see this point. Well, first off, please know that your transferring of your career here to the Centre de Recherche en Cancérologie will always be welcomed with open arms. There are, in fact, no need to discuss specifics. If you join us, I will pen such a ridiculously generous offer that my directors will most likely have my head! That said, Noah, what has led you to this call. I suspect there is something you have not yet told me." I could hear the mischief in Alain's voice. "Your girlfriend, she is pregnant?"

"I do not have a girlfriend, Alain."

"Well, a girl can become with child without the need of any emotional attachment on your part, I suppose."

"No pregnancies involved." I took a moment to compose my thoughts. "There's sort of a shit storm here at the university, and most of what's precipitating is currently directing itself toward me."

"Ah! Politics and intrigue. This is very enlightened of them, I must say. Your country is but young. We, however, have brought such activities to an art form." He corrected himself. "Ah, but now I sound insensitive. My apologies, please. What specifically is going on?"

I provided him a bare-bones version of the situation I found myself in. Most specifically, I reassured him on my honor, that I had done nothing to justify such poor treatment.

"Noah, you must keep in mind the differences between your world and mine. Here in industry, you may arrive naked and pass gas continuously. Similarly, you may be an anarchist and a pig. No one will say a word if you're bringing in the money. You, my friend, will have no problems in this regard, I can personally reassure you."

"Thanks, Alain. You're a good friend. No need to worry though. I promise I will wear trousers if I make the move."

"Suit yourself. Either way is fine with me. So, discuss this please with Karan and call me any time, day or night, with any questions you or she might have. Please know that I tell you as your friend, this is a marvelous place to live, work, and raise a fine family."

I thanked him again. It was good to have at least one outstanding option, should I decide the heat in this kitchen was getting too high. But, I wasn't at all certain Karan would go along with such a drastic move. She and the girls were very comfortable right here. To have them agree to a permanent move to France would be a challenge. Karan had spent a good deal of her younger years in Europe, so if she'd wanted to live there, she could easily have done that. Oh well, I'd jump off that bridge if I came to it.

That only left calling Grace Johansson. No time like the present, I decided. I was on a roll. I saved that call until last, as Yale was the clearest choice for relocation, if that was what it I had to do. Yes, it was two hours away, so the girls would have to change schools. But they could still see their current friends on weekends and holidays. For Karan, it would be fine. Yale was in New England, near her extended family, and that was all she really cared about in a location.

Grace answered after one ring. She was, as always, quick, businesslike, and to the point. "Hi there, Noah. Why am I not surprised you're calling?"

Even for Grace that was a new record for abruptness. "Okay, I'm officially stunned. What draws that remark from the master of tact and nuance?"

"Oh, come on, Noah. You're as predictable as the weather in hell."

"I'll reserve judgement as to whether that, too, is a compliment or not."

"Come off it. You and I go way back. Way, *way* back. I love you, you love me, and we can cut through the crap. Since you're so impressed with my prescience, here's another one. First you called that dirtball Billie, then Alain, and now me. Am I right?"

"Ah, Gracie, you're sort of creeping me out. How can you know any of that?"

"The academic community is a lot smaller than you seem to think it is. Word's been out on your school for several months and on you for at least a month. Well, maybe two weeks."

That did not sound promising at all. "What word?"

"Dude, you work there. The place has gone bananas, and I'm being kind. We all have friends. Which reminds me, thanks for calling me with the latest goings-on concerning your place. Not! Anyway, I know about all the stupid changes and corporatization that are coming down from on high. Your dean, he's a piece of work, and I speak euphemistically."

"And what's the word on me?" I was trembling.

"That you're not a team player and that you're under a microscope. You know all this, right? I'm not flashing the news to you, am I?"

I swallowed hard. "No, I'm just speechless that everyone seems to know my business. How can that happen?"

"I know you're a head-in-the-clouds sort of guy, but really, you should try to be more like the rest of us. If you don't look before crossing the street, bad things can happen. You know academics are hopeless gossips. If there's trouble somewhere, especially if people are suffering, we all want to hear it. More specific to your case, rumors are leaked to poison the well."

Grace could not see it, but I almost dropped the phone. "What does that suppose mean?"

"If your administration gets rid of you, they are doing so because they don't like you. They don't like you because you won't walk lockstep with them and energetically endorse whatever they produce from the depths of their bowel and hold up as a new idea. This makes you a threat. They worry that people like you will negatively influence others, potentially leading them against the bosses. They cannot have that. So, you're, at the least, persecuted and, at most, terminated on falsified charges. They, I don't know, will have painted you out to be a bad apple, right? Any of this apply to you?"

I said nothing.

"So, they want to make sure word is out so that no one else will take a chance hiring you. So, phone calls are made, words are exchanged at meetings, that sort of thing. Plus, what the heck? If firing you is fun, then making your persona non grata is good for even more grins and giggles. Who doesn't want more fun?"

I was dumbfounded. "I had no idea."

"Of course, you didn't, kid. Like I said, your head's in the clouds. There's not enough oxygen up there, I guess. So, that's how it stands. As to knowing who you called in what order, it was an educated guess."

"Do tell."

"You call Billie first, since you don't really want to go there. If you did, you'd have stayed there in the first place. If anyone has an ear to the ground more than I do, it's Billie. Knowing him, I bet he blew you off, right? Oh, I'm sure he didn't say anything you could point at, but I bet he put on a limp-dick song and dance, didn't he?"

"Remind me to never piss you off, Grace. That's exactly what he did."

"And he didn't offer you anything, and he never will. You're a liability, and if he advocated bringing you over, some of your shit might rub off on him. Then you called Alain, who offered everything including sleeping with his wife, his mistress, and his daughter to get you to join his company."

"Absolutely not. He said his mistress was strictly off-limits. Otherwise, let's say yes, he was anxious to have me emigrate to France and was willing to help where possible. By the way, I am beginning to think you have a pretty deviant mind there, Grace."

She laughed. "Ha! I should be so lucky."

"And why did I turn Alain down?"

"I'm guessing you didn't. You left things on hold. But you don't want to pull up stakes and move the family to the land of cholesterol and loose morals. So, after testing the waters, you call me next."

"You know, I've always wondered. Do you gals look into the center of the glass ball, or does the image appear all over the inside, like at Disneyland?"

"Cute, especially for someone in the hot seat you're in, buddy boo."

"If I don't laugh, I'll start crying."

There was genuine regret in her voice. "Poor baby. I'm sorry they're dumping on you."

"So, any chance Yale would have the likes of me?"

There was an uncomfortable silence. Then Grace began slowly, "I...I don't know. That's the honest truth."

"I'd expect no less."

"Especially out of me, right? But, I can tell you this. If you find you are no longer employed by your institution, you let me know. I'll see if I can move heaven and Earth to put together a deal. No promises, mind you."

"And you're not worried I might poison your well?"

"Wow, lame play on my metaphor there, champ."

"I can always count on you to call it like it is."

"What you see is what you get."

"Grace," I hazarded a guess, "sex with you, is it, you know, even fun? I sort of see you giving directions and providing a running commentary the whole time."

"Wouldn't you like to know."

"Probably not. The TMI might be too much."

"Anytime your curiosity gets the best of you, come on over with a bottle of cheap tequila."

"Thanks, but don't wait up, okay?"

"Your call. Anyway, if you get desperate, I can try and work some magic, but the world has gone fairly mad of late. Like you didn't notice."

"It has gone more than mad, Grace. It's really kind of scary." I was tempted to mention my idea about the Corporate Virus but decided not to. I didn't want my best chance to land a good job to wonder if I was losing my mind. "But thanks, Gracie, for your time and your honesty. It is at times like this that you learn who your true friends are."

"Thanks. Sorry again for all the crap you're catching. Is Karan holding up okay?" I must have delayed too long. Grace bristled. "You haven't told her? You are about to be thrown under a steamroller, and you pull a John Wayne. Why am I not surprised at that either?"

"I can't be the cause of inflicting so much pain on her, Grace. It's that simple."

"Well, as your friend, I hear you. But as another person suffering from estrogen intoxication, I can tell you you're taking a mighty risk. The chickens will, at the end of the day, come home to roost."

"At this point, I think I made my bed, so lie in it I must. I'll just have to see if it's in the house or in the garage."

"Well, keep me posted."

So, my situation was worse than I'd imagined. Not only was my administration looking to skewer me, they were blacklisting me too. The fact that it seemed to be effective was not a good omen. But, like a tiny leaf which plummeted over a roaring waterfall, I really didn't have much control over what happened next. I would just have to see what the Corporate Virus had in mind for me, if it had a mind in the first place.

TWENTY-NINE

We've all watched the grisly act of a cat playing with a partially dead mouse. As a child, I asked my mother why the cat didn't just eat the mouse. Why the cruel game? She said that it wasn't cruel from the cat's perspective, only the mouse's. And so it was to be with my persecutors and me. I waited over two and a half weeks to hear back about the aborted meeting and its inevitable follow up.

My chairman, Kent, stuck a cheerful head in my door one morning. "Hey, Noah, sorry it has taken us so long to get back to you about the Action Plan to help you better meet the challenges of the future so that we can all be happy and super-productive."

One sentence. He never even stopped to take a breath. I suspected he had been infected by a powerful virus. Maybe not needing to breathe was an effect of the Corporate Virus?

He went on. "So, expect an email in the next few days regarding the continuation of the session." He puffed out his lower lip and pouted. "I know we all want this matter behind us ASAP. Am I right?"

I continued my fixed stare on him with no other response.

"All right, then. I guess I'll be getting back to the old grind, then. Top of the morning to you, sport." He shot me a Boy Scout salute, turned, and whistled loudly as he perked his way down the hall. What comes after loathing? I had already transitioned from where I *disliked* Kent, to the point I *despised* him, and had, up to that juncture, *loathed* him. My negative emotion toward him had increased, so what descriptor came next? Oh well, I dismissed my quest for a new transitive verb. What good would it do? In no time flat, I'd need the next one after that one and on down the sequence of pejoratives for the waste-of-space.

The foretold email came the following Monday. I was to meet with Kent, some associate vice-chancellor I'd never heard of, and Dean Martin (I still couldn't read his name without a snicker). No Dean Crumpler, however. I wondered what that meant. I thought of calling Grace to find out, but what the hell did it really matter? Whoever's hand manipulated the six-foot pole inserted up my butt, it would feel just as unpleasant.

To allow me sufficient time to twist further on the knife, the meeting was scheduled in two weeks. It was scheduled, as I'm sure necessity demanded it based on everybody's hectic schedules, on Valentine's Day. Funny how a meeting so delayed needed to take place on a day that I might otherwise have been presumed to be happy on.

Kent also informed me that he was no longer my interim union rep. What had happened, I learned, was that once the union learned of that move, they cried bloody murder. He informed me that if I chose to have representation, Henry "Hank" Strazinsky was my man. Hank was a first-year assistant professor in Physical Education and our baseball team's first base coach. I was underwhelmed to his ability to pull my butt out of the fire based on his dubious credentials and made no attempt to contact him.

When the day came for me to be impaled—excuse me, for my help/love intervention—I figured, what the hell? I arrived fifteen minutes late. Who, in their right mind, would voluntarily show up to their own execution punctually? Maybe I'd even piss them off a bit. Who knew? I was ushered into the vice-chancellor's office, where Steve and Kent sat on either side of the man. We did not have to meet in a conference room. No, Vice-Chancellor Percival J. Spaulding's office was spacious enough for us and many others, if need called for it. A Swarovski crystal chandelier, Persian rugs, and a Louis XIV desk set a most affluent tone. All that for a measly vice-chancellor.

The boss started the meeting. "Good morning, Dr. Taylor. I am Dr. Percival J. Spaulding. I do not believe we've met. I am Vice-Chancellor for

Administration and Finance. Drs. Martin and Pearson are well known to you." The other two nodded silently in acknowledgement. He conspicuously inspected his Patek Philippe wristwatch. "You were told this meeting was to begin at ten, were you not? By my watch, it's a quarter past."

I leaned far forward in my chair and stared conspicuously at his watch. In as friendly a voice I could affect, I said, "And that's a very nice watch, if I do say so myself." One. Two. Three. "Is it a knock-off? Ah, no disrespect intended, mind you. I just cannot imagine how much a real one must cost." I looked wistfully at nothing in particular. "Imagine who would be so conspicuous as to buy the genuine article."

Percival J. was a slight man. He wore a Giorgio Armani silk suit that hung on him like a smock. His eyes were small and beady, suggestive of some species of rat. His recessive chin and undeniably prominent nose unfortunately only served to enhance the image of a rodent. His punctate round glasses so set off the impression of social ineptitude, I had to wonder if he wore them as some form of a joke. It was hard to believe anyone would be allowed to inadvertently buy such an unflattering, mocking set of eyewear unless they were positively insistent upon it. His voice was that of a tax auditor, concise, penetrating, and unwelcome. To sum it up, nature had not been kind to Percival. Further, he seemed unable or uninterested in correcting or modifying his plethora of shortcomings.

To my blatantly flippant evasion of his time chastisement, he pursed tightly his thin lips and squinted slightly. "I was warned beforehand that you seem determined to try and play us all for fools. Is my information correct?"

I slouched and crossed my arms. "Percy, are your roots in this fine university's School of Law?"

He balled up his fists. "I must warn you that I will not suffer disrespect. You would be well advised to curtail your Bolshevik tendency, lest you push me too far. As of this moment, that point is not too far off."

"Perce, I'm just trying to make this as easy on all parties as possible. My point is this. If you were familiar with the law, you would understand my response. You asked if I was determined to play you all for fools. My response is that the question is overly vague, that you've not laid a foundation supporting whether I possess knowledge of the supposition, and that I have not been qualified as an expert as to whether you are fools. I will, for now, keep my unqualified opinion as to whether you're all fools to myself."

He placed a hand over his pursed lips and began to massage them softly. I'm not sure if he'd ever been faced with as tough a case, with as malignant an attitude, and as recalcitrant a man as he confronted in me. I felt the entire lot of them had already decided my fate, so why make it any easier on them? Dead men had nothing to lose. We would see what Percival J. was made of. I was determined to make this messenger earn his wages.

Finally, he relented. "Dr. Taylor, we will dispense with further introductory sparring and get to the matters at hand. I have read the records and reports from all parties present at your initial meeting, where it was intended to set up an Action Plan to help you best excel in the bright future that stood before you at this proud institution. That meeting fell off the rails due to your boorish attitude. We are here today to complete the process of assuring your ongoing success, assuming that is still among your present goals and options."

I made no reply. He hadn't, after all, asked a question.

"On the table before you is a six-page document of which we all have identical copies. It is your Action Plan. It focuses our activities and codifies the steps you will need to make in order to achieve the restorative goals spelled out for you. It is a statement of what we expect you to achieve over the allotted period of time. Please read over the document in its entirety. After that, please let us know if you require us to go over any or all points listed."

I scanned the sheets. On it were outlined categories of infractions, appended with more specific accusations and their remediation. For example, under *Gross Disrespect for Proper Authority Figures* it cited my co-opting of Barbara Celestial's committee meeting. The "resolution" was to not show disrespect toward superiors, to apologize in writing to Barbara, and to attend, once more, the PHARS class I had endured not two months earlier. The steps listed were, respectively, impossible to measure, falsely assumed I impugned Celestial in the first place, and nothing but overt punishment. What could be more demeaning?

The rest of the charges were as nebulously phrased. Some were suggestive of events that happened but were either misrepresented or completely overblown. Some were blatantly false, such a Kent's assertion as to what I said to him after the others had left the room. Even if I tried my level best to complete each of their requests, it was going to be impossible to objectively prove I had complied with any of them. The endpoints were so subjective that they could always say I had not fully achieved them.

Other goal in my Action Plan were simply impossible to meet. I was accused of having an excessive number of no-shows in clinic. I was to correct this deficiency. Presumably, a provider with an excessively high rate of no-shows was manipulating his schedule to cause that to happen. The classic example was to repeatedly schedule dead patients, since they were quite unlikely to show.

I had been accused of the no-show business in earlier disciplinary sessions. Therefore, I was able to hand to each man present a graph. It demonstrated that the higher number of no-shows I had was solely due to the greater number of appointments I had compared to my colleagues. We all had around a five percent no-show rate. My performance was shown not to be substandard in the first place, but a purely statistical effect I could not correct.

To my proof of innocence, Percival replied for the group. "We will simply have to agree to disagree as to how we each interpret the numbers. The fact remains, you have the highest number of no-shows, and this number must be reduced. Period."

I rose to try and match his idiocy. "Okay, Percy, here's how I'll resolve this point. I will use all my vacation time exclusively on clinic days. That way I'll see no patients and I'll have the fewest no-shows of any provider. Here," I pulled a pen from my navy-blue blazer and flipped it in front of him, "you can cross that one off your list right now."

For the first time, Kent chimed in. Concerned understanding exuded from his every pore. With his hands folded gently on the table, he said, "Noah, you know as well as we do that your proposed resolution is both impossible, based on access demands, as well as insubordinate. I only wish we could get two points though to you. First, the seriousness of these matters. We are taking about your career here. Second, please know we only want you to be happy."

He looked to the two other inquisitors as he continued. "You know we believe that unhappiness is bad. It is ungood for two reasons. First, unhappy people are unhappy. Now, that's a fact that even you can't deny, Noah. We believe all unhappy people should be helped to be happier, maybe even to be happy. Can you accept that? We know making you happy is why we act here today, but do you also know it to be true of our intentions?"

I cupped my hands over my face and emitted a series of high-pitched sounds to reflect my incredulity. "Oh my gosh, Kent!" I removed my hands from in front of my mouth. "Do you ever, like, listen to yourself? I mean, on one hand, it's better if you don't. It would be damaging to your brain. But, dude, you do the worst impression of Mister Rogers I've *ever* heard. Though, by way of critic, Fred at least made sense with his treacle. You, on the other hand, say words but convey no meaning." I bent over laughing. "Ungood! You said ungood." I cackled some more. "That's not even a word. Oh... my."

I could not help myself. I laughed like a madman. All the anxiety, all my dread and fear shot up uncontrollably. I did not laugh for dramatic effect or to insult. It came from the bottom of my soul, and it felt very, very wonderful.

After a minute or so, a significantly perturbed Percival shouted at me. "Are you quite done with this childish display, Dr. Taylor? I am of a mind to summon an ambulance if you do not restrain yourself!"

I tried to say, "Oka...ha, ok...hu, okay...I got...I gotttt...I got this...ha..."

Kent spoke ominously. "Noah, this is a disgrace. You are putting on an act that not only degrades yourself, but us and the university as a whole. I must insist you stop show-acting and allow us to return to our efforts to help you be happy."

Well, that did it, now didn't it? Kent *had* to say the word 'happy,' didn't he? I launched into another volley of giggling, gasping, and sputtering. I finally regained control and could speak again. "Thanks to all of you. I really needed that. I'm...uhmmh...I'm okay now. I think we may safely proceed."

"One more outburst," warned Percival, "and I will clear this room, Taylor. You got that?"

I saluted. "You bet, judge. I believe Kent had the last correct answer, so he may select the next answer in Double Jeopardy, the round in which the dollar amounts can really mount up quickly."

Percival and Steve looked to Kent, who glowered at me with bestial, primal hatred. "Very well," said Kent. It's your funeral, and you're operating the shovel. My point is that we also believe unhappiness to be contagious. We will not allow unhappy people to remain among our happy employees. It is best for no one's good."

Wow, was he ever numb in the head. He used the words "good" and "happy" in the same sentence to a man who was so recently incapacitated by their very mention. To top it off, he had just fabricated another wondrous nonsense phrase. *Best for no one's good.* I was *so* glad I was taping the farce.

Kent was still speaking. "Your discord can spread to them. They would then become undeniable victims of our not protecting them from unhappiness. You see, Noah, in order for us to make certain everyone *can* be happy, we have to ensure that everyone *is* happy. Otherwise, happy workers might be dragged down to unhappiness, and that would be our fault." He gestured to Percival and Steve.

The first words from Dean Steve Martin were heard. "We will not allow you to drag this institution down with you, Taylor! Do you understand that, boy? You will not be allowed to destroy this entire university because of your selfish petulance and completely amoral lack of team spirit. We will not permit that to happen."

A cacophony of guttural sounds threatened to erupt involuntarily in the back of my throat. Fortunately, I was able to hold them all in check. Steve's regard of me had manifestly declined from complete disgust to profound revulsion. The man, I decided, did not like me.

Before Steve could rally to further righteous indignation, I raised a finger. "So, let me get this straight, Steve Martin. You're saying I, Noah Taylor, can singlehandedly bring down this *entire* university." Steve stood, attempting to control the dialogue, but I would not be stopped. "So, what? This place was founded like centuries ago? It employs fifty thousand people, and it has an endowment larger than the net worth of Africa. But, despite all that, I—little old me—can bring it all to an end? Crash-crunch?" I bobbed my head up and down exuberantly. "Wow! I mean, *wow*! I am one powerful man!" Conspiratorially, I leaned forward. "Are you three sure you want to mess with a force such as me, the man who can bring down dynasties?" I stood up and bowed.

Percival resumed control. "I can see this meeting is to be as unproductive and contentious as all your previous ones have been, Dr. Taylor. This fact is profoundly disappointing. I am forced to ask you to sign the Action Plan, and then we will adjourn." He pointed at the document on the table in front of me.

I sat back down. "Now, don't you boys be too hard on yourselves on account of all the failed meetings you run. Heck, you're trained academicians, not competent human beings. Keep trying, though, please. I'm sure with enough practice and dastardly intent, you will get better at this destroying-people's-lives business." I thumped the document with the back of my hand. "As to signing this mockery of justice, logic, and intelligence, well you can forget about that." I let that sink in a few seconds. "I looked all through our contract, union agreement, and policies and procedure manuals. I see no mention of this process at all. Therefore, the process you are attempting to foist on me does not exist. Therefore, I cannot be compelled to sign this refuse. If you would like, I can take this drivel to my attorney to have her look it over. I can ask her if she thinks I should sign the piece of shit. But, you know, fellows, I'm thinking why waste my time? The woman's going to say, 'Hey, client, don't sign that mockery of justice.' So, what do you say, boys? Maybe I'll just walk on out that door while y'all deflate your egos and jump back into the shower together?"

Percival stood, pushing his chair noisily along the floor behind him. "That is all the insubordination I will stand from you, Dr. Taylor. Please leave. Your refusal to follow a direct order and sign a mandatory document has been so noted in your permanent personnel file."

I elected, then and there, to remain a dignified adult and take the highest road. These were my bosses, and I was a responsible family man. So, I held my hands above my head and waved them around wildly. "Oooooh! Now I'm scared. Not my *permanent* record. Just don't tell my mother, because she's dead." Then I felt bad. My mother was alive and well. But, darn it all, it sure sounded better that way.

Sorry, Mom.

THIRTY

I had most definitely accomplished one thing. The administration was as mad at me as a nest of hornets pounded by a stick on a hot summer's day. Another certainty was that I would not backdown, I would not recant, and I would not—repeat *not*—leave voluntarily. I was going to, for better or worse, come hell or high water, stand my ground. At least on paper, I had rights that protected me. Matters of challenged tenure have frequently been litigated, and the protection afforded by tenure had generally been upheld. The only way I could be railroaded out was if there existed a nebulously termed "good cause." Such cause had to be able to stand up in a court of law. Clearly, I had done nothing to rise to that level.

Still, Kent had lied under oath as to what I had said, so I was on most shaky ground, at best. If they were capable of whipping up false testimony against me once, they sure as hell were capable of doing it twice. They were capable, in fact, of just about anything. I was fairly defenseless. There I stood, alone and resolutely manning the battlements in defense of a castle that I knew would almost certainly fall. I was poised, either foolishly or heroically, to go down in flames or rise higher than imaginable. Okay, maybe not rise super high. Maybe take a serious beating but come out of it with a pulse?

It was time to come clean with Karan. Something bad, worse, or worst was about to befall me. If I waited until after the axe fell, it would be all that much worse, that much harder, to tell her. I elected to bring her up to speed at home as we sat quietly together after the girls were in bed. I also chose to do so on a day when she appeared to be in a good mood. No need to try such a perilous feat when she was otherwise already upset. I may have been crazy, but I was not insane.

I was a firm believer that the best way to enter a body of cold water was to just jump in. To wade in slowly was too painful. Karan was resting her head on my shoulder as we sat on the couch in the den. We both stared lazily into the flames of the blazing fire on a frigid New England winter's day. I began softly. "Hon, there's something I need to discuss with you. I don't think you're going to like it very much, but I think we need to talk."

She shifted her head slightly. "Oh, that sounds ominous. What's her name?"

I popped my shoulder up, tossing her head up gently. "It's not about a girl, silly."

"Sorry, what's *his* name?" She giggled softly.

"It has nothing to do with my interactions with any form of human anatomy located below the belt. I'm trying to be serious."

She nuzzled up closer. "I apologize for toying with you when you were trying to be serious with me. I'm all ears."

Grimly, I began. "Well, it's about work. The university seems to have declared war on yours truly."

Playfully, she said, "Yeah, I kind thought you stopped talking about those 'idiots' pretty quickly. So, what's been happening since we last spoke about them?"

"They have turned the heat up on me significantly. Remember that dried up old wreck of a dean I told you about, Steve Martin?"

"Who could forget? He was pretty rough on you."

"Well, last week he told me he would not allow me to bring the university down with me. Can you believe that? Steve imagines that I am capable of destroying the whole place if the diseased limb named Noah Taylor is not sawed off."

"You'd have to try awful hard to destroy the whole place, wouldn't you? But, maybe if you really set your mind to it, who knows?"

"They're all just so out of touch with reality. It's frightening."

"Heinlein said, 'Never underestimate the power of human stupidity.'"

I harrumphed. "Smart man."

"So, spill the beans."

I told her of my two disciplinary meetings, my confrontation with Kent after the Midnight Massacre, and even my coffee with Tinisha. I related, with trepidation, the conversations I'd had concerning job relocation. She listened intently. About midway through my recounting, she lifted her head off my shoulder and rested back into the cushions, but she never took her eyes off me. She displayed absolutely no emotion the entire time. It was like I was telling her about my first summer at camp when I was ten, not the dismemberment of my career that I had kept secret from her.

I brought her up to date, but I did not include the part where I said my mother was dead. She really loved Mom. If I'd joked about her being dead, I'd be in for a world of hurt. Plus, I wanted to portray myself as the victim as much as possible, and victims worthy of empathy don't make wise ass remarks like that one.

After I had finished, I was somewhat suspicious. "You seem to be taking this better than...I don't know, better than you might have."

She nodded seriously. "I can do righteous indignation, if you want. I'm pretty good at it, you know?"

I grimaced and winced simultaneously. "Yes, I believe you could do a bang-up job, but no thanks. Calm and nonviolent are perfectly fine with me." I breathed deeply. "But, seriously, you're not mad at me? Mildly pissed? Minimally disappointed, even?"

"That's probably the last thing you need, trouble at home to match your trouble at work." She sipped her tea. "Plus, it's not like this is all out of nowhere. Like I said, you clammed up a little too abruptly for me to think it had all just blown over. No, I figured you'd tell me what you wanted me to know when it was time."

"You know, you're one remarkable wife."

She smiled playfully. "Yes, I know. Lucky for you."

She looked back to the fire, then to the other room, and then back at me. She was holding something back. "What," I demanded, "are you not telling me?"

"Oh, nothing, really." She looked to the ceiling, then to me. "Maybe I had a bit of a heads-up from Jill Blodget."

I raised a challenging eyebrow. "What kind of heads-up are we talking about here?"

"Well when I realized you were holding back on me, I sort of called Jill and asked if there was any reason she could think of for you to do so. She did a little pillow-talk investigation and reported back to me."

I pointed at my wife. "Why, you little Mata Hari. Here I'm carrying the world on my shoulders, and you knew it all along."

She pinched up her nose. "Yeah, kinda sorta. It serves you right, you know? Holding out on me may seem chivalric to you, but I think it was a little selfish and definitely childish."

"Touché. I deserved that. Actually, I'm getting off the hook pretty easily, aren't I?"

She slapped my arm firmly. "Yes, you are." She pointed a finger under my nose. "And don't you ever try something like that again, bucko. You got that?" She set as sinister a look she was capable of in her eyes. "Otherwise, you may well find yourself waking up with extreme pain between your legs. Do you take my meaning?"

I saluted. "Yes, ma'am."

"So, what are you going to do? What are *we* going to do?"

I shook my head in frustration. "I have no idea. The administration has made it abundantly clear that they want me gone. They have the money to pay lawyers and the silver coins to purchase false witnesses, so they actually stand a good chance of getting what they want. Still, it's hard to just walk away from the best job I can imagine when I'm so close to key breakthroughs and we live in a community that we love."

"Well, honey, let's break it down in reverse. First, do you want to relocate anywhere?"

My gut said no, but my brain screamed to get the hell out of Dodge. I weighed what I wanted versus what was best for both my family and my piece of mind. "No. There's no place I'd rather be that where I am. While I might settle for elsewhere, I would not prefer it."

248

She smiled energetically. "Great, so we have established that. So, working back some more, what are you willing to do to stay? Are you willing to cave in and play nice, or is that too much for you to stomach?"

"I think we both know that's a rhetorical question, right?"

"Yes," she said, "but we need to at least draw that line in the sand. So, you don't want to leave, but you don't wish to cave. That doesn't leave room for options then, does it?"

"No," I had to admit, "it doesn't. You seem to have framed the picture pretty well." I rolled a balled fist in the other palm. "So, it means I dig in my heels, prepare to take a vicious beating, and hope that I'm left standing in one piece."

"Doesn't that sound like fun?" Then she rose, faced me directly, and curtsied. "Would you be so kind, sir, as to allow me to accompany you in this dubious endeavor?"

I stood and embraced her. "It would be an honor and a privilege to have you along on my fool's crusade, my dearest."

THIRTY-ONE

The next few days passed quietly—too quietly in fact. If an avalanche was going to smite me, I would just as soon prefer it was a fast moving one. I was a ball of nerves, sweating continuously with the pulse rate of a frightened mouse. I had trouble sleeping, thinking, and eating. Karan encouraged me as much as possible, but there was really no way I could chill. That was their intent, right? Making me twist on the knife as long as possible was fun. Well, fun for them.

Finally, I received an unannounced visit from a dowdy, severe looking woman of advancing years. It was clear in her body language that she had never experienced a happy day in all her entire life. Something malevolent about her suggested she made it her mission in life to see that no one else did either. The permanent scowl that sculpted her lips did not waver as she lifelessly informed me that she was the personal secretary to the president of university, the big kahuna himself. The fact that the president chose to work intimately with so dour a soul spoke poorly for his general style. She never actually stated her name, or his for that matter. I was informed, with all due foreboding, that I was to present myself to the president's office in one hour's time.

"Come alone," was the last instruction wheezed by the old witch. After she left, I smiled inwardly because, by that juncture, I kept a navy-blue blazer in my office at all times.

One hour's time was about midway through the lunch hour. It seemed an odd time to begin a meeting—or a beating—but, when the big man summoned, there was nothing to do but go. I gave Karan a quick call to inform her of the latest development.

Her last words to me were, "Good luck, honey, but you won't need it. You'll be magnificent. I feel sorry for the old codger already. And, most of all, don't worry about us. If we stay, we stay. If we go, we go. As long as we're all together, nothing else matters in the least."

That was wonderful to hear. It truly helped soften what was likely to be a pretty painful encounter.

After I hit the restroom, donned the blazer, and started both recorders, I headed over to the main administration building. I arrived fifteen minutes early and was impassively instructed by a more junior, yet no less unpalatable, female secretary to take a seat. Ten minutes after the hour expired, the desiccated secretary rose, on no obvious cue, and walked over to me. "The president will see you now." She extended an arm in the direction of the ornate double doors I assumed marked the opening to his office. In all those renditions of *A Christmas Carol*, there were apocalyptic images of the Ghost of Christmas Future. The ghost always pointed Scrooge onward to a presumably horrific destiny. Yeah, that's kind of how she looked. I don't think it was unintentional on her part.

As I neared the doors, they mysteriously parted. The nightmarish visage of the hag who had summoned me walked backward as the doors parted. As soon as I was past the threshold, she strode past me, turned, and backed out silently. The doors closed ominously. She smelled strongly of mothballs and disdain.

As my eyes adjusted to the subdued light, I could make out a tall man who stood at a broad window. His back was to me as he looked out, his hands together behind his back. The bright light that streamed thought the window made him difficult to see. With no instructions or indicators as to what I was to do, I began to walk tentatively toward a set of lounge chairs stationed in front of the president's desk.

Halfway there, without turning, the president called out, "Yes, please be seated, Dr. Taylor. Make yourself as comfortable as the situation allows."

251

Okay, that was about as creepy a way of saying "have a seat" as possible. After I sat and crossed my legs, I expected the president would join me. At least for the moment, he remained at the window.

He let me fidget at least a minute. "Inspiring view. I never tire of it. Winter, spring, summer, or fall. It is always so stately, so proud out there."

I made no reply, especially since I had no idea what an appropriate response might have been.

After another uncomfortable silence, the president spoke softly but clearly. "I have summoned you here today to finalize the resolution of your unfortunate situation."

"Then, respectfully, sir, I must voice my concerns that due process may have been denied me."

"Due process? You fancy we owe you due process, Dr. Taylor?"

"Again, with all due respect, yes. That is why it is called 'due' process, is it not?"

He rose once to his tip toes. "You will find I am different than those who have dealt with you up until now, Dr. Taylor. I, for example, do not discuss or debate matters with peons such as yourself." He continued to stare out the window. "Neither do I entertain any of the sarcasm or disrespect you are now so infamous for. Your rapier-like wit will, therefore, remain sheathed. Do I make myself clear?"

I rose to the affront. "Or else what, sir? In a challenge, there must logically follow an 'or else.' My wit will remain sheathed or else what?"

"Now, there you go doing precisely what I told you not to do. Dr. Taylor, you will make no other attempt to banter with me." Finally, the man turned to look at me squarely. "As to your pathetic or-else-what taunt, let me simply promise you, young man, that you do not wish to, nor can you afford to find out what consequences I can invoke. If that is not word enough to the wise, then you are a greater fool than I have been led to expect." He waited a moment to see if I had a comeback. "I thought as much!"

Slowly, he walked over to his desk and gently sat down. Knitting his fingers together, he said, "But, a bit of housekeeping. First, I am President Ater. Second, most people in your position conceal a recording device. Some idiots bring two, so that they can proffer up one and still record my words. In your instance, Dr. Taylor, I will make no suppositions. I will ask *once*. Turn any and all recording devices off. And none of your 'or else what' lip." Ater sat back impatiently.

Screw him. I sat back impatiently as well.

"So be it. But, know that I am a man never to be trifled with. Third, I am here to *speak* and you are here to *listen*. Fourth, when you leave here today, your case will be closed. I will reach a final decision, and it will be the end of your tale. Do not impoverish what remains of your dignity by hoping that reconsideration, recourse, or redress are possible. They are not. Furthermore, litigation on your part would be, in a word, suicidal."

What was *that* supposed to mean? Put nothing past them, those were my watchwords.

"Finally, it is critical that you not feel buoyed by that fact that you are a world class talent bringing my university many large grants. These matters are both inconsequential. My university has more than enough talent and money. What you might or might not bring to the table in that regard is ant piss in the sea, Dr. Taylor. Nothing more than that." He rested back and tented his fingers together. "This is the point where a lesser man would ask if that is all clear and whether you had any questions. I am not such a man. I shall proceed."

"As a background, let me state that my father once sat in this very chair, president of this fine university. My grandfather was a provost here, and my great grandfathers were senior deans. My family quite literally built this university. He who builds a thing owns a thing, wouldn't you agree?"

I said nothing.

"I mention this so you understand how deeply I am committed to the ongoing success of this university. I will do anything legal and most things illegal to protect my university's future."

From a very dark corner of the room, came a gargly thick voice. "And, don't forget to mention the university pays your absurdly generous salary."

Up until that moment, I had thought we were alone in the room. I strained to make out who sat obscured in the darkness. By the deep, discordant sound of the voice, it could not have been Kent, Crumpler, or Martin. The man looked indeterminately old. He was twisted into a plush leather chair with his head well below the top. His feet rested on the nearby coffee table. The longer I looked, the more I saw he was puffing and chewing on an enormous cigar. Why had I not smelled that earlier? I guessed the office was just so big and I was so distracted that I had not noticed. The dark man seemed to take no notice of me. His smile directed toward Ater, and it was positively hateful.

I pointed feebly at the figure. "Who's he?"

Ater answered me swiftly. "Never you mind, Dr. Taylor. Please keep in mind that you are only present to listen. You may not ask questions. If it becomes germane, he will be introduced."

He addressed the dark figure. "Up until such point he will, I trust, remain as silent as the grave." Back to me, Ater went forward. "My point in mentioning my personal history is this. I will see to it that this institution excels, period. Nothing shall harm it, and anything that even minimally degrades it will not be tolerated, especially when it comes from within. Your contempt, your negativity, and your ingratitude are just such insults. Further, the little carnival side show you have forced us to conduct sickens me. Do you hear that, Dr. Taylor? It just plain sickens me.

"Consequently, I have before me but two options. First, the one I strongly prefer and the one which is likely inevitable, involves you leaving this university in the very near future. Voluntarily is easier, but involuntarily is perfectly fine with me. Second, you can honestly and sincerely promise me you will be a model citizen of this university. Then you might remain. I would expect you to assume an active role in leadership. You would, of course, support all our ideas and programs with enthusiasm and vigor. To that end, I am prepared to offer you, contingent on your pledge of complete and full rehabilitation, the office of Senior Associate Dean of Research, effective immediately. Your salary would begin at five hundred fifty thousand dollars annually, with the certainty of significant raises as you demonstrate good faith and task orientation. Those are your two options, Dr. Taylor. Which will it be? I am a busy man, as is our guest in the corner, so decide promptly. Please know that whichever choice you make is all the same to me. You are welcome to join us, or you are most welcome to leave us."

I was the very definition of speechless and dumbfounded. I did not know where, in my confusion, to move. That potentate had just offered me two such diametrically opposed and incompatible choices that it was surely impossible I heard him correctly. You're fired or you're promoted to the upper echelons? That hardly seemed to represent a responsible solution to the university's problem. Fired or demoted, yes. But fired or favored? It made no sense. Perhaps it was just a cruel trap? Ah, that had to be it. Ater was going to see me grovel contritely before he put a bullet right between my eyes. What should I do?

"Dr. *Taylor*," Ater said, "I will give you just one minute longer to decide."

Could he be serious? I could stay, stay and be well compensated, not to mention brought into the fold, just that easily? I—

A harsh rustling arose from the corner occupied by the dark man. I looked to see him stand slowly from his chair. I could almost hear his joints creak and his bones grind as he rose. I looked back to Ater, who appeared both annoyed and worried by his silent partner's movement. But those emotions were as incompatible as the offer he had just made me.

The man in the dark arched his back, and began to saunter toward me. He arrived at my side and patted me on the shoulder. "Taylor, let's you and I take a walk."

Ater was indignant. "What's the meaning of this? This is a simple disciplinary meeting. You insisted on attending, but I allowed you to do so *only* as an observer. You are not part of this process and will kindly remain out of it.

The man from the darkness eyed Ater with mild bemusement and more than a little contempt. He pulled up his trousers and then turned back to me. He spoke with convincing authority. "A walk, Taylor. Now." He looked to Ater. "We won't be five minutes, Stuart. Just sit there quietly and try not to get into any trouble while I'm gone. All right?"

I could see Ater ached to say something in response. He raised an indecisive hand, even began to stand, but then flopped back into his chair with clear resignation.

The stranger of darkness took my elbow and directed me toward the exit.

As he opened one door, he pointed. "You can hang your coat there, Taylor. It'll be there when we get back. I promise. Besides, it's such a lovely day outside. Spring is in the air."

It was twenty-seven degrees out there with a wind chill factor five degrees lower. Nonetheless, I did as told. As we cleared the president's entrance, I began to ask the man who he was.

He pinched strongly on my elbow. "Outside, Taylor. We'll talk outside."

Still holding my elbow, we waited for the elevator, descended to the lobby, and braved the cold outside. At least I braved the New England cold. Whoever the man was, he had a three-piece wool suit on. Far better protection than I sported, plus he enjoyed the advantage of insulation with copious blubber. The freezing wind hit me like an angry bull. I found it hard to breathe at first. The man released my arm and began walking casually down the granite stairs. I followed without prompting.

When we were both on the walkway, he spoke casually. "A pleasant walk, a pleasant talk along the briny beach. Wouldn't you agree, Taylor?"

By then my arms were folded across my chest, and I was beating at my back in a vain attempt to keep warm. "I find it neither pleasant nor beach-like in any way, sir. I doubt very much Lewis Carroll had this scene in mind when he penned those words."

He leaned over and smiled wryly. "You know, Taylor, you're probably right."

My teeth began to chatter. "If you don't mind my asking, who are you, and what is the purpose of this death march?"

He thumped me on the back soundly. "Death march! I like that." He pointed to my face. "I'm beginning to like you despite yourself, Taylor."

That made no sense. "Did you mean to say despite *myself,* not *yourself.*"

He shrugged. "Which ever you prefer is fine with me." Oh great, I was to freeze to death accompanied by the Riddler.

"Again, sir, who are you and why are we enjoying each other's company at this icy moment? Won't the president be upset we're keeping him from whatever it is he does all day?"

He pointed at me again and smiled widely. "I can see how that mouth of yours got you into so much trouble." He chuckled to himself. "*Whatever it is he does all day*. That's a good one, my boy! Gun to my head and knowing Stuart as well as I do, I don't think I could tell you how he occupies his narrow little mind."

I turned to him and raised an eyebrow. "Are you certain you should be talking about your boss in such an insolent fashion?"

With a truly amused look on his face, he pointed back toward the building we'd just left. "You think I work for Stewie? Now there's a perverse and disturbing thought."

I had grown numb all over and was highly impatient. "Look, I can see you don't do well in answering compound question. So, let me dumb this down. Who are you?"

He thoughtfully considered my words. "A natural enough question, I suppose. Not important, but not unexpected. I guess I'd ask the same, if the tables were reversed." He looked at me resolutely. "You may call me Limo."

I oozed as much sarcasm as I could muster, poised as I was so close to a hypothermic death. "As in 'a long car one rents for special occasions'?"

Limo jutted him chin forward and frowned pensively. "I suppose so, but not in that context."

I stopped walking, which forced Limo to do the same. I turned to face him squarely. "So, your given name is Limo? Or is your last name Limo?"

He responded obscurely. "Which ever you prefer, Taylor. Either way is fine with me."

"You know that you are most irritating to converse with, don't you?"

"I'm liking you more with each passing moment. You're quite the catch, Taylor."

Quite the catch? *Never mind*, I told myself. Let that odd one go. "And what is it you do here at the university, Limo? What position allows you the singular joy to order the president around and safely call him names?"

He placed his palms flat on his chest. "*Me*, work *here*? No, no Taylor, I don't work here. I'm more of...oh, how shall we put it? I'm more of a consultant. Yes! A consultant, or an advisor." He began to walk again. "Is that good enough for you, Taylor? Or will you be requiring a copy of my CV?"

What a peculiar fellow. "Okay, another simple question. Why are we having this private meeting?"

"Why, indeed?" was his infuriating reply. "Well, it's because you intrigue me, Taylor. Yes, that's it. And as I mentioned earlier, I'm beginning to like you too."

"Not a very forthcoming answer, but I'll accept it for now. Okay, why were you there for my pummeling?"

He flapped his hands in front of himself. "No, I wasn't there for your pummeling. And before you can once again accuse me of being vague and evasive, I'll clarify that. I was there on other business. Stuart mentioned something to the effect that his next meeting was to be a waste of his precious time dealing with a 'feckless malcontent.' He also used the words 'crush the pissant with my boot heel,' if memory serves." He wagged a finger at me. "I think he meant you, Taylor. Stu no like you." He briefly giggled at his cleverness. "I was mildly intrigued, so I told Stuart I'd stay to watch."

"Just like that? On a whim, you decide to attend a life-altering meeting, and Stuart, President Ater, agreed?"

Smugly, he smiled. "Stuart didn't say anything. He just looked pissed off and directed me to the chair you found me in."

"So, you don't work for the university, yet you boss the president around like a henpecked spouse. Ater doesn't seem like an easy pushover to me."

He rolled his thick cigar in his mouth. "That depends, my young friend, entirely on who's doing the pushing." He pushed at the air in front of him. "You, Taylor, didn't have enough footing or weight to accomplish that endpoint."

"Look, Limo, I'm certain that as I look back on this walk, it will seem very charming and enlightening, but I'm actually freezing. What are we hoping to accomplish here?"

"Hey, I would have let you wear you jacket if you had coughed up those recording devices. I could care less if you tape Stewie's ramblings. But me, well, I'm a private sort of guy."

"What makes you think I...?"

"I'd rather not play slap and tickle with you, Taylor." He eyed me up and down. "You're not my type."

"Okay, Limo, I'm literally dying to know. What is it you wish to tell me? I figure I have about five minutes before death ensues."

He swung his head back and forth. "I have three goals, Noah, to be perfectly upfront. First, as I said, I am intrigued to meet someone who Stuart so despises. Second, and my biggest motivation, is simply to piss off Stuart some more. I pulled you out, and he was powerless to stop me. It is an excellent object lesson for that moron. Third, for no particular reason under the sun, I decided to give you a small leg up."

I scrunched my face in doubt. "A leg up? How does that play out? Are you going to reveal Ater's Achilles heel to me, maybe give me some salacious tidbits hiding in his closet to use against him?"

He held out an admonishing palm. "No, nothing that valuable." He looked at me intensely, penetratingly. "You're not worth *that* much, at least not yet."

"So, what leg up?"

"Stuart is a small-minded, provincial dimwit. He's a pompous control freak. Oh, how he loves to throw his weight around. You know the type. He would steal candy from a baby, as long as he thought he could get away with it. He'd go out of his way to step on a bug or stab an ally in the back." His face pruned-up with disdain. "He's a greasy, pointless jerk. So, I take an interest in you, we have a private conversation, and Stuart goes nuts try to figure out why. You see, Noah, a man like that doesn't take a piss without making a complex plan with contingencies. So, pulling you out for a brief walk accomplishes two things. One, I can be a turd in his punchbowl of power. Helps keep him in his place. Second, when you sit back down with him in a few minutes, I've have given you a tiny advantage. Stuart will worry himself sick, all worked up over whether you know something that could hurt him. Maybe he won't be so high and mighty, the self-righteous mushroomhead."

"Thanks, I guess. But, Limo, I'm still knocking myself out here trying to figure out who you are and where you fit in the picture." I hesitated a moment, before I braved, "If I had to guess, I might just think you're a gangster or something, or maybe someone from the government."

He looked at me angrily. "A word of advice, Taylor. Never guess a stranger is a gangster. If he wasn't, you'd sound extremely foolish and hurt his feelings. If he was, you'd sound extremely dangerous and probably end up dead." He eased his expression. "And the government? Why, that's three times as insulting. Fortunately for you, I am not that either. I am a consultant, nothing more, nothing less. I help men like Stuart better run their petty empires. A word to the wise though. Never assume or suppose without great foundation."

"Okay, you're a consultant. But, what do you get in return? What's in it for you? You obviously have nothing but contempt for Ater. Money is only a good motivator to a certain point."

He shrugged. "What's in any of this for any of us, Dr. Taylor?" He reached over and tapped me on the chest. "Today I was privileged to meet one of the last men of principle stupid enough to stand his ground against the machine. You're one of the handful left who risk happiness, security, and the possible wrath of his loved ones to not be pushed around."

I stopped walking and turned toward him. "Limo," I had to ask, "why would Ater offer me that second choice, the one with all the money and power? It makes no sense. It flies in the face of all logic."

He studied my face a moment. "Sorry, kid, you're on your own with that one. If you don't know, I'm not going to be the one who tell you. The fact that you are even talking about it indicates to me his ploy might just work. Look, Taylor, I must be off. It has been nice talking with you."

He began to walk away at a goodly clip. To his back, I shouted, "Which offer would you take if you were me?"

He halted and rotated his torso to look back at me. He rolled his cigar a moment. "I'm *not* you, Taylor. Never have been, never wanted to be. Therefore, the question is mute. I can tell you what you *will* pick, but I cannot say what you *should* pick. Our frames of reference are too far apart."

Limo turned and left. To his retreating image, I said, "You certainly do love to speak in tongues, don't you?" To myself I mumbled, "Riddles and tongues. What good are you to me?" Curious, at that moment, though I could hardly see him in the mist, Limo looked like he raised a finger in some coded reply. How very odd.

He left me standing alone in the frigid, biting wind. I jogged back into the building and stopped over a heating grate. It felt wonderful. Not until I could feel my feet again did I make the pilgrimage back to Ater's office. No sense turning myself in before I was as composed as I could be. When I returned, the outer and inner secretaries were absent, and Ater's double doors were spread wide open.

I tentatively entered his office, uncertain what to expect. Ater was alone in his office. That time, I looked around carefully to be sure no one else lurked in the shadows. He was at his desk, hands folded, and looked straight ahead. It was like he was waiting for a train. When I was halfway to his desk, I cleared my throat loudly. Ater snapped back to attention.

"Ah, Dr. Taylor. It's about time. I'm a very busy man." He looked comical as he peered cautiously behind me to check if Limo was back too. Devoid of his prior bravado and pretense, he asked, "The man you left with…is he gone?"

I thumbed over my shoulder. "Who, Limo? Yes, he's gone."

"Who the hell is Limo? I'm in no mood, Dr. Taylor, no mood for this at all."

I rested my hands on my hips defiantly. "Limo is the cigar-smoking mafioso I left downstairs, St—President Ater," As understanding stuck him, relief poured over him like a warm summer's rain. Seriously, he looked like a man on vacation in the tropics under an inviting waterfall lolling a sunny day. His blissful moment was, unfortunately, all too brief.

Energized now with renewed confidence and sternness, he pointed to the chair I was in before. "Very well. Sit, Dr. Taylor. We are well past the time I've allotted for this nonsense. Hence, I will ask you directly. Which choice is it. Will you depart this proud university or will you commit yourself to joining and upholding its mission?"

Limo said he'd given me a small leg up. Why not see what that might buy me? I slumped back in the plush leather chair and tapped a finger on my lips. After a few seconds, I asked with intended ambiguity, "Just like that?"

Ater's unyielding expression was disturbed, ever so subtly, by a wave of tense ripples. "Yes, just like that." With clear trepidation, he took a deep breath. "Why wouldn't it be just like that?"

As he finished, his eyes were closed tightly. Wow, did Limo have him by the balls, or what? I pressed his uncertainty a bit harder. "So, just those two choices? No wiggle room present here whatsoever?"

"Why would there be any new options on the table? I adjourn this hearing a few minutes for a bathroom break, you finally return, and there's been some change? Did some facts come to light in that brief respite that might suggest that other options might be viable, Dr. Taylor?"

If nothing else, it was entertaining to see how humbled he was before Limo. Too bad I had nothing substantive to lever him with. Oh well, it was at least nice to see the man cower. "What are you babbling about, Ater? How could my taking a short stroll with Limo change any of the lies, half-truths, and fabrications you've brought to bear against me?"

He reassumed his air of immutable disapproval, invulnerability, and superiority. "How *dare* you take that tone with me, Taylor. Need I remind you that…"

I stood. "Stop. Put a sock in it, Stewie!"

He jerked his head back like I'd actually struck him. Nice.

"I have indulged your bellowing and posturing for as long as can be expected of any sane man. I'm really tired of your act and your petulance. Here's the deal. You forgot to mention the third option. The third option, which I most assuredly will take, is that I walk out that door." I pointed to the still open doors. "I am going to return to my daily routine. I will wake up, come to my office, do my job, and return home afterward to my loving family. I will continue to repeat those activities unless some legal force compels me to desist. Your words are nothing to me. At best, they are the prattle of a spoiled child long past need of a spanking. As far as your offer of a promotion, I would ask with all due respect, that you shove it up your ass as far as your overly tight sphincter will allow." I knew that nothing I said could not damage my case anymore than it already was. So, I tossed in, "Finally, as much as I hate to break a promise, I refuse to give you a kiss on the lips good bye. Next time you see Limo, tell him he won the bet. Meeting adjourned."

I felt remarkably pleased with myself. I stormed out of his office and into my very uncertain, tumorous future.

THIRTY-TWO

"You just *had* to throw in the kiss thing, didn't you?" Karan's left hand massaged her closed eyes.

"Oh, come on," I defended hopefully, "you have to admit it was pretty cute. Besides, what more can he do? Fire me twice? Come over here and pee in our swimming pool?"

She removed her hand and looked at me incredulously. "You never are going to grow up, are you, Dr. Peter Pan?"

"Not if I can help it. I have always failed to see the upside." My debriefing proceeded nicely. She understood beforehand that matters were out of my control. Consequently, there really weren't any surprises in the meeting that needed discussion. Well, aside from Limo. She focused a lot on that mysterious figure and his role. She made me repeat the dialogue we exchanged, over and over.

Finally, I had to admit, "I just can't tell you anything concrete about Limo. He was intentionally elusive and evasive. I tried Google searching a bunch of variations of his name, but came up with nothing. The fact that Ater didn't recognize the name I used tells me he gave me a phony name in the first place."

"I just wish we knew more about him. Who he really is."

"Limo's involvement in the meeting was very minor, hon. He made it clear he was not familiar with my case beforehand. He cannot have played any real role in the administration's actions of late. So, why are you so fixated on the man?"

"It's just that I seem to remember my father and uncles discussing a man like Limo with my grandfather, years ago. I couldn't have been older than ten. I don't think they even knew I was listening in. It was at some family gathering. They were at a big table with lots of people I didn't know. I recall being frightened by the man they described, like he was the Boogeyman or something." She shook her head. "Oh well, silly me. I can't put too much stock in a childhood memory, now can I?"

"I'm still stuck on that outlandish job offer Ater made. I mean, assuming he was not just toying with me, it makes no sense."

She tried not to let her incredulity seem overly judgmental. "Really? It seems pretty obvious to me why he'd make that offer. I mean, think about it. You're a boil on his backside. You are not a team player. You're a freethinker and speak your mind freely. So, there's two ways to shut you up. One, the obvious one, is to deep-six you. The other is to force you to join the fold. Don't you see?"

"Of course, I see that aspect of his offer. But, how could he even begin to imagine that I'd change fundamentally just because I had a title and a big salary?"

"Keep in mind the exact conditions he placed on you. You would have to become not just a nominal part of the establishment. You would have to comply with two very critical demands. You'd have to support all their ideas and programs, and you'd have to be active in leadership. That is to say, you couldn't sit on your hands and collect the money. You would no longer be free to speak your mind. You would be required to actively implement their will. Don't you see what would happen?"

I twisted my upper lip and nose. "Probably not as clearly as you do, I'm guessing."

"One of two things would happen. One, you couldn't fake it or take it. You would continue to say things they didn't want to hear and generally not play nice in their sandbox."

"Which is what I sort of think would happen on day two of my ascension."

She agreed snidely. "Most likely."

"And the second alternative?"

"You'd become one of them, just like Kent has."

"No," I protested.

"Yes. If you start walking like a duck and quacking like a duck, pretty soon, you might happily become a duck." She folded her arms across her chest. "Either way, he's solved the problem. That's why he couldn't care less which alternative you chose. Leave or become a zombie. Either way, he washes his hands of you. After all, he can replace you in a heartbeat, and he has plenty of zombies already, so he's not worried about the outcome either way."

I resisted. "No. People can't react like that. I could never become one on them. He has to know that."

"Have you spoken with Kent recently?"

"But he's just playing that role. The man's never taken one thing seriously in his life. He has just decided that acting like a mindless drone beats honest work, so he plays along."

"Are you sure, honey, or is that wishful thinking on your part? I think he drank the Kool-Aid." She shuddered. "I think he is marching in step because he believes in the company. The man you knew is gone, honey."

"Really, Kent? He's a dark overlord now, not a cynical hack?"

She shrugged. "No way to know. That's what I think, but you've been dealing with the man closely, not me."

"Karan, you know me better than anyone, including myself. I understand a corporate structure prefers certain uniformity and that no leader wants to hear dissent. That said, why would those in charge demand zombies? To excel, some element of critical input should be welcomed. It's healthier for the corporation, in the end, isn't it?"

She reached over and stroked my hair. "My poor, idealistic husband. First, you are assuming the people in charge of a big organization actually cares about the organization they lead. They don't. They care for power and money, money and power. They want to make decisions but are positively indifferent as to the outcome of those choices. Most of all, they want to control others' lives. The institution is nothing more than a means to their end. It's a rented mule to abuse as they see fit, advancing their personal agenda at the animal's expense. What do I always tell you power and money are good for?"

I looked to the floor. "More power allows you to get even more power. More money allows you to get younger women with larger breasts."

"Not inspiringly noble goals, but goals nonetheless."

"What's the second thing? You said that first I assume incorrectly what their motives were."

She hardened her expression. "I'm afraid the second point makes me sound cynical, and you know I hate cynical."

"But?"

"Do you know why zombies eat your brain?"

I shook my head slowly, rather blindsided by that question. "No, Karan, I do not. Why do zombies eat your brain?"

"It's not because they're hungry, and it's not because it's the only food they can live off. They eat your brain to make sure no one smarter than them is in the room."

Yikes. "So, you mean to say dumbed-down cooperation is preferable to constructive criticism?"

"Infinitely so. Which is exactly why, my dear, sweet husband, you could never be one of them."

"Well that just sucks. Here I was hoping to ease into their inner circle. There'll be no destroying others' lives on a whim for me."

THIRTY-THREE

At that juncture, there was nothing for me to do but to wait for the other shoe, or more accurately the piano of my career, to drop. I had said my piece. Ater had made his position perfectly clear. I assumed the next thing I would hear would be a notice of termination for cause or a summons to a hearing that concerned such an action. My attorney was certain it would be the latter, which was good. The more light of day the case was subject to, the better, as far as she was concerned.

I tried to go about my days as usual: clinic, lab work, and family time. But, truth be told, my mind was always elsewhere. I worried what would happen next and how I could react to whatever that was. I knew fretting about how to skin fish had yet to catch was completely unproductive. But, understandably, I found it impossible not to dwell on my predicament. Karan was a beacon of love and support, but her magic only worked when I was with her. When we were apart, which was most of the time, I was a burbling, ruminating hot mess.

A week had passed and still I had no inkling of what was to become of me. I half thought of calling Ater and asking what was going on, but that would only document to the evildoers that they were successfully getting to me. Finally, on a Friday early in March, I received a short email from Kent. He instructed me to be in his office late the following Monday. Solo attendance was, he specified again, mandatory. I called my attorney and she advised it was best to go along with the mandate. She would, however, be there sitting outside his office for moral support, whatever that was worth. Otherwise, she and I would simply react appropriately to whatever happened.

I was getting good at showing up for disciplinary meetings. It was a skill I never, in my wildest dreams, thought I'd ever acquire. I was beginning to develop the same familiarity with mismatched confrontations as the school bully was with sitting before his principal. The fact that my punishment was fully undeserved did not help lighten its impact. So, on time, wearing my navy-blue blazer, and with two recording devises ablaze, I presented myself to Kent's office.

He was using the department chairman's office near mine, as opposed to his dean's office in the main administration building. I was unsure if that difference meant anything, but I was about to find out. Harold, the sour, disapproving secretary who worked for the Interim Dean Kent had been transferred to this venue. It was as unpleasant to see the sourpuss again.

As Harold held the door open, Kent rose from behind his desk. He came around to my side and shook my hand in a most manly manner. "Noah! You don't mind if call you Noah, do you?"

As sardonically as possible, I said, "You have been for twenty years, so I guess one more time should be all right."

He was perfectly oblivious to my snark. "Fine, fine, Noah." He pointed to a chair. "Please be seated. Make yourself comfortable. Can I get you something to drink?"

"No, Kent. You can simply get to it, please."

He pretended to be hurt. "Well, all right. But, I hope this meeting can move in a more constructive direction than our last." He returned to his side of the desk and sat down. It was then I noticed none other than Limo sitting smugly the corner, cigar again between his lips. Kent formally began, "Noah, as you are aware, you have been having significant performance deficiencies that we have been looking into and discussing with you. Today's meeting..."

I ignored him altogether. I pointed at Limo. "What are you doing here, Limo? Twice in one lifetime cannot be just an unhappy coincidence."

Kent reacted as if I had struck in the forehead by a cricket bat. His face jerked comically from Limo, to me, then back to Limo. He pointed between us with equal vacillation. "You...you two know each other? Li...Limo?"

The sight of him so discordantly flustered did my heart good. It was so odd, however, that Limo hadn't mentioned me to Kent. And apparently, the man was known as something else not only by Ater but by Kent as well. He was a mystery cloaked in an illusion.

He ignored Kent as fully as I had but pointed his cigar at him. "I'm here for Pearson, Taylor. Not for you."

"Me...m...you're here for me," Kent stammered, "Konrad?"

"Quiet, Pearson. I am not talking to you. When I am not talking to you, never open your mouth. Is that clear?" To me, Limo took a decidedly patronizing tone. "I mean to say I'm present to help Dean Pearson. Your meeting happens, by purest chance, to be on his agenda the morning I was asked to mentor the pinhead. He is to learn at the foot of the master for a spell. My hope is, at least it was, to remain detached and silent if at all possible."

"Why does that not make me feel better, Limo-rad?"

"Toy with me at great risk, Taylor."

Kent finally found his tongue and asked Limo only slightly less moronically, "Why..."

Limo placed a finger over his lips to signal silence.

Kent stumbled verbally but plunged ahead. "If you knew Dr. Taylor, you might have mentioned it to me."

Limo spat on the floor. "Pearson, I agreed to be here today to help you become a more effective tool. My motivations and actions past that are none of your business. Please proceed."

I was not about to allow that. "Hold on, Limo, or whatever your name really is. I'm not so pleased with this setup. If he gets a helper," I pointed to Kent, "I should too. My attorney is right outside. It's only fair."

Limo reacted as if I were mute and invisible. He stared intently at Kent, trying to spur him into action. Finally, Kent stated, somewhat uncertainly at first, "Noah, my advisor is not a part of this meeting, in and of itself. He is here only to observe my performance, generally. Any input he might provide will have no bearing on the meeting's outcome." He was beginning to sound more authoritative and in control. "I am confident that by the end of our meeting you will agree his presence was inconsequential. You will come to believe you had no reason to object."

"I find that very hard to imagine. But, it's your sideshow, so we'll use your freaks." I was surprised to not get a rise out of Limo. Focused man.

Oblivious to my slight, Kent became very serious, even paternal. "Noah, as I was saying, unfortunately, you have had significant challenges in your performance metrics of late. Further, your team spirit has been sorely called into question, not to mention your TEIM spirit, which is equally, if not more, important." He clasped his hands together and shook his head, to reflect deep regret and remorse. "Were these the only issues facing us, we would naturally hope to rehabilitate you and retain you as a viable member of our TEIM's Future." A soulful sigh was peppered in. "But, in the course of our investigation into your unwanted tendencies, we have, with the profoundest of shock I might add, unearthed unacceptable activities—criminal activities."

"Now, the Catholic Church may tacitly condone child abuse by covering up the malfeasances of her employees, but this university *cannot* and *will not* stoop to that level of duplicity." Great, I was no better than a child-molesting priest.

I started to object vehemently, but Kent raised a hand. "Please hear me out. After I've made my statement, you will likely see that any preliminary objections entered at this point will be mute."

"As part of the investigation headed by me personally, felonious activities on your part have literally crawled out from under a rock." He bristled judgmentally. "It is hard, as a friend of yours for so many years, to believe the extent of your illegal behaviors, which were, prior to my investigation, fully unknown and unsuspected by any of us."

Limo cleared his throat. Kent was applying it a bit too thick. Or maybe Limo simply had some phlegm. In any case, Kent reached for a stack of bound documents. With papal severity, Kent said, "I have here *sworn* affidavits obtained at depositions from several of the injured parties. Copies are being simultaneously presented to your attorney, as she is seated in my waiting area. These documents detail actions on your part which will shock and, frankly, disgust any prudent individual."

That was it. "Kent, cut the melodrama. What lies are you trying to proffer now?"

He looked emotively sad and burdened by the weight of his knowledge. "I can understand your anger. When a criminal is publicly confronted with their acts, it is only natural for them to strike out in fear. Your pain is, as an old friend, my pain."

He then provided as genuine a rendition of heartfelt empathy as only a consummate actor might. "I'm here for you, buddy." They were taping the meeting too! He was performing for a greater audience. That's why jerk was being so warm and caring. Son of a thousand fathers.

"You are already familiar with the charges Dean Steven Martin made against you." He held up a rather thick stack of documents in a folder. "These are his words, the words of a frightened, frail, old man describing how you threatened to beat him to death." He paused for dramatic effect. "This is the testimony you force me to have to disclose at deposition, based on the incident my first day on the job as your new chairman. You made it impossible for me to not divulge the threats you made against this institution that dark, dark day. On a day so full of promise, so full of hope, you told me that if the changes planned by Dean Crumpler were not stopped, you would blow up the administration building."

He seemed barely able to speak, he was so upset. He gathered up superhuman strength to continue. "I did not want to believe you were capable of such an act of domestic terrorism, but I cannot deny your very words."

I exploded. "That is it, Pearson! Stop talking and start listening. You are going to rot in prison for this perjury, I'll see to it if it's the last thing I do." Wait, what did I just say on tape? What accusation could they twist that remark to mean? "By that, Pearson, I mean to say I will avail myself of all legal means to redress the slander you have promulgated against me." Okay, nice save.

He looked at me solemnly. With anguished remorse, he could barely continue. "Were that these the only damning accusations leveled at you, dear Noah."

"You have got to be shitting me, Pearson."

271

He reached over and plucked a Kleenex from a box on his table. He daubed at the corners of his eyes. Oh, how I hated the man. He discarded the tissue and picked up an even larger volume of documents. His hand trembled as he haltingly spoke. "This is…it's the most shocking…the most profane testimony of all. Noah, how could you?"

"How could I what, Pearson? You haven't sprung the next set of lies on me yet?"

He could hardly speak, but he somehow managed to march ahead. "This is testimony taken yesterday by me in this very office, Noah. This very office!"

"All right already, you buffoon. What have you fabricated now?"

"I have here *sworn* testimony from Dr. Evan Miller. Dr. Miller is on faculty here in the School of Medicine and was a former friend of yours, Noah, was he not?"

I said nothing. That came at me completely out of left field. I needed to think about this a minute.

"Dr. Evans broke down in my very arms…"

My blood stopped circulating as it froze solid in my veins. I had a terrible feeling, a foreboding of doom…

"Distraught as he was to be forced to relive the harrowing moments inflicted upon him by you, Dr. Taylor. As you know, Dr. Miler is a member of the homosexual community. We at this university advocate for and practice an environment of complete non-discrimination on such matters as sexual preference. Dr. Miller is prepared to issue a complaint with the local police and swear in a court of law that you, Dr. Taylor, forcibly attempted to rape him."

I no longer lived. I no longer breathed. My heart did not beat, and my thoughts did not spark. There was, in that instant, an eternity of nothingness all around me. I had never and would never exist.

Reality flooded back through my eyes with the force and volume of a tsunami. I was pinned back in my chair as my head snapped back.

I had been dead.

I was still dead.

Evan was prepared to charge me with attempted rape. I saw, in an instant, where Kent was headed. I saw all of their conspiring, all their cajoling, all of their lies, and all of their promises.

I saw myself as I stood in an open field. My eyes were closed, but my head was tilted upward. An atomic bomb screamed down ten feet above my face.

All the other charges were unprovable or, at best, petty and contrived. But, to have a man on a witness stand point a finger at me in accusation. There was no way out. Evan would decry, very convincingly, that I had held him and wrestled with his clothes. I would say I had not. He said, he said.

But, given all the other charges, I would appear less credible in the eyes of any rational juror. They had me as bereft of hope and recourse as a bleeding man dog-paddling in the middle of the Pacific Ocean surrounded by sharks.

How could a man I once called friend, a man of sophistication and sensitivity, make such a blatantly false and hateful accusation? The though itself felt like boiling acid poured over my head. It was not conscionable. It was not imaginable. It was not defensible. But, they knew all my trite pleas of innocence would arrive stillborn to the ears of a jury. *Damn you, Evan, how could you?*

"I am forced to ask again, Dr. Taylor. How could you? I thought you were a happily married heterosexual man. What's more, you are the father of two, up until now, adoring daughters. What are they to think seeing their father on the television accused of such heinous acts? I am not ashamed to admit, Dr. Taylor, that you have shaken me to my very foundation with this deplorable act."

Again, Limo could be heard to clear his problematic throat.

"What, and I must insist you speak, have you to say in your defense?"

There was nothing to say. There was only the doing. I spoke in a lifeless monotone. "What is it you want me to do, Kent?"

Despite the facade he had affixed to his persona over the years, I could see then the mischievous, if at times hurtful, Kent of old. It boiled up inside of him with anger and lust and it was insatiable. He felt such ecstasy, such raw sexual gratification at his moment of ultimate triumph over me that he was unable to contain it. Saliva dripped from the corners of his lips and tears streaked his cheeks. The look in his eye was so primal and so removed from my existence that I could not begin to comprehend it. Whatever unrestrained, unbridled joy he had experienced up until that moment of his entire life was insignificant, irrelevant, in comparison to how he felt then and there. I cannot say how I knew it, but I was never more convinced of a truth in my life. Whatever residual vestiges of the human, of the physician, he had once been, were ejected with his subjugation of me. They were lost and forever forgotten.

It took Limo's third throat clearing to bring him back to the present. His hand tremble eased, and his eyes shrank down to a more normal size. Finally, Dean Pearson spoke. "Excellent, Dr. Taylor. That is a very constructive, forward-looking attitude to take. I can see there is hope of redemption for you by the sincerity and depth of your contrition."

As low as I was at that abysmal moment, I could not help but grieve that there would be no redemption possible for Kent.

"Here's one option our legal eagles have come up with that may save us all a world or hurt and regret." He slid a single sheet of paper across the table to me. I scanned it. It said, in effect, that in exchange for my immediate and uncontested resignation, the university would forget about all of my acts that "might be construed as 'sublegal.'" Further, the university guaranteed that formal charges would never be leveled against me by Dr. Miller. Both the university and Dr. Miller were charitable and forgiving by nature, the letter read. The knowledge that I was willing to leave without a struggle confirmed to both parties that my remorse was genuine and lasting. They would, naturally, retain the option of legal recourse if I manifested "reversal of contrition" at any point within the constraints the statutes of limitations placed on such matters.

It was a perfect, clean kill. I had been bloodlessly exterminated.

"Your attorney has already read this document. The relevant portions of several depositions have been provided to her by one of our lawyer-types who has joined her outside these doors. Hang on." He fingered the intercom on his desk. "Harold, can you ask Dr. Taylor's lawyer to step to the doorway, please?"

The door opened and my ashen labor lawyer trembled in the opening.

"As Dr. Taylor's attorney, do you have any problem with him signing this document of his own free will, should he chose to do so?" asked Kent.

"I am not familiar enough with the facts…" she started to disclaim.

"Thank you for the preface, but yes or no? Would you counsel Dr. Taylor *not* to sign this document, despite any burning desire me might have to do so of his own accord?"

Almost inaudibly, she replied, "I would not physically stop Dr. Taylor from signing the document if he feels it is in his best interest and feels he's…"

Kent loudly interrupted her, "Thank you. I believe you've made your position abundantly clear. Harold, please help it leave."

Some of my shock had dissipated. I was obviously beaten, and badly so. There existed no option for me other than to sign the letter. In the end, above all, I had no desire to remain in the employment of a group of demons who could so happily do such horrific injustices to a fellow human. I scribbled my name on the designated line and slid the paper back to him. Again, ingenuously cordial, he said, "I think this is as amicable and fair a resolution to a potentially discordant process, don't you, Noah?"

"One last question and I insist you answer it. What happened to the promise you made me at your wedding, after I saved it from going up in flames? You swore to me *you are my friend forever, Noah Taylor. Please know that. If there is ever anything, however small or however large, that I can do for you, please let me know. It will be done.*" I stood back from his desk. "I want to cash in that favor here and now, Kent Pearson,"

Kent looked at my like the ghost that I was. He stared only briefly, them returned his attention to the documents on his desk.

Kent was fully gone.

All I said was, "I will remove my personal belongings from my office and lab tomorrow. Otherwise, let me state for the record that I hope never to see you nor speak to you again, Kent. Your parents, who are both in heaven, are at this moment crying. They're wishing you were never born. I am so glad I am not you, Kent. So glad I will never have to carry your weight."

With perfectly defensive selective hearing, he was able to reply cheerfully. "No worries, Noah. As you leave my office, you'll find a couple of burly security guards. They have kindly taken the time to pack up your personal belonging. They have kindly offered to carry them to your car as they escort you off site. Please leave your ID badge here with me, along with all your keys. Your access codes and passwords have already been invalidated, so no worries there either. You are perfectly free of this place. Scot-free, in point of fact. I'm almost jealous."

He developed that effected, pensive look I'd grown to hate. He spoke with solemnity. "I'd really like to wish you the best in terms of future luck, old boy. I'd love to bid you a fond farewell and the best of luck finding gainful employment elsewhere. I really wish I could. I cannot, however, actually do so in good faith. I mean, where would you go? Certainly, not San Diego." He chuckled grimly. "No, they wouldn't touch you with a ten-foot surfboard. Some other Ivy League school close by? I doubt that very much." As if apropos of nothing, he told me, "Say, did I tell you President Ater's cousin is a provost at Yale? Not sure why I would have mentioned that, come to think of it, but there you have it." He furrowed his brow. "I guess you might find gainful employment on foreign shores. Who, however, I ask you, wants to uproot entirely and raise children far from their native and blessed soil? Not me, that's for clear-certain. Ah well, Noah, just trust in fate and hope for the best, okay? Hey, I'd shake your hand good-bye, but," he signaled generally to his desktop, "I'm drowning in work and simply cannot spare the time. I'm sure you can understand. So, Harold…"

"So, is it a virus, or is it just human nature? If it's something else, please tell me its name."

He actually looked at me as opposed to through me as he had been up until that point. Confused, "I have no idea what you're—"

I snapped angrily. "That's because I'm not talking to you, moron!" I pointed to Limo. "I'm asking you. The only one who actually counts in this room besides me."

Kent began to say, "Well, I—"

"Silence, Pearson." Kent was immediately silent. Limo spun the cigar between his lips and throated a deep chuckle. "So, you somehow feel I both know what you're talking about, Taylor, *and* that I have the slightest inclination of educating you if I did?"

I threw up my arms. "No. Honestly, Limo, as poorly as things have gone for me today, I just figured I was just due to catch a break. That's the truth of it, sport."

That earned me another throaty grunt of a laugh. A few puffs later Limo sat up in his chair. "You have caught me in an unusually cheery mood today, my boy. Plus, despite my predilection against such sentimentality, you're definitely beginning to grow on me. Sort of like a fungus spreading between my toes. I will indulge you this much. I will answer three yes/no questions, if you guess what comes next." Limo rested back with satisfaction.

I repeated to myself, "What comes next? What comes next, after what? After this meeting? After today?" I addressed Limo directly. "What comes after what? You need to be more specific."

For reasons known only to Kent, though I doubt he will ever recall or admit to them, he spoke up just then. "Gentlemen, may I ask…"

Limo shot to his feet and dove toward Kent. By the time Kent had mouthed "ask," Limo had arrived behind him. He used his momentum to amplify the intensity of his vicious slap to the back of Kent's head. The blow was strong enough to nearly plant his face on the table. Then, without further word or other gesture, he plopped back in his lounge chair and looked to me tauntingly. He clearly awaited my answer and would say nothing more. No clues, no clarifications.

What comes next? I decided take him literally. I stood in front of my chair, after I rose to make my request. Limo said he would allow me three yes/no questions if I "guessed what came next." I might next…maybe sit down? So, if I said, "Next I will sit down." Would Limo gift me my questions? No, that didn't feel quite right. What *will* come next. He could answer me if I stood or sat, so my sitting was not required. What did I need to get, do, or…

I reached my hand into my navy-blue blazer inner pockets and removed the two recorders, one at a time. I set them in front of the astounded Kent, who still rubbed the back of his head. I then picked up the small bronze statue of some generic university president from the desk. I smashed the machines until they were pulverized.

I swept the debris onto Kent's lap with my forearm. He had recovered enough from his head slap to glance up at me with the most precious, befuddled rendition of "dude, why'd you do that" I had ever seen. That look alone was worth the cost of the recorders.

Limo clapped limply. "Bravo, kid. You are smarter than you look. So, ask me three yes/no questions."

Quickly, I asked, "Is it caused by a virus, an actual human virus?"

Immediately, he dismissed, "Stupid, Taylor. Rookie stupid. Yes, it's a virus. The common cold is due to an actual human virus. That's one down, two to go."

Crap! What an idiot. I assumed Limo was going to be helpful and cut me some slack. *Stupid, stupid, stupid.* He would never be that helpful. He was toying with me, no more, no less. I calmed myself. Deep breaths, several deep, cleansing breaths. *Concentrate.* I wanted to know if humankind was being transformed into an army of talking-head, zombie-drones by an infectious agent, a virus. Were the captains of industry transmuted into like-thinking clones by that type of outside force? Did they strive, for reasons unknown to even themselves, to dispassionately operate absent thought, compassion, and humanity? There may have been no "why" of the behavior I was certain I was seeing, but if there was…

I was fairly certain I could never establish so much within my two-question limit. How could Limo be made to say virus, "yes," or virus, "no?" I was never very good at word games or riddles.

Limo warned, "Hurry up, Taylor. If you bore me, I'm gone."

"Okay, can you give me just a little longer?"

"Yes. Two down, one to go."

"No," I howled in protest. "You know I did not mean that to be one of my three questions. Give it back."

Limo tapped his cigar butt to his lips. "Let me see. Is 'You know I didn't mean' a question or a declarative?"

Quickly, I halted that train of thought. "No way. That was a statement of fact. Now, be quiet and let me think." One question. My one and certainly only shot at a gift of information. Then it hit me. Why not just ask. Out of my mouth popped, "Limo, I have a theory. I believe that the leaders of our society are being involuntarily transformed into like-thinking, like-acting subunits. These drones act to satisfy an obscure common good which is not necessarily the best for the group they govern. Decisions are made for their own sake, irrespective of their consequences. Is my theory correct?" I heaved a sigh of relief.

He smiled wryly at me. He was savoring his answer. That could not be a good sign. "You're a clever boy, Taylor, but alas, not as clever as you needed to be. The answer to that monologue is *yes*, and the answer to your rant is *no*."

I was no better informed than before my three questions. That would never do. "Wait, Robert's Rules of Order clearly states that when a true/false question is answered as both *yes* and *no*, either a follow-up question or a specific explanation is mandatory. Your choice." I pointed a finger at him. "I don't make the rules, I just play by them."

He popped to his feet. "I am officially bored. You asked three questions, albeit poorly, and I provided three factual responses. That was our deal. Besides, I doubt very much Brigadier General Henry Martyn Robert bothered to add rules about yes/no questions to his pamphlet. Even if the jerk did, I do not care. I bid you, Pearson, good day. I bid you, Taylor, good life." He grinned ironically at that witticism, then headed toward the door.

Out of nowhere, I held up my hands and shouted. "Wait! Wait one minute longer." He looked murderously at my hands which, though short of actually touching him, were poised to restrain his egress. Apparently, that would not have been a wise move. "Limo, we haven't known each other long. But, I do get this about you. You do not seem interested in typical human emotions like honor, fairness, or kindness. If that's who you are, hey, that's fine with me. You are correct in that you do not owe me anything. No elucidation, education, or edification. I know I will not ask a favor of you. I don't want to owe you anything." He smiled wickedly at that remark. "But, I call on you to perform a random act of kindness. Random acts occur. They are real events, unpredictable, but actual. Please tell me why the answer to my question is yes *and* no?"

He sucked in a torrent of air through his nostrils. "Will it shut you up, Taylor? If I clarify my answer, will you do the unthinkable and shut your trap so I can leave? Boy, and I thought Tricky Dicky talked a lot. You take the enchilada, Taylor."

I shrugged, having nothing to lose. "Sure. You tidy up that last response, and I'll defy the odds and be quiet as a tombstone."

He pointed at me with the macerated mouth-end of his stogie. "Here's the 'no' part of the answer, son. No, there is no infection, possession, or magic that causes *some* people to become the leader of the herd, the mindless herd. Some jokers just look at an ant colony and suddenly desire to be the head ant. They see an easy opportunity, and they grab it. It could be a school, a company, or political machine. They want to boss others around and get rich while doing so because that's what floats their boat, what tickles their fancy. Men like Ater eagerly climb over the backs of their alleged friend to be the top turd on Crap Mountain. Some however," he looked at Kent directly, "join the parade less voluntarily. That's it, kid. With those thoughts, I shall bid you adieu." He brushed past me and sped out the door.

The security guards Kent mentioned earlier stepped forth into the breech left by Limo, curious and uncertain looks on their faces. As if nothing had happened between his dismissal of me without a hand shake and that moment, Kent cheerily called out, "Ah, there you are, fellows, as if on cue. Please escort Dr. Taylor to his car and follow him to the perimeter of the campus, if you will." He then looked down at a few stacks of documents on his desk. "Where to begin?" He then, as an afterthought, glanced over to the chair recently occupied by Limo. He grunted ambiguously and returned to his work.

THIRTY-FOUR

Here I sit, staring out to sea. I am perched on a rough hillock of beach near Homer's Pond. Nantucket lies partially shrouded in the mist off to my left. The endless, cold expanse of the Atlantic is everywhere. The ocean could shrug and reclaim this mote of dryness, swallowing it whole as an afterthought. But, it never quite cares enough to spare the effort. There are fishing boats chugging out to sea and back to safe harbor. Myriad birds fill the air, their discordant protests of some perceived offense echoing all about.

I am oblivious to it all. I stare into nothingness. The late summer's day is far from temperate. A stiff breeze laden with salty spray is sufficient to snuff out any aspiring warmth and to keep my bones rattling. All of this is fine with me. I don't mind the discomfort. I'm not certain I deserve comfort, not now. Maybe never. Comfort, as I see it, is reserved for those who have completed a good journey. It must be earned. I have, to date, traveled poorly. I squandered a career full of promise and a life rich with privilege. For what? My pride? For the doing of what seemed right to me? Does the holding on to some principles in this life, the drawing of some lines in the sand, define a man of merit?

Thoughts and remembrances thunder though my head like jets in a dogfight. Should I have tried harder to fit in? Was it arrogance on my part that made me fail? Did I, for that matter, fail? Were there tenets I upheld that were so high, so dear that they could not be bent a little to better conform to functional practicality?

I wish I could stop ruminating over the rights and wrongs of what happened, the just and unjust of it all. No matter how hard I consider the past, I never quite arrive at any firm conclusions. I never approach resolution.

By what coin, by whose standard, am I to even measure success? I can only hope that with time I'll discover some redemption. Karan stands by me like Mt. Everest. Maybe that's all I really need, all that really matters. Maybe her devotion is the only standard by which I can measure my true success. Still...

It's getting late. Dinner will be ready soon. I should be going. But it's only a short walk back to the compound. I can linger a while longer in my isolation, staring further into nothingness. Karan will be cooking up something warm and fortifying, a dish of classic New England's past. Not particularly healthy but definitely satisfying. Her mother is watching the girls while we spend a week on Martha's Vineyard. The fact that her family is wealthy beyond all reasonable standards is comforting at this difficult juncture in my life. We choose to stay here on Martha's Vineyard, for example, as opposed to the family estates in Hyannis Port or on Nantucket.

There are two unexpected aspects of marrying into great wealth. First, Karan and I have the simplest of tastes. A modest house in a nice neighborhood, sensible vacations, and a minivan. Okay, the other car is a Rolls. Nobody's artistically consistent, okay? But, we who can afford anything live humbly. In terms of my future, Karan keeps saying half-joking that we should buy a university and I can work free of empty-headed bosses. The fact that there is no pressure on me to return to work for financial reasons is both odd as well as comforting. I am not a deadbeat, and I hope I am not kept. I must pay some lip service to protect my dignity.

The second aspect is the knowledge that comes with that wealth. Before I knew Karan, I assumed the mega-rich simply had good jobs, good advisors, and most importantly, good parents. But I learned there was more to it. These families have learned over generations how to not only acquire money, but also how to retain it. To stay rich, they must know who holds power and how to work with them. The system is not open to all citizens on an even playing field. Far from it. Those with money must come to know how the world really works. They gladly pay for political allies as they casually buy inside insights into the financial world. This means they know people. They must learn to tell, if they are to stay on top, the good from the bad. They must discern friend from foe. Knowledge is not power. It is wealth.

So, as news of my tribulations trickled down though her family tree, they were able to help me in ways I could not have anticipated. Remember Karan mentioned a vague recollection of her family talking about Limo or someone similar to him? Well, in fact, they had. I spoke to Cedrick, her father's oldest brother, about Limo. Cedrick said that he couldn't be certain, but he at least knew of men like Limo, if not the actual person I'd encountered. They danced behind the curtains, pulling strings and gathering information always far from the scrutiny of daylight. He said they were dark players who offered no benefits to good people. The Limos of the world could bring down financial empires on a whim if they chose to. I asked him directly if he socialized with this type of man, say in one of his clubs. He looked positively shocked that I'd even ask such a thing. "Never!" he scolded. These men avoided him as energetically as he avoided them. It was always about the power with them, in any case, not the money.

In the end, what am I left with? I have a loving family and financial security. I could eventually land an agreeable job somewhere. Maybe the top schools are off limits to me, but there are many other options. State schools, for example. But, what I'm most poignantly left with is doubt, unrelenting doubt which spawns inaction and indecision. The world has gone mad. I am not mad, so where do I fit in? To paraphrase Milton, is it better to reign in hell then to serve in heaven? Do I want to be part of the insanity even if I try to place firm barriers between myself and the madness? I do have the option to remain apart. What's more, I've proven that I'm incapable of passive toleration of the foolery, of the evil. Of the Corporate Virus.

Can I be a man who looks favorably upon himself in the mirror if I try to function in parallel to the world insinuating itself all around me? I would, with all due male bravado, love to say that I could. But could I, even forewarned as I am now? I don't know. Can I call "boss" a man who has never had nor has ever supported a good idea in his entire inconsequential career? Can I sit through a meeting with duct tape over my mouth where the obvious is being dumbed down to the incomprehensible? If I hear another speaker proclaim that metric-based metrics measure metrics better than metrics alone, could I sit on my hands and not strangle him?

I can't say for certain.

I heard a story the other day, a true story. I ran into an old associate at the store. She told me about a new imperative in Primary Care. Some bean-counter manager calculated the time required to perform an ear wash versus the time "misallocated" in doing one. Some people, unfortunately, can have earwax build up so much that it effects their hearing. Two or three times a year, they need the wax removed. In clinic, the nurse washes the wax plug out with warm water squirted firmly from a syringe. Sometimes, the wax is so dry and it will not budge. In that case, mineral oil is instilled in the ear and the procedure is successfully repeated a day or so later. This process always works. This manager, a credit to managerial ineptitude everywhere, decided to study the time "re-realizations" possible if everyone presenting to clinic for an ear wash automatically received oil drops alone. They were then asked to return in a day or two for the wash procedure. Can you guess what wonders he discovered? Almost no one returned to clinic for the wash. Therefore, he crowed, the entire time "misallocated" in attempting the initial washing was "re-realized." Raise a glass to that visionary. He saved the company many cents.

Keep in mind, putting oil in an ear does not remove the wax, it only softens it. It is then easier to remove. So, I know with certainty that every person receiving oil alone still has wax in their ear and can't hear well. Why, then, did they not return for the wash? I honestly don't think I could hear (pun intended) such a presentation without demanding to know the reason why the patient dropped out of follow-up. I would ask, because I knew the answer. The patient did not return for five reasons.

One, they had already taken two hours off from work to come in and could not afford to do so again. Two, they had already waited forty minutes to be called back for the procedure. They were not so inclined as to spend another forty minutes waiting for what might well be as much a waste of their time as the first visit had been. Three, they could not afford another copay. Four, why go back to a clinic where the staff that didn't know that one washed the ear out first before resorting to the oil (remember, they need the wash several times a year). Five, they were angry. They were never returning to the clinic or the medical care delivery system. The first chance available, they were going to switch plans. So, the upside of "re-realizing" ten minutes' time for one staff member was offset by the downside of the complete revenue loss, not to mention the bad publicity the wax-burdened people of the world would spread. In the end, poor care—bad care—was lauded because it saved a little expense, although it cost the plan a bundle.

I'm not capable of returning to such a world. It's a world gone mad. I'll never be ready for that world.

A new childcare chain with a franchise near the university is named *Las Lagrimas*. They promise, "Lagrimas quality care for each and every child." *Lagrimas* is the Spanish word for "tears." The childcare provider that loving parents are asked to trust their precious children with is called "Tears?" Each child placed there will receive tear-quality care. How was such a thing possible? Why was the name "lagrimas" selected? It turns out the word tested well with groups of young mothers who might find themselves in need of childcare. All but the Latina demographic. They universally designated such a facility as "very unlikely to select." The company was not troubled by this demographic trend. The cost structure of Las Lagrimas was aimed at a higher socioeconomic grouping than Latino averages were projected to support. So, they chose tears to be their standard.

Such a world is not ready for me. I know I couldn't, sit at the board meeting where that decision was made and keep my mouth shut.

It is a world where a mortuary was named *The Tunnel of Love Funeral Home*, because it sounded welcoming for the recently deceased. Metrics proved it. Never mind that a tunnel of love refers to an amusement park ride where young couples steal a first kiss. It is, rightly, a place of wonder and dreams. The phrase may *suggest* a pathway to a better place, but it *refers* to a ride. A tunnel of love is not something you back a hearse up to and drop off what's left of Dad, who was burned beyond recognition after a car accident. But, it tested well with the dead. Please do keep facts and emotions out of the collective thought process.

I'm not ready for that world. How can anyone be? I'm beginning to believe it's actually wrong to be a willing participant in such a decaying environment. Men form tight-knit balls of self-congratulatory bullies who are determined to bolster "the company" by destroying it. They consider themselves above all laws because all laws are of secondary concern when it comes to "the company." Mean-spirited hacks run the world, and it's only getting worse. Maybe the best thing I can do is avoid them by withdrawing as completely as possible into the shelter of a cave. I could cover the cave with rocks and brush, so they'd never find me and never try to "help" me again. But, then I'd be living in a cave. Was letting them win worth it for peace of mind?

Maybe, my defiance of them is really all it takes for me to declare myself the winner? All of my fretting and self-doubt, those emotions paralyzingly me now, are unnecessary trappings. I won. I'll always win. To never give in to the darkness is the definition of victory. Render unto Caesar the things that are Caesar's, yes? But my integrity and my self-worth—my soul—are not Caesar's. Maybe I'll always win because I'm true to myself. Maybe the forces of mindless uniformity are actually incapable of winning. They're only capable of meanness and destruction but never lasting success. Doesn't a snake that eats its own tail soon come to consume itself in the end?

I'm certain that if I rallied now, assaulted their walls and tried to bring down their castles, I would fail completely. No battery of lawyers I could assemble would be able to trump their teams, equipped as they were with perjury and distortion. No public outcry I could make would be credible.

What other weapons existed for me to defend myself? Subterfuge was both beneath me and impossible. I had no real power, no access to people who could destabilize those fools in the least. I couldn't very well lay siege to their fortress.

The only practical manner of defense I can muster, the only way I can win, is to wait for them to go away, for them to self-destruct. So, to me remains the unsexy, passive resolution. I can only walk away and wait. I'm certain ballads about my saga won't be written any time soon. My resolution is not the stuff of legend. It is the stuff of old men sitting in front of fires attempting in vain to warm their bones while they await the inevitable. Mine is the stuff of accountants and stable hands, not wizards and brave knights.

Can I claim a victory if it's one I back into rather than force? Yes, I believe I can. Whether I win by action or inaction, I will not be the one who lost. Supremacy is relative. It can't be declared for me by someone else. It must be declared *by* me. To achieve dominion in the game of life is fundamentally different than mastery on the sporting field. In life, conquest can't be demonstrated on paper. It must be believed by the participant. The competitor in life must seek an internal ascendancy. Harder still, if I'm to be the indemonstrable victor, I must live with the knowledge that few, if any, will perceive my victory. To the masses, I will be seen only as the sad, hapless victim of a poorly played game.

So, mine is to be a semi-sweet vindication. That is an acquired taste. There will be no crown of laurels for my head, no monuments erected to my valor. There will be few who can perceive it. But, I'm one of those with the knowledge, and that, for now, will suffice.

EPILOGUE

No corrupt regime so self-cannibalistic or so inhuman could survive long. And so it was to be for the new order of an old institution. It turned out that the chopping action of a self-propelled axe did not ever stop. When all the wood dubbed dead or diseased by the lords of the mindless axe was removed, it required more targets. So, the next set of false saviors consumed the last set of leaders. They, in due course, were devoured by their faithful. Soon, the axe began to swing without direction or goal. A lumberjack who hacks at his own ankles can't stand for long.

That which began unnoticed propagated itself malignantly and destroyed its own substance, ultimately condemning itself. It died a quiet, unlamented death. The tragedy of the virus, be it real or figurative, was that it didn't turn on itself in time to spare its host. That which remained was so transfigured, so scarred by the disease that it couldn't be recognized as a shadow of its former self. It was referred to, instead, as a notable luminary of times gone by, lost because that was the way of progress. Evolution, they would say, weeded out the weak and rewarded only those most fit.

If this virus had only turned on itself first, well, then there might have been some cheery justice. But, that was not the way of cruelty, not the choice selected by the tyrannical and the foolish. It was, and will always still be, easy to be stupid. Smart, to them, was neither a valid objective nor worthy of the effort.

So, it was, is, and always will be.

AND NOW A WORD FROM YOUR AUTHOR

I hope you enjoyed *The Corporate Virus*. The book was a two-year labor of love. But, like childbirth, it was painful and slow. Like walking through waist-high mud at times. I would love it if you would place a review where you bought it. Yes, even if your opinion is less than stellar. I do learn from all feedback.

If you love medical fiction, please consider my other novel in this genre, *The InnerGlow Effect*

Please consider joining me on the Forever Journey! Space opera at its best. It's only just beginning. Books 1, 2, 3, and 4 *The Forever Life, The Forever Enemy, The Forever Fight, and The Forever Quest* are available now:

The Forever Life
The Forever Enemy
The Forever Fight
The Forever Quest
The Forever Alliance is due out in early 2017.

Please do leave all the books a review. They're more precious than gold.

My Website: craigrobertsonblog.wordpress.com

Feel free to email me comments or to discuss any part of the series. mailto:contact@craigarobertson.com?subject=The Forever Life Follow Up Also, you can ask to be on my email list. I'll send out infrequent alerts concerning new material or some of the extras I'm planning in the near future.

There you can learn about me and my other books. The fun will never stop.

Facebook? But of course! https://www.facebook.com/Craig-A-Robertsons-Authors-Page-943237189133053/

Twitter and Facebook Pages: @craigr1971

My Blog: http://contact.craigarobertson.com/

Wow! That's a whole lot of social media. But, I'm worth it, so it's all right ;)

Don't be a stranger, at least any stranger than you already are...craig

www.ingramcontent.com/pod-product-compliance
Lightning Source LLC
Chambersburg PA
CBHW060539180626

46817CB00002B/638